Someone is Stealing
Children in Paris

Louis Forest

Someone is Stealing
Children in Paris

translated, annotated and introduced by
Brian Stableford

A Black Coat Press Book

ISBN 978-1-61227-252-8. First Printing. January 2014. Published by Black Coat Press, an imprint of Hollywood Comics.com, LLC, P.O. Box 17270, Encino, CA 91416.

Introduction

The version of *On vole des enfants à Paris* by Louis Forest here translated as *Someone is Stealing Children in Paris*, was first published in Jules Tallandier's *Librarie Illustrée* series of *Romans populaires* in 1909. An earlier, substantially longer, version had appeared in the daily newspaper *Le Matin*, running as a *feuilleton* serial from 25 June to 23 September 1906. The serial version began publication in a slot at the bottom of page two in which the paper was then accustomed to running one of its *feuilleton* serials (at the time it was running three), so it was clearly identifiable as fiction; it had a title, "*Le Voleur d'enfants*" [The Child-Stealer] and a by-line, although it was also labeled as "Un Reportage Sensationnel" [A Sensational Reportage] rather than carrying one of the rubrics by which *Le Matin*'s feuilletons were routinely described—usually "Grand roman inédit" [Great unpublished novel]—and employed subheadings similar to those in the paper's news articles instead of chapter headings.

"*Le Voleur d'enfants*" was, in fact, a novel told in the form of daily reportage: the history of an "Affair," as newspapers were wont to call long-running stories whose continual updating provided the papers with one of their principal selling points. Day by day, for more than three months, Forest recounted the history of an Affair that was occurring in a kind of parallel world, similar in all respects to the actual one except with respect to the events described by the hypothetical reportage. It is, in a sense, a kind of "alternate history," referring to a string of yesterdays that gradually accumulated their own momentum and their own significance as a history in their own right—and, inevitably, as a commentary on the actual history unfolding day by day alongside it.

The fictitious Affair in question begins, as so many long-running newspaper stories did, with an account of a series of sensational crimes and the attempts by the police and the examining magistrate appointed to the case to find the perpetrator. Because it is fictitious, however, the hypothetical series of crimes is free to be more extensive, more mysterious and more eccentrically-motivated than any actual series ever was, and can eventually lead to consequences far more extraordinary and far-reaching. Because the story was appearing in the form of reportage, however, in a daily newspaper on a daily basis, it is not merely a commentary on the hypothetical events it describes, but also on the manner in which newspaper reporters involved themselves in the investigation of "Affairs," and the manner in which their reportage helped to guide and shape such Affairs as well as reflecting them. Indeed, in its early phases, the story adopts a cheerfully sarcastic tone that promises to offer a sharp satire on contemporary crime reportage, although that tone shifts gradually and markedly as the story progresses.

Given the vast number of serials that had been published in French daily newspapers since the 1840s, one might think that the idea of mimicking the form and methods of reportage, and formulating a work of fiction as if it were an unfolding news story would have been a tempting one, but the format presents awkward difficulties of narrative organization that would have daunted a great many writers, and it is not surprising that Forest's endeavor is, in fact, extremely unusual, if not unique (I do not know of any other examples). It must have seemed to *Le Matin*'s editor, Stéphane Lauzanne, to be a slightly risky experiment in terms of its format alone, and as the story developed, it became the most ambitious *feuilleton* the paper had ever published, as well as the most unusual.

It is likely that Lauzanne did not know at the beginning exactly how daring Forest's *feuilleton* was going to be—such serials were routinely made up as the author went along, so he is unlikely to have seen more than a handful of sample episodes before it was launched—and it not improbable that the author had no idea either how the plot would eventually develop. There were, however, good grounds for Lauzanne to trust Louis Forest to do something worthwhile, even though Forest had never written a *feuilleton* serial before; he was a seasoned journalist, having worked extensively for *Le Figaro* and *L'Illustration* and he was eventually to become one of *Le Matin*'s leading columnists. In any case, the editor always had the option of telling the author to cut the serial short if the readers did not like it. Given that the paper had two serials well under way in June 1906, by two of the papers longest-serving and most reliable *feuilletonists*, Michel Zevaco and Paul d'Ivoi,[1] the risk of actually alienating any readers by virtue of the eccentricities and extravagances the serial eventually developed was minimal.

The principal reason why the format Forest had chosen is intrinsically awkward is that it puts the pace of the narrative into an effective straitjacket. Conventional narrative allows elastic manipulations of time, permitting the skipping of days, months or years in which nothing relevant occurs, and potentially extending coverage of a single hour to much longer stretches of prose than are conventionally included in a single feuilleton episode (usually between 1500 and 2000 words). Writing a story in which every individual episode has to cover a single day not only reduces that flexibility drastically, but also means that some relevant development of the story has to take place every day, so that the progress of the story becomes rather metronomic. That does not eliminate the possibility of some kind of crescendo effect as the narrative gradually gains tension and builds toward a climax, but it does place restrictions on the manner in which the climax can be orchestrated. Most actual "Affairs," inevitably, tend to

---

[1] Zevaco's *Le Capitan*, one of the historical *"cape-et-épée"* novels on which he had built his reputation, and d'Ivoi's *Le Maître du drapeau bleu*, one of a long series of Vernian "voyages excentriques." The latter was still running when *Le voleur d'enfants?* concluded (the question mark was added to the title in the course of the serialization) but the former had been replaced by Léon Malicet's *Le Coq du village*.

fade away, fizzle out or simply stop rather than reaching a dramatically-satisfactory climax.

French newspapers of the period did occasionally publish fake news stories intended to deceive, at least momentarily, mostly of the one-off "April fool" variety which has long been virtually traditional for 1 April issues. At much more distant intervals there were more elaborate "hoaxes" in the tradition made famous by such examples as the New York *Sun*'s famous "Moon Hoax" of August 1835 (also a big hit when translated into French) and *Le Pays*' publication in 1864 of a series of articles by Henry de Parville about the supposed discovery in America of a "Martian mummy," subsequently reprinted as *Un habitant de la planète Mars* (1865).[2] "*Le Voleur d'enfants*" was always readily identifiable as a work of fiction that merely adopted the form of newspaper reportage, but the use of that format inevitably gave it certain affinities with such hoaxes, which were not without effect on its eventually development.

The whole point of an April fool "spoof" or a hoax series is to extend from the plausible to the absurd, while always maintaining a straight face. Their essential currency is excess. Although Louis Forest's serial was not intended to fool anyone, and was not intended as a mere joke, the logic of the exercise still encouraged, if it did not actually demand, a tendency to excess, and no matter how straight-faced it became as it gradually discarded its initial blatant sarcasm, a certain satirical comedy always lurks behind the mask, never fading away, although it changes its target significantly and takes on a markedly blacker tone.

Thus, although it begins as a somewhat tongue-in-cheek account of serial kidnapping, and progresses to a more seemingly-earnest account of the attempt to discover the perpetrator of the abductions, the logic of the story's presentation and context insisted that its developmental evolution continue, and that it would eventually turn into something rather more exotic—as it most certainly did. This is not the place to discuss exactly what it did turn into, because that would be something of a spoiler, so I shall reserve comment on the eventual substance of the story for an Afterword, but it was perhaps always bound to become the most distinctive, exotic and ambitious item of fiction that *Le Matin* had ever published—or, for that matter, ever would.[3] For that reason alone, it is a work of some historical interest and significance.

In electing to write a serial account of a hypothetical "Affair," Louis Forest was undoubtedly heavily influenced by the fact that he had been intimately involved, both as a reporter and a leading player, in the most famous of all great scandals of that kind, the Dreyfus Affair, which finally reached its conclusion in

---

[2] Translated in a Black Coat Press edition as *An Inhabitant of the Planet Mars*, ISBN 9781934543450.

[3] Oddly enough, the account of the novel's subject-matter contained in Louis Forest's Wikipedia entry at the time of writing, and the publicity blurb employed by the publisher currently offering a print-on-demand version of the Tallandier text, are both extremely inaccurate; obviously, neither writer had read the text.

1906, mere weeks before the serial began. Alfred Dreyfus had been convicted of communicating French military secrets to the Germans in 1894 and sent to the penal colony in Devil's Island, but his conviction was controversial from the start, and the Affair gained new impetus when evidence came to light in 1896 that another officer was actually guilty of the offence. The Army authorities not only attempted to suppress the new evidence—perhaps in an attempt to save face, although more sinister reasons were suggested—but fabricated new "evidence" in order to trump up further charges against Dreyfus. The fact that Dreyfus was Jewish added a further implication of religious prejudice to the appalling injustice, and a fervent campaign was formed to win Dreyfus' release, which the newspapers gleefully reported and refueled on an extravagant scale.

The newspapers' role in the campaign took a uniquely dramatic turn in 1898 when Georges Clemenceau's newspaper *L'Aurore* published an open letter by Émile Zola on its front page with the banner headline *J'ACCUSE*: a scathing attack on the anti-Dreyfusard camp that proved a spectacular *coup de théâtre*. Although the campaign had previously been led by another litterateur of note, Bernard Lazare, Zola's involvement enhanced the celebrity dimension of the Affair considerably, encouraging numerous high-profile writers, artists and actors to bid for leading roles in the fray. Zola died in 1902, and Lazare in 1903, so they were unable to see the eventual success of their cause, but Zola's place as the leading literary celebrity fighting Dreyfus' corner was taken over by Anatole France, the doyen of French letters.

The Dreyfus Affair had another significant dimension because the initial evidence of Dreyfus' guilt involved a handwritten note whose authenticity was certified by an army officer, Major du Paty de Clam, who fancied himself as an expert in "graphology." That evidence was challenged, and several other experts were brought in to assess it, including Alphonse Bertillon, the head of the Parisian Sûreté's "Anthropometric Service," which had led the world in photographing and compiling highly detailed descriptions of criminals. The contest thus became a significant arena in which forensic scientists battled in public over the finer points of their craft.

Louis Forest spent a lot of time in the latter years of the Dreyfusard campaign writing combative articles in its support and attending public meetings, often sharing platforms with Anatole France and other celebrities. Although "*Le Voleur d'enfants*" is not a transfiguration of the Dreyfus Affair, like the famous climactic sequence in Anatole France's *L'Île des Pingouins* (1908; tr. as *Penguin Island*), or even a satirization of it, the influence of Forest's involvement with it is very obvious in the manner in which he constructs and orchestrates his hypothetical Affair, and it is significant that many of the key players in the Dreyfus Affair, including Anatole France and Georges Clemenceau, appear in Forest's story as characters. It is, however, equally significant that many of the real individuals who make cameo appearances in the novel in order to comment on the affair of the child-stealers played no part at all in the Dreyfus Affair, and are summoned as witnesses by Forest because of their known interest in the specific ethical and philosophical issues raised by the fictitious affair.

Although Louis Forest did not enjoy the kind of glittering political career that Georges Clemenceau ultimately achieved, he did hold various political offices later in his career, eventually becoming a councilor for the département of the Seine-et-Oise. His career as a writer began with two books written in collaboration with the prolific Théodore Cahu, *L'Oubli: Alsace-Lorraine 1877-1899* (1899) and the novel *Vers la Paix!* (1900), but he only published one solo novel prior to *On vole des enfants à Paris*, the far more conventional *L'Amour et le naif* (1900), and he never published another thereafter. He directed his primary literary endeavors into the theater, for which he became a prolific writer of *vaudeville* comedies, but those of his works for the stage that reached print have been largely forgotten, as have his novels, although he was by no means devoid of talent and originality. He is best remembered today for his work for *Le Figaro* and *Le Matin*, a number of essays, including *On put prévoir l'avenir: comment? ou la Descartomancie* [The Future is Predictable: How? or, Anticartomancy] (1918), and for the campaigning weekly he founded in his later years, *L'Animateur des Temps Nouveaux* [The Animator of the New Era], which he published from 1926 until his death in 1933.

In spite of its relative neglect, even by the historians who might have been expected to take a keen interest in it—it is not mentioned in Pierre Versins' *Encyclopédie de l'utopie et de la science-fiction*—*On vole des enfants à Paris* is nevertheless a landmark work in the development of the *roman scientifique*. In particular, it represents an important component of a series of modern *contes philosphiques* considering the psychology, sociology and ethics of scientific endeavor and the cause of social progress, for further details of which, please refer to the Afterword.

This translation is taken from the version of the Tallandier edition reproduced on the Bibliothèque Nationale's *gallica* website. *Gallica* also has a complete run of the issues of *Le Matin* containing the serial, but the reduction of the often poorly-printed newspaper pages to the dimensions of a computer screen renders that text very difficult to read, and it was, unfortunately, not practicable for me to use that version for translation, although I would have preferred to do so.

The abridgement of the Tallandier version results in a certain confusion in the time-scheme; the dates added to that version leave the date of the conclusion nine days short of the date of the issue of *Le Matin* containing the final episode of the serial, although only seven days are completely removed from the scheme, two dates being accidentally repeated in the book version, as indicated in a footnote. The cutting and pasting required by the abridgement is occasionally inept in other, less obtrusive ways. I have inserted a couple of dates accidentally omitted from the Tallandier text but have otherwise only made very minor repairs to a couple of continuity errors. There is no way to know whether the abridgement was carried out by the author or by Tallandier's copy-editor, but it is surely safe to assume that the series in which the book appeared was by no means Forest's first choice; he might well have spent the three-year interim between serial and book publication in search of a more prestigious outlet, but found most editors wary of the controversial nature of the book's eventual rhetoric.

I have indicated in a footnote at the relevant point of the text one of the running features of the serial that was dropped from the Tallandier version in the interests of economy. As with most of the other abridgments, that feature is of no great significance to the development of the story, so the Tallandier version is, I think, reasonably satisfactory, although the reader will notice more than one reference in the later phases of the plot to a minor incident that was reported in the serial version but omitted from the book version.

Brian Stableford

SOMEONE IS STEALING CHILDREN IN PARIS

On 25 June 1906 the readers of Le Matin *were able to read on the second page of that great newspaper the following sensational reportage*:

Someone is stealing children in Paris.

They are being stolen every day.

They are being stolen from the great boulevards and the busiest streets.

They have been stolen from the Boulevard Montmartre, the Rue Caumartin, the Rue Royale, the Rue Racine, the Avenue Niel, the Passage des Panoramas and the Cité Rougemont.

They have been stolen in broad daylight, with diabolical audacity and amazing dexterity.

They have been stolen from under the noses of the most attentive mothers.

And this is not one of those tales that made us shiver as children, a story to trouble the nights of the very young with nightmares. It is the most veritable reality, the one in which we live.

It is a certain fact, written in tears and sobs in the weekly chronicles, an undeniable fact, the terrifying gravity of which has been revealed to us by a preliminary investigation.

If this veritable epidemic continues to increase, if a powerful dam does not stop the rising flood, and if the details that we are beginning to discover are unveiled without the key to the mystery having produced a striking solution, it is not difficult to foresee that this new leprosy will make Paris weep, and horrify France and the world.

Seven children have already been snatched from their parents in a matter of days.

That is what we can affirm today, without fear of error—but we have reason to believe that the thefts are even more numerous.

Our information is very incomplete at the moment of going to press. It has been taken from a communication that reached us late in the evening. In spite of our army of reporters, the telegraph and the telephone, immediately put into action, we were unable to wait for fuller details, stopping the machines that were ready to roll for a second time and further augmenting the impatience of our rotary press operators, already irritated by the delay imposed on the printing and perhaps delaying the paper's publication.

Our readers will not miss anything, however.

The affair about which we are informing them today appears to us, at first sight so astonishing and so prodigious that all the informational resources at our disposal will be mobilized in order to arrive rapidly at the establishment of the truth.

We would have been able, nevertheless, in spite of the urgency, to recount a few precise details if we had not, at the very outset of our investigation, run into a new unexpected ill will on the part of the senior police authorities.

A DEPUTY WHO KNOWS NOTHING
A CHIEF CLERK WHO SAYS NOTHING
MONSIEUR HAMARD'S DISTURBANCE

At the Sûreté, no one is saying anything.

Obviously, an order has been issued.

The police, for whom the press is often a precious auxiliary, still believe that they ought to maintain the most rigorous secrecy on the subject of the thefts of children.

We shall see in due course what we ought to think of this silence.

Monsieur Plot, the deputy head of the Sûreté, adopted the most innocent expression when we questioned him.

"Thefts of children? What's this you're telling me? If there had been any, I would know. It's a fairy tale."

The fairy tale in question was not denied so energetically by Monsieur Lounergue, the distinguished chief clerk of the Sûreté. It is true that we had raced to his domicile, so he did not have time to confer with his colleagues, in order to enable him to avoid the little trap that we set for his good faith.

"Monsieur Plot" we told him, coolly, "has told us that children have been disappearing lately in considerable numbers, that no trace has been found of them, that there is anxiety about their fate, that..."

"Monsieur Plot has told you that?" he exclaimed, quite astonished, without taking account of the fact that that interrogative interruption would aggravate suspicions.

"Monsieur Plot has said that," was the reply he received, with the calmness of a lie sure of its effect.

"Oh! Well, yes. But let's not exaggerate. Let's not alarm the public by overstating the case. Numerous declarations have arrived in the offices of Commissaires of Police regarding lost children. There are more than usual. Pure chance! There are weeks when it rains more, others when it rains less. With re-spect to the disappearances of children, we're in a period when it rains more, that's all.

"It happens every day that an excessively curious kid lets go of his moth-er's hand and gets lost in a crowd. When he realizes that he's alone, he cries. A compassionate passer-by questions him. He generally makes no reply. A passing policeman takes the kid, paternally, to the nearest Commissariat, where, nine times out of ten, Mama is in the process of giving a minute description, and in-dicating the location in which the little one must have been separated from her.

"A tender little scene terminates the drama, which finishes, in the final account, with a cream bun at the cake shop. It's rare for a child not to be returned to the parents the same day, or the next, at the latest—except, naturally, when it's a matter of planned escapades, young Crusoes eager for space, deserters from the paternal hearth, dreaming of realizing the exploits of the heroes of certain adventure stories.

"In those cases, the search is more difficult, because the fugitives hide and have generally taken enough food to last for a few days. They're events of an extreme banality. Hazard, I repeat—mere hazard—has multiplied them this week. It's of no importance, none at all, and your reporter's flair can sleep easy."

This little speech would have been fine if the children in question had been found. Unfortunately, they have not.

The head of the Sûreté, whom we succeeded in reaching shortly afterwards, was considerably more disturbed. More forthcoming than his subordinates, Monsieur Hamard did not try to hide the gravity of the situation.[4]

"What? You know? I beg you, don't publish a word about these abductions—for we find ourselves confronted with repeated, systematic, mysterious abductions. We'd like to hide the facts for a few more days. Do us the favor of helping us. I give you my word that you'll be informed as soon as we can reveal everything, that you'll be told before your colleagues and that we'll give you all the information we have. For the moment, though, absolute silence…and if you promise me that, I'll tell you, in exchange, about the capture effected yesterday in Brussels of an entire colony of chloroform thieves who have been terrorizing the hotels of Nice and San Remo this winter.

CURIOUS DETAILS

In spite of the tempting recompense offered to this reporter's discretion, we did not hesitate to fulfill our duty, which is, first and foremost, to keep our readers informed, without worrying about the momentary convenience of the administration at the Quai des Orfèvres.

And why keep quiet about this troubling series of disappearances?

It might be that the police want to bring off a striking coup, trying to attenuate public emotion by announcing the arrest of the guilty party at the same time as the crimes.

Such reasons doubtless have their value.

On the other hand, however, is it not useful to inform parents that a monstrous individual is roaming the city at this moment, in quest of children—very young children—which he steals, for a purpose that has not yet been determined?

---

[4] Octave Hamard became head of the Sûreté in 1903 after some ten years of service in junior positions. MM. Plot and Lounergue are probably fictitious.

Is it, then, a bad thing to shout "Beware!" to imprudent mothers, to shout: "Watch out!"

It is all the more indispensable to divulge the danger because these thefts of children have all the characteristics of those violent events that impassion crowds: the prodigious skill of the villain, the continual repetition of typical methods.

Imagine that, one morning, a warden discovers, in a thicket in the Bois de Boulogne, a corpse bearing a wound on the left temple in the form of the ace of clubs. The newspapers publish a short article about it which appears in the inner pages, and nothing more.

Now imagine that the same warden discovers a cadaver every morning, in the same place, marked on the temple with the same fateful ace of clubs. Immediately, the case becomes famous, will be the object of special issues, will prey on all minds—and at night, before going to sleep, the fearful will look under the bed once again.

The celebrated English murder Jack the Ripper owes his international reputation, above all, to a kind of frightful trademark that he imprinted on his repeated crimes.

Now, the child-stealer also has his trademark.

The first declarations of the parents who were bandit's victims have permitted the observation of identical singularities, which reveal that we are dealing with a tenacious and reasoned determination—unless they are the work of a madman, an odious maniac.

Thus far, the abductor has only attacked little boys.

All the boys in question are between six and seven years old.

All the boys are pale blond, with hair the color of straw.

This is more than coincidence.

Whatever the chief clerk of the Sûreté might think, mere hazard does not repeat itself with that methodical precision.

No. We are in the presence of obscure crimes, whose perpetration must be stopped, as a matter of the utmost urgency. This is a cruel problem, which cannot and must not remain insoluble any longer. It is not acceptable that the Parisian population, the ignorant victim, should abandon more children to the enigmatic sphinx that is devouring them.

LATEST NEWS
THE THEFT IN THE CHAUSÉE-D'ANTIN

At the last moment, one of our correspondents telephoned the following information:

The Baronne de Vautremesse has just signed a statement at the Commissariat of Monsieur Fanguy, of which the following is a summary.

The lady in question was at the crossroads of the Chaussée d'Antin, on the corner of the Boulevard Haussmann, with her son André, when the latter suddenly disappeared, without the mother being able to explain how. After various searches, Madame de Vautremesse decided to inform the police.

The child is six years and three months old. He is slender for his age. He is wearing a jersey sailor suit with a large white collar edged with blue, blue socks and long yellow lace-up bootees. His beret is inscribed with the words *City of Brighton*, in golden letters. Inside, the hatmaker's label is also English: John Chapman & Co., London. All his underwear is delicately embroidered with the overlapping initials A.V. The child is very intelligent.

A significant indication: his long curly hair is a very pale, almost colorless blond.

Will the frightful series continue?

Such was the initial reportage that *Le Matin* published about the extraordinary affair of the *Child-Stealer* who terrorized society for three months.

Following that article, which caused an enormous sensation, *Le Matin* printed new information every day, the series of which forms the most curious, the most extraordinary and the most exciting story that was ever imagined.

We believe that nothing would interest our readers more than the publication of a faithful and complete reprint here.

The facts revealed in yesterday's edition have generated considerable emotion in Paris. Today, the child-stealer is the object of all conversations and all execrations.

Other newspapers are reproducing our article this morning, commenting on it on page one, or even, it must be noted, taking their concern for the new to extreme limits, supplementing it with imaginary details.

The affair that *Le Matin* has brought to public attention has thus become, overnight, the great event of reportage around which journalists are agitating in search of new information.

So much the better.

The more noise there is, the sooner we can expect the exploits of the sinister bandit to be stopped.

It is certainly a matter of a villain or a madman. Everyone is in agreement on that point. None of our colleagues is even discussing the hypothesis of simple disappearances due to deplorable hazards and mere failures of surveillance.

Hazard, we repeat, does not have this troubling persistence. It is quite obvious to everyone that a *child-stealer*, a sinister specialist, is abroad in Paris.

If any optimist, in spite of everything, dares to protest that the unfortunate little ones, gone astray in the crowd, will soon be found, we reply to him that we are now in possession of all the statements made during the last week at various commissariats by tearful parents.

None of those that mention blond children six or seven years old have obtained a favorable solution.

Whereas a dozen children with brown, chestnut, dark blond or red hair have been returned to their homes, none of the ten pale blond children who did not answer their mothers' appeals have been returned to the hearth.

Ten children!

As we foresaw, the figure of seven that we indicated yesterday, is insufficient.

In addition to little André de Vautremesse, whose name was telephoned to us at the last minute, the sad list has had to be augmented with two more young victims.

To the ten questions that everyone is asking with regard to the fate of these ten children, one can only reply with harrowing suppositions.

We shall not develop them today, out of respect for the anguish of the parents.

There will be plenty of time, if nothing occurs to clarify the problem, to print alarming hypotheses.

COMPLETE LIST OF MISSING CHILDREN

1. Bernard Flaquette, aged six, golden blond, answers to the nicknamed "Bobichon." Tall for his age. Obvious intelligence. Gray eyes. Chestnut-colored costume, with large Lavallière cravat in red satin. Father an accountant at the Gas Company, who was returning from a walk with his son when, on turning round, he observed that the child was no longer following him. Probable location in which the theft was committed: Rue Beaubourg, at the corner of the Rue des Gravilliers.

2. Paolo Palavacoccini, walking in the company of his grandmother. Scottish costume. Pitch-pine blond. Six and a half. Medium height. Speaks Italian. Speaks French with a slight southern accent. Very alert and lively. Probable location in which the theft was committed: corner of Avenue Niel and Rue Rennequin.

3. Urbain Godedouin, was with his mother. Pale blond. Abundant hair. Long curls. Six and four months. Blue eyes. Very small for his age, still wearing a dress, richly embroidered, color hazelnut. Hat, socks and shoes of the same color. Nickname Chichi. Intelligence very alert, very artful, above his age. Probable location where the theft was committed: Rue Marbeuf, near Rue François I.

4. Ange Pompaigne, was with his nurse. Light copper blond. Dressed from head to toe in white fabric, very thick. Black felt hat. Six and five months. Brown eyes, very bright. Astonishing intelligence. Probable location of abduction: Rue Racine, corner of Rue Monsieur-le-Prince.

5. Pierre-Isidore-Jules-Marie-Onésime Candelaur, was also with a maid-servant. Ordinarily called, after the fashion of his governess, who is German, "Schaetzen"—which is to say, "little treasure." Milky blond. Six and two months. Small, but sturdy and very vigorous. Sparkling intelligence of Parisian urchin. Dressed in mourning, entirely in black. Round hat with crepe. Probable location of abduction: Rue Royale, corner of Faubourg-Saint-Honoré.

6. Frantz Vetyolle, son of the famous harpist, professor at the Conservatoire; was with his mother. Checkered gray suit, with long trousers and jockey cap. Thin, very tall. Blond hair, almost white. Exceptionally intelligent. Probable place of abduction: Cité Rougemont or Rue Bergère, between Rue Rougement and Rue du Faubourg-Poissonnière.

7. Nicolas Barlatescu, son of third chancellor at Rumanian consulate; was with his mother. Pale gray costume, large flat collar. Opal blond. Six and seven months. Blue eyes. Speaks Rumanian, English, German, French. Remarkable

intelligence. Probable location where he was stolen: Boulevard Montmartre, between Boulevard des Italiens and Rue Vivienne.

8. Jules Bimbaleau, was with his mother. Gray chine trousers. Pleated waistcoat, black and white checks. Tarbe beret. Six and nine months. Large burn-scar on right cheek. Wheat blond. Very intelligent. Probable location where theft was committed: Passage des Panoramas.

9. Fernand Pig, was with his uncle. Beige blond hair. Dressed in dark blue, embroidered collar and ornaments. Yellow lace-up shoes. Russian bonnet. Small, plump. Astonishing intelligence. Probable location where the theft was committed: Rue Caumartin, corner of Rue Boudreau.

10. André de Vautremesse, whose description we have already published.

Such is the list that we have been able to obtain from the notebooks of the police, who, following our article, have not thought it useful to prevent us from doing our job.

What is striking about this lamentable story is the unusual dexterity of the thief. He has abducted ten children without attracting the attention of anyone, without being seen, and without leaving anything on the scene of his exploits that might one day lead to his discovery.

BERNARD, BINARD AND BARBARUS

The drama of the Child-Stealer seems bound to take on a considerable amplitude. Thus, *Le Matin* has decided to establish a reportage race between three of its best reporters.

Messieurs Bernard, Binard and Barbarus have been commissioned by our paper to track the affair of the Child-Stealer from now on. On the day when the guilty party—or the principal guilty party, if there are several—is arrested, whichever of those journalists has furnished the most interesting information will receive a bonus of 25,000 francs.

Our readers will be the judges of this original competition. When the time comes, we shall consult them regarding the attribution of the prize. Their votes will decide the winner. A committee will be appointed to scrutinize the ballot. Our colleague Harduin has been good enough to accept its chairmanship.[5]

---

[5] In the serial version of the story this reportage competition is embellished with a diagrammatic "scoreboard" recording the running tally of the readers' votes, the reputation of which is rather cumbersome and of no real significance, so it is unsurprising that the Tallandier edition omits it, even though the progress of the competition is of some significance to the plot.

TWO MORE THEFTS

Two further thefts have been recorded today.

Monsieur Fanguy, the Commissaire of Police in the Rue de Provence, has discovered a new disappearance, that of little Godefroy Pomme, blond.

On the other hand, Monsieur Péchard, Commissaire of Police in the Gaillon district, has been notified of the disappearance of Charles Clépent, six and two days, pale blond. Charles Clépent is the son of a well known stockbroker.

Godefroy Pomme was abducted at the intersection of the Boulevard Haussmann and the Rue Taitbout, Charles Clépent at the corner of the Rue de Phalbourg, outside the Parc Monceau.

The latter infant was stolen with a dexterity that is near-miraculous. The child was holding on to his mother's dress. She had just taken him in a carriage to see the goats in the Parc Monceau when, almost instantaneously, as she turned the corner of the street, she had the feeling that her son was no longer there.

She looked along the Rue de Phalbourg, by which she had arrived, but saw no one but a few inoffensive passers-by. She ran to the Rue de Thann. The street was almost empty. Only one private carriage could be seen, heading at a rapid pace toward the Place Malesherbes.

Then Madame Clépent ran into the Parc Monceau, found nothing, and came back to wander the neighboring streets, beside herself, then ran toward the Rue des Petits-Champs, where her husband's office is, but changed her mind in order to go directly to the local commissariat.

There she gave a description of her son and details of what he was wearing. At the moment of the theft, the boy was wearing a mastic velvet suit, with large horn buttons ringed with copper, and a matching hat.

Aron Barbarus

STOLEN CHILDREN'S CLOTHING FOUND

The investigation has taken a great step forward.

In various locations, garments belonging to the stolen children have been discovered and handed in to the police.

Many of the people who had found these little costumes had kept them, either out of negligence or indifference, because they attached no importance to them or for other less noble reasons.

It is now possible, therefore, to base deductions on a few tangible clues. Thus, we expect decisive news at any moment.

One very curious thing, which proves that in this great city of Paris, hazard distributes its favors with a certain intelligence, it was our colleague Barbarus who picked up one of these items of jetsam: the last, the little mastic velvet costume of Charles Clépent, which he described yesterday.

BARBARUS' DISCOVERY

At about eleven o'clock in the evening, the *Matin* reporter was going past the Parc Monceau, at the location where, according to his other, little Charles had been abducted. Barbarus wanted to see the place where the theft had been carried out for himself.

He had scarcely taken thirty paces along the Rue de Thann when his attention was attracted by a small object in the middle of the thoroughfare that was scintillating in the light of a nearby gas-lamp.

If it were necessary to stop every time one encounters a stray piece of metal on the roads of Paris one would end up being a full-time rag-picker, so our colleague continued on his way.

Twenty meters further on, however, he changed his mind. Without being able to explain exactly why, the unknown object that he had glimpsed momentarily, doubtless devoid of value, was preying on his mind. One sometimes has these bizarre, incomprehensible obsessions.

In brief, while murmuring "Idiot! Cretin!" to himself, he went back and picked the object up.

It was a button.

That button had an immediate effect on our friend of shock and excitement.

That button was not just any button.

That button was made of horn, with copper trimmings.

That button was probably one of those that had fastened Charles Clépent's costume. *Large horn buttons ringed with copper*, the mother had said. The description fit.

Barbarus immediately reached a conclusion.

The villain who carried out the crime, he thought, *made his escape along the Rue de Thann.*

The button might, in fact, have been carried there after a long sequence of peregrinations, but was it not more logical to deduce that it had fallen off while the thief was making off with his living booty?

It was, therefore, more than probable, so far as Barbarus was concerned, that the mother, in the first moment of anxiety, had not immediately thought of looking in the Rue de Thann and had thus given the abductor time to flee. But these suppositions on our colleague's part, although probable at first sight, were not wholly conclusive, as you will read further on.

Barbarus resumed his route.

Twenty paces further on, he found another button similar to the first, which must have been torn away forcefully, because a shred of fabric was still adhering to it: a fragment of mastic velvet lined with beige cloth.

In the Place Malesherbes, in front of the little triangular garden that brightens the crossroads, the Omnibus Company has had one of those shelters constructed in which its patient customers are accustomed to wait. Behind that construction, the long-sighted Barbarus saw from a distance, in the semi-darkness, a vague white package.

The two discoveries he had just made had sharpened his curiosity. Driven by that clairvoyance of the soul which we call intuition, he went toward that package, picket it up, unwrapped it, and observed, almost without astonishment, that the envelope contained Charles Clépent's clothes, with the shoes, the bonnet, the socks, the sort, the underpants, the braces and one of those flannel bodices beloved by mothers who are absolutely determined to render their children sensitive, delicate and vulnerable to colds.

The buttonholes were ripped. Almost all the buttons had been torn away. The child had, therefore, been undressed violently, by a brutal and hasty hand.

CRUEL QUESTIONS

What, then, can we conclude?

Alas, it is scarcely possible to form a very precise opinion.

The suggestion of our colleague Barbarus, who thinks that the kidnapper must have fled along the Rue de Thann, does not seem irrefutable—far from it.

Even admitting that the thief took that direction, he could not have undressed the child in the middle of the road at four o'clock in the afternoon, and walked on through such a busy neighborhood dragging a naked child by the hand.

One can form more satisfactory hypotheses and reconstruct the drama with greater plausibility.

Quite probably, the thief, after having stolen the child, transported him to his lair, undressed him, and, not knowing what to do with the garments, fearing that they might one day serve as evidence to convict him, got rid of them by throwing them away in a public place. The following night, he must have retaken the route that he had followed with his prey, lost two buttons that had fallen out of the poorly-sealed wrapping-paper in the Rue de Thann and finally discarded his incriminating burden in the Place Malesherbes.

The villain must, in that case, have made the journey twice, at three o'clock to carry out the theft and sometime before eleven to throw away the garments.

In spite of the satisfaction with which we welcome the hope offered by a first glimmer of light in the darkness, there nevertheless remain a few questions, as dolorous as pincers of torture, which will undoubtedly aggravate the general anxiety.

Where are the children?

What has become of them?

What has the child-stealer done with them?

Why does he only kidnap boys?

Why does he only kidnap boys whose hair is a particular shade of blond?

By what method does he abduct them?

Why does he get rid of the clothes?

The only question to which, in the present state of the investigation, it is possible to reply is the last. We have already explained, and the idea must have occurred to everyone, that the thief does not want to keep at home items of clothing that might betray him and serve as evidence in a trial.

But if this hypothesis is plausible, it is followed fatally, with the inflexible cruelty of logic, by a terrible deduction.

We scarcely dare to write it down, remembering that among the readers of these lines are doubtless parents who are still hoping, while we are despairing.

In fact, the presence of the children's clothing would not be any more compromising to the malefactor than the presence of the children themselves. Thus, if he disposes of that which is less dangerous to him, would he not also dispose of that which is more dangerous?

However much tact we would like to employ in order to avoid heaping further distress on families already sorely tried, the events speak for themselves only too clearly, revealing the real meaning of prudent circumlocutions.

Given that it is futile to want to fool oneself, and not to state aloud, in all its brutal horror, what everyone is whispering.

In all probability, the children have been carried away by some sort of vampire, by a being outside humanity, by a mad savage or a savage madman, who, in some ignoble lair, of which he has made a slaughterhouse and a tomb, is murdering them for the pleasure of murdering them, and to destroy the only witnesses to his crimes.

That is what everyone is saying and that is what—we must not, in truth, abandon all hope—is presently most probable. It is certainly not consoling, and will not diminish general impatience.

The government cannot remain indifferent to these crimes. Among other measures, our colleague Bernard informs us that one of the finest agents of the Sûreté, Sub-Brigadier Habischoff, has just been recalled from London, where he was on a mission, and that he will devote himself entirely to the search for the child-stealer.

On the other hand, in consequence of a special request from our ambassador in Washington, a famous American detective, William Trisson, has been summoned by cable. He will embark on the *Savoie* in three days.

And the police are following our example. In the same way that we have offered to reward the skill the skill of our reporters, they have promised a sum of fifteen thousand francs to anyone who denounces the guilty party.

Alone in the face of so many combined efforts, the child-stealer will certainly end up being caught.

We also know that the police now posses certain extraordinarily curious clues of the greatest interest. According to this information, the abductor will prove to be a man of a character even stranger and more enigmatic than the series of crimes suggests.

PLACES WHERE CHILDREN'S CLOTHING HAS BEEN FOUND

We owe to our colleague Bernard, who lays siege to the offices of the Sûreté every day, a list of the places where the garments of the various child victims have been discovered.

We know well enough that with regard to a crime of such enormity, and so fantastic, the slightest details had their significance and are of great interest.

Bernard Flaquette's clothes were found at the corner of the Rue de Maure and the Rue du Faubourg-Saint-Martin.

Paolo Palavacoccini's were in the in Rue d'Artois, at the corner of the Rue de Berri.

Urbain Godedouin's were under the Pont des Invalides, near the Quai de la Conférence.

Ange Pompaigne's were on a windowsill on the ground floor of the Restaurant Foyot in the Rue de Condé. It was in the same place, a few years ago, that a criminal placed the bomb that, by a quasi-symbolist hazard, injured the anarchist poet Laurent Tailhade.[6]

Pierre Camdelaur's were on the Pont d'Orsay, opposite the Gare d'Orléans.

Frantz Vetyolle's crumpled suit was behind the door of the building next door to the Salle Erard in the Rue de Mail.

Nicolas Barlatescu's pale gray costume was at the Palais-Royal, behind the Théâtre-Français.

Jules Bimbaleau's gray chine trousers and black-and-white check waistcoat of were under the peristyle of the Bourse in the Rue du Quatre-Septembre.

Fernand Pig's dark blue coat was in the Rue de Rivoli, almost directly opposite the Rue d'Alger, inside the gate of the Jardin des Tuileries.

Godefroy Pomme's clothes were at the Carrefour Gaillon.

As Barbarus informed us yesterday, the parcel containing Charles Clépent's mastic costume was next to the omnibus stop in the Place Malesherbes.

Our list makes no mention of the garments of André de Vautremesse; they have not been found as yet.

---

[6] The Symbolist poet Laurent Tailhade (1854-1919) obtained some notoriety when he expressed public sympathy for Alfred Vaillant, who threw a "bomb" (little more than a firework) into the Chambre des Députés in December 1893. Several months later Tailhade was injured in an incident involving a much more dangerous bomb thrown by an anarchist, causing a certain amusement among those who did not share his sympathies and resulting in some sharp comments in the press.

FIRST INVESTIGATION
IS THE THIEF A RICH AND COMPASSIONATE MAN?

All the parcels have been carefully examined at the Sûreté, in the hope that the child-stealer, in spite of all his circumspection, might not have left, in one or two of them, one of those trivial items that reveal someone's identity.

First of all, the various pieces of paper in which the garments were wrapped have been examined at length.

Seven of those pieces of paper are daily or evening newspapers: one *Aurore*, two *Matins*, a *Soleil*, an *Éclair*, a *Soir* and a *Temps*.

It is noticeable that the names of these dailies all correspond to natural phenomena of which the heavens are the origin.

As lunatics often take a great interest in astronomical and meteorological data, some people might conclude, on the basis of the comparison of these titles, that the guilty party must necessarily be insane.

Let us pass on to other, more serious observations. Two other parcels were formed with uncut weekly periodicals: the *Annales politiques et littéraires* and the *Presse Medicale*, and two more with wrapping paper, gray on one side and glossy black on the other.

Can anything be made of these observations, in the way of vague clues as to the thief's state of mind?

All shades of political opinion are represented among these periodicals. The bandit, if he has opinions, is singularly eclectic. He goes from monarchism to socialism, passing via medicine.

The simplest thing is to imagine that when he runs short of wrapping paper he buys a newspaper at random.

It is therefore better, once again, to reserve our judgment and not to seek to make too much of what we know, when we know nothing as yet, or very little.

That little is, however, rather interesting.

It unveils an extraordinary little corner of the malefactor's psychology.

Almost all the stolen children belong to well-to-do families.

Four of them were wearing small items of jewelry of a certain value. Urbain Godedouins, for example, had a ring on his finger with a beautiful emerald, and a light bracelet on his left arm formed by a slender gold thread. Pierre Candelaur was wearing a golden hear embellished with diamonds, attached to a little chain, Nicolas Barlatescu a beautiful holy medallion, similarly decorated with diamonds, and Frantz Vetyolle an Asiatic talisman representing the head of a bat, engraved on an opal, whose enormous eyes were made of rubies.

All these objects were found in the parcels.

According to the calculations made by the police, the total value of this jewelry is between fifteen and twenty thousand francs. Young Godedouins' emerald alone is valued at seven thousand francs.

That is a small fortune, tempting enough for an ordinary villain. The child-stealer, however, has scorned it.

Is he a rich man—or, at least one capable of supplying his needs? It is also possible, however, that being poor, but extremely prudent, he prefers not to keep anything, in order to minimize the chances of being caught.

We reported yesterday, by courtesy of Barbarus, how Charles Clépent's garment bore traces of a ferocious and brutal manhandling. The ripped-off buttons and the torn lining are evidence of violence. The clothes discovered since prove that not all the children were maltreated in that fashion. What our colleague reported is the worst case. Three others were in a rather poor state, which demonstrated that the thief had used force to undress his victims, but the other seven boys, probably terrified or in no state to scream or defend themselves, were undressed calmly and without effort.

One other striking and impressive observation has been made, which leaves the field free for a thousand reflections.

The thief has left a lock of hair from the stolen child in each parcel.

To what preoccupation, then, is this singular individual obedient? Is there in his soul one of those contradictions of sentiment, one of those antinomies of sensibility, that one sometimes observes with astonishment in the hardest of hearts?

What does that lock of hair signify?

Does not the bandit seem to be saying to the parents something along the lines of: *I have stolen your child; you will never see him again, but I want you to have something of his, a holy relic that you may kiss every day, while thinking about the little absentee?*

If that is the abductor's thinking, it denotes, in spite of everything, a certain capacity for emotion, unexpected in a malefactor who does not hesitate to commit the worst of crimes.

The story of a brigand with a soft heart, who robs passengers in diligences but is full of compassion for the poor man he encounters in his path, is certainly very old. This time, however, it reappears in a new and bizarre edition, curiously revised and corrected, in which the conflict of sentiments and oppositions of character, after such crimes, surpass anything that the *roman feuilleton* and popular story-tellers have dared to venture. A philanthropic brigand is still plausible, but to accumulate so many tears around oneself, to excite the horror of an entire nation, and then to abandon oneself to that kind of sentimentality is something else entirely!

Can a man capable of stealing children from their mothers, and perhaps of killing them, also be relatively human, gentle and compassionate? Can he be capable of imagining the desolate hearth, the sad meals lacking the chatter of a habitual guest, the gaiety of the household?

And, in representing these scenes of bleak despair or loud lamentations to himself, can the mysterious villain have sufficient delicacy of sentiment to imagine that a lock of hair might often soothe a pain and charm a resignation?

Alain Bernard

NEW DISCOVERIES
LOCKS OF BLACK HAIR, THIS TIME

The child-stealer has not renounced his sinister occupations.

Neither the army of policemen put on the case, nor the more severe vigilance of fathers and mothers, has frightened off the bandit, ready for any audacity.

Our pessimism is motivated by the discovery of three more parcels containing children's clothes.

The first was picked up in the Rue Franklin, almost opposite the Rue des Reservoirs, in front of the Trocadéro palace. It was composed of gray and black wrapping paper analogous to that we described yesterday, containing a brown suit embroidered with large darker brown threads, underwear bearing the initials A.L., polished lace-up shoes and a lock of *black* hair.

Similarly, at the crossroads of the Rues Falguière, Dulac and Delambre, wrapped in a copy of the London Times, was one of those short jackets cut above the buttocks that the English call "Eton jackets," a large white collar, a small bowler hat, and underwear marked B.G.F. with a vicomte's crown and *a lock of black hair.*

Thirdly, the concierge of a building in the Avenue du Trocadéro found, in front of the Musée Galliera, a little blouse in blue cloth with large pleats, a pair of trousers in the same cloth with buckles on the knees, a white belt, a shirt, underpants, a woolen waistcoat, white shoes, and a golden Lourdes medallion, the underwear marked P.-S.

From the pockets of the latter garments a veritable bazaar was extracted: a spinning-top, feathers, a magnet, a penknife, three meters of gilded pastry-maker's thread, two meters of red string, a half-eaten piece of chocolate, one of those tiny little lorgnettes with bone rims, through which one can distinguish, by closing one eye and making strenuous efforts with the other, monuments and landscapes, plus twenty-five centime coin, three glass marbles, an agate whistle, a blue pencil, a shoemaker's measuring-tape, a thimble, half a pair of driving-goggles and a lock of *brown*—dark brown, almost black—hair. All of it was wrapped in an old copy of the Milan *Secolo*.

Alain Bernard, who gave us this information, has emphasized this striking new development.

Among all the other extraordinary particularities of this astounding affair, the thief's initial preference for blond-haired boys was the most curious and the most characteristic.

Either to confuse the search or because blond children are now more carefully guarded, the disconcerting brigand has abruptly changed his predilection. It is now brown- or black-haired children who have the sad privilege of awakening his covetousness.

These new facts are not calculated to calm the public emotion created by the vampire's exploits. It is increasing by the hour.

It is even threatening to become dangerous, by pushing into the background national preoccupation with grave events that are threatening world equilibrium and peace, which would have a profound, enormous and lasting impact of the social and economic fortunes of our homeland.

A LETTER

BOHEMIANS?

We have received a host of letters from our readers. This one is interesting because it is the echo of an opinion very widespread among the public.

Monsieur le directeur,

You might perhaps accuse me of playing an old game. Moreover, I shall not deny that I adore melodrama, its facile tears, and its stories, akin to waking dreams, always exciting and original because they are always the same.

It is because I like these fables that I am suggesting to you an idea that is perhaps, after all, no worse than any other.

Why should the child-stealer be a vampire who must be murdering these poor children?

Since we are reduced to conjectures, may we not think that the little ones who are exciting our pity might have been kidnapped by fairground performers?

You are smiling? That sort of thing no longer happens? Well, I can assure you that it does still happen.

In my travels, and not only to the Théâtre de l'Ambigu, in the midst of troupes of Bohemians, exhibitors of bears and acrobats, I have encountered children of various ages who certainly did not belong to the Romany race. The creaminess of the skin alone revealed a different origin. For these wanderers of the world, who are the true tziganes, a child is still an item of property like a horse, and, just as they steal horses when then do not have one, they steal children when there is a shortage.

One of the circumstances that militates in favor of my opinion is the miraculous skill of the thief.

Who is unaware that Bohemians, pilferers by nature, excelling in the art of deception, know all the tricks, every sleight of hand, and that they are cunning, prudent and subtle?

Far be it from me to pretend that my idea is the expression of the truth—but it might be, and it would be relatively consoling, at least by comparison with the hypothesis of a vampire massacring children.

In these circumstances, please give my letter the hospitality of your newspaper. The parents who are weeping might find a reason for hope therein.

Dr. R. de Rautchild

We have published this letter because it responds to a state of mind much more common than one might believe. Romanticism is not dead in France. We have it in our blood. We love to see, reproduced yet again before our eyes, the beautiful stories that have impassioned generations of theater-goers.

Nevertheless, in spite of our desire and the pleasure we would obtain from telling out readers a tale so certain to have an effect on sensitive hearts, we cannot, even in passing, sacrifice the truth to poetry. The coup has not been carried out by Bohemians. They would certainly have kept the clothes, and especially the valuable items. Returning them is something absolutely contrary to the traditions of their tribes.

It is necessary to search for another explanation.

THE IDENTITY OF THE VICTIMS IS KNOWN

The children with black hair abducted the day before yesterday are:

1. Philippe Soleillaut, aged six years and one month.
2. Léon Aproli, six and eight days.
3. Bouquet de Gobely-Franthéon. Six and three weeks.

The first (the parcel at the Musée Galliéra) was walking with his mother. He was stolen in the Avenue du Bois-du-Boulogne, in the vicinity of the junction of the Rue de la Pompe.

The second (the parcel in the Rue Franklin) was stolen in the Bois de Boulogne, near the crossroads at the end of the lakes, where the path around the lower lake meets the Route de Longchamps and the Route de Suresnes. He was with a young playmate, under the surveillance of the latter's mother.

The third (the parcel in the Rue Falguière) was with his tutor, Abbé Maps. They were coming out of the Institut Pasteur in the Rue Dutot, where they had gone to visit one of Monsieur de Gobely-Franthéon's farmers, who is undergoing treatment after having been bitten by a rabid dog.

Such is the information that Alain Bernard sent us about an hour before sending us the following note:

Isidore Bimorel, a boy between six and seven years of age, has been abducted almost under the very eyes of his father and mother at the corner of the Rue de la Pompe and the Chaussée de la Muette. His clothes were recovered a few hours later in the Avenue de la Motte-Picquet, behind the Galerie des Machines, opposite the École Militaire. The child in question has *red* hair.

BLOND CHILDREN? DARK-HAIRED CHILDREN?
RED-HAIRED CHILDREN?
HAZARD OR PURPOSE

Dry and brief as it is, this information will produce a sensation.

One might think that the thief were amusing himself taunting the public. Could we not expect, after the theft of the last three children, that the series of black-haired victims would continue and extend like the blond series?

Alas, this is where we are. The public remains convinced that, until the author of the crimes is arrested, every day will be marked by the disappearance of at least one poor little mite. No one is any longer expecting to see an end to the sequence of abductions. People are competing in trying to guess what form his sinister whim will take tomorrow.

So long as he was attacking boys with pale blond hair, the parents of children with hair that was less blond, red, chestnut, and various shades of brown or black were only moved by sympathy without fearing for themselves.

After the abduction of three children with dark hair, the parents of blond and fair-haired children uttered a sigh of relief. They breathed a little more easily, thinking: *The capillary preferences of the kidnapper have changed; it's someone else's turn.*

By virtue of the innate need for symmetry that is a malady of civilized humans, many of our readers would have begun to imagine that after twelve very blond children, the sequence of dark-haired children would similarly extend to a dozen.

Now that the fourth of the new series is a red-haired child, everyone feel gravely threatened.

There is no longer a rule that insures some to the detriment of others.

Tomorrow, the sly brigand might go to the left or the right, on a whim, without any longer imposing the bizarre law that struck all imaginations when the crimes began.

Why, after having commenced with a dozen blonds, has he stopped so abruptly?

Why, after having abducted three black-haired children, did he not want to continue with that kind of color?

These are questions that have been added to all the others to which this mysterious affair gives rise at every step, and which, thus far, have remained insoluble.

INTERESTING OBSERVATION OF A READER
THE ABDUCTED CHILDREN WERE ALL VERY INTELIGENT

One of our female readers has made us party to an original observation—which is, doubtless, merely original.

We are printing it as a curiosity.

It proves, according to our correspondent, that a very special particularity characterizes the thefts of children.

Monsieur le rédacteur en chef,

I am one of the individuals of both sexes—and there are many—who exercise their sagacity every day on the prodigious puzzle that the villain is posing to the attentive world. I read with great care, every morning, the article concerning the thefts, in order to try to form an opinion of my own, to divine what kind of man the malefactor must be, to what stratum of society he belongs, to imagine the motive for his crimes, and finally, to discover whether anything in the interpretation of the facts might be escaping the tightly-knit coats-of-mail of your reasoning.

Thus, I have been very disappointed not to read in my newspaper, on the subject of Isidore Bimorel, Bouquet de Gobely-Franthéon, Léon Aproli, Philippe Soleillaut, Godefroy Pomme and Charles Clépent, the tiny psychological detail that you have given with regard to the other stolen children.

I believed that I had picked up a trail. Already I was palpitating with the hope of the hunter who scents a fine prey, and now you have cheated me without warning. I expected further abductions gradually to verify my finding before launching the loud cry of triumph that would have announced my discovery. Perhaps you have robbed me of that glory; let me at least pick up its crumbs.

Not only, as was justly observed, were the ten boys abducted at the start all aged between six and seven years, and not only were they all blond, but they were all very intelligent.

Reread attentively the notes that you inserted after their names.

Bernard Flaquette, alias Bobichon was endowed with "obvious intelligence."

Paolo Palavacoccini appeared "very alert and lively."

Urbain Godedouins, alias Chichi had an "intelligence very alert, very artful, above his age."

Ange Pompaigne possessed an "astonishing intelligence."

Pierre Candelaur had the "sparkling intelligence of a Parisian urchin."

Frantz Vetyolle was "exceptionally intelligent."

Nicolas Barlatescu had a "remarkable intelligence."

Jules Bimbaleau was "very intelligent."

Fernand Pig had an "astonishing intelligence," like Ange Pompaigne.

André de Vautremesse was very intelligent, like Jules Bimbaleau.

Do you not think that the words "intelligence" and "intelligent," repeated like a refrain, signify something?

What?

I shall refrain from writing what I know, because I do not know anything—but it seems to me, something murmurs in the depths of my being, that there is a precious clue here, relative to the mentality of the thief.

People have been wondering since the beginning of this story why the thief only took blonds. No one has wondered why his unfortunate preference weighed—and perhaps still weighs—on children clearly, very or exceptionally intelligent, sparing those of mediocre and low intelligence.

Mistinguette[7] of the Théâtre des Bouffes-Parisiens

We shall leave to our colleague Clovis Binard the prerogative of replying.

RESPONSE TO A READER

The fact that has struck the witty and charming artiste has not gone unperceived by us.

But is it of any importance?

If it proves anything, it is an eternal and touching verity.

All that it demonstrates is that, so far as parents are concerned, no one in the world is more beautiful, witty or more intelligent than their own children.

The descriptions that my friend Bernard collected, with the patience of a beer-drinker, were compiled in accordance with information furnished by the mothers or fathers of the poor vanished children. All of them had a profound admiration for their sons. It could not be otherwise. Did these prodigies not recite fables marvelously, did they not perform calculations over dessert, like Inaudi,[8] to the approving amazement of every guest?

Do not be astonished any longer. The weakness in question is human. It is also exquisite, and charming.

The child-stealer could steal any child in France and it would be the same. He cannot steal children on mediocre or low intelligence. Ask the mothers. There are none.

Clovis Binard

---

[7] Mistinguette (1875-1956), who subsequently preferred to spell her pseudonym Mistinguett, was, in 1906, the highest-paid entertainer in the world, famous for the risqué nature of her performances as an actress and singer.

[8] The uncanny mathematical abilities of the Italian child prodigy Jacques Inaudi (1867-1950) were investigated in Paris by the psychologist Jean-Martin Charcot, and Camille Flammarion was enormously impressed by him.

It is with a veritable discouragement that we conclude this article with the announcement of a further kidnapping.

Alain Bernard's notebook thus bears a seventeenth name, that of Wenceslas Lévy.

Wenceslas Lévy has light chestnut hair.

The mother was sitting on a deck-chair in the Bois de Boulogne, about two-thirds of the way between the Route de Madrid and the Porte Maillot. The child was playing beside her. He disappeared. The mother, who was reading, did not see anything and does not know anything.

The parcel of his clothes was found on the steps of the Metro station at the Porte Dauphine.

Only two of the three striking particularities that we noted in the first article devoted to the child-stealer remain, therefore.

The enigmatic scoundrel, although he no longer limits his audacity to blonds, continues nevertheless to spare girls and only takes children aged between six and seven.

His skill in disappearing, carrying away his prey, is unparalleled—as, in fact, is his astonishing flair for detecting the age of children.

Thus far, that age has varied between six and seven years with a mathematical regularity, the youngest being aged six years and four days, and the oldest fifteen days short of seven.

Instructed by disastrous experience, we shall not hasten to conclude that girls or younger or older boys will be safe from these crimes in future. Doubtless the child-stealer has other surprises in store for us.

Our competition of reportage between Bernard, Binard and Barbarus has been a great success. Why of the three journalists will win the 25,000 francs? No one knows as yet. In the meantime, an anonymous poet has addressed the following lines of verse to *Le Matin*:

Bernard, Binard and Barbarus?
Which of you will equal Croesus?
Who will be running to the bank
Carrying twenty-five thousand francs?
It's worth your while to solve the rebus
Bernard, Binard or Barbarus.

Barbarus, Binard or Bernard?
Who will be the lucky bastard?
The one who'll unveil the mystery
That's the most maddening in history?
The cleverest, the most on-guard?
Barbarus, Binard or Bernard?

Barbarus, Bernard or Binard
Which of you will be starred?
Most certainly I will agree
That one of you must hold the key
Let him not be long in retard
Barbarus, Bernard or Binard.

What can one say of Barbarus?
He has the lynx-like eyes of Argus.
But till today that long clear sight
Hasn't found a guiding light.
The others will be covetous
If he who come first is Barbarus.

But his worthy comrade Bernard
Does not leave much to hazard
He's showing such great expertise
He's sure that it will be a breeze.
Not brilliant but don't disregard,
That's what we think of old Bernard.

But I'm also quite fond of Binard
Who strolls along the Boulevard
While his friends think it a duty
To get their hands on the booty.
He idles with the avant-garde
He's in no hurry, that Binard.

Bernard, Binard and Barbarus
Disregard the superfluous
As they chase the elusive thief
But all of them might come to grief
And success for them is dubious.
Bernard, Binard and Barbarus.

YET ANOTHER THEFT!

Every morning, now, Paris wakes up anxious and anguished, wondering whether the frightful series of thefts of children will ever cease, whether the all-too-real bogey-man has finally been captured or reduced to impotence. And every morning we are obliged to respond to that daily question with the announcement of a new victim.

The last page of Alain's Bernard's notebook bears today the mention of Justin Chipé, a predestined name.[9]

Justin Chipé was abducted from the Jardin des Plantes, in front of the botanical gardens.

The discovery of his clothes preceded the deposition given by the mother to the Commissaire of Police, the customary parcel having been picked up a few minutes after the accomplishment of the theft.

Thanks to a letter found in a pocket, the paper of which bore a printed address, it was possible to learn to whom the clothes belonged before the complaint had been made.

That letter is so touching, so tender in ingenuousness, that we think it appropriate to publish it in all its candid incorrectness.

The latter is addressed by Justin Chipé to his grandmother, the widowed Madame Montrement, the wife of the general who distinguished himself as a colonel at Tonkin and died last year after a fall from his horse.

Paris (France, Europe, the World, the Universe)
2 July 1906
My deer Grandmama

---

[9] "Predestined" because *chipé*, as past participle of the verb *chiper*, means "stolen."

I was very good yesterday, especially with the cod liver oyl. Then Mama made me promise to write to you, and promised me a chocolat niclair to eat.

The wether is fine here.

Bebette has broken the big doll you gave her, but Papa has taken it to the head-mender, which made Bebette very glad, who was afraid you would scold her.

The wether is fine here. It fell with rain yesterday, but today we can go for a walk and play.

That's all I have to tell you. Oh yes! Papa was cross because I said to the minister who came to dinner with us that the minister is going to fall.

It was true, since Papa said it at table the other day, and said that the minister who was coming couldn't be more of an imbiseal than the other. But I didn't say that to the minister, because people don't like being called imbiseals, especially when you're deckorated.

As long as he doesn't hurt himself falling, the minister. He's old. He might hurt himself.

That's all I have to say.

If the wether is still fine, I'm going with Bebette to the Jardin des Plantes. There's a new zebra and a jiraffe with a long neck.

I kiss you very much because I love you.

It seems too that the big elefan at the Jardin des Plantes has the colick. They've given it cathaplasms and cod liver oyl. I take it too but it's not nice. Maman promised me a chocolat niclair because I took two spoonfuls yesterday.

Your little Justin who loves you very much because he kisses you.

Justin Chipé

The reasons why the child-stealer is the object of a unanimous and universal execration, which render his crimes more odious than the most odious, more abject and more infamous than the most abject and the most infamous, are all in this letter, so naïve in its tenderness, so delightful in its innocence.

We cannot imagine that a man exists, created like us, with a mouth, eyes and a nose, who is capable of doing the slightest harm to one of those weak little creatures whose smile is charming, whose gestures of joy and caresses disarm the most hard-hearted.

ALAIN BERNARD'S NOTEBOOK

Nineteenth abduction: Ambroise Riffelard, the son of Dr. Riffelard, a hospital physician. Was with his father. Kidnapped Rue Saint-Ferdinand, at the corner of the square of the same name, at two o'clock in the afternoon.

The clothes were recovered half an hour later at the foot of the Arc-de-Triomphe, at the corner of the Avenue Carnot and the Avenue MacMahon.

A DRAMA
SUICIDE ATTEMPT OF M. AND MME. POMPAIGNE
A BRAVE WOMAN

The affair of the child-stealer has inevitably generated a series of accessory disasters.

Here is one drama!

Yesterday morning, at eight o'clock, a chambermaid in the service of Monsieur and Madame Pompaigne, intending to bring her employers their customary chocolate, was suffocated as she went into the dining room by a strong odor of gas.

Suspecting an accident, she ran to the bedroom, found that it was empty, immediately ran to a neighboring bathroom, opened the door and recoiled in horror.

Monsieur and Madame Pompaigne were lying on the ground, one top of another in the form of a cross.

Practical and courageous, the servant leapt to the window, broke the glass with a thrust of her elbow, closed the gas-tap of the water-heater, which was wide open, raised the inanimate bodies into a sitting position, leaning them against the bath, and ran for help.

I have interviewed this energetic woman.

"I've only been placed with the Pompaignes for four days," she told me. "Good people! They'd intended to keep Maria, in spite of everything—Maria's the maid that let little Ange Pompaigne get stolen in the Rue Racine—but every time they saw her, they burst into tears. So Maria left of her own accord...it broke her heart, poor girl, and she blamed herself...but it wasn't her fault, was it? The same things happened to other kids who were with Papa or Mama. Anyways, Maria's gone...she's in the hospital now, with a bad fever. I took her place, because she asked me to.

"Oh, it wasn't cheerful, the Pompaigne household! I felt sorry for them. Remember that they only had the one child, and he came late, when they were old. One loves them even more, that sort. Since the little one was stolen, they hardly talked any more. They spend whole days looking at one another, without speaking, and when they did talk, it was in low voices, as if beside a death-bed. It was still necessary, at table, to set a place for the little one, a high chair and a silver-plated dish. There are people who need to maintain grief. I said to myself, if this goes on, they'll both fall ill.

"Yesterday morning, they'd lost their appetite for life. They'd spent the night together, without going to bed, and at seven o'clock, they'd had enough. They went into the bathroom. Monsieur stopped up the gaps in the doors with dusters and opened the gas-tap of the water-heater. I arrived an hour later. They would have died but for a little accident.

"Before falling down, Monsieur must have stood up, making a sweeping mechanical gesture. With his hand he must have dislodged a pair of leather reins with which little Ange played at riding a horse. They were hanging from a shelf where the kid's playthings were put. Monsieur pulled them down without meaning to. The reins had dragged an old drum down with them. As it tumbled, the drum, which was near the window, had made a small hole in the glass. A little air had got in. I only had to make the hole bigger with my elbow.

"Really, you see, it was the little one's toys that saved the father and mother...you could even say that it was the boy himself."

Such is the story of the drama, according to the chambermaid.

Monsieur and Madame Pompaigne are recovering. All danger seems to have passed.

Barbarus

LETTER FROM A MOTHER, A VICTIM OF THE ABDUCTOR

You will remember that one of our readers tried, the other day, to discover a tiny part of the solution to the great enigma. Is it not curious that, if one refers to the parents' depositions, the thief only abducts intelligent children?

To that observation, Clovis Binard replied in a tone that was perhaps too light—but he certainly had no intention of wounding the heart of one of the mothers of the bandit's victims.

Although its tone is a trifle sharp, we do not hesitate to publish the letter that our colleague's article prompted.

Monsieur,

It is perhaps not in very good taste to joke about mothers who spend their days, in tears, in an uncertainty that is perhaps more cruel than any mourning.

Oh, you who witness as spectators the events that tear us apart cannot imagine our anguish in not knowing what has become of the unfortunate children.

Every morning, as soon as they appear, I throw myself upon all the newspapers, hoping to find a glimmer of hope and not to have to despair. And when, instead of the consolatory works I seek, I discover the stupid lucubrations of a journalist trying to be witty at our expense, all the emotion by which I am bruised mutates into indignation and anger.

So keep your sarcasm for better occasions.

No, Monsieur, I did not tell the Commissaire of Police that my son is exceptionally intelligent because of maternal vanity.

I said it because it is true and because it might be useful to the investigation.

My son, although very young, precisely because his is endowed in an extraordinary fashion, would not have allowed himself to be carried off like a defenseless little lamb. He would have made rational and serious efforts to escape from the claws of the abductor. He would not have allowed himself to be dragged off God knows where by the lure of some piece of candy or some plaything.

The observation of your reader is not as stupid as you are trying to make us believe. I am personally convinced that she is right, and there is, in the fact that the stolen children are all very intelligent, something typical and striking, OF CAPITAL IMPORTANCE.

Now, if you want proof that I am not letting myself get carried away by a self-esteem that, although quite comprehensible, would nevertheless be a trifle ridiculous, I can give you a formal and categorical demonstration of the brilliant and miraculously precocious qualities on my little Frantz.

I shall copy, for your usage, a passage from a letter that my physician sent to me a week ago. "Frantz," he wrote "amazes me by the incredible maturity of his mind. I fear that his brain might be working too hard. He is an admirable child, worthy of the greatest interest…etc…"

Know, Monsieur, that this letter was written to me by Dr. Flax, who is, incontestably, the greatest medical glory of Paris, and the most reputed specialist for children.

I dare to hope that in the light of this evidence, you will spare us henceforth the Attic salt, too bitter for our taste, of your witticisms.

Accept, Monsieur, my salutations,

Isidora Vetyolle

Madame Vetyolle is the mother of little Frantz Vetyolle, one of the first children to disappear.

THE AFFAIR OF THE CHILD-STEALER IN THE CHAMBRE

Monsieur Georges Larry, the well-known député, has just written the following note to Monsieur Clemenceau, the Minister of the Interior:

Monsieur le Ministre,

I have the honor of informing you that I shall be depositing at the office of the Chambre an interpellation on the subject of the "child-stealer." I hope that you will see for to reply to me as soon as possible. As an elected representative of Paris, I cannot remain indifferent to events that trouble my constituents to this degree.

Please accept, Monsieur le Ministre, the assurance of my very distinguished consideration.

Georges Larry.

ANDRÉ DE VAUTREMESSE'S CLOTHES
A STORY OF CAT-BURGLARS
A TRAIL
THE HOME OF BARON DE VAUTREMESSE

I was lying peacefully in my bed this morning when my maidservant knocked on the door. "Come in," I groaned

"Monsieur Binard," my old Clémence exclaimed, fearfully, "it's a police-man!"

She was not very happy.

Neither was I.

I have thumbed my nose so frequently at so many petty laws that, I confess, the presence in my home of a guardian of the peace suddenly troubled my conscience, previously so tranquil. Which of my victims had sent a representative of public vindictiveness to my home?

"Ask him what he wants."

Clémence went out briefly, and then came back.

"It's on behalf of Monsieur Fanguy, the Commissaire of Police in the Rue de Provence. He asks Monsieur to come immediately."

I leapt out of bed with a single bound.

It was at the Commissariat in the Rue de Provence that, on the day when mention of the child-stealer was first heard, I had obtained news of the complaint made by the Baronne de Vautremesse.

I therefore had the policeman shown in, and I interrogated him while I got dressed.

The policeman in question was the worthy Binette, whom I knew well.

As strong as a Turk and as lithe as a leopard, the fellow in question, a former matelot trained in all gymnastics, was the hero of an unusual chase, which our readers will probably remember.

Last year, he pursued two cat-burglars, climbers of a disconcerting agility, for three solid hours across all the roofs formed by the block of houses limited by the Rues Taitbout, Saint-Lazare, Saint-Georges and d'Aumale. The burglars passed, with an astonishing speed, from outhouses to ledges, from ledges to chimney-stacks, from chimney-stacks to flues, from flues to eaves, from eaves to gutters, from gutters to ridges, from ridges to drainpipes, from drainpipes to skylights, from skylights to mansards, from mansards to pinnacles and from pinnacles to platforms without wearying the indefatigable Binette, without ever finding his muscles or his courage lacking.

Those three men accomplished, above the streets, over frightful slopes, and over slates and tiles, one of the most prodigious sporting exploits of recent years.

In the end, one of the cat-burglars fell into a courtyard and broke a leg. The other surrendered to Binette, who thus holds the record—worth as much as many others—for roof-running.

"So, my worthy Binette, Monsieur Fanguy is summoning me?"

"Yes, Monsieur Binard. All his inspectors are busy, so Monsieur Fanguy asked me to come to find you."

"With regard to the child-stealer, eh?"

"With regard to that blackguard."

"I suspected as much. What's new?"

"André de Vautremesse's clothes have been found. They were the last ones missing from the collection. Now, the Sûreté has them all in its hands."

"Ah!"

"It's me who found them."

"How's that, my brave Binette?"

"Another story of cat-burglars. What did you expect? It appears that the building wasn't a going concern. When a building isn't a going concern, the roofers stop work. When the roofers stop work, one encounters more cat-burglars. That's their business, roofs. So, at eight o'clock this morning I was on duty. A concierge called me. A cat-burglar was at work in his building. That's my specialty. He wasn't difficult to catch. He tried to run away, naturally, but as soon as he saw me, he stopped. 'Binette,' he said, 'I surrender. You can have me, you're too good at this game. I don't want to break my neck.' I took him away like a mate.

"On the way, he gave me a tip. In one of the mansards he'd just visited, he'd broken the lock of a trunk. In the trunk, he'd found a kid's clothes, a sailor-suit, with a white collar edged with blue, and a beret on which he's read City of Brighton, and inside, Chapman & Co., London." (Binette pronounced them "Sitty of Brigton" and "Capman Anco").

"The burglar remembered the details you'd published—no doubt about it! They were André de Vautremesse's clothes. Naturally, I told Monsieur Fanguy about it. We went to look at the trunk together. We found the clothes. The lock of his hair was in the pocket, as usual. We took the sailor-suit away and arrested the maid."

"What maid?"

"The maid who owned the trunk."

"But in that case, Binette, since the costume couldn't have got into the maid's trunk by itself, perhaps we're on the track of the thief!"

"Perhaps, and perhaps not," replied Agent Binette, who, although a native of Brive-la-Gaillarde, can be a Norman at times.

His confidences hadn't calmed my impatience at all. Ten minutes later, I leapt into a fiacre.

At the Commissariat, I was a trifle disappointed; Monsieur Fanguy didn't want to tell me anything. I begged him to let me talk to the maidservant he'd arrested, but he refused, with the gesture of a calm and stubborn man, and a hint of a smile.

"Then why the devil did you wake me up at this ungodly hour?"

The Commissaire looked up at the clock ironically—it was showing eleven o'clock—and replied: "Well, last time I saw you, you told me, if I'm not mistaken, that you knew Madame de Vautremesse."

"Yes—I run into her quite often at dinners at the home of Chocarne-Moreau,[10] the painter of Parisians kids."

"Do me a favor, then. We have strict orders. We have to act with regard to the families with all possible care when we have bad news to give them. Will you take responsibility for telling the Baron that his son's clothes have been found? I can only write an official letter or do the thing brutally. You can use the pretext of a visit, lead the conversation around to it gradually..."

"Some chore! Anyway, I'll do it."

Another cab took me to the Rue de Miromesnil, where Monsieur de Vautremesse lives."

The Baron was out.

I asked to see the Baronne.

A domestic introduced me into a superb drawing room, entirely painted, walls and ceiling, in pale gray with gold trimmings. Everything there is dazzlingly bright. Everything that isn't indispensably opaque is transparent, in glass or crystal. Not many trinkets, but very select, in irreproachable taste: marvelous and sober Chinese vases; a large Gallé cup; a Louis XV pendulum clock in mint condition. Everything there is cheerful, respiring health, aspiring air and light. No frame was every less appropriate to dolor and despair.

I was making these reflections when Madame de Vautremesse came in. Immediately, I noticed that her sincere grief spread more sadness over the surroundings than the surroundings radiated gaiety upon her. Not a single wrinkle, however, not a single line of care had marked the great lady's impeccably beautiful face with its claw. The suffering of the mother was internal, but in spite of everything, she projected a kind of shadow over the bright luxury surrounding her.

As best I could, I tried to attenuate the painful aspect of my mission.

"Oh, Monsieur, we're no longer under any illusion...are we?"

That "are we?" was addressed to Monsieur de Vautremesse, who came back home at that moment, accompanied by a small boy, a second son.

---

[10] The artist Paul Chocarne-Moreau (1866-1931) built his reputation on paintings of Parisian street scenes, many of them featuring young boys getting up to various kinds of mischief.

We brought the master of the house up to date. He was nervous and feverish.

"Oh, if they ever catch him, the swine," he exclaimed, "I'll ask to execute him with my own hands."

"Perhaps he's already been caught. The arrested maidservant must have explained how she came to be in possession of your son's clothes. That's doubtless the beginning of the thread."

"Let's hope so,"

I took advantage of the opportunity to ask Madame de Vautremesse whether she had remembered anything that might assist the investigation.

"No," she replied. "The child disappeared as if by magic. Except..."

The Baronne hesitated. Interrogatively, I repeated: "Except?"

"Except that, when I try to remember the moments preceding the abduction...well, it seems to me that I noticed a man, very tall and very stout, with a big beard—a true giant—who looked at me, for just a moment, insistently. But it's so vague, so blurred! I can't even say whether, by force of striving, of racking my brains trying to remember, I might have imagined it... And yet, I believe, I truly believe, that I'm not mistaken. Yes, I believe...I was just passing a pharmacist's shop, which is at the corner of the Rue de la Chaussée-d'Antin and the Rue de Provence...or the Rue de la Victoire... The tall man looked at me, and then he looked at me again, a little further on. But I'm not sure...I think...simply...there were so many people passing by..."

While Madame de Vautremesse tried once again to reassemble her memories, the Baron, sitting in a large armchair, seemed to be dreaming of terrible vengeances. Between his legs, held against his body in a gesture of protection, as if to defy the thief, he was holding his other son, Gontran, who was following the conversation with feverish interest.

"He bears a strong resemblance to his brother," the Baronne remarked. "There's very nearly the same age. André was six and ten days; Gontran will be seven in a fortnight. They're as blond as one another...and as intelligent..."

I understood the allusion to my article, to which Madame Vetyolle had responded so vehemently. It would have made me smile anywhere but in that desolate house.

Clovis Binard

A BIZARRE ADVERTISEMENT

I was in the process of reading the proofs of my copy when an office boy handed me a letter:

Dear Monsieur Binard, come quickly. The thief has stolen our second child.

Albert de Vautremesse

46

A suspicious detail: the text of the note is composed of letters cut out from *Le Matin* and stuck together.

What does that signify?

C.B.

THE DISAPPEARANCE OF
BARON DE VAUTREMESSE'S SECOND SON
A DESPERATE MOTHER
NOCTURNAL CONSULTATION
IN THE SÛRETÉ'S OFFICES
AN ENIGMATIC NOTE

Everything is becoming increasingly complicated, increasingly strange.

The note signed "Albert de Vautremesse," which informed me yesterday evening of the theft of Gontran de Vautremesse, was quite accurate.

But that note was not sent by Baron Albert de Vautremesse.

And I received the note at the very moment when the abduction was perpetrated, perhaps even before.

There is no point wearing out my typewriter in long commentaries describing the bewilderment and the amazement that seized me by the back of the neck as these various details gradually became clear.

After receiving the short letter that I published yesterday as a postscript, the bizarre characteristics of which intrigued me so much, I immediately went to the Rue de Miromesnil, to the home of the Baron de Vautremesse.

I arrived at half past eleven at a tranquil house in which no drama had caused an upheaval.

The sleepy concierge rubbed his eyes as I questioned him, after which he looked at me with rounded eyes, in which I read that he was trying to determine whether he was dreaming or I was mad.

"I repeat," I told him, "that little Gontran has been stolen, like his brother. It's extraordinary that you don't know that."

"I don't understand a word of this whole story," the porter replied. "Monsieur de Vautremesse went out at quarter at eight this evening with his son. They haven't come back yet. I don't know any more."

A noise of precipitate footsteps cut the conversation short. Two people were running down the stairs. The concierge woke up completely, and became anxious.

A moment later, Madame de Vautremesse and a chambermaid appeared. They were very distressed. The Baronne was bare-headed; in her haste, she had not even thought to put on a hat.

"Open up, quickly!" she commanded the concierge, in a harrowing voice.

I came forward. "What's happened, Madame?"

"Oh, it's frightful, Monsieur. Our second son, Gontran, has also been abducted. I've just been telephoned…"

She is so distressed that she is not even astonished by my presence. At the click of the pneumatic bulb operating the bolt of the front door, she races into the street. I follow her. Outside, there is only one fiacre—mine. I put my carriage at the Baronne's disposal and offer to accompany her. She accepts, and all three of us squeeze into the narrow space the Parisians hirers deign to allow their clientele.

"What address, Madam?"

"The Sûreté, Quai des Orfèvres."

During the entire journey I do not succeed in obtaining a single reply from Madame de Vautremesse.

She weeps, she sobs, she laments.

Does she even know that I'm there? The woman that I saw a few hours earlier, so proud and noble in her grief, is now vanquished to the point of collapse, no longer in control of herself.

As for the chambermaid, huddled in a corner, she allows her eyes to fill with silent tears, which I can see shining as we pass the street-lights.

At the Quai des Orfèvres, at the door through which all the actors in great Parisian dramas are seen to file, Brigadier Tabert is waiting on the sidewalk. He runs to our carriage, opens the door, and says: "Madame de Vautremesse, no doubt?"

"Yes, Monsieur."

"Be kind enough to follow me, Madame."

The Brigadier has not noticed me at first, in the darkness. I make myself visible.

"You!" he cries. "These damned journalists get in everywhere! No point in going up—the chiefs won't let you in. They're working hard tonight."

"Bah! We'll see about that."

Tabert takes us up the large wooden stairway, scarcely illuminated, that leads to the offices of the Sûreté, on the top floor, almost under the eaves. The steps are steep, tiring, and creak as if one were hurting them. Madame de Vautremesse, who had begun the ascent too rapidly, gradually runs out of breath. She stops to get her breath back in front of the office of Monsieur Bertillon, the head of the Anthropometric Service.

I take advantage of the brief pause to asked Tabert: "Where are you taking Madame?"

"To Monsieur Loumergue's study. The Messieurs were there when the news arrived, and they stayed there.

"Which Messieurs?"

"The head of the Sûreté, the deputy head, the chief clerk and Habischoff, who was brought back from London to take charge of the affair of the child-stealer, with me. Monsieur de Vautremesse arrived later."

Finally, we reach the landing on to which opens the long, sad and chilly antechamber of the offices of our great police administration.

The Brigadier invited the chambermaid to sit down in the glass-sided booth in which the office-boys on duty sit during the day. Then he introduces the Baronne into Monsieur Loumergue's office.

I insist on going in.

Tabert opposes it with all his might. The most he will consent to do is to take a visiting card to his chief.

I scribble on the card: *Let me in. Monsieur de Vautremesse has written asking me to come and see him as soon as possible. I know he's there.*

A minute later, the Brigadier brings back my card, with this response on the other side:

Monsieur de Vautremesse is here, but he declares that he has not written anything to you.

"That's too much. What does this signify, then?"

I show the Brigadier the short letter made up on characters from the newspaper.

"Well, well, well!" he says, scratching his head. And he goes back into the office carrying the piece of paper, which seems to have interested him greatly.

The door soon opens again.

"Come in, then, Binard."

It is Monsieur Hamard himself who invites me in. The head of the Sûreté seems stupefied.

"When did you get this?"

"About an hour ago."

"Can you tell me the exact time?"

"Indeed. I had just reread the proofs of my article. I looked at my watch to see what train I could catch. I live in Enghien. The letter was handed to me at eleven twenty."

The last two words are repeated simultaneously in six exclamations.

"What's so extraordinary about that?" I ask, astonished at the effect of my reply.

"It's because," Monsieur Hamard replies, "according to Monsieur de Vautremesse's deposition, that of his chauffeur, and that of the doorman at the Nouveau-Cirque, the child was stolen at eleven twenty-five. *You were notified of the event before it had taken place.* Do I need to explain all the questions to which that fact gives rise?"

At that moment, Monsieur Laudet comes in. He is the examining magistrate charged with the affair of the child-stealer. He has been woken up. The magistrate has come immediately, in his night-shirt. Monsieur Laudet wears pretty night-shirts. It requires the unexpectedness of a nocturnal drama to acquaint us with the nocturnal elegance of our magistrates.

The head of the Sûreté brings the magistrate up to date, rapidly.

The Baron de Vautremesse took his son Gontran to the Nouveau-Cirque. Since the disappearance of his brother, the little boy had been mortally sad. On

50

the advice of a famous physician, Professor Flax, the parents tried to distract the child with the capers of clowns and the contortions of the human serpent.

The Baron left the circus shortly before the end of the performance. At the entrance in the Rue du Faubourg-Saint-Honoré he greeted a lady, the Comtesse de Houdotte, with whom he exchanged a few words.

The child took a few steps toward the sidewalk on his own, in order to see where the open-topped automobile was that would take them home. It was at that moment that the thief pounced. As usual, the nearest witnesses did not see anything, and could not supply the slightest item of useful information.

Having arrived at that point in his narrative, Monsieur Hamard continues, commenting at length, before the eyes of the examining magistrate, on the curious little note that I received. That scene would merit the attention of the brush of a generic painter.

The study of the Sûreté's chief clerk is a small rectangular room whose severity is unrelieved by any refinement. A desk overloaded with papers, an armchair, several other chairs. On the mantelpiece, a few books and a rusty old revolver, doubtless a relic of some crime. The walls are decorated with photographs that I recommend to nervous individuals who are prone to nightmares. They represent various phases of dramas that have remained historic. One sees Lieutenant Anastay, in civilian dress, with a top hat, the knife with which he cut the throats of his benefactress and the maidservant, one glove stained with blood, and the portrait of the victims as they were discovered. On the opposite wall, one contemplates the bailiff Gouffé in the trunk, between his murderers, Eyraud and Gabrielle Bompard, etc., etc.[11]

In that frame, thus decorated with the iconography of crime, scarcely illuminated by an oil-lamp, the ruddy light of which is held at bay by a large shade, the policemen and the magistrate discuss the slightest facts with the passion of huntsmen.

It is necessary to have witnessed one of their conferences to understand the attraction of the police to research, which draws intelligent men of superior talent into time-consuming, perilous, badly-paid functions that are often stupidly scorned by the ignorant public.

In the background, the Baron and Baronne de Vautremesse follow, with dolorous attention, what these men are saying, who are putting all their activity and expertise at their service. Madame de Vautremesse is leaning on her husband, weeping and whimpering. The Baron is trying to stiffen himself. A crease

---

[11] These references are to famous causes celebres. Louis Anastay was guillotined in 1892 for murdering the Baroness Dollard. The murder of the bailiff Augustin Gouffé by Michel Eyraud and Gabrielle Bompard in 1889 was one of the most famous cases investigated by Marie-François Goron, then head of the Sûreté, whose memoirs were a huge success when serialized in *Le Matin*'s rival newspaper *Le Journal*. It was also a benchmark in forensic science because of the vital clues found in a second autopsy carried out by the physician Alexandre Lacassagne.

deforms the corner of his mouth: a kind of rigid smile that denounced internal anguish.

The discussion goes on for a long time.

It will resume this evening, late into the light.

Monsieur Laudet will also interrogate the maidservant arrested by Monsieur Fanguy, in whose trunk Agent Binette discovered the garments of the first child stolen from the unfortunate Vautremesse family.

Clovis Binard

MONSIEUR LAUDET INTERROGATES
THE ARRESTED MAIDSERVANT

The maidservant arrested by Monsieur Fanguy has been interrogated by Monsieur Laudet, in the presence of Maître André Hesse, advocate.

There is no need to describe the surroundings of the study in which the magistrate undertook the assault. Everyone is in a hurry to find out whether the law has finally picked up a promising lead.

Monsieur Laudet arrives at two o'clock. He hastily expedited a few minor items of business. Then he has the maidservant brought in.

Her name is Marie Le Kapelec, a native of Trestraou in Brittany.

She is one of those ageless Breton women somewhere between twenty and fifty. Small and thin, her face is furrowed by a thousand deep wrinkles. Her gray eyes are expressionless. According to the information furnished by her employers, the girl hardly ever opens her mouth, almost never talking to anyone. As hard-working as she is silent, she suits the old couple of rentiers, whom she serves like a docile animal, devoid of soul and intelligence. They are the ones who have hired her defender.

The examining magistrate does not take long to perceive that he is confronted by one of those specimens of the human race nearest to the brute. He practically has to prize the words loose from that thick and rustic skull.

"How did you come into possession of the garments found in your trunk?"

No response. Marie Le Kapelec contemplates the magistrate with a dull gaze.

"Please tell me by what means you obtained this costume?"

No response. In the end, the magistrate loses his temper. He shouts. He rages, He makes threats. Monsieur Hesse also loses his temper. The vocal outbursts of the famous advocate can be heard outside.

The bewildered maid looks at the two men and murmurs, fearfully: "Jesus! Maria!" Finally, she calms the conflict by deciding to confess.

"I found them."

"Ah! Good!" cries Monsieur Laudent, glad to have unclenched the teeth of that living being, previously as rigid as a corpse. "Well, if you found the clothes, tell me where."

It takes twenty minutes of sustain effort to clarify that detail.

In the end, it is determined that a quarter of an hour after the abduction of André de Vautremesse, Marie Le Kapelec was running an errand for her employers, at a house in the Rue Louis-le-Grand, near the corner of the Avenue de l'Opéra. One coming out, she found a parcel propped up against the coaching entrance. She opened it and, finding that it contained a child's clothes, took it away.

From then on, the interrogation loses all interest. It is only too obvious that the Breton has never been acquainted with the child-stealer, however distantly. She is not the one who will enlighten the law.

Nevertheless, Monsieur Laudent, to square his conscience, asked Marie Le Kapelec a few other questions relative to the "great affair." That is what people are beginning to call the matter that everyone is discussing, looking at it repeatedly from every angle.

Everyone?

No.

The police might be on a war footing, the political parties might be making speeches, the reports might be rushing about madly, the telegraph and the telephone might be striving to spread the latest news as quickly as possible, a billion copies of five hundred newspapers and magazines, in France alone, might be reporting the abductions and accessory facts to millions of readers increasingly avid to know more, but there are still people in Paris unaware that twenty children are missing from their homes and the desolation of the patents has almost become public mourning.

A captain scarred from ear to ear by a Prussian saber in 1870 took a trip, once the peace was signed, to a village in the Savoy. He mistook his route, went astray and ended up accepting an hour's hospitality from two old peasants who lived in an isolated house in the mountains. They chatted.

The Savoyard, pointing to the wound across his guest's forehead, asked: "Here did you get that?"

"In the war."

"When was that?"

"This year."

"Has there been a war, then?" the old man asked.

Well, that story is repeated every day, not just in the remote depths of the mountains, far from everyone and everything, but in the heart if modern Paris. One encounters people indifferent to the most important events, people not only incapable of associating themselves in any way with the sentiments that animate the vast majority of people in the country, but capable of ignoring them completely.

And among these beings, phenomenon worthy of inclusion in museums, who did not know that France and the entire would is impassioned by the case of the twenty consecutive, enigmatic and unprecedented thefts, was Marie Le Kapelec, native of Trestraou, a servant in the Rue Taitbout—which is to say, in the very heart of the capital.

It is, in fact, the examining magistrate who is obliged to inform the poor woman about the crime to which some people thought, momentarily at least, she was an accomplice.

Marie Le Kapelec kept the garments she found because she has a child, in the country. Honest but simple, the Breton woman would not steal a centime from another person, but she was unable to resist the idea of one day dressing her little boy, who runs around in rags with his backside hanging out, as a gentleman.

A narrow justice would demand retribution for that touching larceny, but narrow justice is the enemy of broad civilization, as Monsieur Prud'homme says.

Marie Le Kapelec will be released today. Her employers have promised to take her back.

Alain Bernard

HOW GONTRAN DE VAUTREMESSE WAS ABDUCTED
THE INVESTIGATION
THE ABDUCTION WAS PREMEDITATED

After having interrogated Marie Le Kapelec, the examining magistrate occupied himself with the most recent theft of a child. In order to determine the exact circumstances of the abduction, Monsieur Laudet talked successively to all the witnesses, then brought them together. We know more exactly now how the kidnapping was carried out.

Monsieur de Vautremesse was coming out of the arena of the Nouveau-Cirque.

At the entrance to a broad corridor leading to the street, in front of the cloakroom, he met the Comtesse de Houdotte.

The lady in question was waiting for her carriage, which a footman had gone to fetch. The Baron and the Comtesse exchanged a few words while heading slowly for the exit door. Little Gontran, who had just been kissed on the cheek by Madame de Houdotte, was walking ahead of them. The performance had not yet concluded and the vestibule was completely empty. There was no one there but the Baron, the Comtesse, the child and, inside his lodge and sitting at the window, the ticket-seller—who, having made a mistake in his arithmetic, was recalculating his receipts, paying no attention to what was happening outside.

At the door to the Rue Saint-Honoré, Père Mab, the doorman of the circus, was stationed, a worthy man who has been exercising that important function—which is more lucrative than one might suppose—for five years.

Madame de Houdotte's coupé pulled up at the sidewalk, directly in front of the Baron's automobile. Père Mab, leaving the Comtesse's footman to assist his mistress, ran to open the door of the second vehicle. While the Baron was bidding a final farewell to Madame de Houdotte, little Gontran, three meters away, went toward the doorman.

"The kid," said Père Mab, word for word, "turned toward his father before getting into the auto, as if to wait for him. At a certain moment, he stepped behind me. The father arrived immediately afterwards, as the Comtesse's carriage pulled away. Where's the child? We searched for him. Behind the auto there was a fiacre. The coachman was asleep inside. We woke him up. Naturally, he hadn't seen anything either. It's unbelievable."

Opposite the circus, parked at the other sidewalk, there was another vehicle, which pulled away immediately after the Comtesse's. The Baron's chauffeur, who was busy examining the brake pedal, which was sticking slightly, while awaiting the signal to depart, knew no more than Père Mab. He had, however, noticed before it pulled away a man of distinctive appearance, in a dark overcoat and a top hat, who crossed the road and passed behind the automobile.

The Comtesse de Houdotte's coachman recalled having been overtaken, about a hundred meters from the Nouveau-Cirque, by a private carriage whose horse was traveling at top speed.

One can therefore conclude that Gontran de Vautremesse was taken by the child-stealer behind the automobile and then thrown into a carriage parked on the other side of the road, which departed immediately.

But how is it that the child did not cry out?

How is it that the thief was able to cross the road with his prey, dragging the child to the coupé, and get him inside, without being seen?

No one can answer that.

The interest of all these questions fades before the enigma of the short letter that informed me of the abduction of Gontran de Vautremesse.

It is now established, in a definitive manner, that the note in question was sent before the crime was committed—a relatively long time beforehand.

The theft took place at eleven twenty-five. I received the letter at eleven twenty. The office boy who handed it to me had found it in the hallway of the newspaper, on the big table in the middle, at quarter past eleven. It is composed, as you already know, of letters cut out of *Le Matin* and stuck together. To do that takes quite a long time. The letter had doubtless been on the table for some time before being perceived by one of the paper's employees. In brief, all these circumstances prove that it was written at least half an hour before the abduction. But if that is the case, it can only have been written by someone who knew that the theft would occur.

Is it too bold to deduce that that man is the child-stealer himself?

I think not—inasmuch as the fashion of correspondence, by means of scissors, a brush and glue, truly denounces a criminal. The kidnapper has refrained from leaving a sample of his handwriting in my possession. He has employed the most prudent system that a sender of anonymous letters can imagine.

In the same way, he has not dared to hand the envelope to one of the clerks on duty at the entrance to our offices. He has come into the hall and abandoned it at hazard, on a table. Naturally, no one noticed him. Hundreds of people pass through that hallway, which is the antechamber to all our services, every day. One can easily do so unperceived.

It is, therefore, very probably the thief, who, knowing that the Baron de Vautremesse was at the Nouveau-Cirque that evening with his son Gontran, had premeditated his crime, and was absolutely sure of success in abducting the child: so sure that he dared to warn me in advance.

This man must have tremendous confidence in the power and reliability of his means of action. Will anyone ever succeed in capturing an individual so astonishingly well-armed, and so extraordinarily skillful?

Clovis Binard

A LETTER FROM A "FATEFUL REEDER"
GOOD OBSERVATION BUT TERRIBLE SPELLING

We have received the following letter from a reader, which, if it lacks orthography, is not lacking in common sense:

Deer editer,

Excuse my stile, me who as you can see, have not past my ecsamin for antry to the akademy francis (?!?)

Me have no need for ten diploms in arkitekter of govinment to be a nam of common sens.

Your coll-eeg Klovis Binard klames in his artikal of Thurdy that the chile-steeler, after haven stoln por mite Gontran de Vautremesse, prob-ab-lee carrid him away in a carridge. May I permick maysef to point out sumthink vey impotent in the affer, it sims to me. If he has a carridge, he has a cocheman!

Then, this fello, the chile-steeler, is not on but too, since ther is the cocheman and him.

The cocheman and him meks too.

So, ther is not on chile-steeler, but too.

Accep my respecks

A fateful reeder

IS THIS THE ABDUCTOR'S CARRIAGE
THERE ARE TWO THIEVES

The reasoning of the correspondent whose fidelity leads him to make such literary communications is perfectly sound. He will doubtless swell up with pride when he learns that his hypothesis alone, at the present moment, appears the most probable to the examining magistrate and the agents of the Sûreté.

It is assumed that he vehicle that overtook that of the Comtesse de Houdotte was used to abduct little Gontran de Vautremesse. It is also assumed that the thief must have an accomplice, the coachman.

It is very evident that there is still a lacuna to fill in. The fact that no cry, at the moment of the abduction, betrayed the child's terror, remains incomprehensible.

The chances of arresting the guilty parties have, however, increased considerably. A skillful and isolated bandit might escape the police, but two bandits, even skillful ones, will inevitably betray one another eventually. To take an accomplice, when one plans a crime, is the first step on the way to the guillotine.

The problem being thus circumscribed, all the efforts of research are concentrating on the mysterious carriage that carried Gontran de Vautremesse away.

INGENIOUS MUSIC
TAARRRAPATATA! TAARRRAPATATA!
NEW DEPOSITIONS
THE MASTERSTROKE
THE DISTINGUISHED MAN?

The Comtesse de Houdotte's coachman has been interrogated again.

"In my first deposition," he declared to Monsieur Laudet today, "I told you that I was overtaken by a private carriage. I said that without thinking—but Madame la Comtesse de Houdotte has made the observation to me that I risked leading justice astray by an inexact indication. I have come, therefore, on Madame's orders, to retract the part of my statement about which I am not certain.

"In reality, I paid no attention to the kind of vehicle that was going as if the devil was at its heels. I thought that it must be a private carriage because of the speed of the horse. All my attention was drawn to the horse. That beast, I can affirm without hesitation, is a first-rate, solid, ardent animal. It wasn't galloping like a nag that one has to push, and from which only whiplashes can obtain a little speed. It was trotting freely, perhaps a trifle irregularly…trotting stiffly, very fast. I scarcely saw it. My mare, who's sensitive, got excited on hearing the other coming up behind her like a tornado, and pricked up her ears. I had to occupy myself with her when the other went past and stop her capering. That's why I didn't look at the carriage. But I can still hear the sound of that trot. The beast trotted *taarrrapatata, taarrrapatata*. Look, Monsieur le juge, have a thousand horses trot in front of me, and if the one from the other evening is among them, I'd recognize it without hesitation."

"You'd recognize it by the sound of its trot?" exclaimed Monsieur Laudet, very interested.

"Yes, Monsieur le juge. I assure you that the child-stealer's horse trots *taarrrapatata, taarrrapatata, taarrrapatata, taarrrapatata*."

The coachman imitated the rhythm of the gait, Monsieur Laudet, who does not scorn any clue, repeated: "Did you say *tarrrapattata, tarrrapattata*?"

"No, Monsieur le juge, I said *taarrrapatata, taarrrapatata*."

The nuance was slight.

In order to help him to understand, the coachman approached Monsieur Laudet's desk and replayed the tempo of the trot, striking the table successively with his two index fingers.

The magistrate stood beside him and, very attentively, started drumming in his turn. From time to time, the master corrected the student. When the four fingers were beating discordantly, they produced something like the sound of a squadron. Eventually, weary of all that vain cavalry, the examining magistrate sent for a phonograph, and the Comtesse's coachman sang his *taarrrapatata, taarrrapatata* into the recording funnel, which, engraved in the wax, might one say serve as evidence in a trial.

It therefore emerges from the witness's declarations that the child-stealer's horse is a fine beast, impetuous and fast. The quality of his carriage must be similarly determined.

The doorman, Père Mab, believes he remembers that the vehicle that was parked for a few minutes on the far side of the street was a good-looking carriage.

The two guardians of the peace on duty near the circus were a considerable distance away at the time of the abduction, but they are categorical in their affirmations. Before leaving the door, they saw a private coupé stop opposite the circus.

Is that the child-stealer's carriage? Probably.

Remember that the criminal disdains the jewelry and precious objects found on his little victims, which he abandons along with the clothes. Are these not two facts that are evidently correlated, from which it is possible to deduce, without stretching logic too far, a little of the truth? That scorn for gold and costly stones is in accordance with the fortune of which the possession of a fine carriage is suggestive.

Is the thief, therefore, a rich man?

We now have two items of evidence to that effect.

The investigations of the examining magistrate have similarly been directed toward the "distinguished man" in a dark overcoat and top hat whom the Baron de Vautremesse's chauffeur saw crossing the road. No enlightenment, however, has been obtained on that point.

Even so, it seems to have been a good day.

A forward step has been taken.

Clovis Binard

THE FAMOUS NOTE AGAIN!
FINALLY, SOME PRECISE FACTS
AN INCRIMINATING PAPER
THE ABDUCTOR IS WELL-INFORMED

The examining magistrate has been occupied once again today with the short letter that the thief sent me before the abduction of Gontran de Vautremesse.

The Magistrate wanted to associate me with this part of his investigation. I was received by him immediately after lunch. We were still discussing the note at five o'clock.

That long session was preceded by a commonplace preamble—a refrain that my professional obligations have forced me to hear hundreds of time over.

"Give me your word, Monsieur Binard, not to publish our conversation."

"No, Monsieur le juge, I will not give you my word, firstly because I'm a journalist and I've noticed that when someone asks me not to publish something, it's generally interesting, and secondly because I don't, alas, have the means to make you a gift of twenty-five thousand francs."

"What do you mean?"

"That this week, thanks to the abduction of Gontran de Vautremesse, I've got a lead on my colleagues Bernard and Barbarus, who are consumed by rage; that my chances of getting hold of the prize for the reportage competition are increasing; and that I have no intention, Monsieur le juge, of sacrificing the slightest atom of the faintest shadow of the smallest molecule of the most minimal of chances, just to please you."

Monsieur Laudet had the god grace to smile and not to insist. Then he lit a cigarette, scratched his bearded chin momentarily and went on:

"I have the habit, when I find myself in the presence of an obscure and complicated affair, of making a note of the smallest events as I go along. When one conducts an investigation, patience in observing the small details is always useful, often in the most unexpected fashion. I have, therefore, tried to establish, as best I can, the various movements of the Baron de Vautremesse, the child and the thieves before the crime, and, with the aid of the documents at our disposal to attribute them a place in the time-scheme. This is what my initial reasoning produced..."

After a brief pause for thought, Monsieur Laudet continued: "On the evening of the abduction, Monsieur de Vautremesse left the Rue Miromesnil with his son at eight twenty. From there, by automobile, it only takes five minutes to reach the Nouveau Cirque. They arrive at eight twenty-five and they sit down in their box at about eight thirty. It's then that, according to my initial assumptions, the thief, who is watching the performance, perceives his victim. Immediately, the idea of abducting the child germinates in his mind—and also that of notifying you. By *the thief* I mean the one who plans and carries out the thefts. Until further notice, in fact, I consider the coachman as an accomplice of lesser importance."

"Have you thought about the reasons that led the rogue to notify me?"

"We'll discuss that shortly. That's why I've asked you to come. So, for one reason or another, the thief intends to let you know about the exploit he's meditating, but he wants above all to avoid giving himself away. He then recalls a classic means that has proved effective. So he leaves the circus to go and carry out, in a safe place, the work of cutting letters out of an issue of *Le Matin* and assembling them, with the aid of glue."

"Perfect. I'm with you all the way, Monsieur le juge."

"Let's imagine that he goes home to carry out that patient task. I'll allow ten minutes, arbitrarily, for the journey. I've reassembled the letters myself, in the fashion of the thief. It took me seventeen minutes. Allowing for three minutes wastage on this and that, therefore, it's nine o'clock when the bandit has finished his missive. It's now a matter of getting it to you, but not too soon, however. If you had received it at nine o'clock for instance, and had immediately telephoned Monsieur de Vautremesse, the criminal's entire plan would have fallen apart. He has, therefore, to take the letter to your newspaper as late as possible..."

"Perhaps he has it taken?"

"I don't think so. In such a delicate circumstance, it's perilous to address oneself to a commissionaire who might one day give you away...unless we suppose an accomplice...but then that would make three criminals instead of one: the thief, the coachman and the letter-bearer."

"Why shouldn't the coachman have taken charge of getting the letter to me?"

"Indeed. However, it's necessary that someone hitches up and supervises the carriage. But what does it matter, for the moment? The essential thing is that the thief or the coachman has two hours twenty minutes, between nine o'clock and eleven-twenty, to get the letter to you and return to the Nouveau Cirque to carry out his plan. That's the essential thing because, if this is the truth, we know the characteristics of the abduction, and we can hope to pick up a serious trail. But listen carefully, Binard: imagine, for a moment, that it could be demonstrated that the thief had not written—I use the word *written* for want of a better one—the note between the time that the father has entered the circus with his son and the moment when the child was abducted."

"Then he must have done so before the performance."

"Yes."

"But then...?"

"But then, Monsieur Binard, an immense horizon opens up before us. If he had written the letter before the performance, *he must have known that Monsieur*

Vautremesse and his son were going to the circus that evening. If so, the circle of research becomes admirably clear. It would be necessary for us to discover all of those who could have learned, during the day or even in the evening, that the Baron intended to take little Gontran to applaud the performing seals, jugglers and the nautical wedding."

"What is it that makes you think that the note was written so soon?"

"I don't think it—I'm sure of it. My certainty doesn't go so far as to claim that the thief wrote the note before eight-thirty, but I do claim, on the basis of what the investigation has produce, that he had the intention of writing it before then."

"Ah?"

"That exclamatory and interrogative *ah* will receive its response. The head of the Sûreté has found the vendor who, at four o'clock in the afternoon on the day of the abduction, sold the paper and the glue with which the letter was fabricated."

"How?"

"I examined the paper yesterday: a luxury paper—further proof that the thief is unconcerned about money—made in England. I had a drawing made of the watermark, which is quite rare. The drawing was photographed, and copies of the photograph shown by our agents to all the paper-merchants in Paris. Several of the merchants declared that they had the paper in stock. In one establishment, that of Monsieur Veneziani, 8 Rue Menars, a shop-assistant remembered having sold, at the time I've just indicated to you, a box of that paper, at the same time as a small bottle of gum Arabic. The glue on the note, you see, is gum Arabic.

"Naturally, I interrogated the young woman. She has a good memory. The purchaser, according to her, was a man of medium height, rather thickset, dressed in a dark blue or black suit. He spoke with a slight foreign accent, but the young woman was unable to recognize the purchaser's nationality. That's where we are."

"It seems to me that you haven't wasted your time."

Monsieur Laudet smiled in satisfaction.

"Now," he said, "let's interpret the facts. At *four o'clock in the afternoon,* the thief bought what he needed to write that he would abduct Gontran de Vautremesse *at about midnight.* Perhaps the thief, who was aware of what Monsieur de Vautremesse and his son had planned in the afternoon, also knew that you had gone to see the Baron that morning and that you intended to write an article about that visit."

My eyes widened in astonishment. "Is he a sorcerer, then, this animal?"

"A phenomenally clever man, certainly."

"He could have known about my visit, Monsieur le juge—for example, by watching the vicinity of the house in the Rue de Miromesnil. A few people also knew that I was about to go there, beginning with Monsieur Fanguy and his agents at the Commissariat. I also mentioned it to friends, comrades at the Cercle des Capucines, where I had lunch. But what I can swear to you is that the child-stealer could not have known that I would write an article about it. The article was decided between me and my editor-in-chief at eight o'clock in the evening. I didn't deliver my copy to the compositor until rather late, after having received the note. While I was writing it, I didn't speak to anyone."

"In that case," the magistrate replied, "I can explain the sending of the letter, by the boastful impulse that has doomed the most intelligent of criminals, and which is, as experience has demonstrated, almost universal. He wanted to swagger, by notifying you."

The magistrate stood up, in order to dismiss me. "It's a pity," he added. "I thought that your replies might narrow down my investigation further. But bah! There's always tomorrow. Perhaps I'll have need of you. For today, I have work to do. I want to interrogate all of those who could have discovered on the day of the abduction or the day before, that the Baron was taking Gontran to the circus. *Au revoir.*"

If there are still malicious individuals who claim that research is easy, I beg them to imagine, just for a moment, the enormous labor that such an investigation involves.

Clovis Binard

WILLIAM TRISSON, DETECTIVE
DISCONTENTMENT OF THE PARISIAN POLICE
AN UNUSUAL STATISTICIAN

William Trisson, the celebrated American detective, whom our ambassador to the United States has engaged specifically to search for the child-stealers, and to whom the Minister of the Interior, as you will read further on, has made allusion in his speech in the Chambre, has just arrived in Paris.

It was first necessary to find an interpreter, because William Trisson does not speak French.

It appears to me that this ignorance is not exactly fortunate in a man who is going to play Argus on the great boulevards.

It might have been possible to team him up with one of the agents of the Sûreté who knows English, but such reluctance was encountered in the ranks to undertake that kind of work that the idea as abandoned and the authorities are looking elsewhere for a translator who will be allocated to the transatlantic policeman.

One of our finest inspectors told me the reasons responsible for that general refusal.

"Me, help this William Trisson! Never!" he exclaimed. "A fine acquisition the government has brought us there! Paying him a hundred francs a day and putting him up in the Grand Hotel, whereas with us they quibble over every cab fare! To begin with, he isn't even an official detective. He's a private detective. He doesn't speak French, but there's one language in which he's fluent, and that's bluff.

"Interview him, then. To hear him, he's arrested all the evildoers of the Old and New Testaments on his own, from Cain onwards. He's been everywhere, he's done everything, he knows everything, and he holds all the records. He's discovered the more criminals than anyone else in the world; he's made more money as a policeman than anyone else in the world; he has more courage than anyone else in the world, the finest nose in the world and is the greatest musician in the world...the last might be true.

"When, by chance, he succeeds in an affair, the whole world is informed, from pole to pole, and he makes more noise on his own than the good Lord with his thunder. The best thing is that when he's burned to the right, he uses the gift of the gab to pop up on the left. To think that this time, he's got to our ambassador in Washington, and we have to import the package.

"Well, if he only had him to fear, the child-stealer would live as long as Methuselah without being troubled. And you'll see that if Trisson fails, he'll say that it's our fault, that we didn't understand his marvelous plans, and that, if people had listened to him, the most resourceful person on the globe, the greatest phoenix on earth, the greatest virtuoso in the universe and the greatest dentist in the world, it would have been different. In the meantime, he'll have got his hands on thirty thousand francs at the expense of our brave Republic, which will have come out in spots."

"Spots?"

"Yes—idiot's disease."

That judgment, of an eloquent severity, did not appear to me to be definitive, and that is why I tried to get the other side of the story.

After long research, I ended up meeting William Trisson in a bar in the Rue Cambon. He was in the process of concocting, with the precision of a clockmaker, a drink of his own, composed of champagne, mustard, gin, vinegar and pepper. He was phlegmatically drunk. His cold inebriation left him all his presence of mind, however, for the American gave me to understand, as soon as he opened his mouth, that he was granting me a veritable blessing in consenting to an interview, and that he would hold nothing back.

A young barmaid served as interpreter.

"I've come to France," he told me, "on the repeated invitation of your ambassador. For you, I've abandoned affairs of the greatest importance. I have thus consented to make a veritable sacrifice for your nation, and for the sake of humanity—for these thefts of children have excited general interest. It's good to put oneself in the service of such a cause, even if nothing comes of it. I'm glad to be employing the great qualities with which I'm endowed for noble and generous ends."

After that declaration of principle, William Trisson wanted to fill me in on the statistics of his great deeds.

He has personally arrested 80 criminals, who have killed a total of 104 persons, 33 with revolvers, 7 with pistols, 3 with hunting rifles, 3 with military rifles, 2 with blows of the fist, 3 with kicks, 1 with a sling, 2 by drowning, 1 with a bow, 4 with hammers, 3 with clubs, 2 with truncheons, 6 by strangling, 7 with poison, 3 with billhooks, 2 with drills and 22 with knives, daggers, razors, hunting-knives, scalpels, etc. etc. The thieves that he has collared have stolen, in total, 14,760,852 dollars. 8 forgers, 5 arsonists, 84 burglars, 9 blackmailers, etc. etc. have been delivered to justice by him, etc., etc. 58 of these bandits have been subjected to the death penalty. The others have received, in total, 4,800 years in prison, which is 48 centuries.

The young barmaid who was translating seemed wonderstruck by all these exploits, which the detective enumerated with a bored expression, and, from time to time, an accusatory hiccup. The honest Englishwoman had surely fallen in love at first sight.

Alain Bernard

It was at the beginning of yesterday's session that Monsieur Georges Larry questioned the government about the measures taken to put an end to the abductions of children.

The intervention of the Parisian député was bound to have the result, in default of any other, of permitting the Minister of the Interior to give an exact account of the matter.

M. Larry: "I have no need, Messieurs, to tell the Chambre the details of the multiple abductions that have evoked an echo of pity in all hearts. I shall content myself with recalling that at this moment, twenty-one children have been snatched from their hearths and the love of their parents, and that the criminal is still at liberty. So long as the villain has not expiated his crime, and so long as we do not know what has become of the children, the wound will bleed, and it is not possible for us to remain still, indifferent to so much suffering and desolation. You are not unaware, Messieurs, that the infamous deeds of the child-stealer are now absorbing the attention of the entire world, and that they belong to the category of those rare events that awake universal consciousness. People would therefore be astonished, in France and abroad, if the assembly that directs the destiny of the nation..."

M. Basies: "Some direction!"

M. Anthide Renard: "The direction of a café-concert."

M. Larry: "...remained indifferent and silent with regard to such events. I have no intention of enumerating here the criticisms that governmental action merits. I am content to ask the minister what measures he intends to take to put an end to the abductions. I assume that it is necessary to oppose exceptional crimes with exceptional means of repression."

The Minister of the Interior went up to the podium and settled the matter in a few sentences.

M. Clemenceau: "I observe, to begin with, that the honorable Monsieur Georges Larry has reduced his interpellation to a simple question. I shall reply swiftly. The government has not remained insensible to the crimes of the wretch who has succeeded thus far in holding all the forces of repression at bay. I must say, in praise of our agents, that there has been no need to stimulate their zeal, and that they are wholeheartedly devoted to a difficult and ingrate task.

"Special instructions have been given to all the guardians of the peace. They are keeping watch as best they can on the children abroad in the streets. Monsieur Hamard has received orders to occupy his finest sleuths exclusively with the search for the kidnapper. A reward has been promised to anyone who denounces the guilty party. We have summoned a detective from America whose reputation is universal. We are ready to employ any means that are indicated to us to hasten the arrest of the guilty party.

"Let those who criticize our inaction and lack of intelligence so bitterly place their activity and intelligence at our disposal. We shall not refuse any useful collaboration—but I must declare here that the administrations at work are capable of doing their job well and that they doubtless have as much skill and sagacity as those who, with their feet on the fire-irons, fulminate facile anathemas or distribute patronizing and often imbecilic advice from afar to responsible men.

"What must be admitted is that the police have never before encountered a criminal of such savant finesse and, if one might put it thus, such general mastery, and such ingenious perspicacity. He has never left the slightest useful clue in his wake, and it seems that, when he does abandon some clue to us, it is of his own volition, either to taunt us, or perhaps to lead us astray. I demand that the Chambre should immediately approve our efforts and our vigilance. Nothing is, has been or will be neglected to give full satisfaction to public opinion so justly aroused."

After this speech by Monsieur Clemenceau, no one asked to speak and the discussion was closed; the debate was thus reduced to a simple conversation.

Monsieur Hamard attended the session in which the Minister of the Interior defended him energetically.

The head of the Sûreté gave me to understand, as he left, that he hopes to justify, soon and entirely, the confidence of his superiors, and that the affair of the child-stealer might well soon enter a new phase.

Barbarus

ON A TRAIL
PRECIOUS INDICATIONS OF A TRAVELER IN BARRELS
THE QUARTER DISCOVERED IN WHICH
THE THIEVES' LAIR IS LOCATED

Little Gontran de Vautremesse's garments, which had not yet been recovered, are now in the hands of the examining magistrate. The Prefecture of Police received a parcel this morning accompanied by the following letter:

To Monsieur Lépine, Prefect of Police.[12]

On the evening when the abduction of Gontran de Vautremesse took place I went home at about eleven thirty. I live in the Rue de Bourgogne, not far from the Palais Bourbon, and I was going along the Rue de l'Université.

Apart from me, there was no one about.

Suddenly, a carriage traveling at an exceedingly rapid trot emerged from the Rue de Bellechasse, on the side of the Seine. As it flew past me, a rather voluminous packet was thrown out of the window on to the roadway.

Very intrigued, I picked it up and ripped off the paper enveloping the contents.

They were garments, undergarments and a pair of children's shoes, with a lock of hair. That says it all. I carried my find away.

At seven o'clock in the morning I was woken up by a telegraphist. My employer asked me to take the first train in order to pick up an order of barrels at Bordeaux. (I'm in the wholesale barrel business.)

Downstairs, on reading the newspapers. I realized that the clothes that I had left on my table in Paris were those of Gontran de Vautremesse. I only returned from the trip today, and am sending them to you immediately.

Please accept, etc., etc...

Gilbert Bartoulou
Commercial traveler in barrels
(wine, beer, oil and gasoline)

Half an hour after the receipt of this letter, Gilbert Bartoulou received a visit from an agent, and at ten past eleven exactly he was interviewed by Monsieur Laudet.

The deposition of the barrel-dealer has been very important to the investigation.

---

[12] Louis Lépine was the Prefect of Police in Paris from 1893-97 and from 1899-1913; he supervised he modernization of the French police forces, greatly encouraging the use and advancement of forensic science.

Many doubts are now lifted.

Many suspicions have become certainties.

The carriage from which Gontran de Vautremesse's clothes were thrown, which Gilbert Baroutou encountered in the Rue de l'Université, is the same carriage that was parked opposite the Nouveau-Cirque and the one that was noticed by the Comtesse de Houdotte's coachman, Père Mab and the agents on duty near the door of the arena.

It is definitely a private carriage hitched to a very fast horse.

It is, moreover, evident today that the hypothesis of the "fateful reeder," who is definitely not stupid, is exact and in conformity with the facts.

We can no longer talk about the child-stealer. It is necessary henceforth, with complete certainty, to talk about child-stealers.

It is now proven that little Gontran was drawn into the carriage by one man, who undressed him and immediately parceled up his garments, while the coachman, evidently an accomplice, drove the beast at top speed.

Thanks to Gilbert Bartoulou, it has also been possible to determine the direction in which the children are taken.

The Comtesse de Houdotte's coachman, whom Monsieur Laudet has summoned for a third time, has completed his initial declarations. While he continued to go along the Faubourg Saint-Honoré, the mysterious carriage passed him at the corner of the Rue Cambon, into which it steered.

It was seen again a few minutes later by Gilbert Bartoulou as it entered the Rue de l'Université, emerging from the Rue de Bellechasse.

The intermediary trajectory, therefore, certainly includes a small section of the Rue de Rivoli, the Place de la Concorde, the Quai des Tuileries and the Pont de Solférino.

According to Gilbert Bartoulou, the carriage continued straight along the Rue de l'Université, where he lost sight of it during the night, before ceasing to hear it.

To reach that part of Paris, coming from the Nouveau-Cirque, it would have been just as convenient, if not more so, to take the Rue Castiglione, the Rue de Rivoli—in the opposite direction—the Rue des Tuileries, the Pont Royal, the Rue du Bac and the Rue de l'Université.

Why did the abductors choose the less simple route rather than the other? Simply because the horse was stationed with its nose directed toward the Rue Cambon. The coachman, in a great hurry, no doubt, probably did not want to take the time to turn round. He found it more practical to go straight ahead.

The examining magistrate—and this is hardly a masterpiece of reasoning—was able, having thus fixed the points of reference, to draw the borders of the quarter containing the house to which Gontran de Vautremesse must have been taken.

Except for intersections with the major arteries, the Boulevard de la Tour-Maubourg, the Boulevard Saint-Germain, the Rue du Bac and the Rue des Saint-

Pères, the Rue de l'Université is one of the quietest streets in Paris, because it does not connect to any of the quarters essential to the life of the capital.

One is therefore confronted with the following question:

Toward what goal is a carriage heading that, arriving via the Pont de la Concorde, turns left into the Rue de l'Université.

That is the problem.

Examine a map of Paris.

The entire right bank of the Seine is excluded from the response, in the same way as the entire south-west of the capital. There remains the south-eastern part, below the Seine. But the fact that the carriage, emerging from the Pont de la Concorde, did not take the Boulevard Saint-Germain limits its destination to the long stretch of territory limited by that artery and the river.

It is possible to reduce that area by a further half, by eliminating all the streets that are north of the Rue de l'Université—the Rue Jacob, the Rue de Buci and the Rue Saint-Andre-des-Arts—because, to go there, the coachman would undoubtedly have gone along the quais after crossing the Pont de la Concorde.

Let also remove from the area the block of buildings contained between the Boulevard Saint-Germain, the Rue de l'Université and the Rue du Bac, Gilbert Bartoulou affirms that he carriage continued its route along the Rue de l'Université. It therefore did not have as it destination a house forming part of that block or the Rue Villersexel

By virtue of successive eliminations, the quarter to which the child-stealers' coupé was going—must have been going—is bordered by the Boulevard Saint-Germain, the Rue du Bac, the Rue de l'Université, a short section of the Rue de Seine, the Rue de Buci and the Rue Saint-André-des-Arts.

It is within that narrow and restricted area that the thieves' house is doubtless located.

The research would therefore be limited and relatively easy, if it were not necessary, in order to be on the safe side, to add in the area between the Boulevard Saint-Germain, the Rue Saint-André-des-Arts, the Place Saint-Michel and the Quais Saint-Michel, Montebello and de la Tourelle.

In fact, a coachman arriving via the Pont de la Concorde might have the idea of going there via the Rue de l'Université, although, to tell the truth, he has other routes at his disposal equally advantageous, if not more so. It is therefore better, although it inevitably complicates the research, to extend to the maximum the area to which the child might have been taken.

I have only inflicted these topographic deductions on our readers in order to give them an indication of the school of dialectics and the difficult logical game to which an examining magistrate and the police must devote themselves. These men, whose job obliges such mental efforts, require an incredible maturity of mind and a marvelous lucidity.

If the truth ever becomes known one day, it will be interesting to compare it with the seriously calculated hypotheses that are generated by the hour today, as the child-stealers allow little clues to escape and that untiring Ariadne, the examining magistrate, extends his thread through the labyrinth.

Such threads often break.

The magistrate has not, for example, been able to extract any conclusion from another promising trail.

On the assumption that the child-stealers knew, before the performance that preceded Gontran de Vautremesse's abduction, that the child would be taken to the circus by his father, the judge had taken it upon himself to seek out those who might have been able to obtain knowledge of the Baron's intention.

That enquiry has been rendered absolutely impossible by the large number of people in the category in question.

Madame de Vautremesse had gone to the booking office in person, the day before, to reserve a box for her husband and son. She had given her name to the ticket-seller—a name that had been in the full glare of publicity for some time. The ticket-seller immediately told Père Mab, who transmitted it to a groom, and by the end of the afternoon performance the entire personnel of the circus knew that seats had been booked by Madame de Vautremesse. It would therefore have been necessary to interrogate everyone to whom all those people might have communicated the information.

Furthermore, all the servants in the Baron's residence had been informed by the chambermaid.

It is, as you can see, virtually impossible to determine how many ears the information reached as it was passed on repeatedly.

The police, whose zeal and patience are untiring, intend to visit every building in the small area that has been marked out on the map of Paris in consequence of the deposition of Gilbert Baroutou.

Let us hope that that indefatigable zeal does not end in further disillusionment!

Clovis Binard

My colleague Barbarus reminds me that Madame Clépent, when she was searching for her son in the Rue de Thann immediately after his abduction, noticed a private carriage that was heading for the Place Malesherbes.

That is more than coincidence. It is proven now, beyond all doubt, that the child-stealer owns a luxurious coupé.

C.B.

TO THE GAMBLERS: LET UP, IF YOU PLEASE

The abduction of Gontran de Vautremesse and the latest incidents of that abduction have permitted my friend, collaborator and competitor Binard to grab the headlines regarding the child thefts. Barbarus and I have remained silent for a few days.

All three of us having been launched into a reportage competition that demands great honesty, we have sworn, with our hands on our inkstands, that we will act in accordance with the highest principles of French chivalry, and the most absolute sporting rectitude.

So we have decided that when one of us obtains information of great interest he will have all available space at his disposal until the complete exhaustion of his subject, and that the other two, save for information requiring immediate publication, will mark time, and will not clutter the paper with facile copy.

That is why Barbarus and I have left Binard have the spittoon almost to himself for five days.

That explanation is necessary to appease the exaggerated ardor of the gamblers who continue to bet on our chances, and who, it seems to me, given the number of letters I receive, are now legion. As soon as I stay silent for a single day, they imagine the most shameful double-dealing.

This week, for example, I have been vehemently accused of entering into a conspiracy with Binard to let him win. These days, people accuse their fellow citizens of being thieves and bandits with a deplorable ease.

This unfortunately tendency is extremely disagreeable for the unfortunates who have some responsibility in the sporting trials and competitions on which gamblers have seen fit to wager their savings.

It is understood between the players, as an eternal verity, that all kitties are stolen, that all horses are pulled, that all races are fixed. It is impossible to find one among them admitting that he has only fallen victim to himself, that it is his own recklessness, colossal stupidity, phenomenal idiocy and monumental egotism that drives him to go on betting, on anything and everything, when the dice are so obviously loaded.

I have no particular esteem in the eyes of the gamblers who bet on me. If they win, they will not be grateful to me, and will be content to congratulate themselves on their flair. If they lose, they will heap abuse upon me. I therefore beg them now to wait for the end of the competition to applaud me or throw me to the lions. Let them leave me in peace until then. I spend an hour every morning that could be better employed in opening mail that lacks charm and originality.

For our readers who are interested in the reportage competition without seeking to augment their emotion by putting money on it, and for them alone, I consent to say and repeat that neither I, nor Barbarus, nor Binard, has at any time thought of gaining less but more surely by simply dividing between us in advance the prize of 25,000 francs that will reward the most adroit. Binard, Barbarus and I are each doing our best, and following our own inclinations, in fighting for the gilded laurels.

Besides which, we would take just as much trouble if those laurels were painted cardboard, enfevered by zeal alone.

Alain Bernard

THE ADBUCTORS OF ÉMILE LOUBÉ
THE SUSPICIOUS AUTOMOBILE
DEPOSITIONS OF A SENTRY AND TWO CHILDREN

The audacity of the child-stealers has not yet declined. Their odious insolence does not recoil before public force or universal reprobation.

At the corner of the Rue de Bienfaisance and the Rue Portalis there is a large communal school. A little boy who bears exactly the same name as a former President of the Republic,[13] young Émile Loubé, came out of it after classes yesterday at four o'clock, in order to go home to his parents, concierges in the Rue Laborde. He was abducted during the journey, in front of the Église Saint-Augustin on the Rue Portalis, almost opposite the Pépinière drill-square.

The information collected regarding this abduction adds solid mesh to the net that the Sûreté is endeavoring to weave around these subtle wretches.

Along the broad sidewalk, almost always deserted, in front of the church, in front of the public garden, a closed automobile used by the kidnapper was parked for at least a quarter of an hour before the abduction. It was observed throughout that time by the sentry on duty at the Pépinière barracks.

A worthy lady—I am using a distant metaphor for the sake of modest readers—watching from a small rectangular building situated at the gate of the drill-square and composed of a corridor bordered by little booths that do not contain telephones—in other words, the attendant collecting the ten centimes that citizens of both sexes pay, who, it seems, on examining their faces as they go in and out, have bought for that modest price the repose of their conscience—also saw the vehicle.

However, the directress of that chalet of necessity—another metaphor, more immediate and more appropriate but no less elegant—absorbed by the demands of her commerce, was not much interested in the presence of the vehicle and only cast a distracted glance at it.

By contrast, the soldier on sentry duty at the gate of the barracks was more curious. He is a former chauffeur. He was naturally interested by the sight of a beautiful four-cylinder, which, after having passed in front of him, came to a stop not far away, next to the sidewalk of the Église Saint-Augustin. Interrogated as to the reasons why his attention was especially drawn to the automobile in question, he responded as follows.

---

[13] Only phonetically; the former president in question was Émile Loubet, whose term of office, begun in 1899, ended in February 1906; he played a major role in settling the Dreyfus affair, and was once violently assaulted by an anti-Dreyfusard at Auteuil racecourse.

"Can you give me a description of the chauffeur of the automobile?" Monsieur Laudet asked the young soldier, who was brought to the Palais de Justice immediately after the abduction of Émile Loubé.

"My God, Monsieur le juge, he was like all chauffeurs. I'd have difficulty recognizing him. He was dressed in a dark uniform and wore a flat cap of the same cloth, in the same color. I think he had a moustache...yes, he had a moustache."

"And the vehicle? What was it?"

"I told you, a four-cylinder."

"Did you recognize the make?"

"I don't remember. Perhaps a Prima...but I can't be sure."

"Did you get the number?"

"No."

"What about the bodywork?"

"A big, very comfortable limousine. Dark green paint."

"What did you see after the automobile arrived?"

"The chauffeur stayed in his seat for a good five minutes. I thought he'd had orders to wait for someone there. I thought the someone wouldn't be long, because the chauffeur hadn't stopped his motor. You know that when one prefers, in an automobile that's stopped, to be shaken by the engine turning over at speed, it's because one's thinking about getting away again soon. One prefers, in that case, the nervous juddering of the engine to getting out and turning the starting-handle to get it going again. I was quite surprised, therefore, on seeing that the wait was prolonged, and that the chauffeur was suffering all the flatulence of the pressure. That astonishment increased when a man got out of the vehicle. I'd thought it was empty. The driver must have been amusing himself jolting—in the literal sense of the word[14]—his boss. The monsieur who had accepted being shaken up in that manner without protest didn't say a word to the mechanic and started marching back and forth. The chauffeur continued, with his hands on the steering-wheel, to endure the vehicle's somersaults. That went on for nearly a quarter of an hour. That's all I know."

"What? You were intrigued by the performance, and yet you turned away?"

"Well, I didn't do it deliberately. The time came to change sentries. I was relieved of duty and had to go back into barracks."

Two schoolboys have completed this testimony as best they could.

Having emerged from class first, they ran rapidly forward, followed by the comrade who was about to be abducted. When they reached the statue of Jeanne d'Arc they turned round, just in time to see their friend seized by a man in front

---

[14] *Vanner* [here translated loosely as jolting] has, in addition to several literal meanings referring to various different kinds of shaking or stirring, the metaphorical meaning of making rude remarks.

of whom they had just passed, and thrust into the automobile, one of whose doors had remained open.

The vehicle departed immediately and disappeared in the blink of an eye in the direction of the Madeleine. The coup was executed with a disconcerting rapidity.

Neither the soldier nor the children, petrified by the spectacle, could give an exact description of the man who had made off with the unfortunate boy so swiftly.

The soldier had seen the abductor in a top hat.

The young witnesses declared that he was wearing a soft felt hat

These divergences do not permit us to trust any observations of detail. It is necessary to stick to the broad outlines of the event.

Clovis Binard

ONE OF MONSIEUR HAMARD'S SUSPICIONS
IS CONFIRMED
THE LONG PREMEDITATION
OF THE EVENT'S MOTIVES????

I was lucky enough to run into Monsieur Hamard as he was coming out of the school in the Rue Portalis. The head of the Sûreté had just questioned the teachers. He was accompanied by Inspectors Habischoff and Gambin.

"Be assured," he said to me, "that we will succeed, one day or another, in catching these villains. They might have a diabolical skill, but they leave further slight evidence at each of their manifestations, which we are following up carefully."

"A lot of small traces end up making a big trail," observed Inspector Gambin, sententiously.

"The depositions of the soldier and the schoolboy," Habischoff remarked, "prove that all these abductions are premeditated, calculated. The thieves waited for the end of classes. They had observed that the child went along that sidewalk every day at four o'clock, and..."

"Oh yes!" the head of the Sûreté interjected. "Each abduction is evidently the result of a mature and careful plan. The thieves know the habits of their future victims and those of their parents. They make preliminary arrangements. I have an idea about that, which is further corroborated every day. The most recent theft reinforces it further. I'm convinced that the thieves choose their victims a long time in advance. They weren't lying in wait for just any child on that sidewalk. They had positioned themselves there with the objective of kidnapping little Émile Loubé."

"What makes you think that?"

"All sorts of petty observations I made regarding the previous thefts. Look, Émile Loubé's two comrades passed in front of the abductor, within arm's reach. Why did the man let them go? They were easy prey. No—he was waiting for the third child, because it was Émile Loubé he wanted, and not someone else."

"Why him rather than another?"

"I don't know. I'm stating a fact; I haven't yet discovered the reason. In the beginning, when the thieves only took blonds, we knew their preferences."

"How old is young Émile Loubé?"

"Six years and two months. The thieves are remaining faithful to their rule of only taking children between six and seven years of age. But one of the two kids the kidnapers let past was six and one month, the other six and four months. They were, therefore, in the same category as the stolen boy. I'm trying to figure out the reason why they spared them and attacked little Émile. Oh, if we only knew the specific objective that has determined their enterprise! We're marching on the spot as long as we can't work out the abductors' motive."

"Émile Loubé's teacher has said that the child was uncommonly precocious," Gambin remarked. "He was at the top of his class."

There was a brief pause while Monsieur Hamard seemed to be reflecting profoundly.

"Yes," the head of the Sûreté replied, eventually, "perhaps it's necessary to look in that direction. We began by laughing and making fun when the parents affirmed that their lost offspring were all exceptionally intelligent for their age. I laughed like everyone else. I think it will be necessary to make honorable amends. That mental maturity might be the quality that attracts the abductors, the criterion that determines their actions. But then the problem throws up a further question, even more insoluble than the others."

As he left me, the head of the Sûreté added: "This succession of crimes is unique in the annals of the police. The affair bears no resemblance to any other. But the further the investigation progresses, the more convinced I am that it's necessary to expect extraordinary surprises. My policeman's flair tells me that there is, in spite of the proverb, something new under the sun—and I have a suspicion that the motive for these thefts of children is strange, unexpected, incredible, unique, singular, extraordinary and formidable."

Barbarus

Paris, 12 July

THE FOREIGN PRESS AND
THE PARISIAN ABDUCTIONS

The press of the entire world continues to concern itself with the child thefts with the greatest interest.

Every day, another special correspondent disembarks in Paris. If this continues, the international news syndicates will be submerged by the demand for information, and will burst their bounds. The devoted president Monsieur Blasco, that master of journalism who has already done so much to facilitate his colleagues' task, will not know which way to turn.

There are small newspapers in the depths of Africa, the remotest areas of the Americas and the heart of Australia that are following this affair like an affair of State, and devoting as much space to it as our Parisian gazettes.

A CURIOUS PRECEDENT IN PUERTO RICO
THE VENGEANCE OF A MAROON

A newspaper in Puerto Rico, the *Voz de la Patria*, which is published in Mayaguez, recalls, with regard to the Parisians abductions, an analogous event by which the island was turned upside-down some fifteen years ago.

A maroon successively abducted half a dozen white children, who were only found a long time afterwards, when all hope had been lost and the shroud of forgetfulness had already enveloped the victims.

The black man was living with them in an isolated spot that no one penetrated. He was haunted by the idea of reducing to slavery some of the whites who had submitted his race to vile servitude for so long.

It was with the objective that he had created a troop of little servants, whom he maltreated with a ferocious cruelty. He made them pay dearly for all the miseries of the great black family, sold to the yoke and crushed under the boot of its masters. He reigned by terror, directing the children by blows of the whip, obliging them to talk to him on their knees, like a god, imagining all kinds of petty tortures for the slightest faults. He had even extended his vengeful rage so far as to brand them with a hot iron.

One evening, one of his young captives succeeded in escaping, arrived at a farm, dying of starvation, and denounced the criminal.

And expedition of volunteers was immediately organized, and the native, having been received half a dozen bullets in the body, was hanged by way of supplementary justice, without any other form of trial.

UNJUST AND BILIOUS ATTTACKS
A SOUVENIR OF MOUNT PELÉE

If all the foreign newspapers were content to inform their readers in that manner, we could only cry bravo. But it is necessary to observe, with regret, that a few papers are taking advantage of the affair of the child-stealers to denigrate our homeland.

France has the singular privilege of serving as a focal point of universal censure. There is no other country so closely monitored, whose slightest gestures attract the attention of the entire world. There is no nation that encounters more aggressive and more persistent detractors everywhere. Her spirit of frankness and clarity aggravates the very individuals that she attracts into her orbit, and incites petty resentments and sly jealousies in their hearts.

Their excuse is that we are the people most willing to criticize ourselves, so loudly that uninformed outsiders, themselves habituated to washing their dirty laundry in private, can only imagine with great difficulty that we might be exaggerating in the opposite direction.

A few German papers, among the most important, which, as if following orders, have been baying at our heels for some time, are taking further advantage of the affair of the child-stealers to try to denigrate us. "It is only in France that such crimes are possible," cried one Hamburg newspaper. "The French genius consists above all in astonishing the world with automobile follies and news items," declares a colleague in Munich, amiably.

In the same way, a United States daily directed by an Austrian, one of the very few organs in free America that pursue us with sarcasm and hatred, has attacked the organization of our police and our press in a recent issue.

"One of our detectives would have got to grips with the child-stealers, or one of our reporters would have discovered their lair, a long time ago," it says, with a hypertrophied pride that is so characteristic. Let us not in passing that the famous American policeman William Trisson, entertained at the Republic's expense, has not yet discovered anything, and respond with a simple story

During the eruption of Mount Pelée in Martinique,[15] the epidemic of journalists that in invading Paris today afflicted that unfortunate colony. One of the American reporters who had come in such haste showed such prudence that he amused the population of Fort-de-France, who did not, however, have the heart to laugh. Under the pretext of the heat he lived in a cave and sent a negro to gather news. That did not prevent him from telegraphing bitter criticisms of the authorities—who, according to him, showed neither courage nor any hint of initiative.

---

[15] The eruption in question, in 1902, killed 30,000 people, the town of St, Pierre being completely destroyed by a pyroclastic flow.

One day, we learned—for I was there—that he was claiming in his newspaper to have made an ascent of the fuming mountain, whose threats of death were rumbling beneath us through the ground.

A few hours later, the jet of hot gases sprang forth noisily, passing over poor Saint-Pierre for a second time. A man was then seen in Fort-de-France, scarcely dressed and seized by panic terror, with his eyes bulging out of his head, running at top speed toward the harbor and throwing himself in the sea. He swam and swam, until, exhausted, he was picked up twelve hundred meters out—a local record—by a ship at anchor.

That was the reporter from the cave, who reproached us in our dispatches for lacking a cool head, the subterranean climber whose bravery had looked the fire-monster in the mouth! People in Martinique still talk about him: the swimming journalist has remained legendary.

Now that reporter worked for the newspaper that claims that its reporters would have interviewed the child-stealers a long time ago. And what is more, we know that it is that same reporter who has written the article that vituperates against us so inelegantly.

Perhaps this story will recall our bold colleague to modesty.

Clovis Binard

ÉMILE LOUBÉ'S PARENTS
POOR PEOPLE
THREE MYSTERIOUS THOUSAND-FRANC BILLS

I have just paid a visit to little Émile's parents.

They live in the sad and somber lodge of a house in the Rue de Laborde, between the Boulevard Malesherbes and the Boulevard Haussmann—one of those lodges that are too often found in our buildings, in which certain architects seem to have taken pleasure in fabricating night in broad daylight, with vitiated air and tuberculosis.

What misery there is in that gloom, poisoned by a poor oil-lamp.

The father has been in bed for a week. Without employment for two months, he was searching in vain when, by an excess of ill luck, he broke a leg in the street. The physician has now condemned him to a month of immobility.

And now someone has taken their only son!

The mother weeps softly beside the man who cannot move. "My child! My child!" she moans, incessantly, in a prayerful tone that breaks the heart.

I try to revive the courage of these unfortunates slightly.

"He's so intelligent, our little Émile," groans the father, whose eyes are shining with fever in the depths of sunken orbits. "Always top of his class!"

"Oh, yes, Monsieur," the mother adds, raising hr ravaged face toward me. "The schoolmasters said that he would become someone. Monsieur, Monsieur, make them bring him back to me!"

79

Our conversation is interrupted by the arrival of Brigadier Gambin. The policeman had come to tell the parents that Émile Loubé's clothes have been found, scarcely a quarter of an hour after the abduction, on the Quai des Tuileries, a little before the terrace of the Orangerie.

"One more item of evidence," the Brigadier says to me, "that the thieves' base is in that direction."

"Since you have my little one's clothes," the mother cries, all of a sudden, "Why haven't you brought them to me?"

"But Madame, we're keeping them as evidence for the court."

"Oh! Well, I want them right away—right away, you hear!" she shouts. "It's all that I have left, Monsieur, you understand...to remember him by..."

The poor woman is overexcited, threatening and moaning.

Brigadier Gambin exhausts himself trying to make her understand that the law cannot yet release objects that might help guide the investigation and serve to establish the truth.

"They're my relics. I want my relics."

"You need to address yourself to my superiors, Madame," Gambin ends up replying. "It's not up to me."

In fact, why not return to the parents the garment that will remind them of the dear little ones for which they are shedding all their tears?

As Gambin and I are preparing to take our leave of the unfortunate woman, who has never ceased to weep, the postman come in.

"A letter for you, my dear lady."

The concierge snatches the envelope feverishly and utters a cry.

"What is it?"

Trembling with amazement, she shows me three thousand-franc bills. That sum is accompanied by a piece of paper on which there is a text made up of letters cut out from *Le Matin* and stuck together in exactly the same fashion as the note by which Clovis Binard was informed of the abduction of the second Vautremesse son.

Overwhelmed by astonishment, I read:

To relieve your misery slightly, poor people, whom we pity with all our hearts. On behalf of the child-stealers.

"This is unimaginable!" cries Gambin, his eyes rounded by astonishment. "These rascals don't lack cheek! Three thousand francs! Are they millionaires, then?"

Barbarus

ON THE AUDACIOUS CHARITY
OF THE CHILD-STEALERS

My article about the parents of little Émile Loubé has fortunately attracted considerable compassion to them. They have been visited by charitable people who, with all possible tact and delicacy, have attempted to relieve the pain of the unhappy household.

The husband is now assured of a good job on the day when he is able to go out. His wages will be paid from today.

The Loubé family has decided not to make use of the three thousand francs sent by the child-stealers.

"I'd rather die of starvation than touch that money," the mother declared to me, grimly. "I won't buy a mouthful of bread with that gold. It would seem to me, as I ate it, that I'd be devouring my child. Let them keep their money and give me back my boy."

As soon as he was informed of the audacious charity of the child-stealers, Monsieur Daltorf, the local Commissaire, had the consignment seized as evidence.

Aided by Monsieur Bertillon, the head of the Anthropometric Service, Monsieur Laudet immediately set to work. They rapidly reached agreement.

The two notes—the one addressed to Binard and the one containing the three thousand francs sent to the Loubé family—have the same origin. The paper is indisputably the same, the nature of the glue is the same. No doubt is possible.

This, therefore, is a great step forward. The question of whether there is one thief or more is now clarified by the confession of the guilty parties themselves. There are at least two.

The hypothesis that the guilty parties belong to the wealthy class has also received a striking confirmation. They have sent three thousand francs to their unfortunate victim! Three thousand francs is a tidy sum in itself!

The sending of that gross and insolent alms opens up the field yet again to all sorts of discussions.

The child-stealers who are acting with such implacable cruelty are soliciting attenuating circumstances with a curious constancy.

Those hearts of stone have occasional refinements of tenderness.

Their habit of leaving a lock of hair with the garments of the stolen children already indicates an extraordinary sensitivity in the crime. And now they have sent help to poor people whose distress they have multiplied tenfold themselves, as if they wanted to attenuate mental suffering by means of greater material wellbeing.

Barbarus

IN WHICH THERE IS MENTION OF A GIANT

Monsieur,

I have no wish to be summoned to the Palais de Justice a hundred times over for the needs of the investigation. That is why I am maintaining my anonymity. However, I ought to communicate a small item of information to you that will doubtless not be worthless.

At the moment when the theft of little Émile Loubé was taking place, I was going from the Rue du Rocher to the Église Saint-Augustin, passing via the stairways that descend to the Rue Portalis.

There, I was struck by the presence of a kind of giant who, stationed a certain distance away from the school, seemed to be on watch. He was walking back and forth, five steps one way and back again. He seemed to be watching someone or something that I could not see.

It was before the end of classes. Unfortunately, I did not have time to stop to clarify this small matter. I am convinced that it is not unconnected with the abduction of Émile Loubé.

The giant was a man well above the average, without, however, being as thin as almost all the monsters of great height that are exhibited in fairs. Although of exceptional height, the man was well-proportioned; his breadth was in proportion to his height. His face was completely clean-shaven, and he was wearing a summer overcoat of neutral hue.

I cannot give you any further details. It is therefore unnecessary for me disturb myself for the examining magistrate.

A reader who wishes to remain anonymous

It is not the first time that "a giant" has been mentioned in connection with this affair. If you remember, Madame de Vautremesse made allusion one day to the presence of a man whose height had struck her. She told me that she had noticed (I quote her own words) "a man, very tall and very stout, with a big beard—a true giant—who looked at me, for just a moment, insistently" before the abduction of little André. The Baronne could not remember a more precise description.

Let us note, however, that Madame de Vautremesse's giant was bearded, while the one denounced by the anonymous reader was clean-shaven. The two might well be the same man, however. There is nothing easier than shaving off a beard.

Perhaps this is an important clue. Fellows of that size are very rare. The police would be undertaking a useful investigation in searching out all the giants in Paris who once had a beard but are no longer wearing one.

Clovis Binard

MONSIEUR LAUDET'S INVESTIGATION

With unalterable patience, Monsieur Laudet is continuing to have the entire neighborhood to which he believes the vehicle identified by Gilbert Bartoulou was heading searched, house by house.

Although the agents charged with this fastidious duty are almost at the end of their task, having methodically explored the area assigned to them, the searches have produced no result, either because they have been poorly conducted, or—which is more probable—because the deductions of the examining magistrate, although interesting, were hazardous.

C.B.

THE ABDUCTION OF A LITTLE GIRL

I have been notified of an event, the certainty of which I cannot yet guarantee, which I shall hasten to verify.

It appears that a little girl has disappeared, in the same circumstances as the recent abductions. Her clothes have been found, with the usual lock of hair, this time left in the child's blue ribbon. If this is true, the abductor, after having only attacked little boys to begin with, had changed his tactics and is menacing little girls.

That is not calculated to calm public alarm.

C.B.

AN ARREST

An arrest has been made, which undoubtedly has some connection with the affair of the child-stealers. The accused has already been locked up for three days. The secret has been religiously kept. In spite of the most urgent insistence, this time I have not been able to obtain either a confirmation or a denial of the news.

Alain Bernard

LAST MINUTE NEWS
ANOTHER ARREST

Was the government right to have the famous American detective William Trisson come all they from America?

The transatlantic policeman has just arrested a man whom he has taken to the police station in the Rue de Provence. William Trisson affirms that he is one of the child-stealers.

Barbarus

A SCANDAL
ARREST OF THE COMTE VAN DEN PLAYGS
A STUPID DIPLOMATIC INCIDENT

He's quite something, William Trisson!

For his trial run in Paris he has brought off a true masterstroke, which will leave a durable reputation here.

What flair he has, this policemen—in verity, what flair!

It is not possible to imagine, for a detective, a greater gaffe than the one he has committed.

William Trisson has had arrested none other than His Excellency Comte Van den Playgs, secretary to the King of the Belgians.

No police blunder has ever been more ludicrous or more leaden.

Here are the facts:

On the formal orders of Monsieur Hamard, two inspectors able to speak English, Raoul Mirovitch and Sever Contamps, were put at the disposal of the American, who, since his arrival in Paris, seemed to have found a savant trail in the major bars. The work of the agents accompanying him seemed to consist mainly of ingurgitating cocktails.

When he had thus enlightened his ideas by a notable absorption of complicated alcohols, William Trisson went out into the streets with his two companions, nose in the air, waiting for hazard to put the child-stealers in his path.

"When William Trisson ordered us to arrest a very elegant gentleman who was turning the corner of the Rue de Maubeuge," Raoul Mirovitch told me, "he had absorbed a good dozen glasses. The Comte Van den Playgs—for it was him—having just made a movement toward an old lady who was holding a little boy by the hand, our worthy Trisson immediately imagined, by virtue of a drunken inspiration, that the monsieur who was thus increasing his pace was about to snatch the child.

"It was as simple as that: 'Seize that man for me,' he said to us, in English. Contamps and me, we looked at one another. What should we do? We'd been given the order to obey the American. We obeyed. Just as I put my hand on the Comte's collar, I remembered that I had seen his face somewhere before, but I couldn't remember where.

---

[16] At this point, the dating of the Tallandier edition becomes confused, the dates 12 and 13 July being repeated, thus accounting for two of the nine days separating the final date in the Tallandier edition from the date of the issue of *Le Matin* featuring the conclusion of the serial. There is no easy way to correct the mistake without changing all the subsequent dates, so I have left it as it is.

"Monsieur Van den Playgs, naturally, protests with all his energy, and equally naturally, we're immediately surrounded by a crowd. Trisson, whose picture has been published, is recognized and—I don't know why—the drunkard is always likeable at first glance. People side with him. Finally, the secretary says, very reasonably, that it's much more practical to go and explain himself at the police station. There, everything becomes clear. The Commissaire of Police makes his excuses, and alerts the Minister of the Interior.

"The worst of it, you see, is that for five hours they keep us, Contamps and me, at the station, as if we were guilty. Even today, we still fear that we might be sacked. I ask you, what should we have done? We only knew the orders. They can't punish us for following them. It just that, we've been told, what if American has gone to our chiefs today and told them that, thanks to our reluctance, the child-stealer he's caught had got away? We'd be in a jam!"

William Trisson has been kept at the disposal of the authorities. Does his mistake, which his drunkenness explains but does not excuse, really merit punishment? If so, what?

As soon as he learned about this absurd event, Monsieur Pichon, our Minister of Foreign Affairs,[17] went to see the Belgian Ambassador, to present the apologies of the government of the Republic.

Either I'm much mistaken, or the famous William Trisson's career in Paris in over.

Clovis Binard

THE ARREST OF A SPY, PIETRO PALAVACOCCINI
HE IS THE FATHER OF ONE
OF THE ABUCTED CHILDREN

Today we know the name of the person arrested a few days ago in such a mysterious fashion. It is that of Pietro Palavacoccini, the father of Paolo Palavacoccini, who was one of the first children to be abducted by the child-stealers.

At the Sûreté, there is still silence on this subject. I have been able to ascertain that the arrest has no direct bearing on the affair of the child-stealers. It is, however, Monsieur Laudet's investigation that provoked this measure against Pietro Palavacoccini.

It appears that the investigations of the police into the "Great Affair" have led, in an unexpected fashion, to the proof that Palavacoccini is the leader of a veritable spy-ring.

Alain Bernard

---

[17] In fact, Stephen Pichon (1857-1933) did not take up that post until October 1906, when Clemenceau was promoted to President of the Council; this name was presumably mistakenly added to the 1909 edition.

THE KIDNAPPER IS NOW SNATCHING GIRLS
THE ABDUCTION OF GERMAINE PLAIZANCE

In the midst of all these events, the abduction by the child-stealers of a little girl is not the least resounding.

Yesterday's news was correct.

The abducted child is named Germaine Plaizance.

She is the daughter of Commandant Plaizance, who has just departed for Madagascar, where he has been dispatched on a topographical mission.

The little girl was abducted as her mother was buying two tickets at the Metro station in the Place de l'Europe. By chance, there was a considerable crowd in that station, which is not usually busy. To avoid the little one being jostled, the mother had left her in front of the barrier behind which the queue for tickets had formed.

Germaine Plaizance disappeared at the moment when her mother took her eyes off her to slide her money through the window.

Terrified, on observing the disappearance, the unfortunate woman uttered loud screams. People crowded around her.

The searches of the people present produced, as usual, no result. Important depositions were, however, collected.

Henri Keroul, the well-know dramatic author,[18] as he was about to descend into the subterranean Metro station, saw a very elegant woman coming out. She was holding a little girl by the hand, in a slightly violent fashion, whom she dragged away rapidly in the direction of the Place de Londres. The little girl was wearing a beige mantle with a lacy collar. That description corresponds with the one given by the mother.

Little Germaine was, therefore, abducted by a *female* thief.

Henri Keroul was unable to give an exact description of the features of the woman he saw. He only remembers that she was wearing a hat garnished with a large brown ostrich-feather undulating around it. She was wearing a simple dress tailored with refinement, almost certainly the product of one of the best fashion-houses.

The giant was also seen—or, to be strictly accurate, the giants, for, almost at the same moment, immediately before and immediately after the abduction, two men were seen in the vicinity who respond to the description given yesterday by an anonymous reader.

However, the two abnormally large individuals perceived by different witness, whose statements coincide, were both bearded—like the giant that Madame de Vautremesse remembered vaguely.

---

[18] Henri Keroul (Henry Queyroul, 1854-1921) sometimes spelled the forename of his pseudonym Henry, thus confusing bibliographers. Although best-known for his dramatic works, many of them vaudevilles in the same vein as Forest's, he also contributed at least one feuilleton to *Le Matin*, *Le Secret de Madeleine* (1902).

As in the case of the abduction of little Émile Loubé, an automobile was parked in the vicinity, quite a long time before the theft, this time of the Pont de l'Europe, at the corner of the Rue de Londres.

A newsvendor saw a woman getting into that vehicle, in which a man was already present, with little Germaine.

That automobile was not the same one that was observed during the kidnapping of Émile Loubé by the soldier on sentry duty at the Pépinière barracks. The latter had a long chassis, whereas this one had a short chassis.

All the facts now accumulated prove that we are not dealing, in the affair of the child-stealers, with two people, as it was previously possible to believe, but with a whole gang.

It is almost proven today, according to the various witness statements, that there are at least six accomplices:

1. The man who, for want of anything better, we shall call "the elegant man," who appeared during the thefts of André and Gontran de Vautremesse;

2. The coachman of the carriage that as seen outside the Nouveau Cirque

3. The chauffeur of the automobile;

4. A very tall and very strong man;

5. The man who went to buy the paper and the glue to write me the note by means of which I was alerted to the abduction of Gontran de Vautremesse;

6. Finally, the lady whom Henri Keroul saw emerging from the Metro.

Germain Plaizance's garments were found behind the Église de la Madeleine about twenty minutes after the abduction.

A PUBLIC MEETING AT THE TROCADÉRO

A veritable stupor has overtaken the city.

People had gradually become accustomed to the idea that the child-stealers only kidnapped little boys. They are disturbed to discover that they are now abducting little girls.

The emotion is all the more profound because the event was so unexpected.

We know that the impatience of the public to put an end to these crimes, whose repetition, constancy and audacity are frightful, will soon be translated into action.

Meetings are being organized.

It has been announced that a well-known society lady, Madame la Comtesse de Houdotte, will hold a big public meeting on the matter in the hall of the Trocadéro. All the months of the kidnappers' victims will be invited to it, as well as various important figures in literature and the arts. There will be a public discussion of the means of putting an end to an intolerable situation.

We also know that at the surgical conference that was held yesterday in Paris, several scientists proposed that they come together to form a scientific research committee to aid the police in centralizing information.

Everyone is in agreement. It is not possible, in our era, that such crimes can continue to be perpetrated in the heart of Paris with such impunity!

Clovis Binard

NEW CRIMES

Public apprehension has been brought to a peak by the news that five abductions were carried out in a single day yesterday, of three little boys and two little girls.

1. Vincent Montiers, abducted outside the Gare de l'Est. His clothes were found under the Porte Saint-Denis.

2. Louis Maneuil, abducted at the corner of the Avenue Victor Hugo and the Rue des Belles-Feuilles. His clothes were found in the Rue de Magdebourg, outside the gardens of the Trocadéro, a short distance away from the place where those of Léon Aproli were found.

3. Philippe Ordin-Rosier was abducted at the corner of the Rue de Téhéran and the Boulevard Haussmann. His clothes were found in the Avenue Marigny, against the wall of the Palais de l'Élysée.

4. Victorine Artesy was abducted in the Boulevard Diderot, in front of the fire station. Her clothes were found on the Quai Saint-Bernard. In a fold of her dress, a small medical thermometer was found, broken.

5. Alice Poliarre was abducted in the Place des Ternes. Her clothes were found in the Rue Lamennais, not far from the Rue Washington.

All these thefts were committed in the afternoon.

The police and the examining magistrate are at their wits' end, and no longer know what to do.

Barbarus

THE ILLUSTRIOUS WILLIAM TRISSON

After a night spent in the Conciergerie, the celebrated American detective has been released. He is protesting his innocence energetically, and declares, in spite of all the evidence, that the two French agents are solely responsible for the unfortunate error.

"On the contrary," he said, "I did everything I could to prevent the arrest of Monsieur Van den Playgs. It was those imbeciles who insisted."

In spite of all he might claim, William Trisson will be occupying his leisure time in other research than that of the child-stealers. The government has canceled its contract with him on the grounds of blatant incapacity.

The American detective has nevertheless made a great deal of noise, demanding that he be paid generous parting compensation in order to keep quiet. It has been recognized that the two French agents, victims of their orders, were only obeying him. They will keep their jobs.

Alain Bernard

THE PALAVACOCCINI AFFAIR

The arrest of Pietro Palavacoccini has been maintained.

It has gradually been confirmed that the capture was justified. A nest of bandits has been discovered, of whom Palavacoccini was the leader.

The Italian had constituted a veritable syndicate of spies, whose information he was centralizing. It was in pursuing his investigations into the child-stealers that Monsieur Hamard discovered that vast conspiracy organized against national security.

There is talk of further arrests, consequential on that of Palavacoccini.

I have been able to converse for a few minutes with this Palavacoccini in the antechamber of the Anthropometric Service, where he was preparing to submit to Monsieur Bertillon's measurements.

The Italian, a short, stiff dark-haired man, seemed to me to be profoundly depressed. He made no difficulty about telling me his story.

"Yes, Monsieur," he said, "I organized a large-scale espionage service. I won't deny it. Let them punish me—I don't care. But they won't get any more out of me. For whom was I working? How was I working? With whom? Let them search. As for me, I shall stay mute, and my fate is indifferent to me. I only devoted myself to that vile profession in order to be able, one day, to make my little Paolo rich. That child was everything to me. Now that the kidnappers have taken him from me, they've killed me…because, in my opinion, they've killed him…

"I no longer have any appetite for life, and everything is indifferent to me. Go to my home. You'll find my wife and my mother-in-law there. They'll tell you details about the abduction of Paolo that might be very important to the discovery of the guilty parties. Until now I'd forbidden them to speak. My duty obliged me to have as little as possible to do with the police. I owed that silence to my accomplices, to those who had confidence in me. That's why I'm keeping quiet, in spite of the desire I have to talk."

PAOLO PALAVACOCCINI'S MOTHER
AND GRANDMOTHER
THE TWO GIANTS AND THE SOCIETY LADY
PRECIOUS INFORMATION

I did not have to be invited twice.

As quickly as I could, I went to the Avenue Niel, where the two tearful women that I have just left reside.

The loss of their child and the unexpected arrest of the husband has been a double catastrophe for them.

They received me in a drawing room whose windows were shuttered, only illuminated by a night-light.

"Since these events," the poor grandmother told me, in a tearful tone that did not impede her Italian accent or her volubility, "I can no longer bear the light. I have to remain in darkness. Imagine! We had no idea that Pietro was following that vile profession. He told us that he was engaged in land speculation. We weren't curious. We never looked through his papers. If he hadn't confessed, I wouldn't have believed it."

"Yes," the wife added, "we only had a suspicion that something shady was going on here when my husband forbade us to tell the examining magistrate what we knew about the child-stealers. He forbade us very forcefully and would never give us any explanation. We obeyed reluctantly, without understanding, with the sentiment that there was something terrible behind it. Oh, what a frightful existence we have led since then!"

"But now that your husband has been arrested you no longer have any reason to hide information useful to the law."

"No, Monsieur, and I will gave it to you. Our little Paolo was abducted at the corner of the Avenue Niel and the Rue Rennequin, where he was walking with his grandmother..."

"Yes," the grandmother interjected. "I was walking in the sunlight. In the Avenue Niel I passed a tall man, a giant with a large beard. What struck me the most was that at that moment, as I looked across the Avenue at the opposite sidewalk, I saw another giant, who was looking at us.

"The giant on my side stopped me to ask for directions to the Place Pereire. At that moment, the child, who was rolling a hoop, turned the corner of the Rue Rennequin. We have not seen him since. In the Rue Rennequin a private carriage was speeding away at a fast gallop. The little one was inside—I was sure of it. I shouted to the giant to give chase, but he didn't budge—and suddenly, I saw that the other giant was beside us, that the two men knew one another. They were immediately joined by a woman, a very beautiful woman with refined manners.

"I was distraught because of the disappearance of the child. I didn't know what to do. I was weeping. But there were only the four of us at the street corner. The lady advised me to go to the Commissaire. I asked them to go with me. They refused, saying that they didn't have time. Then I went home instead, to alert my son-in-law. That's all."

"But in that case," I exclaimed, "there are definitely two giants and not one! And you have had direct contact with the three accomplices?"

"Yes, Monsieur. The proof is that we received, perhaps only three minutes after I returned to the house, a letter brought by a commissionaire. Here it is."

The grandmother got up, painfully, and went to open a drawer, after which she handed me an envelope bearing the address: *To Madame Palavacoccini senior.*

Inside there was a visiting card on which the printing had been scored with a pen-knife. Written in pencil was: *Please do not say anything about the abduction of Paolo until you have talked to Palavacoccini senior, or something unfortunate will happen.*

"At the moment when we received that letter, my son-in-law was there. We were about to go to the Commissaire of Police to tell him everything, but after receiving that card, my son-in-law, trembling all over, told us that it was necessary to keep quiet, not to say what we knew about the people who were, I sensed instinctively, accomplices to the kidnapping. All that he would permit us to do was to report the little one's disappearance to the Commissaire, without giving any details that might lead to the thieves being caught. We had to obey—reluctantly, as you can imagine."

This time, the law finally possesses some precise information, precise and categorical details.

The conversation I had with the two women clarify the situation.

The police research will finally be guided by concrete indications and not abstract suppositions.

The complicity of a woman, two men of well above medium height and two men of ordinary stature in now definitely concluded.

One has a vague sensation that the affair of the child-stealers will soon take a new turn.

Clovis Binard

Paris, 14 July

A POSTER

The walls of Paris are covered today with large yellow posters, of which we received a sample yesterday evening.

This is the text:

To the Mothers of Paris,
We cannot tolerate any longer the dolorous situation in which all the mothers of Pars have been placed.
There is not one who is not in fear for her child.
The promenades are deserted.
The public gardens are empty.
Children are now kept at home, cloistered and imprisoned.
When mothers are obliged to go out with their children, they tremble in every limb until they get home.
We admit that the public powers are doing their duty, but in such circumstances, it is necessary to do more than one's duty.
In consequence, a committee of ladies met the day before yesterday under the convocation of the Comtesse de Houdotte. It has been decided that a public meeting will be held tomorrow in the hall of the Trocadéro.
All the parents of the missing children have been invited.
Numerous celebrities of the artistic and literary world have already given their support. They will be there to lend their presence to the organizers of the meeting.
We cannot urge the mothers of Paris strongly enough to respond to our appeal. It is urgent that we study together the means of liberating the city from the frightful bandits who are terrifying families.

The chairwoman of the Committee of Women
Against the Child-Stealers
Comtesse Geneviève de Houdotte
The Committee:
Blanche de Vairlette
Cautet, of the Comédie-Française
Mme Léopoldine Israël-Kahn
Baronne de Vautremesse, etc., etc.

The meeting will be held at two o'clock in the afternoon. The doors will open at one-thirty. Free entry.

A COMMITTEE OF SCIENTISTS

In yesterday evening's *Le Temps*, we read:

The affair of the child-stealers has, in truth, surpassed the range of news.

These crimes that are incessant and remain unpunished, the audacity of which confounds the imagination, have gradually upset the entire social equilibrium of Paris.

Now, private initiative has been set to work. One of those great movements of social solidarity has been established, such as one sees at moments of large-scale calamity.

Yesterday, in one of the rooms of the Cercle Volney, a large meeting of scientists was held, at which almost all those illustrious in the exact sciences and the observational sciences were present.

It was decided, after a discussion that lasted no less than two hours, to form a scientific committee to investigate the child-stealers.

Some of our most highly-reputed scientists have promised to devote themselves body and soul to this new endeavor.

It is truly a sign of the times to see, in grave circumstances, science hastening to the rescue of the impotent police.

THE SCIENTISTS AND THE CHILD-STEALERS
THE CELEBRATED SURGEON PROFESSOR FLAX
IS ELECTED PRESIDENT OF
THE SCIENTIFIC COMMITTEE OF INVESTIGATION

The first meeting of the committee that our colleague announced in these terms took place at ten o'clock this morning in one of the rooms of the École des Sciences Politiques.

The scientists gathered in the great amphitheater in the Rue Saint-Guillaume numbered approximately fifty. The list of their names is a veritable honors list of French Science.

Present were:

Dr. Arsonval;

Dr. Bruyère;

Dr. Pozzi;

M. Branly, the inventor of wireless telegraphy;

the celebrated bacteriologist Professor Metchnikoff;

Dr. Bertillon, the head of statistics of the City of Paris;

Dr. Flax;

M. Cruppi;

M. Lavisse of the Académie Française;

M. Alfred de Foville, former director of the Monnaie, director of the Cour des Comptes;

M. Bréal of the Académie des Inscriptions et Belles-lettres;

M. Alfred Croiset, doyen of the Faculté des Lettres;

M. Edmond Théry, the eminent economist;

M. Painlevé, of the geometry section of the Académie des Sciences;

M. Monins, of the astronomy section;

M. Bouquet de La Grie, of the geography section;

M. Lippmann, of the physics section;

M. Michaud, of the chemistry section;

M. de Lapparent, of the mineralogy section;

M. Prillieux, of the botany section;

M. Schloesing, fils, of the economic and rural section;

M. Perir, of the zoology section;

M. Poincaré, the most celebrated mathematician in the world;

Dr. Marie, chief of medicine at the asylum of Villejuif;

M. Bouvard, director of the architectural service of the promenades and plantations of the City of Paris;

M. Bienvenu, chief engineer of the technical service of the Métropolitain;

M. Mercadier, inspector general of telegraph services and director of studies at the École Polytechnique;

M. Émile Prélat, director of the École d'Architecture

M. Pelletan, subdirector of the École Nationale Supérieure des Mines;

M. Camille Flammarion;

M. Henri de Vorigno;

Dr. Paul d'Angliney;[19]

Etc.

Such are the names jotted down at hazard in pencil.

It was M. de Vorigno who opened the session.

"I beg you to excuse," he said, loudly, "if I permit myself to speak first; someone has to start, but I have only one hasty task, which is to abandon my place to someone more worthy. During the conference on surgery, which I attended in the capacity of recorder, the opinion was expressed that science had a duty to fulfill in the affair of the child-stealers. That opinion received such an enthusiastic welcome that, on the initiative of a few friends, I have invited you here. The letter by which you were invited explained the purpose of the meeting. Your presence is, in itself, proof that you approve. Before beginning any discussion and endeavor, it is, I think, urgent to constitute a panel of officers to direct the debates. That is a necessary of any assembly. I therefore propose to appoint a

---

[19] Almost all of these names are those of real individuals, although it is not obvious that Forest's readers would have recognized them all, or been immediately conscious of the exceptions; the last two are, however—like that of Dr. Flax—fictitious.

president, two vice-presidents and two secretaries. I shall begin the putting the presidency to the vote."

On all sides, as if in response to an order, the name of Dr. Flax was shouted almost unanimously.

M. de Vorigno then wanted to proclaim the celebrated surgeon elected, but the latter protested. "No," he cried, "I cannot admit that election. First of all, I say quite frankly that I do not want the great honor that has been done to me. I am at overwhelmed by work at the moment; I need all my time. If I have come here, it is only because I am accomplishing a veritable civic duty by my presence. I fear, however, that the work of research would exceed my capacities and the time I have available, and I beg you to redirect your suffrage to someone else."

The assembly did not want to hear it.

M. de Vorigno having proposed a show of hands, every arm was extended unanimously to designate Dr. Flax once again.

The celebrated surgeon, who, as everyone knows, is no ordinary individual, went to the green baize table and said in a loud voice: "You give me no pleasure at all by this proof of confraternal confidence. But all in all, too bad. The wine is uncorked; I shall drink it." And he went to sit down at the table.

The election proceeded of the vice-presidents, Messieurs d'Angliney and Marcel Dapran, and the secretaries, Messieurs de Vorgino and Hacrin. Thus constituted, the committee commenced its routine functions.

"I hand the floor to Dr. d'Angliney," said Dr. Flax. "Our eminent colleague will explain to you the reasons why science ought to intervene in the question of the child-stealers."

"Messieurs," said M. d'Angliney, "the police investigations have been carried out with an intelligence to which I render homage. We consider, however, that intelligence without method is like a thoroughbred horse without a rider. It runs to the right and it runs to the left, but it incapable of heading of its own accord toward a distant goal. Some of us are convinced that if a committee of scientists were to apply to the facts the inflexible methods of observation to which we are accustomed, we would succeed in binding together a useful sheaf of indications.

The kidnappings have been so numerous that it is undoubtedly not impossible to discover *the law* of these abductions, to find consistent relationships, as there always are in the repetitions of the same actions by the same individuals. Skillful as they are, the thieves cannot isolate themselves from the laws that govern the activity of entities, the physical and psychological laws that govern human beings. They are obliged to obey those laws, which are the very form of our lives. They are, by the very fact that they are skillful, forced to submit to the inflexible pressure of logic.

"The role of the Scientific Committee of Investigation will be to discover the permanent features of the thefts and to extract therefrom a set of deductions from which we might hope for the finest fruits. Our action does not, I repeat, imply any criticism of the police or the examining magistrate. I merely say that the habitude of the sciences gives us a turn of mind that permits us to unravel problems that simple common sense and clarity of mind cannot succeed in solving."

After this speech, the meeting of scientists decided that a sub-committee would be charged with seeking authorization from the Garde des Sceaux to obtain communication of all the evidence concerning the affairs of the abductions. The documents would be categorized, analyzed and discussed in a plenary session.

The first meeting of that sub-committee will take place the day after tomorrow.

Can the intervention of the scientists hasten the end of the nightmare in the midst of which Paris is writhing?

Clovis Binard

INTERVIEW WITH DR. FLAX
A GREAT PHYSICIAN
ENORMOUS HONORARIA
DISSIMULATED GENEROSITY
SON OF A SHINA-CHALA

This morning I presented myself at the home of Dr. Flax, whom the scientists who met yesterday chose unanimously to direct their discussions and their efforts.

A member of the Institut, professor of pathology at the Faculté de Médecine, Commander of the Légion d'honneur, etc., etc., Professor Flax is a man heaped with so many honorific distinctions that he no longer knows where to put the medals and ribbons.

His 104 decorations doubtless do not add anything to his merit, but they prove that his medical reputation is one of the most solidly and universally established. All the kings in the world and all the billionaires have solicited his care. The most splendid monarchs, the sovereigns who love to dazzle people with the luxury of their parades and their costumes, have donned medical gowns before him, and it appears that the medical gown confers no more advantage on princes than anyone else. Dr. Flax has seen all the miseries that a great name or a fat wallet might bear pass before the celebrated gleam of his searching eyes.

But aristocrats and plutocrats, the rich and the powerful, without exception, have been obliged, before consulting the physician, to leave all pride and arrogance at the door. More than one anecdote has been related about the way in which the scientist treats his august clients. It appears that he does not spare them wounding remarks or displeasing observations. He tells them the brutal and cruel truth.

A man who permits himself to speak as bluntly to noble lords used to seeing everyone bow down, and only hearing certain truths disguises by courtieresque circumlocutions, is certainly not banal. That indomitable character has made no small contribution to the professor's worldwide glory.

What has struck the public most of all, however, are the fantastic sums of money that the doctor demands from his patients. A recent lawsuit has revealed them.

He charges 100,000 francs for a routine consultation. A voyage to Ems cost a rich German who summoned such a costly master 30,000 marks. The American Abel Strussel, who made millions in the construction of certain powders that earned him, a trifle ironically, the title of "the insecticide king," was oblige to sign a check for 50,000 francs for a minor operation.

Professor Flax—I permit myself to record this because the facts are in the public domain and he has redeemed himself by so many virtuous deeds—is ferocious in the fixation of his honoraria. The doctor taxes his clients in accordance with the fortune he supposes them to possess, and only consents to undertake treatment if paid in advance. I have held in my hand a letter received by a great refiner who wanted to be examined by the scientist. This was the curt text:

Monsieur.

6,000 francs. Pay in advance. Then come Sunday evening at 10-15 precisely. Compliments.

Flax

One might think, in truth, that the doctor gladly exercises a special kind of cynicism in questions of money, that he takes pride in displaying an implacable avidity, in manifesting a malicious cupidity in order better to mislead those who are unaware of his inexhaustible generosity and his ever-alert charity.

For this miser, who seems to take pleasure in publishing his vice, hides the fact that he distributes to others what he extracts so brutally from some.

Let the doctor's clients not protest too much. They have been, doubtless in spite of themselves, the collaborators in generous and praiseworthy endeavors. The professor does not accumulate money for himself. He considers himself as a simple intermediary, charged with taking from overloaded coffers that which is necessary to relieve those who have excessively meager resources, or no resources at all.

Professor Flax is, in fact, the benefactor of our great hospitals in Paris and the provinces. They owe to his generosity a thousand ameliorations that their own budgets would not permit them to realize.

In particular, he had aided, with all his might and all his fortune, the services for the care of children. It is well-known that the beautiful hospital recently inaugurated at Montretout and reserved for children was constructed by courtesy of the generosity of an anonymous donor. I can reveal his name today; that secret philanthropist is none other than Dr. Flax.

Every morning, the professor goes to that hospital, where he remains until midday, caring for his young invalids or working in his laboratory. Since the creation of the establishment at Montretout, the professor has specialized in the maladies of childhood.

Such is the individual to whom I went in search of a few clarifications regarding the projects of the Scientific Committee of Investigation into the affair of the child-stealers.

Dr. Flax resides at number 26 Rue Cassette, a somber town house of unappealing appearance. The street is not lively; it gives the impression of having gone to sleep during a previous regime and not yet having woken up. The professor's house certainly does not make it any more cheerful. From the outside, one only perceives and enormous wall, bisected by a huge black door, tinged with green, that seems to belong to one of those prisons of yore from which one never emerged. Not one window, not one loophole.

I ring the bell

The sullen door opens immediately. I go in. Behind the door there is only an enclosure, which one enters by way of a large and badly-paved courtyard. At the back is the house, an old building of grandiose appearance, but cold and morose.

On the threshold stands a sort of colossus with green eyes, who, in a voice that would cause someone less courageous than me to flee, asks me in a strong German accent: "Vot do you vant?"

"To interview Dr. Flax."

I hand my card to the Cerberus, who turns it over in his huge hands. His little finger is thicker than my thumb.

"Parparus? *Matin?*" he mutters, hesitantly. Then, after a moment's reflection, he shouts: "Chrysostome!"

A mighty voice replies with a question in a language that I assume to be a German dialect. I deduce that it signifies: "What do you want, Wolfgang?"

"There's a journalist here," howls the said Wolfgang in French, "who wants to interview the doctor."

The thunderous voice replies, but this time I don't understand.

At that moment, a man of medium height appears, whose gaze is keen, almost scintillating. More jargon. Finally, the new arrival, who responds to the name of Numérien, says to the colossus, in good French with a hint of a foreign accent, in an admirable voice with the sonority and extension of a bell: "You can take Monsieur to the doctor, Wolfgang. No need to announce him."

"Give me your hand," says my guide, and engulfs my thin phalanges in his broad palms.

He opens doors, closes them again, takes me through rooms whose shutters are closed and in which I cannot see a thing. Finally, in front of a door-curtain that he lifts up, my guide declares: "Here it is. I'll wait for you to take you back."

And he pushes me into a large room whose walls are decked from floor to ceiling with bookshelves. To the left, at a window, seemingly gazing out into the courtyard, the skeleton of a monkey is suspended by the top of the skull from a wooden frame.

That is all the decoration of the doctor's study. An exceedingly worn Persian carpet; old leather armchairs, which, caved in, seemed to have retained the trace of the innumerable heavy posteriors to which they have been subjected; a similarly dilapidated sofa; Gothic chairs made entirely of wood; and an immense table that serves as a desk make up its entire furniture.

Dr. Flax has risen to his feet, throwing off a traveling rug that was protecting his knees.

"Good!" he says, with no other preliminaries, offering me a seat. "I can guess what brings you here."

He does not give me the time to get a word in, and continues: "There is nothing more stupid than an interview in which a man who generally knows something chats to a journalist who generally knows nothing., but who will be obliged to write a column on a subject that is as foreign to him as the theory of the lancers' quadrille is to me."

"Oh, Monsieur, I haven't come today to ask for transcendent information. I'd just like to know what the plans of the Scientific Investigation Committee are."

"So you don't know, then, damn it? You haven't read the newspapers, you who fill them? There was no need to disturb me. We're investigating the child-stealers."

"Yes, but this famous scientific method...?"

"You're an idiot. Go to school. Do I have to repeat a lecture that you didn't take in during your studies in philosophy? No. All that I ask you to tell your readers is that it's necessary, in spite of everything, not to have too many illusions about our scientific sagacity. It's not impossible that we won't find anything. The rigor of our deductions might weaken if we're not in possession of certain data. My opinion is that the investigation will be terribly difficult. The child-stealers do not appear to me to be ordinary intelligences. *Au revoir*, Monsieur—that's all... no! Repeat once again that I've very annoyed by the honor that has been done to me by acclaiming me president, and believe that I'm not speaking out of false modesty. *Au revoir*, Monsieur."

"One more question. It's said, Doctor, that you're not French, and..."

"That's said because I have dark skin. I was born in Chile, where my father, a Frenchman, was established as a pharmacist. My mother was a Shina-Chala, famous for her beauty and an exotic complexion. She bequeathed me the complexion, but certainly not the beauty."

"A Shina-Chala?"

"For those who don't know—which is to say, for 999 of your readers in a thousand—learn that a Chilean Shina-Chala is the daughter of a Chilean Zambo and a Chilean Chola, that a Chilean Zambo is born of the mating on an Indian with a black woman and that a Chilean Chola is the result of a marriage between an Indian and a white person. My blood is thus a mixture of Spanish, French, Indian and African blood. With that, Monsieur, get out. I have work to do."

Without paying any more heed to me, Professor Flax goes to sit down at the table he left a few moments before, and resumes writing, as if I were not there.

It only remains for me to salute that bizarre and arrogant scientist, whose bony and desiccated face, with dark eyes and pronounced eyebrows, is heightened by the harshness of the features, the superb contours of the forehead and a gaze that plunges into you to the marrow. If ever that steely gaze comes to rest on one of the guilty parties, the judges will immediately learn the long and the short of the matter. The victims of the child-stealers will be on the eve of their vengeance.

Barbarus

THE MEETING AT THE TROCADÉRO
A SPEECH BY THE COMTESSE DE HOUDOTTE
A MOVING PRESENTATION

The meeting at the Trocadéro took place yesterday.

The crowd and the enthusiasm were enormous.

The meeting had been advertised for two-thirty. More than an hour before, when the doors had not yet opened, a considerable mass of curiosity-seekers, mostly women, have laid siege to the vicinity of the Trocadéro.

The immense hall rapidly fills up.

Soon, not a single corner remains.

The spectators are impatient, noisy and loquacious. There is nothing astonishing about that, as most of them are female.

The sound of voices rumbles like distant thunder.

Finally, the curtain goes up. The conversations die away. The mothers of the abducted children are sitting in a semicircle on the stage, around the notable individuals who have lent their collaboration to the organizers of the assembly.

All the mothers, as if responsive to a formal instruction, are dressed in black. That row of afflicted women is touching to behold. Some stand out, in particular; I will mention Madame Clépent, Madame Pompaigne, the Baronne de Vautremesse, etc.

The Comtesse de Houdotte, who is in the chair, is surrounded by the ladies making up the committee. One picks out Madame Cautet, whose silhouette has so much elegance, and Blanche de Vairlettes, whose fine gaze is examining the crowd curiously. Around them, and in front of the mothers, one also notices:

Marcel Prévost, whose clear, plain and frank face is the complete reflection of his literary work;

Anatole France, whose soft and pensive eyes belie the appearance of a retired cavalry officer;

Camille Flammarion, sympathetic and benevolent, with his wife beside him, whom one sees everywhere that devotion to a noble cause is necessary;

Dr. Flax, whose powerful temples seem to be sculpted in brown marble;

Séverine, a marvelous mask of intelligence, generosity and energy;

M. Dubief, the former Minister of the Interior;

Dujardin-Beaumetz, the Undersecretary of State for the Fine Arts;

André Antoine, the director of the Odéon, who has left the architects with whom he studies the reflection of his theater to run to the Trocadéro and add luster to the stage of its Napoléonic effigy;

Adolphe Brisson;

Gaston Deschamps;

Paul Deschanel;

René Baschet;

Massenet;

Louis Forest;

Marcel Lhereux

Francis de Croisset, whose ironic lips have an expression of gravity today;

Adrien Bernheim, etc.[20]

With a brief and authoritative shake of the hand-bell, which proves that the Comtesse de Houdotte is well-equipped to direct an assembly, the president puts an end to the final whispers.

"Mesdames et Messieurs," she cries, in a voice no less firm and no less categorical, "let us not waste time repeating facts that are common knowledge. For nearly a month now, Paris has been living in a kind of terror, lamenting like the cities of old whose surroundings were devastated by the Hydra. We want to slay the Hydra. We are appealing to you for help.

"This appeal has been heard from the top to the bottom of Parisian society. We are surrounded here by the most noble talents, and if I read you the letters of apology that all the notable individuals who, whether invited by us or not, wanted to assure us of their sympathy, I would be reading for an hour. We have the entire world with us. We have all of France, and everyone else.

"Before giving the floor to one of our friends, however, before proposing myself an action that will be the consecration of our discussion, I want to introduce to you the unfortunate mothers whose misfortune has gradually become a national misfortune."

Then, in a beautiful display of eloquence, with incredibly sovereign and engaging gestures, the Comtesse de Houdotte introduced, one by one, the mothers whose children had been abducted in recent days.

At each name, one of the poor women stood up, and a great murmur of sympathy rose up from the depths of the crowd.

For each one, the Comtesse de Houdotte finds a new word of emotion, of comfort. At each name, she relates the story of the abduction, gives the details, offers descriptions of the children, recounts their beauty, their gentility, their tenderness. Every time, too, the designated mother dissolves in tears, recalling all her grief—and those communicative plaints draw the spectators in; one hears, among the breathless crowd, sad echoing sobs bursting forth.

Never before have I seen a crowd so forcefully gripped, so ardent and so vibrant.

What an unforgettable memory!

---

[20] Again, the majority of these names are those of real individuals; the exceptions are the members of the committee. Those who will eventually have speaking parts in the novel are the novelists Marcel Prévost and Anatole France, the popularizer of science Camille Flammarion, the Socialist journalist and feminist Séverine (Caroline Rémy de Geubhard) and André Antoine.

That enumeration of subjected miseries, before those who have suffered them, in the presence of several thousand hearts beating in unison, was a superb and grandiose spectacle.

The mothers were all there, save for one whom the Comtesse de Houdotte designated last, and for whom she found words of pity even better chosen. Madame Palavacoccini, stopped by the shame that has fallen upon her since her husband as implicated in espionage, has not dared to confront the curiosity of the crowd. She was undoubtedly wrong. No one would have dared to reproach her for a crime of which she was ignorant, and which perhaps redoubles the general compassion for her.

That introduction terminated, Marcel Lheureux takes the floor. In a few sonorous and well measured terms, he explains that the successive crimes of the child-stealers dictate a new duty to all hearts that public misfortunes do not leave indifferent.

"It is," he adds, in conclusion, "perhaps the greatest virtue of democracies that every misery immediately finds around it an active pity."

The preliminaries concluded, the Comtesse de Houdotte resumes speaking. Certainly, there are few orators who could match that noble woman for eloquence, and boast of having such a suggestive influence by means of word and gesture.

The extracts of that marvelous speech that we are publishing cannot give an idea of the impression that it made. The phrases seem to me, as I reread them, as if they are chilled. Their soul is lacking The Comtesse de Houdotte is able to communicate to words a force, an ardor, a gift of conviction and an unimaginable emotion.

AN EXTRAORDINARY IDEA
THE MOTHERS' PROCESSION

"Mesdames et Messieurs," proclaims the Comtesse, "the words that you have just heard confirm the universal sympathy that is gathered around us like a fortifying atmosphere of spring. But it is not with cordial wishes and sincere prayers that the world can be moved, and the brigands arrested. It is absolutely necessary to take action. What can that action be?

"We have no desire to involve ourselves with the investigations of politics and the law. The Committee of Investigation organized by the greatest scientists in France, which is represented here today by its president, Professor Flax, will fill that need better than we can. Let us allow it to do so. To us, women, another role is destined: that of exerting all our ardor, all our fervor, upon the public powers.

"We are told that they are doing their duty. According to the formula of our poster, one can do more than one's duty. That is what we want to obtain. We want to ensure that the affair of the child-stealers is now the principal preoccupation of the government and that all others vanish before it. We want the government to organize around the abductors such a formidable network of forces that they will no longer be able to escape, that Paris will finally have peace, and that our unfortunate children will once again be able to play in the public gardens, without fear of the all-too-real bogeyman that is abroad in the city.

It is therefore important today to give our emotion a form that will oblige all the newspapers to multiply tenfold, a hundredfold, the enormous propaganda that they have already spread. It is necessary that there should not be any prefect sure of his future, any député sure of his reelection, any minor functionary who feels safe from the sack, if they do not all collaborate, to the fullest extent possible, in the work of discovering the abductors. It is necessary, in an affair of this sort, that everyone connected with the administration feels himself to be a policeman at heart, asking questions in all directions, trying to discover new information, etc.

"To that end, it is necessary for us to put pressure on the entire country, to maintain emotion in a considerable and constant fashion. In consequence, this is what I propose:

"In a Republic, great ideas are manifest in the streets. The long processions in which thousands of people, advancing at a steady pace, affirm a collective opinion, are necessary to the life of a free people. What a marvelous force animates them, the motionless crowd of the dormant, the hesitant and the indifferent says to itself, since they are marching with no other discipline than a beautiful common thought.

"Thus, on two occasions, triumphal processions have been organized, one of which ended in a banquet with thirty thousand place-settings, the other in a feast with fifty thousand guests. *Le Matin*, which does not haggle over giving its gigantic publicity to the affair of the child-stealers, thus gives impetus to a superb principle of mutuality. The obscure abstraction that the principle of mutuality was for the immense majority of citizens, became concrete for everyone during these miraculous deployments of energy. The dormant finally awoke with a new idea, a beautiful idea, in mind; the hesitant made up their minds, the indifferent were shaken up.

"In the same way, let us demonstrate in the streets; let us wake up the dormant, make the hesitant ashamed, jostle the elbows of the indifferent. Let us organize for the day after tomorrow, through Paris, an immense cortege, *the procession of mothers*, which, marching from one boulevard to the next, will end up at the Élysée and Parliament, bringing the supplications of all the women of Paris. At our head will march all the victims that you see here behind me. We shall be a hundred thousand, two hundred thousand strong, and it will be very improbable if, out of all that generated movement, some small decisive clue does not emerge that will put an end to the public calamity."

The Comtesse de Houdotte's proposal was acclaimed, voted with a noisy and resolute unanimity. The enthusiasm for action, as the eloquent woman counseled, terminated in a kind of frenzied delirium when, at the end, our friend Bernard brought a piece of paper to the Comtesse de Houdotte. She read it rapidly, and then, pale and trembling with emotion, she read it out.

A further abduction had occurred at one o'clock in the afternoon, that of little Aristide Peinassols, kidnapped outside the Gare Saint-Lazare. His garments were found behind the Madeleine, at the same place where Germaine Plaizance's had been discovered.

Thus, the day after tomorrow, Paris will see the unique spectacle of a hundred thousand women marching through the city, a supplicant procession, an imposing cortege, whose slow march will be a kind of protest against destiny and a hope for the future.

Clovis Binard

Paris, 17 July

TOMORROW'S GREAT DEMONSTRATION

I have witnessed the final meeting of the ladies who took the initiative of organizing the public meeting at the Trocadéro. They have spent the day preparing for tomorrow's great procession, which will traverse the city along the line of the great boulevards.

This is the text of the new poster that Parisians will read on the walls this afternoon:

To the Women of Paris,
According to the information received at the headquarters of the committee, the demonstration by the women of Paris, decided in consequence of the meeting at the Trocadéro, will form a monstrous procession.

The organizing committee asks all women who would like to take part in the demonstration to wear mourning dress or black clothing, or, at least, to attach black armbands to their sleeves.

The cortege will set off from the Place de la République, and head via the great boulevards toward the Opéra, where the Municipal Council of Paris will be waiting for it. It will continue its route via the Madeleine, the Rue Royale and the Faubourg-Saint-Honoré, in order to pass in front of the Élysée. The President of the Republic has promised to receive a delegation.

The demonstration will resume its route along the Avenue Marigny and the Champs-Élysées, to disperse in the Place de la Concorde, after which a delegation will also be greeted on the steps of the Palais Bourbon by the President of the Chambre, who will be joined by the President of the Senate.

The cortege will depart from the Place de la République at nine o'clock in the morning. The demonstrators will gather in the adjacent streets from eight o'clock onwards. All the necessary directions can be read on placards.

The route along the great boulevards will be cleared from seven o'clock onwards and the circulation of vehicles stopped, by order of the Prefecture of Police.

The Organizing Committee
Accurate reproduction by Alain Bernard

THE COMTESSE DE HOUDOTTE
AN INTERESTING INDIVIDUAL

The Comtesse de Houdotte, who revealed herself yesterday to be an orator of genius, the woman whom thousands of voices acclaimed at the public meeting at the Trocadéro, is one of the most curious personalities of Parisian high society.

It is worth writing a complete portrait of the socialite in question, who has no fear of becoming involved with the passions of the crowd.

Before yesterday, the name of the Comtesse de Houdotte was not completely unknown to the wider public. It has cropped up on numerous occasions, in connection with charity fêtes, artistic and sporting events, and family dramas. The Comtesse de Houdotte's talent as a singer is much appreciated in the world of music. Not until today, however, has the woman who roused an unprecedented enthusiasm yesterday ever stepped so forcefully into the limelight.

Scarcely thirty years old, the Comtesse de Houdotte has already been married three times and is presently a widow.

Her first husband whom she married when she was only sixteen, Captain MacLerton of the Colonial infantry, died at Saint-Louis in Senegal shortly after his return from a long exploration in the hinterland of Sierra Leone. At the time, his death caused a good deal of ink to flow, especially in the medical journals; the officer had, in fact, contracted during his expedition the terrible disease of sleeping sickness, which was then thought to be unique to negroes. His death, proving that whites were susceptible to perish under the influence of the disquieting trypanosome that is the microbe of sleeping sickness, was the cause of a great deal of discussion and dread.

The Comtesse de Houdotte's second husband was the young Japanese Prince Kamayatsu, who astonished the scientific world by his scientific abilities, so universal that they recalled the legendary glory of Pico della Mirandola. The patents for which he applied during the three years in which he was attached to the Japanese legation in Paris embraced all the branches of human knowledge. His death, which was also one of the most dramatic, is still remembered. He perished after breaking his back in a session of jiu-jitsu with his teacher.

The lady's third husband, the Comte de Houdotte, a charming old man whose witty remarks ran the length of the boulevards, died in the church of a ruptured aneurism on the day of the marriage. That tragic ceremony, which took place six years ago, was the object of a great deal of commentary in the press at the time.

Afflicted by all these tragedies, the Comtesse de Houdotte went into seclusion in Switzerland for a year, in a large villa that she bought in Lungern, on the Brunig. When she returned to Paris, she reopened her salon, today one of the most interesting in the capital. Its renown is considerable, although the bizarre recruitment of its guests has caused more than a little astonishment. One encounters there, in an eccentric frame an even more eccentric society.

One detail to set the scene: in the exact center of the room—a large octagonal room constructed at the extremity of one of those rounded houses that architects built at the curtailed corners of streets—one perceives, fixed in the floor, a simple stake.

It is a historic instrument.

An ancient Laotian prince, having previously displeased his subjects, was condemned by them to be impaled in great ceremony. As the great lord had particularly discontented his people by his virtues, a grateful contingent, against al the odds, obtained an attenuation of the punishment. It was decided that the stake, instead of being made of vulgar wood hardened by fire, good enough for a commoner, would be made of gold.

With a little imagination, the Comtesse's guests, while sipping fine wines, or tickling their taste-buds with the voluptuous aroma of a unique tea, can imagine the spectacle: the twitching prince threaded on that sparkling pike, while the crowd dances around him, madly amused.

The Comtesse de Houdotte receives every day, except Sunday, and the fashion in which she selects her guests is not at all banal.

On Monday evening, she invites them at random, unselectively, in accordance with their requests to be introduced. She calls them the "sampled." The majority of them do not receive an invitation to return, only entering the famous salon once.

Others, more fortunate, are admitted for a period of varying length, at the end of which they might be admitted to the ranks of the Tuesday evening guests. If not, they become the object of so much sarcasm and mordant mockery on the part of the Comtesse that they prefer never to reappear in the presence of a hostess so wittily malicious.

The Tuesday evening guests, the "decanted," are, therefore, the results of the filtration of the Monday guests.

After having been studied by Madame de Houdotte, if they are judged worthy, they pass into the class of the "proven," who are received on Wednesday evenings.

Those of Thursday evening, the "potent," are veterans of Wednesdays who have become even more intimate.

The "illuminates," admitted to present their tributes on Friday evening, are Thursday friends who have been promoted yet again.

To be received on Saturday, among the "profound" is the supreme recompense of the friends of the Comtesse de Houdotte. Let us add that, according to renown, the profound form a unique collection of beautiful characters of great intelligence.

These Saturday guests, about thirty in number, are all men of genius, and of the most varied genius. Our great scientist Berthelot; Anatole France, the pianist Mroczkowski; Tristan Bernard; the painters Henri Martin, Dagnan-Bouveret, Monet, the marine engineer Laubat; our ambassador to London, Monsieur Cambon; the engineer de Bousquet of the Compagnie du Nord, the inventor of the most marvelous locomotives ever designed; François de Curel, Antoine of the Odéon, the mathematician Poincaré, etc., etc., rub shoulders there with Barnum, Jacquelin, the racing cyclist, the jockey Stern, etc. etc.[21]

All these men, truly superior in all the branches of human activity, have been given the entrée to the Comtesse de Houdotte's Saturdays.

That organization of her salon makes no small contribution to the reputation that the organization of the procession of mothers has acquired in Paris. Tomorrow's extraordinary demonstration, which will turn the entire existence of the capital upside-down for a day, will increase and popularize the strange renown of the Comtesse de Houdotte.

C. Binard

THE WORK OF THE COMMITTEE
OF SCIENTIFIC INVESTIGATION
A STORMY SESSION

The scientific committee of investigation went to the Garde des Sceaux yesterday morning to ask him to authorize the examining magistrate and the police to communicate the physical evidence and documents of their enquiries.

The minister made the remark that a communication of that sort was abnormal, but, the circumstances being equally abnormal, he agreed. The delegation of scientists then went to the Palais de Justice to meet with Messieurs Hamard and Laudet. In order not to oblige anyone to futile transportation, the Republic's prosecutor had an office installed in the Palais itself that the scientific committee can use for its research. Only the larger general sessions will be held at the École des Sciences Politiques.

We know that the first working meeting took place his morning.

The scientists examined all the children's clothes at length.

It appears that a very important observation has been made. I do not know its precise nature. Monsieur d'Angliney, whom I met in a corridor, simply told me: "We've already found one detail that escaped the examining magistrate. It's of great interest."

According to other indiscretions, the meeting of scientists was very stormy. Dr. Flax tried to steer the investigation in a direction that, it is said, the majority of the committee deplored.

Bitter words have been exchanged.

The celebrated surgeon threatened to resign.

One of the opponents, whose name I have promised not to reveal, told me that Dr. Flax wanted to impose a method that was too slow. In his view, each participant ought to record his impressions of the investigation in writing. These

---

[21] The individuals cited were all real. "Mroczkowski" subsequently dropped his surname and became better known as Felix Ostroga. The diplomat Jules Cambon was actually the French ambassador in Madrid in 1906.

impressions were to have been discussed at the following meeting, and there would only have been two meetings a week.

"With that system," my interlocutors claimed, "the investigation might last ten years. We're more impatient than that. By a majority, we've decided to meet every day and discuss every day. Dr. Flax observed that vote with a certain ill grace, but he had to submit to it or resign. The resolution of the scientific committee is a god one; we want to discover the thief by the most rapid means, and we shall."

Barbarus

Paris, 18 July

THE PROCESSION OF MOTHERS
A MONSTROUS DEMONSTRATION

Thanks to the prodigious activity of the Comtesse de Houdotte, the immense procession that Paris has witnessed today was organized within thirty-six hours.

No disorder!

Not a single hitch!

All precautions had been well taken.

Monsieur Lépine, who had met with the organizing committee, drew up the timetable personally, and, as usual on such occasions, the Prefect of Police was seen everywhere at once, multiplying his instructions, rapidly and clearly, remarkably calm, intelligent and decisive.

How many demonstrators were there? It is difficult to give an exact figure. 250,000 is certainly not far from the truth.

Almost all the women obeyed the instructions of the committee. Nine-tenths of those who went to the Place de la République for the procession were wearing mourning dress. Many had even put on hats with crepe veils.

At nine o'clock in the morning, the Place de la République, which had been cleared in advance by the Gardes de Paris, offered an unforgettable scene.

From all the neighboring streets and all the boulevards, converging toward the statue as if toward a beacon, the demonstrators were arriving in long somber files. The bands, whose benevolent participation has been so prompt, met at eight o'clock at the foot of the monument.

At the appointed hour, the procession sets off, heading toward the Opéra along the great boulevards.

At the head, preceding a band that was playing slow marches, are two rows of mounted guards; then come a small group that attracts all eyes: the mothers of the children abducted by the kidnappers.

They advance slowly, preceded by a cordon of agents directed by three peace officers.

The sidewalks are black with crowds.

At every window, spectators are huddled.

Everywhere, there is a kind of atmosphere of sadness and compassion. No cries, but a mute, magnificent homage is imposed, as the mothers pass by, on all the men who are contemplating them.

As the procession advances, all heads are bared in a great salute of condolence and fraternity.

Behind the band that separates the demonstrators from the mothers of the children march the Comtesse de Houdotte and the other organizers of the demonstration of the mothers of Paris.

As the woman to whom that monstrous parade is owed passes by, discreet applause rings out.

With one of those curt gestures that dominate crowds—no one knows why—scarcely raising her hand, the Comtesse de Houdotte stops that nascent applause dead.

The women participating in the cortege patiently wait their turn in the streets adjacent to the Place de la République. Everything is accomplished in accordance with the plan that the organizers had prepared.

As they pass *Le Matin*'s offices on the Boulevard Poissonnière, the mothers are saluted by our editor-in-chief.

Madame de Houdotte speaks then, and in a few words, warmly approved by the mothers surrounding her, she thanks the newspaper that was the first to reveal the affair of the child-stealers, the first to denounce that public misfortune, and which, finally—as usual—has maintained an ardent campaign for the public good during the affair.

After that short pause, the cortege resumes its course, now without interruption, as far as the Place de l'Opéra. There it makes a deviation around the macadam square containing the entrance to the Metro station. The Municipal Council has assembled on the steps of the Opéra. Monsieur Chautard[22] comes down and, going toward the group of mothers, assures them of all the good wishes of the council. He declares that he approves with all his fervor of the procession, which will, by its resonance, certainly lead to the best results.

Having spoken thus, Monsieur Chautard places himself, with the Municipal Council, as anticipated, at the head of the cortege, which pursues its slow and impressive march. It proceeds in that fashion via the Madeleine, the Rue Royale and the Faubourg Saint-Honoré to the Élysée.

The Municipal Council, followed by the group of mothers and organizers, then goes into the courtyard of the palace, and two minutes later, they are received by Monsieur Fallières.[23]

M. FALLIÈRES' SPEECH

The President of the Republic pronounces the following words:

"Mesdames, like the entire world, I have borne my share of your griefs and your dolors. I have, in the course of many sleepless nights, evoked your pain and sought means of remedying it. I have summoned to my presence the principal individuals on whom the task of riding Paris of the child-stealers is incumbent. I

[22] Paul Chautard became president of the Municipal Council of Paris in 1906 before being elected to parliament as a radical socialist député in 1907.

[23] Armand Fallières became President of the Republic in January 1906.

have exhorted them personally as best I can, in order to augment their zeal. I then took account of the fact that they have done everything that it was humanly possible for them to do. Their efforts have run into a kind of implacable fatality, but it is the property of strong souls not to be discouraged by failure, and to become more valiant as obstacles emerge. So be assured that that all those who are charged with discovering the guilty parties and recovering your children will not weary, and will only relax momentarily in order to refresh themselves and steel themselves again. I think, Mesdames, that your children will be returned to you one day. Until conclusive proof is brought to me that misfortune has befallen them, I shall persist in the belief that they are alive and that they will come back to you. You will then find them scarcely changed, as if they were simply returning from a long journey."

On behalf of all the women, the Comtesse de Houdotte thanks the President of the Republic for his speech, which the tone of his voice rendered so pathetic.

That visit concluded, the mothers emerge from the Palais de l'Élysée to resume their route.

However, exhausted by emotion, Madame Pompagne, who fainted during the President's speech, was retained at the Élysée for several hours. Madame Fallières, who lavished a thousand cares upon her, took her home personally, by carriage.

BEFORE THE CHAMBRE
THREE FURTHER CRIMES
THE DISAPPEARANCE OF SOEUR THÉRÈSE

After having passed along the Avenue Marigny, the cortege turns left, along the Champs-Élysées, and heads for the Chambre des Députés, on the threshold of which it is welcomed by Monsieur Brisson,[24] beside whom is Antonin Dubost, the President of the Senate. After a further round of speeches, the procession returns to the Place de la Concorde, where the dispersal of the immense crowd of women in mourning begins.

The procession of mothers will remain in the memory of Parisians for a long time, as one of the most moving demonstrations that has ever moved the heart of the capital.

As if they have sought to exasperate the population, however, as if they want to sneer at all efforts and thrown down a challenge to the nation, the child-stealers have signaled their again existence today by sinister exploits.

They have exercised their frightful industry during the procession.

Three little girls have disappeared. Alice Change, Fernande Bonnéglise and Louise Accesson have been abducted during the demonstration. All three of

---

[24] Henri Brisson, elected President of the Chambre des Députés in May 1906.

them were with their parents among the spectators. At the moment of their abduction the first was at the crossroads of the Boulevard de Sébastopol and the Boulevard Saint-Denis, the second at the corner of the Rue Poissonnière and the Boulevard Bonne-Nouvelle, and the third at the corner of the Boulevard Montmartre and the Rue Montmartre. As usual, the garments were found, with locks of hair.

One truly dare not, in confrontation with all these crimes, calculate the number of children abducted in the last month. These kidnappings, carried out on the very day when the entire city was protesting by means of a cortege against the crimes of the child-stealers, will have an echo more lugubrious than the others.

We have also been apprised of another disappearance, which has no obvious relationship with that of the children, but is nevertheless particularly curious. It has, in fact, been revealed by one of the principal persons engaged in the search for the child-stealers. Dr. Flax has just informed the police that Soeur Thérèse, who was in charge of the infirmary at his children's hospital at Montretout, has given no sign of life for three days. She was seen leaving the hospital on Tuesday, at eleven o'clock in the morning, and has not returned since. In spite of all the steps that have been taken and enquiries made, no trace of her has been found.

Clovis Binard

The abundance of material obliges me to put off until tomorrow the publication of a long study that I have just completed.

I have undertaken, with regard to the child-stealers, a patient enquiry that has led me to an unexpected, amazing and implausible conclusion. I am frightened myself by the result that I have obtained.

May I be permitted not to say any more until tomorrow.

C.B.

THE ASTONISHING WORK OF CLOVIS BINARD
WITH THE MAP OF PARIS

I announced yesterday a curious endeavor with an amazing conclusion. It is, unfortunately, merely curious. It is, unfortunately, only amazing. The whole thing might prove that, when one seeks to make an investigation with an accumulation of petty proofs, one sometimes ends up deceiving oneself, with the best will in the world; and that a sheaf of petty proofs is not proof, and that it is necessary to be very prudent when one accuses people and affirms categorically, citing the name, that someone is guilty.

Since the beginning of the affair of the child-stealers, I have adopted the habit of marking on a map of Paris, day by day, with a little cross, all the places where, according to the parents, the children were abducted.

Why did I devote myself to that petty task?

I don't know.

I did not suspect that I would arrive by that means at some very interesting observations.

My father was a maniac who left me many of his habits by way of an inheritance. He even left me that one. He was one of those people who follow wars by planting little flags on geographical maps. Like him, I take pleasure in those innocent little diversions.

That was why I sowed my map of Paris with little crosses. To begin with, my little crosses led me to a new observation.

Almost all the children were stolen at street corners. That detail had not yet been noticed. In itself, it is of no importance. It is merely a previously unnoted datum. The child-stealers have calculated that it was most convenient for them to kidnap the children at a crossroads than in the middle of a street. It would have been astonishing if it were otherwise.

A much more important observation: the children have only been abducted in certain quarters, and these quarters are not distributed, on the map of Paris, in a fashion irrelevant to the investigation.

To render my pseudo-demonstration clearer, it is necessary for me to offer here a few considerations regarding the topography of Paris.

EGG, BALLOON, SOLE OR TADPOLE?

Paris has the form of an egg, the larger end of which, considerably flattened, is to the east, and the smaller end, slightly deformed, to the south-west, with a sort of cap formed by the Bois de Boulogne.

The maps sold commercially all include certain parts of the surrounding communes, in such a fashion as to enclose the central egg in a rectangle.

The northern extreme and the southern extreme of the ovoid almost touch the two bases of that geometrical figure at the Porte de Gentilly, the Porte d'Italie, the Porte Pouchet and the Porte de la Villette.

To the west, the frontier is marked, as we have said, by the line that is formed by the Bois de Boulogne; to the east the Porte de Vincennes would mark the extreme frontier, if the Bois de Vincennes did not form a very emphatic projection.

That appendage of verdure obliges editors to publish, in the margin of the map of Paris, part of the maps of Saint-Mandé, Bagnolet, Lilas, Pré-Saint-Gervais and Pantin, with which they could dispense but for that excrescence. I have noticed, however, that a few printers, to the unintelligence and economy of whom it is necessary to render homage, leave blank spaces in the location of neighboring towns. Paris thus looks like an immense dirigible balloon, of which the Bois de Vincennes is the rudder.

In a few lines, I have already compared Paris to an egg and a dirigible balloon, and I perceive that one could also compare it to a tadpole or a sole. The Bois de Vincennes would constitute the tail. But I shall stop there, for fear of leaving, in the minds of my readers, some doubts about the precision of geographical comparisons.

Egg, balloon, sole or tadpole, Paris can be divided into four approximately equal zones by drawing two lines that cut the middle of the four sides of the great rectangle with which the city is ordinarily surrounded at right angles.

That great rectangle is divided by this procedure into four smaller rectangles, comprising the north-west, north-east, south-west and south-east of the capital.

THE TOPOGRAPHY OF THE ABDUCTIONS

Now, while eighteen children have been abducted in the north-western rectangle, and eight in the north-eastern rectangle, only three children have been abducted in the south-eastern rectangle, and only two in the south-western.

Of the two children kidnapped in the south-western rectangle, Isidore Bimorel was taken almost on the edge of the line that divides Paris in two. One can therefore count him among the children abducted in the north-western rectangle. Similarly for Bouquet de Gobely-Franthéon. It is purely by hazard and exceptionally, his parents living in the Rue Pergolèse, that he happened to be in the vicinity of the Institut Pasteur.

In sum, no abducted child belongs to the south-western rectangle, while twenty belong to the north-western rectangle.

Let us examine the north-eastern rectangle.

The bisection of the angle of the major east-west and north-south lines that is in the middle of Paris divided this rectangle into two equal parts. Now, all the children abducted in this rectangle have been in the sector closer to the north-western rectangle, which is already the one most afflicted by the child-stealers.

Thus, Paris has been very unequally affected by the thefts.

That observation gave me a new idea—that the child stealers must live in one of the rectangles almost spared by the kidnappers. That idea was corroborated by Monsieur Laudet's enquiries into the direction taken by the coupé in which Gontran de Vautremesse was carried away after the abduction at the Nouveau-Cirque. That carriage headed for the south-eastern rectangle, where the thieves rarely operate.

BIZARRE CONVERGENCE OF CERTAIN LINES TRACED ON THE MAP OF PARIS DOCTOR FLAX'S HOUSE

Having made these observations, I drew lines on my map joining the places where the children were stolen to the places where their clothes were discovered.

It has been noticed, in fact, with regard to several of the abductions, that the garments were discovered very soon after the kidnappings—in some cases, only a few minutes after the crime.

We may assume that, once the capture has been effected, the child-stealers hasten to take their victims to their lair as rapidly as possible. Therefore, they get rid of the clothes on their way. The general direction of the habitation to which they take the victims ought, therefore, to be indicated by lines linking, I repeat, the places where the children were abducted and the places where their clothing was found.

Having connected those two points, I extrapolated the lines and observed that almost all of them converged, like the spokes of a wheel, on a single vicinity, situated slightly to the left of the Jardin du Luxembourg, close to the Rue Vaugirard, in the vicinity of the Rue d'Assas.

The majority of the lines, however, do not cross at exactly the same point. Some are a little to the left, others a little to the right. A certain number, however, intersect at a single point, and that point is none other than the one occupied by the house of Dr. Flax, the president of the Scientific Committee of Investigation.

The Bouquet de Gobely-Franthéon, Isidore Birmorel, Wenceslas Lévy, Philippe Soleillaut, Alice Poliarre, Philippe Ordin-Rosier, Pierre Candelaur, Germaine Plaizance, Fernand Pig, Frantz Vetyolle, Ange Pompaigne, Victorine Artesy and Justin Chipé lines all intersect precisely at the house of the famous surgeon.

You see!

You see how one can deceive oneself when one tries to bend dry and brutal facts to the purse reasoning of logic, to preconceived principles.

If my lines had converged on any other house than that of Dr. Flax, I would certainly have accuses the child-stealers of having made their lair in that dwelling.

I would have accused them of heading toward that habitation, following the shortest route to go from the place where the children were abducted to the place where they are hidden.

I would have accused them remorselessly and in all conscience of abandoning the garments without losing time, along the straightest route.

Fortunately, hazard, which sometimes does good things, directs those lines to the house occupied by the president of the Scientific Committee of Investigation, to the house of the man who had taken the most trouble to discover the child-stealers, the man whom the general confidence of his colleagues has charged with directing the discussions that ought to concluded with the punishment of the crimes that Paris is bewailing.

And all my beautiful calculations have dissolved.

That renders me very modest, and augments my long-held suspicion of all expert labors, of all the scrupulous research by specialists, splitters of hairs, in the name of which so many innocent people have been condemned.

Clovis Binard

The divergences of opinion between Dr. Flax and certain members of the Scientific Committee of Investigation are augmenting and becoming aggravated. It is reported that a violent argument has taken place between the president and Dr. d'Angliney, which will doubtless have serious consequences.

Our sister paper the *Rappel* even claims that one of the members has criticized the doctor in these terms:

"One could swear that, after having accepted the presidency of our assembly, charged with discovering the child-stealers scientifically, you are now trying to delay our work. This situation cannot go on. But don't worry. We will find the abductors in spite of you…and perhaps within twenty-four hours."

An enigmatic threat, giving rise to various comments, of which the public anticipates an explanation with keen impatience.

AN EXTRAORDINARY ACCUSATION

I only published my article yesterday to prove how accumulated coincidences can be deceptive.

I never had the slightest intention of accusing Dr. Flax of having abducted the children.

It was the very absurdity of that idea which drove me to show how error can sometimes be born, in good faith, in the minds of those charged with rendering justice.

But now the affair has become complicated, and I no longer know what to think.

The following document is signed by Monsieur de Vorigno, in the name of eight of the most eminent members of the Scientific Committee of Investigation. Nevertheless, we are not publishing it without a certain hesitation.

It is not possible that these scientists are right.

It would be so extraordinary!

Let us therefore transmit the text to the public without further comment:

A FORMAL ACCUSATION

To the people of France, and the magistracy,

We, the undersigned, declare that we have discovered the child-stealers, and we are exposing them to public condemnation.

We agreed to take part in the Scientific Committee of Investigation in good faith and in all sincerity.

We devoted ourselves to a rigorous enquiry with all the force of our intelligence and our patience.

It is, therefore, not lightly that we have come to accuse a man of having committed one of the most monstrous crimes of humanlty.

In spite of all the prudence we have imposed on ourselves, however, the facts that have come to our attention are sufficient to motivate immediate, energetic action.

The present denunciation will strike the entire world with astonishment and indignation.

The man that we are about to offer to general anger is perhaps the last that opinion would have imagined. He was, according to all appearances, above suspicion.

But, if the truth is implausible, it is nevertheless the truth.

Our formal, categorical accusation has been scrupulously studied. It is not the work of hatred, paradox or extravagance.

We accuse Dr. Flax, member of the Institut, Professor of Pathology at the Faculté de Médecine, commander of the Légion d'honneur, of being the author of the numerous thefts of children that have saddened Paris.

We accuse the president of the Scientific Committee of Investigation of being the criminal that the committee was mandated to discover.

We accuse, in addition, the Comtesse de Houdotte of being the accomplice of Dr. Flax, the child-stealer.

We accuse the President of the Women's Investigation Committee of being the accomplice of the criminal that committee gave itself the mission of discovering.

We also accuse the three Windernunhut brothers, in the service of Dr, Flax, of having assisted in the perpetration of the abductions.

Such is, in a few clear and curt proposals, the unexpected result of our labor.

We owe it to the truth to admit that several of our colleagues on the Scientific Committee of Investigation have refused to add their signatures to this formal accusation. They are obeying very honorable scruples, before which we bow down.

Some have been inhibited by their great admiration for the scientist that Dr. Flax is; others plead an old friendship that renders the accusation odious; yet others have abstained because their convictions are not yet sufficiently solid.

For ourselves, we consider that, no matter how indisputable the scientific genius of Dr. Flax might be, we cannot refrain from the duty we have imposed on ourselves, in the name of the public conscience.

The proofs of the complicity of Dr. Flax, the Comtesse de Houdotte and the Windernunhut brothers are numerous and concordant.

We shall indicate, in the first place, the marvelous work that Clovis Binard published yesterday. It is a masterpiece of sagacity, which has corroborated in our minds a latent suspicion that we scarcely dared communicate.

It has given sudden substance to an accusation that some of us have vaguely sketched, without daring to pronounce it categorically.

FIRST PROOFS
ONE OF THE GUILTY PARTIES MUST BE A PHYSICIAN

From the very beginning of the Scientific Committee's investigations, as soon as the legal evidence was handed over to us, some of us thought that the child-stealer must be a physician, and probably a surgeon.

Firstly, all the garments of the stolen children had a slight odor of iodoform. The children had been abducted by hands impregnated with that professional perfume, so tenacious and so penetrating.

One of the members of the Scientific Committee of Investigation is endowed with an exceptional sense of smell. We shall not designate him in any other way, because ours is a collective endeavor. Nevertheless, we ought to say that the finesse of his nose is prodigious. He belongs to that rare category of physicians who "scent death." It is sufficient for one of them to enter a room where there is a dead person to observe the decease, simply by virtue of the atmospheric odor. Furthermore, they are often capable of prognosticating imminent death. Our secretary, Monsieur de Vorigno, has published a curious paper on the very particular sense of smell.

It is thanks to the subtlety of our colleague's olfactory sense that the iodoformic exhalations were revealed to us.

Once our attention had been attracted to that odor, we were all able to observe, with varying degrees of difficulty, the reality of the circumstance.

The idea that the abductor might be a physician came into all our minds.

Secondly, in the parcel containing the clothing of little Victorine Artesy, which was found on the Quai Saint-Bernard, the debris of a medical thermometer was found. That instrument could have fallen by chance from the doctor's pocket and broken when the abductor wrapped up and sealed the parcel.

Thirdly, the examination of the pieces of paper in which the children's clothes were wrapped added further support to the idea.

At the time of the first thefts, there was long discussion in the press of the subject of the newspapers that the thief had used to wrap his parcels.

They were mostly political daily newspapers, but a copy of the *Presse Médicale* was also discovered. Since that era, the thieves have made use of several other newspapers, and a second copy of the *Presse Médicale* was found.

Now, that is the only specialist periodical that has been discovered in this way. Among the documents of the investigation, neither the *Moniteur de Métallurgie* nor the *Journal d'Épicerie* has been found, and yet, if, as was thought, the thief bought the first periodical that came to hand, it is probable that other professional gazettes would have been discovered. We are therefore led to think, by a third item of evidence, that the thief is a physician.

We know, in addition, that Dr. Flax is a great reader of newspapers, that he buys all the political papers, that he reads them in his carriage and that every morning, when he arrives at the hospital, the concierge, following orders, comes to clear the coupé and distribute the copies to the staff.

Obviously, if we only had evidence of this kind against the surgeon, we would not have dared to make our accusation. We record these details to show the path that we followed.

WITH REGARD TO THE THIEF'S FORTUNE

Faithful to our method of beginning with the strongest evidence in order to end with the most certain proofs, we recall, in the second place, that, according to the observations of the police and the magistrate, the thief must be a rich man.

Remember that he returns his victims' jewelry, and that he sent three thousand francs to little Loubé's parents.

No one is unaware that Dr. Flax has a large fortune, that his clientele is very extensive, and that he demands exorbitant fees for his consultations.

We add that the three thousand-franc bills addressed to Monsieur and Madame Loubé seem to have the characteristic odor of iodoform that we found in the parcels.

THE DISTINGUISHED MAN

We accuse Dr. Flax of being the "distinguished man" who has been mentioned several times in the depositions of the witnesses who have been heard.

It will be easy to verify this assertion by means of confrontations.

THE VEHICLES

Since the beginning of the "great affair" there has been mention of three vehicles.

Near the places where the children were stolen, there have been successive sightings of a well-kept private coupé, an automobile with a long chassis, and an automobile with a short chassis.

Dr. Flax possesses three vehicles answering these descriptions.

His coupé is an elegant vehicle, extremely well cared-for and highly polished.

The automobile with a long chassis that Dr. Flax owns is painted in two colors. Against a dark blue-green background, discreet red lines are designed, similarly reproduced, similarly reproduced around the wheel-rims and along the spokes of the wheels. The soldier who observed that automobile while it was parked in front of the Église Saint-Augustin before the theft of Émile Loubé declared that it was dark green. If he did not mention the red lines it is because they are not very apparent, and at a distance, or when traveling at speed, they would not be perceived. The young soldier can therefore be put in the presence of Dr. Flax's larger automobile in order that he might recognize it.

The third, smaller automobile that was seen on the Pont de l'Europe during the abduction of Germaine Plaizance is doubtless the third vehicle of which Dr. Flax makes use from time to time.

This, our accusations are becoming specific, and we emerge from the domain of deductions to enter the realm of precise facts.

THE TIMING OF THE THEFTS
TELLING COINCIDENCE

Little attention has been called to the fact that the abductions all took place in the afternoon, with the exception of those that took place during the procession of mothers.

Now, according to our suspicions, we believe that Dr. Flax carried out all the abductions personally.

Is it not curious, given that, that none of the thirty-one thefts was committed at a time when the surgeon was, as is well known, occupied with other tasks?

Every morning, the professor goes to the hospital he has founded at Montretout, and does not come back until midday. The concierge of that establishment keeps a record of all those who go in and all those who come out. The presence of Dr. Flax is noted every day, with the exception of the day of the mothers' procession. By a striking coincidence, three children were, exceptionally, abducted that morning.

We have further proofs at our disposal but, judging that, in such grave circumstances, we shall have to combat all sorts of polemics, we do not want to exhaust all our munitions in one blast, and we shall await the enemy with a firm foothold.

In our opinion, the arrest of Dr. Flax, the Comtesse de Houdotte and the Windernunhut brothers is imperative, and this very day.

H. de Vorigno
On behalf of eight members
of the Scientific Committee of Investigation

EMOTION IN PARIS
FLAXISTS AND ANTI-FLAXISTS
THE OPINION OF THE NEWSPAPERS

The document published by the dissidents of the Scientific Committee of Investigation has provoked intense emotion throughout Paris.

This morning the capital has woken up divided into two equal camps, the Flaxists and the anti-Flaxists.

The Flaxists consider that the accusations leveled against the celebrated surgeon do not stand up.

The anti-Flaxists are of a diametrically opposed opinion, and support the accusers with an infectious ardor.

The *Lanterne* demands the immediate arrest of the persons designated in the scientists' formal accusation. Many accused individuals, it says, have been arrested on the basis of weaker evidence.

The *Humanité* observes that it is necessary to be very prudent. There is a risk, Monsieur Jaurès' paper says, of giving birth to a kind of medical Dreyfus Affair.[25]

The *Echo de Paris* is straightforwardly Flaxist. "We cannot believe," one reads in that paper, "that the accusations brought against the most celebrated surgeon in the world are true. In sum, no decisive proof has been presented to us. There are suggestions, and some of those are not even serious."

The *Figaro* is of the same opinion, and takes a position in favor of Dr. Flax, while the *Gaulois*, on the contrary is opposed to the professor.

The *Temps* reserves its judgment. "One cannot yet form a precise idea of the facts," it says. "The question is far too serious for it to be permissible to obey the suggestions of Dr, Flax's accusers, or to follow his defenders without reflection. We await the further evidence that we have been promised.

"We shall merely observe that, to date, no one has mentioned a motive. If the surgeon has kidnapped children, if his accomplices have assisted him in his abductions, it is doubtless with some objective. We confess that we cannot perceive any. We would be very glad if someone would explain that to us."

We shall observe the sage attitude of our sister paper and content ourselves with exposing opinions for and against, leaving our readers, until further notice, to draw their own conclusions.

Barbarus

---

[25] The leader of the French Socialist Party, Jean Jaurès, became one of the staunchest Dreyfusards once he was convinced of the lieutenant's innocence. He contrived to unite all the disparate French Socialist movements briefly, early in 1906, in order to make a bid for political control of the Chambre, but was outflanked by Clemenceau, who put together a radical program that excluded any specifically socialist goals.

AT DR. FLAX'S HOME
AN ENERGETIC DEFENSE

I have tried to obtain an interview with the Comtesse de Houdotte, but in vain. An implacable order has locked her door.

I have been more fortunate at Dr. Flax's home.

His enormous porter—one of the Windernunhut brothers that the dissident scientists accuse of complicity—welcomes me with his most generous smile and immediately takes me to his master.

I cannot help recalling, in passing, that there has been mention of giants in this affair, and that, as giants go, Dr. Flax's introducer is, in truth, a giant.

Still troubled by this remark, I am introduced into the doctor's study; he receives me with the utmost calm.

"Without being a sorcerer," he says, "I can divine what brings you here. It's the ludicrous accusation of which I am the object, along with other persons. Oh, Monsieur, it would be laughable, if it were not so sad to see veritable scientists, minds that one might have thought serious and reflective, launching themselves recklessly into an accusation of this sort. That is the sort of thing that ought to make us timid when we talk about the progress of the human brain. Look, I shall help you put your finger on the incoherence of the reproach made against me. Can you tell me why the Comtesse de Houdotte has been introduced into the matter?"

"Do you know the lady?"

"Yes. I'm one of the guests that she is kind enough to receive on Saturday evenings—one of those known as "the profound." But from there to obtaining from a woman of the world the strange complicity of which she has just been accused is a big step to take! Our intimate friends, who know what our relationship is, must have laughed out loud on reading such heresies. As *Le Temps* has wisely remarked, the scientists who have put forward these ridiculous charges have refrained from saying what reason I might have had for abducting children..."

"Indeed."

"Abducting children! But I repeat, why? Why? At Montretout I've founded a children's hospital. There are three or four hundred out there, for whom I care as best I can, and—I can declare this publicly today, since I'm obliged to do so—at my own expense. So what? All these accusations, you see, are born of the jealousy of a few colleagues. Not all the signatories of the accusation are hypocrites. There are at least two among them who have allowed themselves to be carried away. But the rest! They simply resent me for having had more success than them, and are seeking to bring me down by this futile and grotesque means.

"Have you noticed one remark? I am reproached for my extensive clientele and the supposedly exorbitant process that at charge for my treatments. Extravagant prices? Is it an extravagant price, then, when one cares for hundreds of children gratuitously, paying all the expenses—which are considerable—from my own funds? Certainly, I have made a few rich men pay dearly, but that money has allowed me to do good to others. For myself, I have few needs. I live in this old, worm-eaten and tranquil house, whose rent is not extortionate. I sleep in an iron-framed bed. I live on cutlets and boiled eggs. It isn't, therefore to satisfy appetites for luxury that I exploit my rich clients. It's uniquely to subsidize the expenses of my hospital, and those of my scientific research..."

"Master, some of the evidence advanced against you has a certain appearance of verity."

"I do indeed own three vehicles: a coupé, an automobile with a short chassis and another with a long chassis. What does that demonstrate? It proves nothing, any more than the amusing work that you've carried out with the map of Paris. You've been more prudent, yourself. You haven't concluded, from the fact that all the lines you've traced converge on the Rue Cassette, that I must be the kidnapper. Fundamentally, what is happening in my regard at this moment is what generally happens in cases of judicial error. One imagines that fifteen coincidences are worth as much as a fact. Now, that isn't so. Voltaire said, with regard to Calas, that a hundred shreds of evidence don't add up to a proof, and that truth is an eternal verity that ought to be inscribed on the frontons of all Palais de Justice."[26]

"What to do intend to do to counter your accusers?"

"Nothing. I shall await events. I shall place myself at the disposal of the magistrates. This matter has been exposed too publicly for the court to treat it with indifference. I'm ready to furnish explanations when they're demanded of me. It will all end with the confusion of my detractors.

"Understand that if I were guilty of anything whatsoever, I would have packed my bags immediately after your article regarding the map of Paris. I would have put a long distance between myself and the law. Note, also, how implausible it is that the two people who are at the head of the movement intended to maintain public agitation to obtain the discovery of the child-stealers are precisely those who are accused today.

"You can well imagine that the Comtesse de Houdotte, if she had participated in any way in all these abductions, would not have drawn attention to herself, would not have organized the meeting at the Trocadéro and the procession of mothers, and mobilized with so much courageous energy a movement of opinion that has no other objective but to stimulate the investigations of the law.

---

[26] Jean Calas (1698-1762) was a Protestant sentence to be broken on the wheel for having murdered his son Marc-Antoine because he feared that he might follow his brother's example and convert to Catholicism. Voltaire became interested in the case, and mounted a scathing attack on the circumstantial evidence on which the conviction had been based, initiating an important debate about the value of various kinds of evidence. He succeeded in exonerating Calas—posthumously, alas.

As for myself, I was one of the first to step forward when it was proposed to create a Scientific Committee of Investigation. I thought that my duty obliged me to take part. I did not hesitate. Is that the attitude of a child-stealer?

"In brief, Monsieur, we are floundering in incoherence, drowning in illogicality and absurdity. It seems to me that it is a joke to have to defend myself against such accusers, who seem to have made a pledge to accumulate all the contradictions of human reason against their thesis."

After these words, pronounced with a sort of snigger equivalent to a smile, I take my leave of the man whom this business seems to have moved to amusement—to the extent that such a man is capable of showing signs of hilarity.

The readers of this newspaper are generally very demanding. They will not admit that a reporter does not have an opinion on a problem that he has studied.

As I write, I am thinking that tomorrow, hundreds of thousands of Frenchmen will be wondering whether I believe in the surgeon's culpability, or whether I do not.

I am tempted to respond that I belief in the guilt or innocence of the doctor in accordance with the last person to speak. When I examine the arguments of the Scientific Committee of Investigation, they seem convincing. When I meditate on the reasoning that Dr. Flax has given me, I immediately think that it is excellent. In those conditions, how can one decide?

Nevertheless, as the equilibrium of a balance is never perfect, and one of the pans always tilts, even by a hundred millionth of a millimeter, I have a certain tendency to believe in the innocence of Dr. Flax. His final argument appears to me to be striking.

The Comtesse de Houdotte would not have risked unleashing public opinion against the child-stealers if she had been part of that sinister gang herself. The same applies to Dr. Flax. Perhaps one might object that in acting thus, the accomplices wanted to deflect suspicion by means of a masterstroke, but that thesis hardly seems plausible.

Clovis Binard

DISINTEGRATION OF THE SCIENTIFIC COMMITTEE

The formal accusation against Dr. Flax, the Comtesse and the surgeon's domestics which appeared in our columns yesterday, has put an end to the existence of the Scientific Committee of Investigation.

It was Dr. Flax himself who presided over its final session, which took place yesterday evening, at the École des Sciences Politiques.

The scientists who had separated themselves from the principal group to sign the evidence they believed they had discovered against the great surgeon were naturally absent. All the others were present. They were curious to know whether Flax would arrive to take the chair. A letter of apology was generally expected. His entrance therefore caused a sensation.

He immediately took the floor, very calm and composed.

"Messieurs." he said. "In the present circumstances, I can only hand in my resignation as president of the Scientific Committee of Investigation. I did not seek that honor. I even considered it as a burden. I accepted it because it was not possible to retreat before the unanimity of your marks of confidence. In a matter of hours, everything has changed. I am now the object of the hatred of the very people who voted for me. I am, therefore, withdrawing, not only from the presidential chair, but from the committee. It will not be possible to accuse me of preventing, by my presence, light being case on this affair. My attitude is natural. I think that you will all approve of it."

Applause burst forth, but it was much less energetic than might have been expected. A certain chill was visibly affecting the meeting. Dr. Malouino got up, and replied to Dr. Flax from his place.

"I am speaking on behalf of my colleagues who were unable to follow those of our friends who are being described by the press as 'dissident scientists.' I deem that it is incumbent on all of us to measure our words carefully today. It will suffice for me to describe as...regrettable, the step taken by our colleagues, who so abruptly separated themselves from us when we did not want to accompany them on to the reefs of hazardous deduction.

"We understand perfectly that our president, in the presence of the situation in which he has been placed, is resigning, and renouncing the work that he had begun. But we all owe him a mark of solidarity, in order that there should be no doubt about our sentiments. I therefore propose, Messieurs, that we disband, and no longer sit, since Dr. Flax can no longer preside. We shall leave all responsibility to the small group of dissident scientists—both the responsibility for their accusations, and the responsibility for the disintegration of an assembly whose efforts might have been very useful in the affair of the child-stealers."

Dr. Malouino's proposal was accepted with alacrity. The scientists, it seemed, were in a hurry to rid themselves of the annoyance of having to take a position in the midst of all the disputes that have arisen and will arise. They are, for the most part, as closely linked to Dr. Flax as to his adversaries. The majority is certainly and very visibly in favor of the surgeon, but that sympathy is not manifest loudly and in an expansive fashion. It is, if you wish, a cool sympathy.

To be fair, it is necessary to add that, even in the meeting, some scientists considered that it was necessary to await further events before coming to a decision, and that, however absurd the accusation might seem, it was similarly absurd to think that the notable individuals who drafted it had thrown themselves into the affair recklessly and without reflection.

It is evident to all those who witnessed that last meeting of the Scientific Committee of Investigation that, although Dr. Flax has admirers, he has no friends.

Clovis Binard

NEW INTERVENTION OF THE DISSIDENT SCIENTISTS

The dissident scientists have communicated the following notes to the press:

We promised not to limit ourselves to the evidence spelled out in the document published the day before yesterday.

In addition to the necessity of not blunting our weapons in the first skirmish, we have also been obliged to conduct delicate enquiries in order to corroborate some of our suspicions.

We are presenting the public today with a new batch of proofs.

THE ATTITUDE OF DR. FLAX
A RUSE
WHO LAUNCHED THE IDEA OF
THE SCIENTIFIC COMMITTEE OF INVESTIGATION?

Before anything else, we want to invalidate and argument of which the Flaxists have made abundant use. The objection has been raised that Dr. Flax would not have had himself named president of the Scientific Committee of Investigation if he had been the guilty party.

Our response is simple.

We are convinced that Dr. Flax wanted to deflect suspicion by this maneuver, and that the Comtesse de Houdotte founded the Ladies' Committee with an analogous aim.

Their calculation was accurate. The ruse has worked marvelously. The facts demonstrate that.

We would not be struggling today against a majority of Flaxists, opposing a powerful current, if the surgeon and his accomplice had not taken the precaution of flattering public opinion. Our accusation seemed pure folly to all our fellow citizens who, for several days, had been accustomed to considering Dr. Flax and the Comtesse as the most determined enemies of the child-stealers.

Critical intelligence is a quality with which the French are incredible well-endowed. The art of discerning the true from the false by the study of documents and the sifting of probabilities and improbabilities is rarer among us.

We have seen very clearly that our imputations have lost all their force in consequence of the deception thus foisted on the public.

In our view, we repeat, Dr. Flax had himself appointed as president of the Scientific Committee of Investigation with the sole objective of leading opinion astray.

It is certainly true that the surgeon protested when we nominated him as president of the assembly, and allowed himself to be begged, but his protest did not go so far as renunciation. He allowed himself be persuaded.

We are certain that in the depths of his heart, in spite of his appearance of annoyance and his irritated language, he was delighted with a vote against which he protested only in playing to the gallery. The honor we did him realized his dearest wish, the secret project that would prevent the truth from ever coming to light.

Another aspect of the same question: the rumor has run around in the press that the Scientific Committee of Investigation was born by a kind of spontaneous generation. During the recent conference on surgery, a few scientists, whose names remain unknown, had proposed the meeting of that committee, and the idea had taken its course without anyone knowing its author. In fact, that author was Dr. Flax. He was the first to talk about the application of the scientific method to police investigations. He was the one who voiced the opinion that a syndicate of scientists might arrive at a result where the police and the magistracy had so far failed. He was the one who launched the project, negligently, as if he did not attach any importance to it, but with great subsequent intelligence and dissimulated persistence.

We have witnesses.

Dr. Netter remembers very clearly that it was the surgeon, today in the dock, who was the first to mention the Scientific Committee of Investigation to him. The eminent scientist would not deny it, in spite of his amity for his colleague.

Such a prodigious trick, such an adroit tactic, might seem impossible to worthy people who do not know Dr. Flax. We have no difficulty in admitting once again that the professor we have accused is one of the most astonishing brains of modern humankind. All his conceptions are stamped in the coin of genius. It is therefore not at all astonishing that, in the affair of the child-stealers, he pre-armed himself with a unique and exceptional defensive weapon.

THE AS-YET-UNKNOWN MOTIVE

When he interrogates an accused individual, against whom charges weigh, one of the first preoccupations of an examining magistrate is to discover the motive for the crime. His conviction is only definitively acquired, his mind is only satisfied, when he has understood the true motives for the action.

We have been summoned to explain the reasons for which Dr. Flax, the Comtesse de Houdotte and the Windernunhut brothers have abducted thirty-one children.

Our partisans are crying out to us from all directions: has not the celebrated surgeon abducted the children in order to carry out scientific experiments on them?

We do not believe in the truth of that accusation.

In what way could scientific experiments of that sort interest the Comtesse de Houdotte, Dr. Flax's accomplice? Would that great lady expose herself to the exemplary punishments that medical research of such cruelty would merit, for the glory of discovering some new remedy or some new physiological law? We do not think so.

We therefore confess our absolute impotence to explain, *for the moment*, the moral causes of the abductions.

Only investigation, pursued to a conclusion, can reveal a secret that we have not yet succeeded in penetrating.

We anticipate that our honesty in expressing these hesitations will attract a thousand attacks on the part of the Flaxists. Nevertheless, we shall continue the accumulation of evidence. Our demonstration seems to us to be sufficient to persuade the hesitant. It will remain until later to discover the motive that still remains unknown to us.

THE ROLE OF THE COMTESSE DE HOUDOTTE
PORTRAITS RECOGNIZED

The name of the Comtesse de Houdotte was seen to appear for the first time in this affair during the abduction of Gontran de Vautremesse at the Nouveau-Cirque.

By virtue of a hazard that we can easily explain today, that lady was in the corridor of the circus at the moment when the Baron de Vautremesse, accompanied by his second son, was coming out. The Baron greeted the Comtesse de Houdotte, with whom, according to the newspapers he exchanged a few words. It was during that short conversation that the child went out on to the sidewalk on his own and was suddenly snatched.

Since that time, the investigation had revealed that a woman has participated in the majority of the abductions. That woman was seen by Monsieur Kéroul, the dramatist, and by Madame Palavacoccini, the grandmother.

We have shown a portrait of the Comtesse de Houdotte to Monsieur Kéroul. Without affirming in a categorical fashion that he recognized the thief, the man of letters declares nevertheless that he is struck by a certain resemblance.

As for Madame Palavacoccini, she is much more affirmative. According to her, the person whose image we presented to her was definitely the one who met the two giants at the corner of the Rue Rennequin a few seconds after the abduction of little Paolo.

We are keeping in reserve a few proofs even more convincing for the incredulous who are not immediately persuaded.

H. de Vorigno
For the dissident members
of the Scientific Committee of Investigation

THIS MORNING'S PAPERS

This morning's papers are continuing the campaign and hardening the attitudes that they chose the day after the formal accusation of the dissident scientists.

"Arrest the guilty parties!" cries the *Lanterne*. "For us, the proofs are sufficient. We wonder in vain what the police are waiting for. If they wanted to permit Dr. Flax and his acolytes to escape, they would act no differently. If, during the famous Humbert case,[27] the law had acted more energetically, if they had followed the precise indications of those who could see clearly, they would not have had to organize a hunt for the crooks all over Europe, many thousands of francs would have been saved, and the course of justice would not have been delayed.

"What influences, then, are impeding action?

"The demonstration of the dissident scientists is very clear. The Comtesse de Houdotte has been formally recognized by Madame Palavacoccini the grandmother. There is no reason to defer police action.

"There is too much abuse, in the camp of the surgeon's friends, of the ignorance in which we remain of the motives for the crime.

"The crime exists.

"We know its authors.

"Even if we remain ignorant of the reasons for their evil actions until the end of eternity, that would not be a reason for not punishing what ought to be punished, and for not thus reassuring the Parisian population."

The *Echo de Paris* protests, with equal force, against the claims of the anti-Flaxists.

"They continue," that paper says, "to heap us with the gossip of concierges and stupid anecdotes. And that's what they call proof!

"Monsieur Kéroul did not recognize the Comtesse de Houdotte from the portrait that was shown to him. He simply thought that he observed certain resemblances. And that vague testimony suffices for some to accuse a woman of the world whose devotion to the cause of the victims of the child-stealers has been admirable!

---

[27] The "Humbert Affair," which concerned the financial frauds of an adventuress named Thérèse Humbert, launched when she obtained a huge bank-loan in 1881 on the basis of an inheritance obtained with the aid false documents, dragged on for twenty years. *Le Matin* played a major role between 1883 and 1901 in demanding an investigation of her claim but her father-in-law, who was the Minister of Justice in 1883, blocked all the early attempts and the lawsuit launched by the real heirs was stalled until the money had all been spent.

"There is also the deposition of Madame Palavacoccini, the mother of the celebrated spy. That old lady, who wears spectacles, did not hesitate. But, even supposing that she is sincere, and not seeking to help the spy Pietro Palavacoccini profit from the sympathy inspired by little Paolo Palavacoccini, it is not possible to admit her assertions without well-founded doubt."

THE THIRD SERIES OF
THE DISSIDENT SCIENTISTS' PROOFS

Continuing their campaign, in spite of all the anathemas, the dissident scientists have today delivered to publicity a further series of proofs. Here they are:

THE ATTITUDE OF DR. FLAX
FURTHER ARGUMENTS

We return today to the question of the attitude of Dr. Flax when the Scientific Committee of Investigation was organized.

We have revealed that it was by means of petty intrigues and adroitly sown words that Dr. Flax launched the idea of that group of scientists and was eventually nominated as its president.

We add today that from that moment on, he had but one aim, that of thwarting the efforts of the devoted scientists desirous of taking the task seriously.

At the first meeting of the sub-committee, Dr. Flax proposed a method of working that would have postponed any results to the Greek kalends, and prevented us from ever achieving anything.

We protested, and the echo of those arguments resounded in the press.

It was only by a small majority that we succeeded in imposing our will on our president. From the very start, therefore, he made every effort to prevent us from seeing clearly. His maneuvers were, as always, very skillful. We only understand now the motives for his adroit obstruction and the impractical and unproductive methods of working with which he attempted to immobilize us.

THE QUESTION OF THE GIANTS

Dr. Flax has three strange men in his service, three bizarre characters, utterly devoted to their master.

We have accused the Windernunhut brothers of complicity. We repeat our accusation today with further conviction.

All those who have been to Dr. Flax's home, in the house in the Rue Cassette, have noticed those three bodyguards, two of whom are phenomenally tall.

What are they, exactly? Who are they?

We do not know yet. One of us, who had dealings one day at the hospital at Montretout with the eldest, was struck by the erudition of the colossus. He is a veritable scientist. He astonished our colleague with his bacteriological knowledge. Dr. Flax is assisted in his laboratory at Montretout, sometimes by one of the Windernunhut brothers, sometimes another.

At the children's hospital, everyone knows that the three men are endowed with remarkable aptitudes for medical study, that Dr. Flax listens to their opinion with a reverence equal to that which they testify to him continually. Nevertheless, they also serve him as domestics, coachmen and automobile drivers. They introduce visitors into the house in the Rue Cassette, and, as no one has ever seen a cook enter the dwelling, it is also supposed that they prepare the food for the midday and evening meals. That opinion is also corroborated by the observations of the neighbors.

One of the brothers goes to the market every morning to make the purchases necessary to the household. The delivery men who go to the house in the Rue Cassette are always paid by one of these three extraordinary beings. By the same token, many clients have placed the physician's fees in the hands of one of the Windernunhuts.

Two of these men are giants, as ample as they are tall. Now, is there any need to recall that giants have been observed several times in the vicinity of places where children have been abducted?

The Baronne de Vautremesse remembers—vaguely, it is true—having been passed by a man of abnormal height a few moments before the abduction of her first child. Giants were seen during the abduction of Germane Plaizance. Two more giants were similarly found, as if by hazard, at the corner of the Rue Rennequin at the moment at Paolo Palavacoccini disappeared in so sudden a fashion.

The objection will be raised that, according to the witnesses, one of those giants was bearded, while the Windernunhut brothers are all as clean-shaven as actors. Similarly bearded were the two colossi who were seen in the vicinity of the Europe Metro station at the time of the abduction of Germaine Plaizance, but there is no proof that those beards were not fake. We continue, therefore, to claim that the giants of the investigation are the two brothers Wolfgang and Chrysostome Windernunhut.

The third brother Numérien, who is of medium height, is, in our view, the automobile driver who was seen outside the Église Saint-Augustin. He is also the man who bought a bottle of glue in the paper shop in the Rue du Havre, which served to fabricate the note by means of which Clovis Binard was notified of the abduction of Gontran de Vautremesse. The shopgirl who gave a statement to Monsieur Laudet affirmed, in fact, that the buyer had a slight foreign accent. Numérien Windernunhut, although he speaks French fluently, does not pronounce certain words with an absolute purity. His two brothers have much thicker accents. That was observed by Madame Palavacoccini during the conversation she had with them in the Avenue Niel. We have just received this information straight from the old lady's mouth. It appears to us to be of the utmost importance, and should convince the most incredulous.

WITH REGARD TO DR. FLAX'S INDISPOSITION

We have reason to believe that Dr. Flax participated personally in each of the abductions. We have two reasons for thinking that, the first of which is that the surgeon was indisposed for four days, during which he remained in bed in a room set up for him at the Montretout hospital. If we refer to the police record, no abduction took place during those four days.

WITH REGARD TO THE ABDUCTION OF
GONTRAN DE VAUTREMESSE
THE DIRECTION OF THE SUSPECT VEHICLES

The examining magistrate was led, as is well-known, by all kinds of deductions to think that the child-stealers knew that Baron de Vautremesse's son would go to the theater on the evening of the crime, and that the abduction was premeditated and prepared.

It is confirmed today that among the people who knew was Dr. Flax, who is the Vautremesse family's doctor. The professor met the Baronne on the day before the abduction, asked for news of her son and advised her to procure a few distractions for little Gontran, downcast by the grief of having lost his brother. He even suggested the Nouveau-Cirque. That is a very astonishing coincidence!

We also want to draw attention to another point: the direction taken by the vehicles in which the children were taken away.

The coupé that carried away Gontran de Vautremesse and which, because it went along the Rue de l'Université, inducing the examining magistrate to make an error, could easily have been heading, by means of a slight detour, toward the Rue Cassette.

The automobile in which Émile Loubé was taken away went along the Boulevard Malesherbes. That is also in the direction of the Rue Cassette.

In the same way, the other automobile that was used for the abduction of Germaine Plaizance departed via the Rue de Londres. That is also the route one would take to go from the Pont de l'Europe to the Rue Cassette.

These proofs add to those that Monsieur Binard has gathered by studying the places where the clothes were abandoned, in relation to the places where the abductions had taken place.

In the same way that all those lines traced on the map of Paris by Monsieur Binard converge on the Rue Cassette, all the accusatory evidence converges toward Dr. Flax, the Comtesse de Houdotte and the Windernunhut brothers, with an implacable and vengeful rigor.

Why wait, in fact, to act energetically against them and perhaps finally dis-cover what has become of the children?

H. de Vorigno
For the members
of the Scientific Committee of Investigation

INTERVIEW WITH THE BARON DE VAUTREMESSE

I have been to the home of the Baron de Vautremesse in order to obtain his impressions of the debate that has surged forth.

"I'm very perplexed," he told me. "What to think? Several times, Dr. Flax has been called to the beds of family members who have fallen ill. Although I have not always been delighted by his abrupt manners, I could not have been more satisfied with the care he has rendered. He's a physician of genius. I dare not believe in his culpability. First of all, why would he abduct children? So long as that question is not clarified, everything remains obscure. Is he not the victim of an extraordinary series of coincidences? Such things have been seen before. I have no need not remind you of numerous judiciary errors that were due, not to the incompetence of the judges, but to a veritable conspiracy of circumstances. And yet, when I read the proofs published by the dissident scientists, I feel convinced...

"It's certain that Dr. Flax knew that our little Gontran was going to the circus on the night of the abduction, that he had advised that distraction. It's true, too, that I met the Comtesse de Houdotte a minute before the abduction, that I stopped to say a few polite words, and that she climbed into her carriage at the very instant I perceived the abduction. If I hadn't paused like that, I would never have left my son for a single second, and the kidnapper could not have carried him off in the dark. Is it permissible to conclude that the Comtesse de Houdotte, whom I've known for a long time, who is a woman of great intelligence and heart, was there expressly to separate me from Gontran? I can't believe it, and yet, at times, I believe it anyway."

The Baron de Vautremesse, a nervous and violent man, seems utterly depressed by the uncertainties in the midst of which he is living.

"Well, Monsieur," he added, when I took my leave of him, "at any rate, the kidnapper will pay us for our tears. I swear that in addition to the penalties of the law, he'll have to deal with me, directly."

Barbarus

AT THE HOME OF THE COMTESSE DE HOUDOTTE
DR. FLAX IN LOVE

I have had the favor of being received briefly by the Comtesse de Houdotte.

The implacable order that closed the door to all journalists has been lifted for me. I owe that preference to the benevolent intervention of Madame Sarah Bernhardt, who is one of the Comtesse's friends.

The Comtesse appeared, superb and majestic, at the door of the reception room where I was waiting. Welcoming me in the frame of the parted door-curtain, she invited me to pass into another room—the one containing the famous golden stake.

"Monsieur," said that remarkable woman, whose every attitude is a seduction. "I'm seeing you on the insistence of my friend Sarah Bernhardt. She says that I'm wrong not to defend myself. She thinks that, in my situation, it's necessary to make friends in the press, under pain of making enemies...

"I've known Dr. Flax for a long time. I've always had the greatest admiration for his genius. He's part of the circle of the 'profound' that I receive on Saturday evenings. Dr. Flax has been, and perhaps still is, in love with me. He has asked for my hand. I refused. I consider that, after three experiments in marriage, I ought not to try again." She smiled as she said that. "Since the time when I was obliged to explain my decision to Dr. Flax, there has been no further question of love between us...

"You will notice that I'm expressing myself frankly, without shame or embarrassment. Will that count to my credit? Oh, Monsieur, how extraordinary it is to have to recount details of that sort to a journalist—but am I not obliged to shut the mouths of the malevolent?"

"Can you not, Madame, add a decisive word to prove your innocence?"

"No. It's up to my accusers to prove my guilt."

"They consider that they have proved it."

"That's because they're content with very little. We'll emerge victorious when the time comes."

With these words, tranquil, self-assured and smiling the Comtesse de Houdotte offered me her hand and I took my leave.

Such calm, in the midst of hostile clamors, at a moment when it seems certain that the law, under the pressure of public opinion, will have to proceed with an investigation, willingly or unwillingly! I confess that after that visit, I am wondering increasingly whether the dissident scientists have not been misled and gone astray, in spite of all the good reasons they seem to have, on a trail as resounding as it is false...

Clovis Binard

AT THE HOME OF DR. FLAX
THE THREE OGRES PLAY CARDS
THE DOCTOR'S PROJECTS

I have just returned from the home of Dr. Flax.

Before penetrating into the surgeon's study I went into a room on the ground-floor, where I conversed for a few minutes with the Windernunhut brothers.

They seemed as calm as their master and the Comtesse. The two giants, milder this time, welcomed me with pleasant smiles and replied amiably to my questions.

The two colossi have enormous voices. When they laugh, they make the windows shake. I observed, by contrast, the harmonious voice, with a metallic sonority, of the third brother, the one of medium height, Numérien Windernunhut.

"Where do you hail from?" I asked them.

"We're from Swabia," Chrysostome replied. "Our story doesn't take long to tell. Our father emigrated to Paris. He was a manufacturer of wooden blocks for shoemakers. One doesn't become rich in that line of work. We wanted to study. It was a veritable itch, but we didn't have the means. One day, our father broke his leg in the street, just as Dr. Flax was passing by. The surgeon brought him back to the house. We became acquainted. We pleased him, and he paid the expenses of Numérien's studies, in Zurich. There, my brother passed all his examinations at the Faculté. Numérien is the only one of us who has diplomas. As for us, we trained in medicine by assisting Dr. Flax. We learned as much from him, believe me, as any master in the hospitals, but as we don't have the parchments we can't practice. Besides, there's no need. It's sufficient for us to participate in the doctor's laboratory research. That life pleases us. We live here with him, partly collaborators, partly friends and partly servants.

"And too bad," added Wolfgang, shaking the table with a blow of his fist, "for those who don't like it!"

"Now," Chrysostome went on, "we can't deny that we're giants. Wolfgang and I are excessive by a few dozen centimeters in height and girth. Does that prove that we're child-stealers? We're very big, very sturdy, very strong. But at the end of the day, if specimens of our kind are rare, they exist. Why are people obstinate in only harassing us, out of all the giants in the world?"

"I don't say," Numérien continued, "that the evidence accumulated by the dissident scientists isn't troubling. When I read the newspapers, I try to step outside myself, to examine the arguments objectively. Well, if I weren't sure that we're all innocent—because I am sure of it, quite simply—perhaps I'd be in doubt momentarily. I can understand the attitude of the dissident scientists, given that the coincidences are amazing. Those three vehicles, the coupé and the two automobiles…the lady one encounters in the affair and who resembles the Comtesse de Houdotte…the elegant man who resembles Dr. Flax…those two giants who resemble my brothers. I notice, however, that the giants are described as bearded, while my brothers are clean-shaven.

"All in all, these multiple petty details, which appear to be concordant, might easily deceive sincere men. So, for myself, I don't consider them as malevolent, or even jealous. They're simply men who are mistaken, who have been logically induced to error by a series of indications that are convincing, but false."

"Personally," said Chrysostome, laughing, in a fashion that shook all of his formidable thoracic cage, "I always repeat the same question: why would we have abducted the children? My God, why do it? We care for four hundred at our hospital at Montretout. They lead us a merry dance, the little scamps. Now, what do you think we'd do with more?" He forced another gross laugh. "Everyone knows that ogres are giants, so, reciprocally, giants ought to be ogres. So write in your paper that we eat them, these little children, that we make pâtés out of them, in which we delight at lunch and dinner."

"If you want to see Dr. Flax," Wolfgang put in, cheerfully, "you'd better go now. It's time. Another time when you come again, we'll show you my seven-league boots, which we keep in a cupboard."

"Yes, come along," said Chrysostome. "I'll show you up."

And, still laughing at his leaden jokes, he took me to the surgeon.

"You've come at the right time, Monsieur!" the doctor exclaimed. "In fact, I've just made a decision of which I want to inform the public. It's necessary to put an end to all these tales of brigands. I can see now that it's only possible to combat an unleashed public opinion by permitting a thorough investigation and putting everything in daylight. Have I any need to tell you that the police and juridical authorities don't believe in my culpability? I'd have been arrested a long time ago if my innocence weren't recognized in high places. But it's not sufficient to be innocent. It's necessary to succeed in convincing others of that innocence. In a Republic, where everyone has his say, the man believed to be guilty is guilty, and the man believed to be innocent is innocent. It's therefore necessary that I succeed in convincing everyone. So, please make a copy of the letter that I've just written to the public prosecutor. Here it is."

Monsieur le Procureur de la République,

Having decided to put an end to the agitation to which the accusation made by some of my colleagues has given rise, I am writing to ask you to charge Madame la Comtesse de Houdotte, the brothers Windernunhut and me. A formal, official charge will permit the law to mount a profound investigation.

Let us be confronted by all the individuals who claim that they have seen us.

Let all the searches be carried out that their professional experience suggests to the investigators.

We submit, in advance, with the best will in the world, to all the disruption indispensable to the manifestation of the truth.

This is the only way for all of us to reply to our enemies and put an end to this lamentable affair.

Please accept, etc...

Flax

After having dictated that letter to me, the doctor added: "I hope that afterwards, people will be prepared to leave us in peace."

I got up to leave, but Dr. Flax retained me.

"One more word," he said. "Yesterday, during the visit you rendered. Madame la Comtesse de Houdotte revealed to you, with admirable frankness, my sentiments toward her. Well, yes, I love the Comtesse de Houdotte. I don't deny it. I have asked her to be my companion in life. She refused the offer. And that's all. So much the worse for the scandal-mongers and the jackals of the salons; they will not be able to unearth any infamy in my relationship with the Comtesse de Houdotte."

"Do you think," I said to the surgeon, as I left, "that the court will follow your direction and lend itself to this investigation that you are demanding for the benefit of the gallery?"

"Certainly, Monsieur. I have no reason to hide from you that I'm acting with the agreement of the examining magistrate."

"Then will not public malignity claim that the investigation will not be serious?"

"It will not be able to do so, for the slightest documents will be published."

As I went past the large lodge on the ground floor, a vast and spacious room painted in gray, I perceived the three Windernunhut brothers placidly playing cards.

For a woman accused of the blackest sins, and men accused of all sorts of crimes, the Comtesse, Dr. Flax and the Windernunhut brothers are maintaining—I cannot repeat it often enough—astonishing attitudes of composure.

Clovis Binard

The dissident scientists are continuing to accumulate evidence against Dr. Flax. These are the latest documents that they have sent us.

FURTHER PRROF OF THE CULPABILITY OF DR. FLAX
THE PROOF OF THE BALLOON

To the series of our demonstrations, we add today a direct proof, an irrefutable testimony.

Dr. Flax has been seen, in person, during one of the most recent abductions signaled to the police.

On the day of the mothers' procession, the Comte de La Vaulx, the celebrated aeronaut,[28] was making an attempt on the record for a balloon journey from Paris to Algeria. That attempt was, as we know, crowned with success. The bold voyager came down in the desert south of Biskra. He has sent us the following dispatch:

Biskra. Learn from local newspapers of accusation against Dr. Flax. Offer my testimony. Was passing in balloon over Boulevard Montmartre, departing for Algeria, when I saw with binoculars, at the location where Louise Accesson was abducted, Dr. Flax and Numérien Windernunhut, long familiar. De La Vaulx.

This is *in flagrante delicto.*

It will be necessary, one day, before our continual listing of evidence, for the magistracy to explain its inaction, and for the Flaxists, who have thus far considered our efforts with disdain, to discuss the precise, certain facts that we do not cease to reveal, and will not cease to reveal, as long as the law maintains its incomprehensible attitude of indifference and immobility.

H. de Vorigno
For the dissident members
of the Scientific Committee of Investigation

---

[28] Comte Henry de La Vaulx (1870-1930) was one of the co-founders of the Aero Club of France in 1898 and wrote numerous books on aeronautics. He set a distance record for balloon travel of 1,200 miles in 1900 but did not make a flight to Algeria in 1906. There is now a medal named for him.

Paris, 26 July

A COUP DE THÉÂTRE
THE CULPABILITY OF DR. FLAX

The Flaxists will receive this morning, on opening their newspapers, one of those blows from which they will not get up.

As improbable, as incredible as it might appear, Dr. Flax, the Windernunhut brothers and the Comtesse de Houdotte are the guilty parties.

No doubt is any longer possible.

Last night, a certain hesitation still weighed upon the Minister of the Interior, when the Minister of Justice, in company with the public prosecutor and Monsieur Laudet, the examining magistrate, went to see Monsieur Clemenceau.

It was during that conference that a decision was taken: to proceed the following day, and not for form's sake this time, with the arrest of the surgeon and his accomplices.

What had happened to move the government and the judiciary so suddenly to action?

Very little. Last night, there was no more proof against the doctor than there had been the day before.

The decision of the two ministers simply translated the triumph of Monsieur Hamard, the head of the Sûreté.

Monsieur Hamard had been convinced personally, since the very first day, by the proofs of the "dissident scientists." He had tried, with all his influence, to bring about the immediate incarceration of the criminals, but he had collided with the incredulity of the magistracy.

That conflict had become so bitter that it had ended up disturbing the ministers.

It was that antagonism that had provoked a nocturnal conference between Messieurs Clemenceau and Briand. For a long time, they had discussed and analyzed the proofs furnished by the dissident scientists. The Minister of the Interior's private secretary proposed, in order to get out of the difficulty, applying Bentham's calculation to the discussion.

To each proof for or against, a numerical score as awarded, as our readers do on a weekly basis for Bernard, Binard and Barbarus. All these scores were added up, and the means calculated.

If our information is accurate, the arrest of Dr. Flax was decided by 244 points to 214.

THE ARREST WARRANTS
A SURPRISE FOR THE MAGISTRATE
THE DOCTOR AND HIS ACCOMPLICES

The court was thus obliged to submit, and finally to sign warrants for the imprisonment of the brothers Windernunhut, the Comtesse de Houdotte and Dr. Flax. The arrest warrants have been executed this morning—or, to be precise, have *not* been executed.

In view of the immediate search that he wanted to witness, the examining magistrate went in person to the Rue Cassette this morning, at eight o'clock.

He rang the doorbell of the house in vain.

No one responded to the summons of the bell, whose heavy and sinister ring could be heard in the street.

The judge did not persist; he was soon obliged to yield to the evidence; either the house was empty, or its inhabitants were refusing to show themselves.

Now, according to the promises that he had made to the examining magistrate the day before, Dr. Flax ought to have been at home, at the disposal of the law.

Very disappointed by that silence, and beginning to suspect the truth, the magistrate had the hospital at Montretout telephoned, in order to discover whether the doctor had gone to visit his patients. The response was that neither the doctor not the Windernunhut brothers had been seen there since the previous day.

Before having the door forced by a locksmith, Monsieur Laudet went in haste to the house of the Comtesse de Houdotte, in the hope that he might have more luck there.

The magistrate was received by the domestics.

They told him that their mistress had left the previous evening, at six o'clock, at which time she had taken a train from the Gare du Nord.

She had, according to them, gone to the country, to a small property she owned on the edge of the woods near the little village of Pierrefonds. The Comtesse often went there to rest, in peaceful retreat.

A telegram sent to the gendarmerie at Pierrefonds rapidly convinced the magistrate that if the Comtesse de Houdotte had, as her chambermaid affirmed, boarded the train, she had not arrived at her destination.

Her description was immediately sent to the intermediate stations between Paris and Compiègne.

It was proved by this means that the Comtesse had got off the train at Chantilly and had left the station, where she had climbed into an automobile that had sped away through the forest, toward an unknown objective.

After having failed at the Comtesse de Houdotte's house, the magistrate, disturbed by his initial findings and very nervous, returned to the house in the Rue Cassette.

There, a locksmith attempted, without result, to break the bolt retaining the enormous battens of the door. The workman only succeeded in breaking his tools.

Confronted by the impossibility of opening the door, they tried to get into the house via the neighboring houses. That attempt was equally vain.

All the walls overlooking the courtyard of the surgeon's house were armed with large spikes, by which anyone who tried to get in that way would surely be lacerated. They wondered why the doctor had armored the vicinity of his house with spikes in that way—for he was the one who had ordered the defensive work carried out, several years before.

It will therefore be necessary to go in by the door to the Rue Cassette. It will be opened tomorrow, by means of a dynamite petard.

I have talked to Monsieur Hamard, who is naturally triumphant.

"Of course," the head of the Sûreté said, "they were expecting us. It won't be easy now to catch these rogues, who will be running over the roads of Europe. My idea is that they'll try to reach Greece, a country with which we have no extradition treaty. They can live there is peace, unless the father and mothers who were their victims send a maritime expedition against them."

But what has become of the children?

Clovis Binard

The anti-Flaxist newspapers are having a good day. They are singing victory songs, with little care for modesty.

"We were right," cries the *Lanterne*. "As usual, people didn't want to listen. And now, it's the taxpayers who will pay the price. Once again, we shall have to spend hundreds of thousands of francs sending telegrams to alert the international police. Inspectors will be sent here, there and everywhere, traveling at our expense. That is the first result of the extraordinary amiability and suspicious benevolence with which Dr. Flax and his sorry friends have been treated in recent days.

"Shall we not find anyone in Parliament to ask where the responsibility lies, to ask who will pay, at least morally, for this monstrous blunder?—if one can call a kind of complicity in events, politely, a blunder."

The Flaxist papers are naturally disappointed and embarrassed. The majority do not hesitate to admit their error frankly.

"The flight of Dr. Flax and his friends," writes the *Figaro*, "remains for us a problem whose obscurity is not yet dissipated.

"Even if, in spite of everything we were able to believe, the surgeon is guilty of these abductions, if the dissident scientists really are right and have discovered the truth, it is not yet possible, in spite of everything, for us to admit that the professor is the frightful criminal that some describe.

"Dr. Flax, the Comtesse de Houdotte and the Windernunhut brothers abducted the children—so be it! Those are facts that seem proven today.

"But with what objective?

"To murder them?

"That is too implausible.

"Although events have proved them right, we cannot follow the anti-Flaxists, who do not hesitate to launch extreme accusations."

THE OPINION OF M. D'ANGLINEY

The celebrated physician, who was one of the first, in contrast and opposition to everyone else, to discover a new truth, is very sober and modest in victory.

"My God!" he said, when I went to disturb him in his laboratory, where I told him about M. Laudet's check at the door in the Rue de Cassette. "All this doesn't astonish me. We foresaw and predicted it, my dissident colleagues and I. One always marches on the right path when one is guided solely by concern for the truth and does not allow oneself to be dragged right and left by one's desires, one's sentiments or one's friends—but it's not without a certain sadness that I observe how right we were.

"Whatever the motive was for which the guilty parties abducted thirty-one children, it is nevertheless true that Dr. Flax is a scientist of profound genius, perhaps the finest brain that has ever added luster to French science. It's heartbreaking that such a mind should founder in an affair to which—I don't want to explain myself on this subject—one detects a rather nasty underside. As for our role—those of us who have been called the 'dissident scientists'—it's concluded. Now that the law has decided, belatedly, to swing into action, we have only to let it take its course. I shall telegraph my colleagues to tell them not to release the new proofs that we intended to publish today. We shall give them to the examining magistrate, who will act as he sees fit. We shall fall silent now and go back to our laboratories, which we have neglected too much in recent days."

And, as if to illustrate his words, Monsieur d'Angliney leans over a Bunsen burner, with the aid of which, in the blue and white flame, he draws out a long tube of glass into a tapering point, which weeps incandescent tears.

Barbarus

An artillery officer has just been appointed to blow up the door of the house in the Rue Cassette with dynamite. The operation is imminent. It will doubtless have taken place by the time these lines appear.

Will the children by discovered in the house so hermetically sealed by Dr. Flax?

B.

THE SEARCH OF DR. FLAX'S HOUSE
OPENING THE DOOR
DYNAMITE

The operation announced in the evening editions for eight o'clock actually took place at four o'clock in the morning.

The police wanted, by means of a false indication, to avoid having to protect a crowd of gawkers from their own imprudence. It was a wise precaution because from six o'clock onwards—when it was already all over, and frightful observations had already been made—an army of curiosity-seekers tried to mount an assault on the Rue Cassette.

All day long, solid police cordons had barred entry into the Rue de Vaugirard, the Rue de Rennes, the Rue Carpentier, the Rue de Mézières and the Rue Honoré-Chevalier. The invasion of Professor Flax's house was thus prevented, which would doubtless have been sacked, not so much by thieves or the furious as by souvenir-hunters, the frantic demolishers that one encounters in all catastrophes.

The order was so strict that it gave rise to an amusing incident. The President of the Senate, returning to his home, was obliged to negotiate with a Brigadier who was obstinate in preventing him from passing through. It required the intervention of a very confused officer of the peace to permit Monsieur Antonin Dubost to cross the quarantined zone and reach his domicile.

It had not been possible to maintain absolute secrecy regarding the moment chosen for the explosion of the petard. Was it not necessary to warn, as well as a few journalists of the major press, Dr. Flax's neighbors? The shock wave of the detonation might have broken windows; debris hurled by the blast might have injured a few people guilty of nothing but living in the vicinity. Precautions were thus indispensable.

A notification from the Prefecture of Police, delivered yesterday evening, had therefore warned all the interested parties that the explosion would take place at four o'clock in the morning, and that it would be prudent at that moment to keep all their shutters closed and the windows open.

Thus, when Monsieur Touny arrives at midnight to post his agents, he already has to drive back four or five hundred curiosity-seekers who have been tipped off.

It is half past three when Monsieur Lépine, accompanied by one of his secretaries, the colonel of the fire brigade, the public prosecutor and Monsieur Laudet meet up at the house that is now world famous with Monsieur Hamard and his men, who have already been on duty for some time.

A few minutes later, Artillery Lieutenant Lombarol arrives, with a corporal, a few soldiers and two large trucks filled with sandbags.

There is a brief deliberation, after which the officer goes to place beneath the door, in a hole pieced the previous evening, the petard fitted with a white fuse about a meter and a half long.

That task completed, the men construct a large barricade by piling up sandbags on the sidewalk and in the street. It is designed to absorb the impact of pieces of wood and stone that the petard will transform into projectiles.

It is obvious that all precautions have been taken to avoid damaging the adjacent buildings. Nevertheless, Monsieur Lépine is anxious, and looks up at the nearby windows repeatedly.

"Experience teaches suspicion," he tells me. "Behind those shutters, there is more than one young monsieur and more than one old demoiselle burning with the desire to know what is happening in the street. I fear that, in spite of my urgent recommendations, curiosity getting the upper hand over prudence, one of those lovers of new sensations might stick their nose outside at the exact moment that it is necessary not to do so."

The silent agitation of all the soldiers toiling outside Dr. Flax's house, all those magistrates and policemen coming and going in the darkness, by the light of torches carried by firemen, has something fantastic about it.

It seems to me that one of those strange tales in which certain writers with a feverish imagination delight is coming to life there in the darkness. Perhaps that is an absurd thing to say, but I write it without hesitation, for it expresses my thought.

The immobility of Professor Flax's house is exceedingly impressive. It will doubtless be objected that houses that walk, or are even content to fidget, are rather rare—obviously—but nevertheless, the one before which we are strolling like attentive shadows seems more immobile than the others, and its immobility more powerful and more hostile. One might think that it conceals a trap into which we will all disappear, that an abyss yawns behind the heavy door.

At five to four, we leave the artillery to their final preparations and go around the corner of the Rue Cassette to take shelter behind the thick walls of the convent of the barefoot Carmelites.

And we wait, without breathing a word, hearts gripped by a vague and irrational apprehension. I have taken care to synchronize my watch with that of the officer responsible for lighting the fuse. By the light of successive matches, I watch the jerky movement of the second hand.

At four minutes past four, a feeble, abrupt sound reaches our ears. We all stand there, quite astonished.

The detonation has made no more noise than a bursting pneumatic tire.

It appears, however, that the shock-wave has been much more considerable. In the direction of the Place Saint-Sulpice, several buildings have shaken from top to bottom.

We all run to examine the results of the explosion.

They are satisfactory.

The little hole of the mine has been enlarged into a gaping gap through which a man can slide. Part of the wall has been torn away.

None of the surrounding houses has been damaged, thanks to the barricade, in which some of the bags have been split. Red sand is running out abundantly; they look as if they are bleeding.

I pick up a twisted, flattened, torn piece of one of the formidable hinges that held the right-hand batten in place. It will be exhibited today in one our display-cases, along with a few other small objects that I found in the doctor's house and appropriated for the curiosity of our readers. You will thus be able to contemplate a scalpel, the femur of an antediluvian animal, an ebony pen-holder, a page of one of Flax's manuscripts, at the head of which can be read: "Essay on the Essential Substance of the Brain," etc., etc.

I also took possession of a wooden pipe that must have belonged to one of the Windernunhut brothers. It is marked with an H and bears the German inscription: *Liebe mich, ich liebe dich* (Love me, I love you).

An idyll was cultivated in that house of crime.

A FRIGHTUL SPECTACLE
A TRAGIC DISCOVERY

As soon as the breach was enlarged, I penetrated into the house, in the wake of the magistrates and the police authorities.

What an extraordinary and funereal visit!

I shall remember it until my dying day.

To begin with, we examine the complicated armature of the bolts on the door. No entrance to a fortress was ever more solidly constructed. Iron bars are overlapping in all directions, supporting and reinforcing one another so that their arrangement ensured the maximum resistance.

In single file, illuminated by lanterns carried by policemen, we inspect one room after another, quite rapidly, from the large lodge where the Windernunhut brothers were stationed to the study and the drawing room that I have already had occasion to describe.

Nothing has changed.

At the most, it seems a little tidier.

We do not find anything extraordinary until the moment when Monsieur Hamard opens the door to a small room adjacent to the doctor's bedroom.

Oh, the frightful vision of horror!

I cannot explain the terror that grips us all by the neck.

By the miserable light of the lanterns I see men go pale who have never gone pale before. Monsieur Hamard is as white as a sheet. The examining magistrate feels sick. The prosecutor cannot remain.

The acclamations uttered by those who came in first are answered by the interrogations of those who are still outside, bringing up the rear of our little cortege.

There is jostling, pushing, shoving.

And everyone, at the fist glance cast into that infamous chamber, feels his heart beat more rapidly, abruptly and brutally panicked.

It is there, the much-sought solution to the enigma!

The response to all the anguishing questions of the affair of the abductions is in front of us, frightful and sinister, surpassing anything of which one could dream in terms of the macabre.

Monsieur Hamard, overexcited by emotion, curses. "Damn it! Lift up your lanterns, then, so that we can see!"

The agents obey, raising their lanterns as high as they can.

They are trembling with emotion.

Their disturbance is detectable in the magnified vacillations of the shadows projected on the walls.

The room is hung with light blue wallpaper on which are scattered innocent bouquets of myosotis. It does not contain any furniture. It is only ornamented by a single picture-frame that gives the impression of having been abandoned there and forgotten a long time ago. It contains an old *image d'Épinal* representing the first railway train on the line from Paris to Saint-Germain.

Save for that picture and a shelf running along the wall opposite the door, at the height of a man, the room is quite bare—except, also, that on that shelf one can see carefully arranged in a row, approximately thirty skulls: thirty small skulls, of children.

We gaze at them, shivering.

So, the professor has killed his little victims.

All insults, all execrations, all maledictions are permissible against the name of Flax, which has only been pronounced thus far with admiration and respect.

The certainty of one of the greatest crimes against humanity is now acquired.

It is written on that shelf, in the immobile rictus of those little jaws, in the fixed gaze of those little eyeless orbits.

"It's necessary to count the skulls," says Monsieur Lépine to the head of the Sûreté.

We understand the thinking of the Prefect of Police. Thirty-one children have been abducted. Are they all represented here, by these frightful bones that seem a caricature of life? If the number is found to be larger than thirty-one, it will prove that there have been abductions still unknown.

Monsieur Hamard counts, in a dull voice: "One, two, three, four..."

We listen to that dramatic enumeration, more halting as it approaches the figure of known abductions.

"Twenty-five, twenty-six, seventy-seven..."

Eventually: "Messieurs, there are thirty-one skulls."

That lugubrious discovery terminated, Monsieur Lépine ushers us out and seals are applied to the room's only door. Two agents will guard it until further notice.

The remainder of the tour of the house reveals nothing further to the law.

As for me, oppressed, my heart heavy, it seems to me that in quitting the threshold of that accursed house, I am entering another world: a world of joy and liberation. The gray day that is beginning is, however, scarcely calculated to inspire such ideas. Everything is relative, though.

The day's work has been decisive. The affair of the child-sealers has entered a new phase.

Clovis Binard

ON THE HEELS OF THE GUILTY

So, Dr. Flax, the Comtesse de Houdotte and the Windernunhut brothers have committed one of the most frightful crimes against humanity. Thirty-one children have been stolen from their parents; thirty-one small skulls have been discovered in the house in the Rue Cassette, famously sinister henceforth.

When I recall that spectacle, of the flickering lanterns held by the agents, licking the lugubrious bones with their vacillating gleams, I am gripped by frissons. It seems to me that I am having a terrible nightmare, dreaming while awake.

At the risk of passing for a weakling and a sissy, I do not hesitate to write that those grinning and grimacing skulls have pursued me all night through my slumber, that they have danced sinister quadrilles before my eyes.

Even now, it is sufficient for me to close my eyes to see before me, lined up by a meticulous hand, those thirty-and-one bony masses, which were the frames of thirty-one living brains. In spite of the rather fleeting nature of the vision, I retain such a violent image of the spectacle that I could give names to those skulls, recognize them if they were mixed up.

Oh, however moving my experiences as a journalist might be, the little room with the blue myosotis wallpaper will always remain one of the most atrocious memories.

The duty of the authorities is now clearly traced. They have allowed those criminals, unique in history, to escape; it is necessary that they do not pause or rest until they have made them expiate their monstrous sins.

I am not one of those who will heap abuse on the people who allowed Flax to make fools of them.

That would be ungracious.

I have followed the investigation faithfully, and passionately. I have collaborated with it. I am one of the first people to have taken an interest in the affair of the child-stealers. I know all its ins and outs. And yet, without being explicitly Flaxist, I estimated until yesterday that it was necessary only to advance with the greatest prudence.

It would ill become me, therefore, to accuse the magistracy of negligence, or even, as some people are not hesitating to write, of complicity, because it was dazzled by the professor's fame to the extent of leaving the nevertheless-convincing evidence of the dissident scientists in the shadows.

Descriptions of the guilty parties have been sent telegraphically to all the police forces of Europe. We may hope that these precautions will have a good result. Two men of an appearance as characteristic as Chrysostome and Wolfgang Windernunhut cannot go unnoticed for long. The crime has made too much noise for a thousand denunciations not to burst out wherever they go.

Naturally the police have taken the usual measures. Special agents have been sent to all the great sea-ports.

The general opinion, in the administration at the Quai des Orfèvres, is that the guilty parties will have split up and are each traveling in a different direction.

Dr. Socquet, the medical examiner, has been charged with the medico-legal examination of the little skulls. His investigation will begin tomorrow. The seals are still in place today on the door of the room in which the mutilated children are sleeping their motionless slumber.

Barbarus

FURTHER SEARCHES

The search has continued al day in Dr. Flax's house. The initial visit had, in sum, been very superficial. The discovery of the skulls had elucidated the doubts to such a extent that it had not been judged worthwhile to carry it much further forward.

In the stables, the two automobiles of which there have been much mention were found, along with the coupé and the horse, all of which were used in the abduction of the children.

The young soldier who saw the large automobile outside the barracks on the Rue de la Pépinière when Émile Loubé was abducted has formally recognized it.

Similarly, the witnesses who saw the smaller automobile that Flax used for the abduction of little Germaine Plaizance have declared that they have identified it without a shadow of hesitation.

Many difficulties have been encountered with regard to the coupé, which is very similar to many other vehicles of the same type. Madame Clépent, Gilbert Baroutou, Père Mab, the doorman at the Nouveau-Cirque, Madame Palavacoccini senior, and Madame de Houdotte's coachman and footman, could not be certain. Perhaps it was that coupé, they said, and perhaps another.

THE COMTESSE DE HOUDOTTE'S COACHMAN
THE "TARRRAPATTATA" AGAIN

The deposition of the Comtesse de Houdotte's coachman, however, has permitted more precise and very curious reconstitutions.

They prove once again that it is necessary, in an investigation, never to neglect the little details.

To begin with, that individual's story demonstrates how studied and prodigious the guilty parties' cunning was.

The coachman in question is a very worthy man, a good Lorrain with no pretentions.

"I've only been in the Comtesse de Houdotte's employ for a short time," he declared to Monsieur Laudet. "She only hired me a few days before the abduction of Gontran de Vautremesse—exactly a week. I won't take anything back, no matter what happens. I assure you that I took Madame to the Cirque d'Hiver and brought her back without having the slightest suspicion that she had just been an accomplice in the abduction of a child. The footman who was beside me will tell you exactly the same.

"And how could I have believed that she was guilty? As soon as she read the newspapers the day after the theft of little Gontran, she summoned me to her drawing room. 'Can you read?' she asked me. 'Yes, Madame,' I said. 'Well, look at all these papers. You'll learn than an abduction---one of these abductions of children about which there's so much talk at the moment—took place at the very moment when we were leaving the Nouveau-Cirque.'

"So I read the papers and I told Madame what I know—which is to say, nothing. 'It's necessary nevertheless,' she replied, 'to put yourself at the disposal of the law. They need to have even the slightest indications in order to follow the trail of the guilty parties. I'll write to the examining magistrate that you're at his orders.' After that conversation, Monsieur le Juge, you can easily imagine that I was a thousand leagues away from thinking that she as the guilty party, or an accomplice. It would have been truly extraordinary."

That part of the coachman's deposition shows that everything in the adventure of the kidnappers of children was planned and arranged.

By sending her coachman and footman to the examining magistrate, the Comtesse de Houdotte inaugurated the process that led her and Dr. Flax to place themselves in the forefront of the affair of the child-stealers, and to manifest such zeal for the discovery of the criminals.

How could one suspect a man and a woman who were going to so much trouble to enlighten the law and steer public opinion in the right direction?

After having taken the coachman's deposition, Monsieur Laudet carried out a conclusive experiment. He had Dr. Flax's horse and two other mares borrowed from a large livery stable brought to the Quai des Orfèvres, outside the little fire station that backs on to the Palais de Justice,

"You claimed before," he said to the coachman, "that you would recognize Dr. Flax's horse by the sound of the animal's hoof-beats. According to you, the horse that went past your carriage outside the Nouveau-Cirque, made a characteristic sound: *tarrrapattata!* Well, here are three horses; we're going to have them run past you. You tell me, by listening to the sound of the horseshoes on the macadam, which is Dr. Flax's horse."

"Hang on, Monsieur le Juge," the coachman replied. "I'll only recognize it if it's the same horse that went past me on that famous night..."

"Of course."

"Well, if one of those animals makes the sound *tarrrapattata tarrrapattata* as it runs, I'll surely recognize it."

The experiment was carried out immediately. Dr. Flax's horse was first. The coachman did not take long to have the beast stopped.

"Of course! That's the mare!"

The magistrate then had the phonograph brought on which he had recorded, some time previously, the *tarrrapattata* sung by the coachman during his first deposition. That experiment too was conclusive.

So much for the mockery lavished on the investigator at the beginning of the affair, for learning to repeat the *tarrrapattata tarrrapattata*! All the newspaper caricaturists have shown him to us, on all fours, learning to paw the ground and trot. All the café-concert reviews devoted an issue to that fashion of discovering evidence.

The result is there today to demonstrate that the experiment was not so silly, and that it is too easy to mock when one does not understand the reasons for things.

The Comtesse de Houdotte's house was also searched, but no interesting discovery rewarded the patient research of the magistracy.

Neither the police not the examining magistrate have yet been able to determine the motive for the crimes.

We should like to know, or to guess, but all hypotheses seem ludicrous and do not stand up to scrutiny.

For what reasons did the criminals kill? Under the influence of what madness, what monstrous obsession? And why did they conserve all the skulls in the room with the blue myosotis wallpaper, stripped like anatomical specimens?

Clovis Binard

Paris, 29 July

FURTHER SEARCHES
A LETTER TO THE COMTESSE DE HOUDOTTE

The searches, both at Dr. Flax's house and the apartment occupied by the Comtesse de Houdotte, have continued with the greatest care. Every little corner has been visited and searched. Even the paving stones of the cellars in the Rue Cassette, formed of large slabs that had not been disturbed for two or three centuries, have been taken up.

So far as the examining magistrate has been able to determine, Dr. Flax lived in the simplest, almost the most ascetic, fashion.

In the larger rooms of the house the items of furniture are all large and coarse, peasant furniture in white wood. Only the study that I have described and the waiting room for clients exhibit a certain luxury, albeit pale, worn and faded. The bedroom only contains a narrow, iron-framed bed and a student's washstand.

The rooms occupied by the Windernunhut brothers are the most comfortably-furnished in the entire house.

Flax's bodyguards possessed large brass beds appropriate to their size, and sculpted wood furniture. Let us not exaggerate the luxury of the sculpting in question; they are due to the heavy labor of those Swiss workmen who carve wood in a particularly leaden fashion. In each room one also sees a large Swiss cuckoo clock, from the top of which a cockerel emerges from time to time to crow the hours, the halves and the quarters.

The papers seized have not revealed anything new. Flax had the habit of burning all his letters and documents. All that has been found are abundant notes, written day by day, about the maladies of children.

In the laboratory, the investigators have discovered, amid the usual apparatus of surgeons, physiologists and chemists, a jar containing a hundred small teeth that once belonged to the jaws of children.

The continued searches at the Comtesse de Houdotte's house have been longer and more meticulous. The activity of the policemen has been put to a severe proof by the unusual abundance and luxury of trinkets.

In the drawer of a small writing-desk the magistrate found a short letter addressed by Dr. Flax to his accomplice; it is dated 15 January 1906.

My dear friend,
Oh, how I would have liked to be able to send you, as a seasonal gift, something better than the banal bouquet of flowers that I brought you!

I had promised you that I would finish, by the end of the year, my great work on human genius. I thought that I would be able to offer it to you as a tribute for the new year.

I know how interested you are in it, and with what passion. I often recall your great dreams, realizable if my theories are correct.

But you are discretion itself. I have not observed any reproach in your gaze for my belatedness.

And yet, all the curiosity of your soul is extended toward that labor! Be patient. You will not be required to wait much longer. I am in the process of adding the final touches to the whole picture.

And afterwards, we shall see...

Now I am sure my dear friend, that the future is ours.

All best wishes,

Flax

This letter proves that the relationship between Flax and the Comtesse de Houdotte, at least at the epoch in which it was written, was purely amicable. It does not contain the slightest amorous expression. It is merely the letter of a scientist writing to a woman interested in his work.

The Comtesse de Houdotte must have a particular predilection for the surgeon's studies, since a series of notes taken by her has been found in a file, on the first page of which is written, in capital letters:

THE MAN OF GENIUS
THE FUTURE OF THE WORLD VIA THE MAN OF GENIUS

Under this title observations and thoughts are transcribes regarding the man of genius and his destiny on the earth.

For the most part, they are rather paradoxical ideas. For instance: "The superior peoples are those in which there exist, proportionally, the greatest number of men of genius. Frenchmen are superior to negroes not because each individual compared to another individual is essentially better, but because we possess more compatriots of genius than the negroes do. The mentality of the Chinese, Russian peasants, and some French workers or peasants gorged with alcohol, is not intrinsically superior to that of negroes. That superiority is uniquely due the proximity and the reflection of more men of genius."

These specimens of the Comtesse's *pensées* show that the extraordinary woman in question was scarcely occupied with the thousand frivolities in which Parisian socialites routinely delight.

Clovis Binard

There are still Flaxists—which is to say, partisans convince of the innocence of Dr. Flax

Among others, there is Jean Ajalbert, the man of letters who, not content with literary notoriety, has attempted to conquer the laurels of the explorer.[29]

I met him in the Boulevard Malesherbes as he was bathing his sturdy Auvergnat frame in the sunlight.

"I'm an old friend of Flax," Monsieur Ajalbert told me. "He's a man absolutely outside the banal, the common—a man who does not resemble anyone. But he's incapable of any kind of crime. I do not think I am taking any risk in sustaining, energetically, unlike and in opposition to everyone else, that there has been no murder. Evidently, skulls have been found; evidently, the evidence is concordant; evidently, it seems convincing at first glance. Personally, though, I remain convinced that there is a mystery underneath all this, which, when it is eventually revealed, will astonish the world. Friends and enemies will then obtain an explanation satisfactory to the most demanding, and the surgeon's innocence will be crystal clear. I'm sure of it."

"But what about the lugubrious discovery in the Rue Cassette?"

"I repeat, without wanting or being able to explain further, that in spite of the most violent appearances, I do not believe in the culpability of the celebrated surgeon."

"But Monsieur, Dr. Flax has fled; the Comtesse de Houdotte has fled; the Windernunhut brothers have fled. Have they not confessed, by virtue of that precipitate, unexpected departure?"

"They had reason to flee. I disagreed with my friend when he proposed to submit to a kind of voluntary inculpation, in order to convince the public. It would not have changed the opinion of his adversaries. He would, in spite of a favorable judgment by the tribunal, always have remained the child-stealer so far as the majority of Frenchmen were concerned. In the meantime, he would be exposed to all possible and imaginable slanders. The formula is always the same. Accused, in a sense, of having stolen the towers of Notre-Dame, it was better to go abroad.

"The doctor and his friends have seen organized against them one of those enormous, anonymous, collective accusations that are sometimes spontaneously generated in Republics, explosions of the mental firedamp of democracy. They would have been stupid to continue to brave the popular clamor that had con-

---

[29] Jean Ajalbert (1863-1947) began his literary career in association with the Symbolist and Decadent Movements, but cultivated a different kind of fame when he mounted strident opposition to French colonial adventures in the Far East, after visiting Laos and Indochina. In 1906 he was writing regularly for Jean Jaurès' newspaper *L'Humanité*, along with another writer who has a walk-on part in the present text, Tristan Barnard.

demned them in advance. But let's wait and see. The hour of justice always chimes in the end."

After the terrifying search in the doctor's house, Monsieur Ajalbert's optimism appears somewhat exaggerated. Our readers will doubtless wonder whether the sympathetic litterateur has allowed himself to be blinded by amity.

Barbarus

Paris, 30 July

The attempts by the police to discover the whereabouts of Dr. Flax, the Comtesse de Houdotte and their enormous accomplices are continuing with all desirable activity.

One of the agents of the Sûreté has obtained information that will hopefully permit the precise determination of the direction in which Dr. Flax's strange female friend has fled.

The magistracy has been equally preoccupied with trying to discover what the criminals have done with the bodies of the children, since only the skulls have been found.

WHAT HAS BECOME OF ALAIN BERNARD?

We have received a number of letters from readers complaining about the rarity of articles by Alain Bernard. It is, of course, the eternal gamblers who are writing to us, hoping thus to stimulate the zeal of the reporter on who they have put their money.

For several days, in fact, our collaborator had been silent. He had only taken part in our investigation in the most cursory fashion.

We had all been struck by a change in his character. The big fellow, ordinarily tranquil and placid in appearance, seemed preoccupied and nervous.

Now, Alain Bernard has disappeared, in a disquieting fashion, and we can no longer hide our anxiety on his behalf.

The day before yesterday, he brought us the few lines that we published in which he related the sentencing of the demonstrators in the Rue Casette.[30] Our editor-in-chief, who wanted to give him an assignment, had asked him to call in at the paper that same evening, at eleven o'clock. Alain Bernard agreed to the meeting, but did not turn up. An errand boy was sent to his domicile, but did not find him.

Alain Bernard has not returned to his home since that morning. His concierge, who also serves as his housekeeper, has sworn to that. We have been expecting a word of apology, a telephone call or a telegram. Nothing has arrived. As on the day before, Alain Bernard did not appear at the paper yesterday.

I have gone to his domicile several times. The tearful concierge has only been able to repeat to me that Alain Bernard has not come back. I let myself into his apartment with the key he leaves in the lodge, and found no trace of his passage. We have thus had no news of our colleague since he brought us the last petty item of judiciary reportage.

---

[30] Dropped from the Tallandier edition.

That say, he said to me feverishly, accompanying his words with small nervous gestures: "Old man, I think I'm on the track of something wonderful." And he repeated, three times: "Wonderful, wonderful, wonderful, old man."

After which he left in a hurry. What has become of him since? And does his disappearance have anything to do with the affair of the child-stealers?

Is it necessary to dread that the search for something wonderful has drawn out friend into some ambush? Some of us fear so.

We have notified the police of the disappearance of Alain Bernard, although, at present, they have a great deal of work to do.

Barbarus

REPORT OF THE MEDICAL EXAMINER
SCIENTIST'S ASTONISHING REVELATIONS

Dr. Socquet has not taken long to place his initial report in the hands of the law. He sent it to the magistracy this morning. The celebrated specialist did not want to give me a copy of the actual text, but he kindly answered my questions.

"What have you discovered, Doctor?"

"A superficial examination sufficed for me to make an observation of the greatest importance. I believe that the result of my investigation will amaze everyone. Tell me how many boys and how many girls the child-stealer abducted?"

"He abducted thirty-one children, of whom twenty-five were boys and six were girls."

"Well, among the skulls that were brought to me from the surgeon's house, I only found two girls' skulls, and twenty-nine boys' skulls."

"What does that signify?"

"It signifies that it might not have been the skulls of the thirty-one abducted children that were found in Dr. Flax's house."

"Oh! That will revive the courage of the few partisans who have remained faithful to Dr. Flax. But are you quite sure that you can determine sex exactly from skulls?"

"Perfectly sure. It's elementary. For the sake of greater certainty, I repeated the experiment with three or four experts in anatomy. I replaced the girls' skulls among the boys' and asked my colleagues to sort them out. They did not hesitate. No matter how many times the experiment was repeated, we always obtained the same result: twenty-nine boys and two girls."

"But in that case," I exclaimed, "you don't have all the skulls of the abducted children. The abduction of four of the boys you've examined haven't been reported to the police. Another four boys must therefore be added to the total of known victims. In the other hand, as we know that six girls have been stolen and you only found two female skulls, it's necessary to add another four victims to the list of remains.

"The total number of stolen children must, therefore be thirty-five: twenty-five boys whose abduction was reported, and of whom we possess the skulls; four boys whose abduction was not reported, and whose skulls we have; two girls whose abduction was reported and of whom we possess the skulls; and four girls whose abduction was reported but whose skulls haven't been found. Total: thirty-five. So Dr. Flax hasn't killed thirty-one children, as e thought, but thirty-five."

"No," replied Dr. Socquet, "because in my opinion, none of the skulls from the Rue Cassette belong who any of the children that have been in the news of late."

"What!?!?!"

My eyes must have expressed a profound amazement, because the doctor smiled as he asked me; "that astonishes you, eh?"

"Indeed. Dr. Flax's crimes seem to me to be large enough in number without increasing the list any further. Think of that hecatomb of poor little things! He must have murdered, in addition to the thirty-one children whose disappearance has been reported to the police, thirty-one other children, whose remains have been found. That makes sixty-two in al!"

"You're reasoning too rapidly, my friend. Nothing I've said could lend itself to the belief that the skulls in the doctor's house belong to murdered children."

"But..."

"No, they are, in my opinion, children who died naturally. They're anatomical preparations, of which Dr. Flax made use in his studies. I have the proof—evidence that was initially overlooked in the midst of all the emotion and confusion. The first item has nothing medical about it—anyone could have seen it. Under the lower jaw of each skull the doctor has stuck a little label on which figures can be read that have nothing cryptic about them. They simply represent measurements of the length and breadth of the cranial cavity. But there are much more serious proofs. These anatomical preparations are not recent. They date back three, four or five months, perhaps much more but certainly no less. There was no mention as yet of child-stealers when these skulls were doubtless already where they were found."

"Your findings are going to cause a fine racket, you know? The Flaxists, momentarily disappointed by the recent discoveries, will resume their campaign."

"Personally, I'm neither a Flaxist nor an anti-Flaxist," said the doctor. "I'm content to do my job and relate what I know for sure. If Flax hasn't murdered the thirty-one children whose skulls are on my table, that doesn't prove that he hasn't murdered the thirty-one who haven't been found...

"Anyway, publish without hesitation the fact that the bones I've examined are simply an anatomist's working specimens. The majority have marks of trepanation under the left ear. Doubtless the surgeon was either practicing his operational skills or trying to discover some new scientific verity. It is, however, not beside the point to add that all the skulls recovered are those of children about six years old, the same age as the children who have been successively abducted in recent weeks."

So, here we are, brought back to our point of departure by Dr. Socquet's work.

The discovery of the skulls in the hose in the Rue Cassette no longer signifies anything. The alarm was probably false. Al the problems we thought solved are back to where they were a few days ago.

What has become of the abducted children?

What have the doctor and his accomplices done with them?

Have they murdered them or not?

"Everything about this affair," *Le Temps* writes, "continues to be profoundly mysterious and worrying. As soon as a solution seems close, as soon as the objective seems to be within reach, it draws away again. The police and the magistracy are running after a mirage."

Clovis Binard

PROGRESS OF THE INVESTIGATION

The investigation continues with the greatest activity.

The policed have circulated the details of the automobile used by the Comtesse de Houdotte to flee Chantilly railway station.

It is, in fact, important to determine the itinerary of that vehicle.

The deputy station-master having declared that the bodywork was painted apple green, it has been possible to recover the tracks of the conspicuous vehicle.

The automobile belongs to a garage in the Avenue de la Grande-Armée.

We are now sure that it was Numérien Windernunhut who went to hire the vehicle. It was agreed between him and the garage-manager that the apple green vehicle would wait for a lady at Chantilly station. According to what Numérien said, the lady was a foreigner desirous of visiting the area around Chantilly.

"The Comtesse de Houdotte," said the chauffeur who drove her, "played her role very well. After a tour of the locale she had me take her to the château, which she visited. Like everyone else, she threw breadcrumbs to the ducks and the famous carp in the moat—after which she gave the order to take her back and set her down at the Gare d'Orsay."

These facts, confirmed today, demonstrate that there is, whatever impenitent Flaxists might say, a certain complicity between the Comtesse de Houdotte and Dr. Flax, since it was one of the doctor's servants who went to hire the automobile for the Comtesse."

That trip to Chantilly also proves the skill of the guilty parties. Evidently, it only served to distract the police. The vehicle was brightly colored in order to be noticed. The Comtesse did not appear to be hiding, although she was. Perhaps she feared that she might be being followed by the police, and it was a means to deceive the pursuit can cause her trail to be lost.

It is not generally believed that the Comtesse de Houdotte, after returning to the Gare d'Orsay, took a train on the Orléans line. It is thought that that was another cunning subterfuge.

It is only fair to add that others think, on the contrary—and for the same reason—that she did leave by one of the train on that line. The true cleverness, according to them, would consist, after deceiving the police by all kinds of subtle means, in deceiving them once again by the simplest means. Having put off the police by means of a simulated journey, it would be more cunning to put them off again by means of a real one, for it is always difficult to discover a truth hidden in a pile of lies.

Barbarus

We still have no news of our colleague Alain Bernard.

His inexplicable disappearance is causing the gravest concern.

We have sent colleagues to all the places he normally frequents. All research has so far been in vain.

Meanwhile, according to a rumor that is going round, which it has not been possible for me to verify, he had said to one of his lady friends: "Expect a *coup de théâtre* I haven't had much luck so far in the reportage competition. I'm a long way last, but perhaps I can rehabilitate myself by a resounding exploit. All the hypotheses made about Dr. Flax are false. There must be a prodigious secret at the bottom of this affair. Perhaps I'll soon be able to reveal it to my readers."

If these words are accurate, they leave the way open for all suppositions. A few of Bernard's friends, in fact, claim that their friend, in the course of his investigation, must have run into Dr Flax, and has doubtless fallen victim to his own zeal.

Barbarus

ALAIN BERNARD IS FOUND

All the news that the agencies and our sister papers have brought us today is, according to the letter from Alain Bernard that you can read below, of purely documentary and historical importance.

We know our colleague, who has finally been found, to be a conscientious and serious man. He certainly would not lead us astray. Given that he expresses no doubt about the success of his expedition, we consider that it will not be necessary to wait for long before obtaining, on the subject of Dr. Flax, information that will satisfy all curiosity.

THE REVIVAL OF THE FLAXISTS

As anticipated, Dr. Socquet's observations on the children's skulls have revived the ardor of the Flaxists.

This morning's *Figaro* expresses succinctly the general opinion of the surgeon's partisans, whom the accusations of the dissident scientists and the flight of the accused had momentarily depressed and confused.

"Like everyone else," one reads in that paper, "we ended up being troubled by reading every day the evidence accumulated against Dr. Flax, the Comtesse de Houdotte and the Windernunhut brothers.

"But today, a muted voice repeated to us more than ever the eternal questions that, without destroying the evidence of the dissident scientists, leave us nevertheless uncertain and perplexed.

"First of all, the motive! We always come back to that same mystery. Let us imagine, for a moment, that Dr. Flax has killed the thirty-one children.

"Why has he killed them?

"Some people reply: he was obedient to some unknown atrocious aberration.

"It is then necessary to admit that he has succeeded in drawing into his madness the Comtesse de Houdotte and the three Windernunhuts—who are, however, according to all the evidence, models of calm, tranquility and reason. Monsieur d'Angliney, who knows them well and who certainly cannot be suspected of benevolence in their regard, said himself to one of his colleagues: 'Those Windernunhuts are men exempt from nerves!'

"Other anti-Flaxists suppose that Dr. Flax has taken possession of the children, in order to carry out scientific experiments on them. That is even the opinion that tends to be prevalent. It seems to us to be equally absurd.

"If, as has already been said and repeated, the surgeon wanted to carry out experiments on young children, has he not an embarrassment of choice in his hospital at Montretout? He is the absolute master there. Even if he had wanted to take experiments on the little invalids beyond the limits of prudence and sound moral authority, no one would have permitted themselves to raise any objection. He could always have disguised such wretched studies so as not to give rise to any indiscreet questions.

"And in this hypothesis, as in all the others, the role of the Comtesse de Houdotte would remain completely inexplicable. That woman of the world is not occupied in surgery or medicine. The doctor's experiments could not interest her. Why would she risk, in the abduction and murder of children, a thus-far-spotless reputation, one of the most enviable social positions, and an agreeable, comfortable and peaceful life?

"There still remains against us, unfortunately, a strong argument derived from the flight of Flax and his friends.

"We gladly confess that it has considerable weight.

"The response that we in the Flaxist camp make almost unanimously is rather weak and limited in range. The surgeon must have wanted to avoid the annoyances of an inculpation in which he divined that he would have all public passion against him. But when it is opposed to us that he had requested himself to submit his case to the sagacity of the judges, our argument buckles, we willingly admit.

"Perhaps, nevertheless, that is the truth. It is not the first time that a man—even a man of Dr. Flax's breadth—has changed his mind in a capital circumstance of his existence. That about-turn is quite natural. It might be the key to all these events.

"Let us not forget, either, that the doctor, in making the decision to have himself officially charged, was dragging a woman into the adventure: that the Comtesse de Houdotte would have been constantly in the dock with him. It is therefore possible that, after having weighed the inconveniences that would result from such a frank attitude, not for him but for a woman to whom he was utterly devoted, the doctor went back on a decision made in haste and in a moment of unreflective generosity.

"Finally, the findings of Dr. Socquet have thrown new doubts into our minds. His report is clear and categorical. The thirty-one skulls in the Rue Cassette are not those of the thirty-one children that have been abducted from the streets of Paris.

"A notable observation regarding the psychology of public opinion is that the great majority of anti-Flaxists refuse to believe the medical examiner. The figure thirty-one has carried away all convictions.

"One can only admit that the coincidence might permit the fantasy a certain regularity.

The hazard that determined that Dr. Flax, with the objective of study, gathered on a shelf the skull of thirty-one children who died of natural causes, juxtaposed with the hazard that determined that thirty-one children have been kidnapped, demonstrates, for the crowd, that those hazards are not hazards, that they must be due to the reflective actions of human will.

"Nothing can reduce that public opinion to nothing.

"But we, persisting increasingly in the conduct from which we have never deviated, follow Dr. Socquet in his entirely serious reasoning and his entirely precise deductions.

"Not only do we not understand as yet why Dr. Flax, the Comtesse de Houdotte and the Windernunhut brothers would have murdered children, but we think that it is not yet proven that the abducted children have been murdered by anyone at all.

"Our hope that they might be found one day, alive and well, is therefore still legitimate."

We have published that article from the *Figaro* in full to show our readers where the Flaxists are, and the fashion in which the enigma presents itself to them today.

NEWS OF ALAIN BERNARD

The letter you are about to read has come as a great relief to us.

Our joy at having found Alain Bernard is double, since he announces to us at the same time that he is sure that he is on the right track, and that we might, thanks to him, discover the place where Dr. Flax and his accomplices have taken refuge.

My dear Editor-in-chief

I have been following your anxieties in my regard in your paper.

I have been very flattered by them.

There is nothing like it to show who one's friends are—to such an extent that I regret that I am not believed to be dead. I would then have been able to read the obituaries, which would surely have tickled my self-esteem

But I do not want to continue any longer to worry our comrades and the few gamblers who have bet on the outsider that I am.

I was obliged to leave Paris in a hurry, in hiding. It is, in fact, absolutely necessary, for the moment, that I am not disturbed in my task by meddling colleagues.

Believe that it is not solely the sentiment of egotism that is impelling me. I do not want to keep the fruits of my discovery for myself alone, but I do not want anyone to prevent me, by making maladroit moves or premature revelations, from arriving at the truth.

You will, therefore, understand all the precautions I have taken to leave Paris in the greatest secrecy.

I beg you not to publish the name of the town from which I am writing, in order not to indicate, even vaguely, the direction in which I have gone. It would be necessary to charter a special train for all the reporters that would race to that place, if you identified it even by a single word.

I am on the track of Dr. Flax, the Comtesse de Houdotte and the Windernunhut brothers.

I think I shall be able, before long, to tell you how the trail was revealed to me, and by what fortunate combination of circumstances I have been able to obtain precise and reliable details.

I was due to dine on the evening of the day after tomorrow with Monsieur Porci, the director of the Théâtre de Vaudeville. Please be kind enough to send him the enclosed letter of apology. I did not want to entrust it to the post for the same professional reasons, in order not to indicate to anyone where I am.

It is for the same reason that I have not sent you a telegram. The telegraph operator would have been tempted to spread the news of my resurrection and my firm hope of soon being able to send you great and sensational news.

Alain Bernard

ALAIN BERNARD EXPLAINS
THE FATE OF THE CHILDREN

Either I am much mistaken or the letter I sent to you yesterday must have made its way across the world.

My information was sound.

I shall know tomorrow exactly where Flax is hiding. I shall attempt the unimaginable to see him.

I deem that there is no longer any inconvenience in revealing where I am, how I got here and why I am here. No matter how diligent my competitors are, they will arrive too late. I no longer fear being "scooped" by any other reporter.

I am writing to you from Sarnen, a small town in Switzerland, the major town of Obwalden in the canton of Unterwalden. It is situated on the Brunig line that links Lucerne to Meiringen and Interlaken, almost equidistant between the great city of the Lac des Quatre-Cantons[31] and the culminating point of the famous pass.

Although Sarnen also has its tranquil blue lake, tourists rarely pause her, in haste as they are to reach the landscapes that the editors of guides and itineraries have recommended to the compulsory admiration of travelers. The town therefore rests in the calm of it provincial life, a pious and tranquil place asleep in the midst of convents.

My sudden departure for Sarnen was provoked by two telegrams received a few days apart, whose texts read: *Prepare depart, case doctor, Hermlein* and *Come see me tomorrow afternoon, Sarnen. You will know doctor's whereabouts. Curious expedition. Am following. Silentium. Salve. Hermlein.*

It had been four years since I had heard mention of Rudolph Hermlein. We had once made twenty or thirty perilous excursions together, among the Alpine summits. He had initiated me into the unique joys of great ascents, the vivifying domination of high places, gulfs and glaciers. We had overcome a thousand dangers in one another's company, had been caught in an avalanche together, had been exposed to terrible landslides by one another's side. He had nearly been carried away before my eyes by a torrent suddenly rising underfoot as if by magic. I had nearly been killed before his eyes by a mountain bull, and he had saved my life.

But all that frank camaraderie, which had linked two very different characters together, had not resisted the handshake of the departure. He had stayed in the mountains; I had been drawn into the trepidant gears of Parisian existence.

---

[31] More familiarly known as Lake Lucerne. It is probably not coincidence that the area indicated here is the geographical center of Switzerland.

We had not given one another any further thought. One does not write, after having promised to write.

Hermlein's telegram revived emotional memories in me, and gave rise to many hopes. *You will know doctor's whereabouts.* Those four words gladdened my heart.

Ah, that Hermlein!

He does not often send news, but when he sends any, it's worth the trouble.

Rudolph Hermlein is a very interesting man, with a child-like soul, an artistic mind , a will of granite and the most obstinate brain in the world. He was born in Switzerland, in Ober-Rickenbach, a hamlet lost in a circle of mountains where the main road from Wolfenschiessen, at station on the line from Engelberg to the Lac des Quatre-Cantons, suddenly stops as if one has reached the limit of the space permitted to human beings. Two enormous, impenetrable walls loom up at that place, which seem to seal off the world.

Raised until the age of ten in the midst of that forceful nature, Rudolph Hermlein then went to the Benedictine school at Engelberg, where his masters perceived that he had an aptitude for the plastic arts. They sent him to study drawing and painting in the studios of Munich. He specialized there in religious subjects. At the time when I met him, he was filling all the chapels in the canton with his Madonnas and his John the Baptists.

To his talents as a painter, Rudolph Hermlein joins that of knowing all the mountains around Engelberg, summit by summit and pass by pass. He is also well-known as a chamois hunter, and his reputation as an eagle hunter extends even further. He is the man who once, in order to take eaglets from a nest, had himself hoisted all the way down to the aerie, along a frightful wall of rock, at the end of a rope measuring more than three hundred meters. That terribly dangerous enterprise, infinitely complicated in its execution, accomplished with admirable composure, made a great deal of noise at the time, among those mountain people in whom boldness and audacity are not rare virtues.

Such is Rudolph Hermlein, who has put me on the trail of Dr. Flax.

I arrived in Sarnen in the middle of one of those athletic festivals that stir up certain Swiss cantons, from the humblest peasant to the highest functionary. Hermlein having not sent me his address, I was obliged to search for him in the midst of the merrymaking crowd.

As soon as I disembarked, I asked an employee at the station: "Do you know Rudolph Hermlein?"

"The painter?"

"Yes. Can you tell me where I might find him?"

"He's one of the organizers of the fête. You'll doubtless find him at the *Hornussen*. He's the chairman of the jury."

"What's the *Hornussen?*"

The station employee looked at me with profound disdain. He was certainly thinking: *Where did this one spring from?*

"Go to the fête," he said. "You'll see."

So here I am, reaching the meadow where the athletic competitions are taking place.

The town is decorated with a hundred painted banner extended from house to house. One can read thereon in capital letters all the possible welcomes to strangers required of a people welcoming the care of pleasing their guests.

Peasants are passing by, cheerful and familiar, broad-backed and heavily-built, hirsute or freshly-shaven, and bourgeois and bourgeoises who have put on their best clothes—which does not mean that the clothes are beautiful.

Sons of families are circulating on horseback, proud of their beribboned armbands, of the honor the town has done them in making them responsible, exceptionally, for maintaining order during the fête.

The games have attracted the entire canton, and many enthusiasts from neighboring cantons.

The Swiss adore cavalcades and historical processions. The program of the festivities has therefore brought out the most reclusive. Imagine, then, a vast defile representing spring, summer, autumn and winter: spring represented by a herd of cows with cowbells, accompanied by shepherds and goatherds yodeling in the Tyrolean manner; summer represented by groups of gymnasts going to the harvest festival dance, by a carriage containing an entire high-alpine cheese-making factory, by cheese-porters, tourists, guides, photographers, landscape painters, seekers of edelweiss and gentian roots; autumn represented by musicians in costumes of the last century, musicians costumed as modern wrestlers; winter represented by a ancient peasant room reconstituted on a truck, by hunters, woodcutters, old women with spinning-wheels, etc. Picture also the wild man, the necessary clown of local fêtes, pronouncing extravagant speeches and cutting a thousand capers, after having offered a beautiful cheese to the old curé. And picture fresh-faced peasant girls, adorable slender, delicate and virtuous, parading in their rich national costumes.

How can one rest all those attractions?

How can one resist the pleasure of "the game of flags," a fatiguing sport in which one sees robust young fellows juggling with enormous shafts around which they have to undulate their fabric in harmonious folds. How can one resist the pleasure of Swiss wrestling, which consists of felling one's adversary by taking hold of him simply by a pair of improvised underpants? How, above all, can one resist the pleasure of the *Hornussen*, a formidable and extremely curious sport, special to a few villages that challenge one another with a fervent rage, my ignorance of which earned me the scornful gaze of the station employee.[32]

I finally discover Rudolph Hermlein on the vast arena of the *Hornussen*.

---

[32] Hornussen was not so very esoteric even in 1906; the Federal Hornussen Association had been founded in 1902 to organize regular competitions, but that news might not have been reported in *Le Matin*.

175

"Bonjour!" he shouts to me, without any other formula of politeness. "Don't disturb me. Later! Later! I'm very busy."

He is attentively watching the course of a kind of hard wooden ball, which, with the aid of a long staff swollen at the end and held in two hands, a peasant is projecting forwards with a prodigious force. A long way away, facing the launcher, in several rows, are about forty players, each armed with a wooden shield.

When the ball passes overhead, they try to interrupt its trajectory by throwing their shields into the air. It is a strange spectacle, as much by virtue of the ferocious cries that accompany it as by the implausible skill of the players, who stop the invisible little ball and have then to dodge a heaven rain of shields capable of demolishing the most solid skulls.

I try several times to extract a few words from Rudolph Hermlein. The interest of the contents does not make me forget Flax and his crimes.

"We'll talk tomorrow!" Hermlein shouts. "No time today. Too many things to do."

"But Flax?"

"There's a big dinner this evening, performances, etc. I'm making a speech. We'll talk tomorrow."

I know my Hermlein. He's as stubborn as a rock. I beg: "One detail? Just one?"

"Oh well—your Dr. Flax is in Switzerland." He indicates the mountains with a gesture.

"Far away?"

"Enough! Tomorrow! Tomorrow!"

"I beg you, Hermlein, is he alone?"

"He's with the Comtesse, his three male accomplices and another woman."

"What other woman?"

"How do I know? And there are children."

I leap into the air.

"What do you mean, children? He hasn't killed them all, then?"

"If he's killed them all, he didn't kill them all in Paris."

"I beg you, Hermlein."

"Leave me in peace, Bernard. I'm fulfilling an important function today. If you don't leave me in peace until tomorrow, I'll shut up completely, and *bon voyage*. Tomorrow, I'll accompany you to a certain place, and you'll learn a great deal."

That is all that I have succeeded in obtaining—and how did I get so much?—from my friend Hermlein. He has an iron head; his obstinacy is famed throughout the land. Nothing can bend him; it's impossible to get one word out of the man that he does not want to say. If there were a hundred people like that in Paris, all reporters would go mad.

176

I hope that my readers will consider, however, that I have not made the journey in vain.

I am leaving tomorrow with Hermlein for Interlaken. You will soon receive, I think, further information about Dr. Flax and his incredible accomplices.

Alain Bernard

ARE THE CHILDREN ALIVE?
THE PUBLIC'S IMPRESSIONS
THE FATHERS AND MOTHERS COME FOR NEWS
A SPECIAL TRAIN

Alain Bernard's telegram has revived general curiosity, although it scarcely had any need of that further leaven.

Our colleague's dispatch, like all those we receive, was pinned up in a display-case at the door of our building. Thousands of people filed past, to reread incessantly, on the little strips printed by the telegraphic apparatus, the text that they had already read, much more comfortably, in their morning paper.

In the morning, we received visits from all the parents from whom the cruel surgeon of the Rue Cassette has stolen children. Because their successive arrivals provoked stirrings in the crowd and overexcited the curiosity of the idlers, it was necessary for us to ask the prefecture for a squad of men to protect our offices.

Having run to obtain news, the mothers and fathers laid siege to our employees, our errand boys and our reporters, who, knowing nothing more than what we published yesterday, were incapable of replying to that vain harassment.

To put an end to the confusion, our administrator had the idea of bringing the parents together in a large room on the first floor. When all of them had been thus assembled, Barbarus climbed on to a chair and, after having obtained silence—not without difficulty—he expressed himself in these terms:

"Mesdames et Messieurs, I shall answer in a few words all the questions that are rising to your lips from your hearts.

"Mesdames et Messieurs, we have published everything that Alain Bernard has sent us, exactly—absolutely everything. On the other hand, we are expecting a further communication from him before this evening. Indeed, Alain Bernard leads us to anticipate that he will spend today gathering information. It's probable that he will draft his communication rather late, in order to send as much as possible at once, naturally taking account of the local telegraphic conditions and the necessities of our print run. We therefore have reason to think that it is necessary not to expect more complete details before ten o'clock at night."

That statement is welcomed by a great murmur of disappointment, which Barbarus quickly suppresses by alleviating the bad impression with a few comforting remarks.

"Nevertheless," he resumes, "We have no pretention to infallibility. A dispatch might arrive before the time that we anticipate. We would not dream of suggesting, when you are all trembling at the possibility that your children are alive, and might be returned to you, that you do not have a right to your legitimate impatience. In consequence, this room will be reserved for the parents of the stolen children. They may either wait here at their ease or come back for news when it pleases them. As telegraphic communications come in, the information they contain will be communicated to them without delay."

A thunder of applause greets this announcement. Barbarus was getting down from his podium when a voice shouts: "I demand to speak!"

The abruptly-improvised president of an assembly, Barbarus does not lose his composure, and immediately slips into his role.

"Monsieur Horace Clépent has the floor."

At that name, a keen curiosity raises a small swell of excitement among the audience.

"It would be extraordinary," shouts the stockbroker, "if none of us rose to his feet to thank, on behalf of all of us, a newspaper whose constant ambition is to serve the public good..." (*Enthusiastic bravos. Acclamations.*) "...the newspaper that was the first to talk about the child-stealers, the first to denounce the probable culpability of Flax, and which, since the commencement of the abductions, has been the perfect interpreter of our anguish and our hopes..." (*Sustained applause.*)

"This just tribute having been paid to gratitude, I shall permit myself now to make a proposition that will, I think, be favorably welcomed. Alain Bernard's telegram has reawakened in us the hope of recovering our children..." (*Cries: "Yes! Yes!"*) "...and the illusions that we are perhaps still nursing no longer seem to be merely deceptive mirages. So, our duty is clear. Let all those of us who can depart as soon as possible for Interlaken!" (*Cries: "That's right, let's go!"*) "We ought not to wait another minute to join Alain Bernard and save the children that the surgeon still has with him..." (*"Yes! Yes!"*) "I therefore propose to charter a special train for us. In such circumstances, the question of expense does not arise. If there are any among us who are not fortunate enough to share the cost, let them come anyway; just let me know. We shall facilitate their journey with a fraternal and discreet good will."

Unanimous bravos greet these words.

The ordering of a special train is immediately decided.

Then an organizing committee is appointed. M. de Vautremesse is president, Horace Clépent treasurer. Alfred Flaquette, Marius Candelaur, M. Joly de Gobely-Franthéon, Sigismond Lévy and the widowed Madame Peinassols are the committee members.

Thanks to the diligent kindness of the Compagnie de l'Est, the parents gathered in our offices were advised, at three o'clock, that the train would leave at five thirty-five.

Clovis Binard

To our great astonishment, we have received the following brief telegram today, still originating from Sarnen:

Serious setback! Nothing can be extracted today from Rudolph Hermlein. Serious discussions in the festival committee. Multiple protests by competitors. Hermlein places that before everything, not listening to pleas or supplications. Am becoming enraged. Hope that we will leave this evening for Interlaken and mysterious abode of Flax, Comtesse, giants and children, perhaps all still alive.
Alain Bernard

Paris, 4 August

NEWS FROM BERNARD
WIDERNUNHUT BROTHERS REALY CALLED HINGERTIL
FLAX IS AT FRUTT

Let me first apologize to our readers. Two days ago I knowingly and voluntarily sent a false item of information.

I never went to Interkaken

I never had any intention of going there.

I only telegraphed that detail to put off the reporters who must, at present, be going to search for me on the banks of the Aar, while I have actually plunged into the mountains in a south-westerly direction, along a sinuous torrent, the Melchaa.

I already anticipated, the day before yesterday, that the stubbornness of Rudolph Hermlein—who, according to his own expression, "never does two things at once"—would inflict the loss of a precious day's endeavor on me.

And indeed, absorbed by a hundred recalculations of accounts, arbitrations, etc., etc., my friend let me down again yesterday and put off until today the first stage of our expedition in search of Flax.

I shall not attempt to describe my state of mind during that day of inaction.

I was within sight of port. In five minutes, Hermlein could bring me up to date, but I ran into the obstinate silence of a man who "never does two things at once." I could have killed him.

I was obliged to gnaw on the bit, the first evening in Sarnen, and the second day in a little village nearby, Sachsein, where I had taken refuge to avoid encountering any Swiss reporter who might have taken it into his head to pass through the town. I had a good nose, for Hermlein was obliged this morning to escape from some German journalists arrived from Munich. He had to employ all kinds of ruses to dodge them. They were already on his heels.

Rudolph Hermlein joined me today in Sachsein at about four o'clock.

"Finally!" I cried.

"Oh, you're always in a hurry. You spend your life running to the fire!"

I grab the collar of his large brown coat. "Not one more word, Rudolph. You're killing me with impatience. Flax, Flax, Flax! I only want to hear about Flax."

Hermlein looks at me and, with a calm and placid smile, says: "It appears that they're very interested in him in Paris."

"Somewhat, Rudolph. You haven't read his story, then?"

"Yes, yes! That's how I knew that you were mixed up in the affair."

"Where's Flax?"

"Out there!" With a gesture, Hermlein indicates the high mountains to the south-west.

"How do you know?"

"I've known the Hingertil brothers for a long time."

"What Hingertil brothers?"

"The ones you call the Windernunhut brothers. A funny name, by the way. Look."

Hermlein takes an ordnance survey map of the region out of his pocket. He points to a chain of mountains. "Read the names of these three adjacent mountains."

I read: *Widderfeld, Nunalphorn, Hutstock...*

"You see! Flax's accomplices have adopted a pseudonym. They didn't look far, and forged a name from the first two syllables of the Widderfeld, the first syllable of the Nunalphorn and the first syllable of the Hutstock. Wider-Nun-Hut. Is your curiosity satisfied?"

"Rudolph, I'll strangle you. It's necessary to tear information out of you. For the love of God, go on, go on...tell me everything you know. So the Windernunhut brothers are really called Hingertil?"

"Yes, that's what it's necessary to call them henceforth. But Bernard, old chap, it's time to set out *en route*."

"To go where?"

"To go and spend the night at Melchtahl, a little village three leagues from here."

"And when we've spent the night at Melchtahl?"

"We'll leave very early the following morning, with a local guide, Werner Dürrer, for Frutt, in the high mountains. We don't really need a guide, but Werner Dürrer is a friend of the Hingertils. We might learn a great deal from him. Let's get going."

"Is there a telegraph at Melchtahl?"

"And a telephone, Bernard. We're in Switzerland, and the smallest places are linked to the big ones by all the wires imaginable. Let's go!"

Hermlein and I start walking, slowly, along easy slopes. The country is pleasant and charming. One can fill one's lungs. I could gladly describe the rich valleys, the prosperous forests and the sound of the waters if my thoughts were not exclusively and constantly orientated toward the child-stealers.

"We're going to follow the left bank of the Melchaa. The path clings to the mountain side and follows al the caprices of the torrent."

"No literature! Flax! Flax! Flax! And more Flax!"

Hermlein, who has never been impatient in his life, not even once, looks at me once again with his placid gaze. I detect a hint there of the idea that he's making fun of me by keeping quiet. I reply immediately to that temptation.

"Old man, I like you a lot, but I swear that if you oblige me one more time to beg to for information, I'll immediately throw you into that ravine."

"Damn! A ninety meter jump! I'd rather chat. So, it was the name Windernunhut that gave me the key to the mystery. I've climbed the Widderfeld eleven times, the Nunalphorn fourteen times and the Hutstock, a superb mountain from which the view is splendid and where the chamois are abundant, some thirty times. You can well imagine that, in those circumstances, that 'Windernunhut' must have struck me.

"I told myself than that Flax's three bodyguards must know the country very well to have baptized themselves in that fashion. Now, there was once a family in Melchtahl reputed for the giant stature of its members, the Hingertils. These Hingertils have all disappeared from the region—except that three brothers born in Melchtahl returned to the locale from time to time in recent years for five days at a time. They astonished us every time the returned by the strangeness of their attitudes.

"It was known that they lived in Paris. They corresponded to the descriptions indicated in *Le Matin*. One was called Chrysostome, the second Wolfgang, the third Numérien, like the Windernunhuts mentioned by your friend Binard. Were they spinning a yarn in telling him that they were Swabians and the sons of a maker of shoemaker's equipment? Of course! They wanted to fool everyone. If Hingertils had been mentioned in the newspapers, we would have figured out that what they were doing here had some connection with Dr. Flax's abductions.

"So, the Windernunhuts were the Hingertils, and those three individuals had been the object of many conversations in the region for more than a year, because they had bought Frutt, and had built up there, on an isolated and deserted plateau, a kind of bizarre fortress, which is an extraordinary puzzle for all our peasants. That's where he surgeon is, with the Comtesse and a company of children."

"Alive?"

"They were five days ago. I saw, with my own eyes, a dozen of those children, very much alive. I don't know what might have happened since." Without transition, Hermlein continues: "Oh, my old Bernard, I'm happy to see you again."

"Tell me about Flax, damn it!"

"Bah! You'll hear enough about him in the days to come. You see, Bernard, the only means of being happy in life is always to stay calm, not to get excited about anything, never to hurry, to be ignorant of haste and fever, and to tell oneself that what one doesn't know today, one will learn tomorrow, unless one dies in the meantime."

"Rudolph, you're making me jump out of my skin."

"Be careful—it's very difficult to get back in once you're out. Come on, my friend, Flax's story might be exciting, but is it worth as much for a healthy soul as this pleasant walk in the veiled light of the falling dusk? Let's be quiet. Our conversation is preventing us from hearing the regular sonority of our footsteps, which are accompanied by an indiscreet echo. There's no joy more profound for those who love nature than to hear oneself waking a long a woody path...

"Come on, Bernard, can all the Flaxes in the world, all the Comtesses de Houdotte, all the Hingertil brothers and all the dramas of civilization compete in interest with the roseate and milky sky that poses over the darkening summits?"

I am obliged to leave Rudolph to his lyricism, and then to his mute contemplation. All my questions are breaking against the inalterable patience of that man, which is like a wall.

And now that he has been gripped by the poetry of things, I realize that nothing will change the course of his thoughts. No one who has not heard one of these big mountain men, men of strength and character, admiring familiar nature, the well-known forest and the beloved peaks—beloved like lovers—can ever have any idea of how dear their country is to them.

I am writing these lines in a little hotel, the Alpenhof, in Melchtahl. A maidservant has warned me that the telegraph office is about to close. I am therefore forced to terminate my dispatch forthwith.

Alain Bernard

THE PARENTS' SPECIAL TRAIN

We have arrived in Interlaken. No Bernard. He is not registered in any of the hotels. What do we do?

Barbarus

BERNARD'S DISGRACE

We have immediately telegraphed to Barbarus to take the entire caravan of parents to Melchtahl.

On the other hand, we have ordered Bernard to cease his functions as a reporter as soon as Barbarus is on the spot and return to Paris as soon as possible.

We cannot admit that, even to put foreign reporters off the track and conserve a lead on certain news, one of our correspondents has caused us to print inaccurate information. Alain Bernard doubtless thought, in falsely informing us of his departure for Interlaken, that the joke was quite innocent. It has had the result of making the parents of the little victims make a long detour, a needless and cruel journey. Alain Bernard will doubtless realize himself that it was in bad taste to amuse himself at the expense of those unfortunate families. He will therefore return to Paris, leaving to Barbarus the honor of discovering Flax's retreat and explaining to us the as-yet-unimaginable mystery of the affair of the child-stealers.

The Editor-in-Chief of *Le Matin*

Paris, 5 August

WITH REGARD TO THE RECALL OF ALAIN BERNARD

In the note that appeared yesterday we announced our intention to recall Alain Bernard as a disciplinary measure. That reporter had failed in his foremost duty, that of exactitude.

Did he not deserve to be published for his incomprehensible neglect, for having, by way of a petty lie, unimportant to him but dolorous in its consequences, steered the parents to Interlaken, who thus wasted a precious day?

But the public has pleaded so fervently in his favor that we have been obliged to renounce that recall.

Fourteen hundred letters have been addressed to us to protest against our severity. Almost all of them, it is true, are signed by gamblers who had bet on Bernard's chances. They would find themselves indirectly handicapped if we persisted in our rigor.

We have, in addition, deemed that the importance of news sent by Bernard, which will take the story of the child-stealers into a new phase, merits some indulgence of an incorrection that is certainly blameworthy but perfectly understandable.

We have given in to these reasons.

The Editor-in-Chief of Le Matin

ALAIN BERNARD'S TELEGRAMS[33]
TOWARD FRUTT

Melchtahl, 3 a.m.

I am to meet Rudolph Hermlein and a local guide, Werner Dürrer, at four-thirty this morning, in order to travel together to Frutt, where Dr. Flax is hiding. We shall arrive soon enough in the morning. I am taking four errand-boys with me who will bring my telegrams to the office at Melchtahl as I write them.

What follows the end of yesterday's article, which I could not send because the telegraph office was closing. It relates to my arrival in Melchtahl and my meeting with Werner Dürrer.

Once Rudolph Hermlein has launched himself into his description of the marvels of the mountain, nothing can stop the flight of a lyricism that is both calm and ardent.

---

[33] It is perhaps worth noting, with reference to the manner in which the fictitious reportage is conveyed from this point onwards, that in 1906 *Le Matin* carried an advertisement beneath its front page masthead boasting of being the only newspaper in Paris to receive news telegraphically from all over the world.

While all my thoughts are extended toward the enormous masses of stone, behind which I divine that the fantastic surgeon is pursuing some unknown work of malediction, I am obliged to listen to a hymn to the dark verdure of the fir trees, the splendor of the maple forests, and the snowy mountains where the chamois, perched on a protruding rock, contemplates with its astonished eye the distant gleams lighting up in the depths of the valleys.

After having traversed a wooden bridge covered by a roof in the Swiss fashion, every plank of which is strewn with the inscriptions of tourists, we pass from the road that goes along the left bank to the path that goes along the right bank. Soon afterwards, we encounter a sawmill, and the village appears in its happy solitude.

Rudolph Hermlein knocks on the door of one of the first houses with his staff.

A voice replies to him from a first floor window. It is that of Werner Dürrer, the guide who will accompany us to Frutt tomorrow.

Soon, Werner Dürrer opens the door and we go up to his dwelling on a wooden staircase that makes the devil of a racket under our heavy boots.

In the upper room we sit down at a humble table, on which an odorous soup is steaming. We have interrupted the family meal.

The wife hastens to fetch glasses.

Three bright-eyed children look at us, half curious and half fearful.

Werner Dürrer is one of those guides who have left a warm and grateful memory in the minds of tourists. He has become the fried of all the travelers he has guided over the hazardous routes of the passes, across disquieting landslides, precipices and the blue crevasses of glaciers. The man is astonishingly handsome, tall and strong, with limbs in perfect proportion. He bears no resemblance to his gnarled and stunted colleagues whom one encounters on the esplanade in Interlaken. He is an athlete whose symmetrical and proud features ennoble the strength of his muscles and bones.

Rudolph Hermlein introduces us.

"Well, Dürrer, what's new?"

"New? Nothing much. I haven't been up to Frutt since the day we went there together, but a friend, Hans Gelper of Kaegswyl, was curious enough to climb up there. Like us, he ran into the walls, the impenetrable barrier that now encloses the property that the Hingertil brothers have built at Frutt. He knocked and shouted at the door, but no one responded. He came back empty-handed, like us. This morning though I had a moment of excitement—my God yes. It was about five o'clock, when I met Wolfgang Hingertil on the road."

"Ah!"

It was me who pronounced that "ah!"—an "ah!" of satisfaction and joy. I finally have them, then, these phantasmal beings who have escaped all searches for many days. I have that unique prey, on the trail of which a thousand reporters have launched themselves in vain.

Involuntarily, I smile at the faces that all my colleagues would pull, who, since the commencement of the affair of the child-stealers, had exhausted themselves without succeeding in getting ahead of my newspaper, which always, always cocks a snook at them and cuts the interesting news from under their feet.

I also think, not without malice, about your noses, my dear friends—your nose, O Barbarus, which is long and pointed, and your nose, O Binard, which is short and obtuse—when you read this dispatch and see melting away, line by line, the hope of winning the bonus of 25,000 francs.

As an everyone down here builds his castles in Spain, I also think about mine, which I shall be able to acquire with that money, my own castle in Spain, which is a little rustic cottage at Moret, on the banks of the Loing, where, on days of rest, one can fish for roach to fry from one's bed, through the window.

Those are all the sentiments expressed by the "ah!" with which I interrupt the guide's story—who looks at me, a trifle astonished by that sharp exclamation.

"Yes," he said. "Wolfgang Hingertil came down from Frutt yesterday evening."

"Did you talk to him?"

"Yes, of course. I asked him what he was looking for in the valley. He told me that he wanted to buy some honey. As I had some to sell, we made a deal—but he wanted three hundred pots and I only had sixty. I promised to get him the rest by tomorrow morning, so I need to go up to Frutt with a mountain cart."

"If you're delivering the honey to him, he'll have to open the door in the wall."

"Obviously."

"And you'll go into the enclosure?"

"If Hingertil lets me, yes. I'll see…we'll see, if you're still determined to climb up with us…"

"Of course—I've come from Paris with that express purpose. Did you question him about the inhabitants of Frutt?"

"Of course—but Wolfgang isn't chatty. He simply replied: 'My dear Dürrer, we were, I believe, born on the same say in adjacent houses. You ought to know me, in spite of the recent years I've spent far from the valley. Well, I tell you that you'll never hear anything from me about our boss. I advise you to repeat that to others who look at me with curious eyes or ask me stupid questions.' That, Messieurs, is almost exactly how Wolfgang Hingertil expressed himself. Then he loaded the sixty pots of honey into a big basket—a tidy weight—and slung the basket over his shoulder. That's all I know for the moment, Messieurs."

After that conversation, Rudolph Hermlein and I leave the guide and go to dine at the Hôtel Alpenhof

We leave at dawn for Frutt, where Dr. Flax, the children, the Comtesse de Houdotte, the Windernunhut/Hingertil brothers and an unknown woman are leading God knows what strange existence.

Alain Bernard

On the road to Frutt, 6 a.m.
Rudolph Hermlein, Werner Dürrer, the four errand-boys whose services I've hired and I are climbing slowly, along a crude, steep and stony path. The vehicle containing the pots of honey is one of those very narrow carts that the Swiss postal service uses for difficult journeys.

The horse climbs one step at a time. It stops abruptly every twenty meters. A grapnel drawn underneath the vehicle digs into the ground then and holds the vehicle on the edge of the precipice. It is bitterly cold. We'd advance more rapidly without the horse.

Alain Bernard

On the road to Frutt, 6.30 a.m.
Professor Flax has been the owner of the entirety of the immense region of Frutt for four years. The Hingertils have served as front men for his purchase of that estate.

Frutt, a high Alpine valley, extremely interesting and wild, is at an altitude of eighteen hundred sand eighty meters. It is surrounded by high peaks.

Once, tourists came in fairly considerable numbers to stay in two hotels. Today, the doctor has had all the passes walled up and an immense structure has been built on the shore of the little Lac de Melch, which is at the entrance to Frutt. No one goes up there any longer, neither tourists not shepherds. The local people have always been intrigued by the mystery constructed up there. No one knows its purpose.

Alain Bernard

On the road to Frutt, 7.30
The Hingertil brothers have been in the locale for several days. No one can tell me exactly how long.

They went up to Frutt via Melchtahl, and have taken up residence there.

In their turn, the doctor and the Comtesse came to "the Fortress"—as the bizarre property is known throughout the region—by another path, whose point of departure is Meiringen, at the end of the Brunig line.

A number of children have been taken to Frutt, one by one, by a woman whose description does not correspond to that of the Comtesse.

Alain Bernard

On the road to Frutt, 7.45

Six days ago, Hermlein and Durrer, as we know, climbed a summit from which one can look down on Frutt. From a distance, with the aid of binoculars, in a large courtyard surrounded by walls, they saw a dozen children who were marching back and for in two rows, in a strange fashion, like automata. They also saw Flax with two women.

Alain Bernard

(On return) Melchtahl, 2 p.m.

Hermlein, Dürrer and I arrived on the plateau, before a wall six meters high, fitted with an enormous iron door.

The three Hingertil brothers were waiting.

Impervious to all questions, they unloaded the pots of honey without saying a word.

After having paid for them they said "*Au revoir!*" and shut the iron door behind them.

I was unable to see anything through the open door. An immense lock situated directly behind it masks the landscape.

I have received orders to return to Paris.

I am desolate, but I shall depart.

Alain Bernard

Melchtahl, 5 p.m.

The parents of the stolen children arrived in Melchtahl at four o'clock, in the midst of an indescribable confusion.

More than seven hundred people, curiosity-seekers, reporters and so on, have already taken this little village by storm.

Horace Clépent, the Baron de Vautremesse, the Comte de Gobely-Franthéon and Madame Peinassols are leaving immediately for Frutt, in spite of the advice of Harmlein and Alian Bernard, who have returned. Werner Dürrer is with them.

So am I.

Barbarus

Melchtahl, 6 p.m.

I have received your countermanding order. I am delighted. The telegraph office is overwhelmed. I fear delays. The crowds in Melchtahl are increasing in volume. Everyone wants to see Dr. Flax's "Fortress." We are waiting for the police to liberate the children.

Alain Bernard

A VILLAGE TAKEN BY STORM

Melchtahl, 7 a.m.

The entire village has been turned upside-down.

Ordinarily, its inhabitants number about three hundred. Eight hundred and fifty people demanded dinner and sleeping accommodation yesterday evening.

The two small hotels, naturally, were inadequate. By eight o'clock it was impossible to obtain, for gold or for silver, the slightest mouthful of bread or slice of sausage.

My fear of seeing a mass influx of journalists and curiosity-seekers has thus been fully justified.

In spite of the good will of the local people, many strangers have not found accommodation in the chalets and have been obliged to leave again, almost all of them on foot.

They have scattered throughout the surrounding area, in particular to Flühli-Ranft, were there are two comfortable hotels and the curé keep a boarding-house. It is more than an hour away; that walk, ordinarily very pleasant, must have seemed very hard to a few travelers, already weary when they arrived in Melchtahl.

I have advised the mothers who came in the special train to seek accommodation at the entrance to the valley of the Melchaa, because it is foreseeable that existence in this small area will become very difficult for a few days. The majority have listened to me. By telephone, I reserved for them all the remaining beds at the Hôtel Nunalphorn, which is set in a delightful landscape not far away, and the Hôtels Krone, Roessli, Sonne and Hirsch in Kerns, another village two and a half hours from Melchtahl.

That precaution having been taken before the great influx of foreigners, the mothers of Flax's victims will have shelter, and will not be subject to any privation.

The famous American policeman William Trisson has been seen.

The greatest bungler in the world, as he is now known, has come this time in the capacity of reporter, on behalf of a large popular Chicago newspaper. A quarter of an hour after his arrival, he sent a long dispatch. One of our colleagues, who had the indiscreet notion of reading over the American's shoulder, was surprised to find Trisson already cabling an interview with Dr. Flax. I would be very interested to know its contents.

Alain Bernard

OUR EXCURSION TO FRUTT
MADAME PEINASSOLS INJURED

Melchtahl, 7.20

We should have listened to the sage advice of Rudolph Hermlein and Alain Bernard, who strongly advised us yesterday not to go up to Frutt so late, with the prospect of returning in the dark.

Preceded by the guide Werner Dürrer, who was making the journey for the second time in one day, we—Horace Clépent, the Baron de Vautremesse, the Comte de Gobely-Franthéon, Madame Peinassols and I—climbed the slope that leads to the mysterious roost that Flax has built at Frutt. We went in a carriage as far as the place where the mountain-path branches off. That accursed route is, it seems, negotiable by a cart, since Dürrer went that way in the morning with a horse-drawn vehicle. How the devil was a horse able to traverse that goat-path dragging a load?

Parisian that I am—and it is true that I already find it difficult to go up the Rue des Martyrs—I huff and pull lamentably in climbing along those stony mountain paths. A thousand sharp corners pierce your skin, insinuating themselves through the excessively thin soles of those who are, like me, venturing over those spikes in bespoke patent-leather shoes. The pebbles cut, bruise, slip, fall and collide with one another, seemingly mocking you, with malevolent little trills. One gets annoyed, taking two steps backwards while trying to take one forwards, with excessively furious energy.

The whole of that ascent, child's play for a man with a little experience, was very long—dolorous, even—for men and a woman who had not slept they night before. Everyone was so stressed in anticipation of the next day that none of the passengers on the special train had given any thought to sleep. The disappointment of not finding Bernard at Interlaken, the departure decided two hours later one receipt of your telegram, the further railway journey from Interlaken to Sarnen, punctuated by the ferry crossing of the Lac de Briens, and then the journey by carriage or on foot to reach Melchtahl, had not permitted anyone to get a moment's rest.

The ascent to Frutt has completely exhausted our little group, courageous enough to attempt the adventure without delay. I have come back done in. Every movement makes me want to cry out; all my joints are agonized.

And our excursion was in vain.

Like all the reporters who followed us, we ran into the wall that Dr. Flax has built at Frutt, which seems insurmountable.

The descent was even more difficult than the ascent. The night was black, absolutely black, and our march uncertain and cruel. The vague light of the lantern that Werner Dürrer had taken the precaution of bringing was insufficient. As for the cold, it was so penetrating that I could hear the Comte de Gobely-Franthéon's teeth chattering alongside me.

To complete the ill luck, Madame Peinassols' valor was poorly rewarded. The courageous woman slipped on a stone and incurred a serious sprain as she fell. We were obliged to hoist our unfortunate companion on to Werner Dürrer's back.

That man is devotion personified. He carried Madame Peinassols for several kilometers.

When we arrived at the place where the mountain path joins the main road, we fortunately encountered a landau that had brought my colleague Galtier of *Le Temps*, Siegmund Feldmann of the Berlin *Lokalanzeiger*, his colleague Levin of the *Boersen Courier* and a woodcutter from Melchtahl. The three journalists intended to go up during the night in order to be at Frutt in the morning.

Scarcely was she laid down in the carriage than Madame Peinassols lost consciousness and it was in that condition that we brought her back to Melchtahl. There, a further hitch! Madame Peinassols had not booked a room. Fortunately the headmistress of the local school took pity on her distress and offered her own bed to the injured woman, who has received the most devoted care.

Madames Clépent, de Vautremesse and de Gobely-Franthéon, having followed the advice of Alain Bernard, who had booked accommodation for them at the Hôtel Nunalphorn in Flühki-Ranft, had not been able to reserve beds for their husbands. They were obliged to spend the night as best they could in the landau.

To restore our spirits, we were only able, on our return, to obtain hot tea and liqueurs—not so much as a crouton!

Barbarus

THE ARRIVAL OF M. HAMARD

Melchtahl, 8.40

Monsieur Hamard has just arrived by carriage. The head of the Sûreté, whom I immediately brought up to date, has told me that an extradition request has already been addressed to the Swiss government, and that the arrest of Flax and his accomplices cannot be more than a matter of hours away.

Three trucks carrying food supplies have arrived from Sarnen.

Bernard

POLICE MEASURES

Melchtahl, 1 p.m.

The flood of curiosity-seekers is still rising.

The disorder is great. The Sarnen police have had to intervene.

The two parallel roads following the torrent of the Melchaa have been blocked. They are the two most important access-routes to the village. The other routes that lead here are only mountain paths, some of them perilous, which the crowds cannot use.

Gendarmes posted at the point where the two roads diverge have orders only to let food trucks, authorities and reporters through—all those, in a word, whose functions or veritable interests have brought them to this remote spot.

Bernard

MADAME PEINASSOLS' ACCIDENT

Melchtahl, 3 p.m.

Madame Peinassols' injury is worse than first thought. It is not a sprain but a broken ankle. The reduction will be carried out by Dr. Stockmann from Sarnen.

Barbarus

Melchtahl, 3.40

A meeting is taking place at this very moment in the dining room of the Hôtel Alpenhof between Monsieur Hamard, Monsieur Bergenholder, the Chief of Police in Sarnen, the Baron de Vautremesse, Sigismond Lévy and Rudolph Hermlein. They are discussing the means of liberating the children as soon as possible.

Bernard

THE MYSTERY OF FRUTT

Melchtahl, 4.30

The numerous reporters who have been to Frutt have all met with the same result. They have stopped at the door in the wall. Then they have come back, without having been able to break the agonizing silence that it the sole response to their appeals.

The question everyone is asking is why Flax has constructed the Fortress of Frutt. With what end? What kind of life is being led by those who have locked themselves away, or have been imprisoned, on that deserted plateau? Everyone is lost in conjectures.

Alain Bernard

THE ARRIVAL OF THE LANDAMMAN

Melchtahl, 5 p.m.

I have been informed that the Landamman, Adalbert Hochberger, the principal magistrate of the canton of Unterwalden, has just arrived at the Hôtel Kurhaus in Melchtahl.

Alain Bernard

Melchtahl, 5.20

Monsieur Hamard has gone to see the Landamman. The forces of the gendarmerie are standing by.

Bernard

Melchtahl, 6 p.m.

No one is in any doubt that the extradition of Professor Flax and the Comtesse de Houdotte will be granted with the briefest possible delay.

But what will become of the Hingertils, who are Swiss subjects? Will Switzerland surrender its nationals to a foreign court?

My friend Rudolph Hermlein, who has just read this telegram, has remarked that we are all talking about extradition, as if the surgeon had fallen into the hands of the authorities. "You're selling the bear's skin," he says. "At least wait until the beast is caught. That might be difficult."

His opinion is that Flax would not have built the Fortress is an inaccessible region is he did not plan to stand firm.

Alain Bernard

Melchtahl, 7 p.m.

Madame Peinassols is as well as can be expected.

Barbarus

Melchtahl, 8 p.m.

Monsieur de Gobely-Franthéon tells me that a police operation against the Fortress of Frutt has been scheduled for tomorrow, at four p.m., so the arrest of Flax and the liberation of the children still alive ought to be imminent.

Bernard

Paris, 7 August

FRANCO-SWISS NEGOTIATIONS
THE QUESTION OF EXTRADITION

The French authorities have been diligent. They have been reproached for their slowness too many times for them not to be granted an honorable mention for their speed on this occasion. Let us therefore congratulate the Ministers of the Interior and Foreign Affairs for the rapidity with which the two administrations have acted since, thanks to my indications, the surgeon's retreat has been revealed.

Monsieur Hamard has departed, as soon as he was able to do so, with the most categorical instructions, to obtain in haste, and by any means, the arrest of the guilty parties and their extradition.

The head of our Sûreté has orders not to quit Flax and the Comtesse until the doors of a Parisian prison have closed upon them.

The plenipotentiary minister of France in Berne has been asked to occupy himself with the extradition of the guilty parties and the repatriation of the children, if there are any.

The Swiss government will not raise any difficulty with regard to surrendering the surgeon and the Comtesse to us with the briefest possible delay.

The Swiss are bringing the best will in the world to the accomplishment of their international duties. The president of the Confederation has given our envoy a formal assurance that the federal authorities will not mount any procedural hindrance.

It was possible to imagine, a few hours ago, that the extradition of the Hingertil brothers might prove complicated, in view of their status as Swiss subjects. It has transpired today, however, that the surgeon's accomplices were granted French nationality two years ago. The objection collapses of its own accord. Since they have abandoned their nationality to adopt ours, the Swiss will treat them as foreigners, in the same way as Flax and the Comtesse de Houdotte.

They will be treated in that fashion when they are caught. The two governments have come to an understanding in order not to drag things out, but it ought to be remembered that there was a third interested party whose opinion was valuable. Was Rudolph Hermlein right to claim that it is necessary not to sell the bear's skin too soon?

According to the latest news, the bear seems to be prepared to defend itself energetically.

Clovis Binard

DR. FLAX WILL RESIST
A BIZARRE LETTER

Melchtahl, 2 p.m.

Twelve gendarmes arrived in Melchtahl yesterday evening.

They have been joined this morning by a crew of firemen from Sarnen.

Assault equipment—ladders, ropes, grapnels, etc.—has already been transported to the wall at Frutt. Since the inhabitants of the Fortress do not want to open the door, entry will be gained over the wall.

Some would prefer to see a repetition of the procedure employed when the house in the Rue Cassette as opened by a dynamite blast.

The expedition is ready to depart, but the authorities and Monsieur Hamard are still hesitating. I have only just learned the reasons for that indecision, the proofs of which we have had for a few hours and which are most astonishing.

The Landamann has received, in the morning mail, a letter signed by Dr. Flax, ostensibly from Frutt, but posted in Lucerne. It was thought at first to be a practical joke, but it has been necessary to yield to the evidence after comparing the handwriting with that of an authentic letter that Monsieur Hamard chanced to take the precaution of bringing with him.

It really is the surgeon who has traced those elongated and cramped lines.

This is the letter, which I have just copied from the original:

Frutt

Monsieur le Landsman,

You are in the process of organizing a small expedition against Frutt and have mobilized gendarmes, policemen and firemen.

I am writing to you in order to spare all those brave men many inconveniences, or, at least, a wasted journey.

Today, I am absolutely unassailable in my fortress.

It is materially impossible to penetrate into my domain with the means at your disposal.

My little garrison will not have to make a great effort of self-defense, because I have domesticated the forces of nature, of which to make use in order to keep out intruders.

I am writing all this as simply as possible, in order to convince you, and to avoid you considering me as a madman.

If you persevere in your project, I shall be obliged to oppose it.

I am therefore washing my hands of the responsibility.

I will strive to avoid disastrous events, but only in the measure that is necessary in order not to compromise my security.

If anyone dies, you will only have yourselves to blame.

You will only be able to avoid accidents and interests by staying away and leaving me in peace, in my home.

I shall only come down from Frutt when it pleases me, at a time of my choosing, when my projects have been fully realized. No one can bend my will.

Only know that the goal that I am pursuing interests humankind entire.
Please accept the assurance of my very distinguished consideration.

Flax

Melchtahl, 3 p.m.

Flax's letter has made a deep impression.

The police operation is becoming more delicate. Everyone wants to avoid bloodshed. The surgeon seems disposed to defend himself in his fort, no matter what the cost, and is now believed to be capable of anything.

The local authorities have asked for instructions from Berne, by telegraph. They intend to cover their responsibility, in the case that any serious accident ensues.

Alain Bernard

Melchtahl, 4 p.m

The expedition has been postponed until tomorrow, perhaps in the afternoon. The Swiss government has given the order to wait. An artillery officer from Thoune has been appointed to command a small attack force, which will be augmented by twenty men.

We have all been very surprised to learn that Dr. Flax's letter bears a Lucerne postmark on the envelope.

That city is several hours from Frutt. How was the letter transported there? By whom?

None of the surgeon's habitual emissaries have been seen in the valleys. If one of the Hingertil brothers had so much as taken ten steps outside, we would know, so closely are the environs of the Fortress watched, night and day, by an army of curiosity-seekers and reporters, who are no less curious than the curious.

Does Flax have means of communication of which we are unaware?

I have had the honor of being received by the Landamman.

The president of this little republic within the greater one, the canton of Unterwalden, Monsieur Adalbert Hochberger, is one of those Swiss dignitaries who, while maintaining an elevated idea of their functions, do not distinguish themselves from their fellow citizens by attitude, costume or ostentation.

He received me with all the simplicity in the world and offered me a glass of beer at a corner of the table. Then he lit one of those huge porcelain pipes that are the glory of German smokers, and I lit a cigarette.

"I can't take it on myself," he said, "to risk those men in an assault on Frutt. That accursed surgeon incontestably has the positional advantage. Inside his Fortress, a single man armed with a rifle could carry out a massacre before being captured by assailants. And we only know the external appearance of the work he's carried out. Perhaps there's an entire system of defense inside that will take us by surprise.

"In order to leave nothing to chance, we're going to reconstitute, if possible, the entire plan of that extraordinary domain of Frutt. All the contractors and workmen who labored on it will be interrogated, and their depositions combined into a collective study. We're also trying to discover the name of the Parisian architect whose designs served for the construction of the principal buildings.

"We hope to discover, by that means, not only the topography but also the purpose of the Fortress, I can't understand, in fact, what motives led Dr. Flax to raise the walls of a fortified castle in such a wild region."

"One assumes that he wanted to make an unassailable refuge in order to retire there with the Comtesse de Houdotte, the Hingertil brothers and the stolen children."

"Obviously. The hypothesis is plausible, but it only answers half the question, and the less interesting part. What remains to be clarified is the goal the surgeon is pursuing. He has not locked himself away up there with a troop of children for the pleasure of it. He has an objective. What? Until we know that, Flax is putting us in a very awkward situation."

"Hasn't the proposal been made to break down the walls with cannon fire?"

"Yes—and it's truly amazing that such a ludicrous idea has come into the minds of so many people. Not one of those advisers has considered that we'd be risking the lives of the children hidden in Frutt and that the remedy might be worse than the disease. A little patience, therefore! It's necessary to wait a day, perhaps two, for the moment to terminate this adventure, which is turning the whole region upside down. It's been a long time since our peaceful countryside was so agitated."

"Do you know, Monsieur Landamman, that the fathers gathered in Melchtahl are beginning to get impatient? There's a great deal of nervousness in their camp. The mothers, who are staying further away, are besieging the telephone, overexciting their husbands with their tearful words."

"Of course! Put yourself in their place. They know that children are sequestered in the Fortress, that among those little prisoners might perhaps—probably—be the one that has cost them so many tears and such desperation, the one that they have raced here at top speed to find. And you want them not to be impatient! It would be simply monstrous if they weren't. But our role, by contrast, is to preach patience. That is, in general, the role of all governments. Knowing all the difficulties, they try to restrain the impulsiveness of those who don't know, or who, knowing imperfectly, hurl themselves head first at the obstacle at the risk of breaking their neck."

"What will you do, Monsieur Landamann, if a private expedition is organized against Frutt?"

"We'll prevent it," replied Adalbert Hochberger, energetically. We cannot allow any individual to carry out a police operation, weapons in hand."

"Don't you fear, though, that the fathers will band together to mount an assault on Frutt themselves?"

"No. They'd need weapons and tools. They don't have them."

Such are the Landamman's declarations. They have their importance, for, if the assault on Frutt is delayed it is necessary to expect loud protests here. The fathers of the stolen children are revolted by the slowness of the Swiss police. It is to be feared that their anger might lead to violent and regrettable actions. Tomorrow might well be turbulent.

Barbarus

Melchtahl, 7 p.m.

Madame Peinassols has spent a peaceful night. Slight fever during the day.

Barbarus

INDIGNATION OF THE FATHERS AND MOTHERS
A PRIVATE EXPEDITION AGAINST FRUTT
THE BARON DE VAUTREMESSE AT THE HEAD
OF THE VOLUNTEERS

The postponement of the assault, telegraphed yesterday by the authorities in Berne, has caused considerable anger to flare up in our little village.

The fathers of the families did not cease, for several hours, to complain violently about the lack of urgency that the Landamman was devoting to the satisfaction of their impatience. If they had had their way, an armed expedition would already have invaded the territory of Frutt.

The official decision, learned in the midst of the effervescence already created by the excessively cool zeal of Adalbert Hochberger, thus therefore provoked clamors of revolt.

That evening, a public meeting was improvised in the restaurant hall of the Hôtel Alpenhof, where almost all the fathers were dining.

They have reached dessert, and clouds of cigar smoke are already rising, when Horace Clépent taps on a glass to demand silence.

"Messieurs," he cries, in the midst of excited acclamations that greet him as soon as the speaks, "the situation that we are in here is intolerable. After a thousand emotions and a thousand agonies, we finally have news of our children. We know that they are not far from us, all or nearly all of them. We want to see them again, and without delay. And just at the moment when we imagine that the Swiss authorities are going to aid us with all their might, we run into prevarications, hesitations and truly monstrous delays.

"Well, Messieurs, I ask you whether we ought not to do without help for which it is necessary to beg, although it ought to be offered to us wholeheartedly. The Landamman Adalbert Hochberger is a charming and devoted man, but he is timorous. If we don't do anything, we won't achieve any result; we'll remain for weeks on end at the foot of these mountains; we'll go up every day to that frightful wall behind which the little beings we cherish and imprisoned, and we'll continue to fret, impotently, in this hotel.

"The pretext that has been given to us for delaying the taking of the Fortress by force does not exist. It is pitiful. How can the threats of the child-stealer stop us? On the contrary, they ought to hasten the assault. The surgeon's letter is the letter of a madman! Our children have fallen into the hands of a lunatic! That opinion ought not to delay the measures to be taken. On the contrary, we cannot tolerate the notion that our little ones are defenseless in the hands of people capable of any delirium, general paralytics, monomaniacs from whom society preserves itself by isolating them in special asylums.

"I don't want to exaggerate. I don't want to increase your anxieties with lightly-uttered suppositions, but nevertheless, the facts don't permit us to close our eyes and blocks our ears. One sentence in Dr. Flax's letter seems to me to be characteristic. 'My little garrison,' he writes 'will not have to make a great effort of self-defense, because I have domesticated the forces of nature, of which me make use to keep out intruders.' If, after that, anyone still claims that Flax, the Comtesse de Houdotte and the few unfortunates that they have drawn into their aberrations are not insane, fit for a straitjacket, I wonder what proof they need.

"And it's before a man who has domesticated the forces of nature that the police and gendarmerie of an entire country are hesitating! It's ridiculous. Well, Messieurs, let us leave them to their timidity. As for us—forward ho! It's necessary to liberate the children as soon as possible, no matter what the cost."

This speech is interrupted by frantic applause.

Monsieur Clépent sits down.

His idea has been understood. The project of mounting an assault on the Fortress of Frutt by means of a private expedition, independently of the governmental forces, is in every mind. They do not even feel the need to formulate it in a precise fashion. They discuss the ways and means without even agreeing the principle.

The Baron de Vautremesse, whose nervousness is ill-adapted to the necessities of the present moment, then cries in a strident voice, in the mist of the tumult: "Let's not wait another minute, Messieurs. Let's go up to Frutt this very night, and take the Fortress by storm. Since yesterday evening, I've been convinced that we can no longer count on rapid action by the public force. I have taken my precautions in consequence. Let those who want to wait, wait. Personally, I shan't wait any longer.

"We have no weapons—we shall have them tonight! The Landamman has said that we wouldn't dare attack Frutt without rifles—and, indeed, it would be reckless to attempt such desperate means without having a bullet handy for the lunatics that Monsieur Clépent has just described to us. But those rifles, I repeat, we shall have.

"We have been told that the local people will not give us the military weapons that Swiss law leaves at their disposal in every hearth. That's true, but we have something better. Forty of these mountain men, among whom heroism is an atavistic quality, have offered me their aid. They will not lend us their rifles. That would seem to them to be an antipatriotic crime—but they will come themselves, arms shouldered."

At this moment, Rudolph Hermlein protests sharply against the Baron's speech. "The local men who have promised your their collaboration were wrong to do so," he cries, indignantly. "Our republics can only survive if the citizens obey the authorities. I oppose the projected expedition with all possible fervor. When the government, which doubtless has excellent reasons, has given us permission to act as we please, you can count on me for anything, and I won't cede first place to anyone else, but for the moment, I beg you, remain tranquil in Melchtahl. It's better to advance slowly but surely."

In spite of all the sympathy that the Swiss painter inspires, Hermlein's proposal obtains no success with the majority. It is nevertheless supported by Alfred Flaquette, who pronounces a few reasonable words.

"Do I need to affirm that I share the general impatience?" he says. "But I think that we would be wrong to hurry our decisions. If Dr. Flax really is mad, it's important not to overexcite him by an improvised attack that cannot succeed. A setback would be disastrous. Let's not forget, Messieurs, that he has hostages in his hands. If we give him the time, between the attack and his capture, to exercise some kind of vengeance against them, we might perhaps end up with a disaster that will make the world tremble.

"In those circumstances, my advice is to leave all responsibility to the Swiss authorities. The children will remain in the Fortress for a few more days. I deplore that with all my heart, but we will have preserved the best chance of finding them safe and sound. It's not with forty local men that we can think of storming Frutt. If we don't intervene in overwhelming fashion, by invading the Fortress from all sides at once, in order to submerge the lunatics under the flood of assailants, we risk, I repeat, the worst catastrophes."

While speaking, Monsieur Flaquette realizes that his opposition is not having the slightest effect.

The great majority is in favor of violence.

I ought to add that the mothers of the children, who are living some way away, and following our discussions by telephone, are urging their husbands to extreme measures.

The party of violence holds sway over the sage.

Furious, Rudolph Hermlein threatens to leave Melchtahl and return to his brushes in his studio at Engelberg. Alain Bernard and I spend a whole hour begging him to stay. And it is not, as is well-known, an easy matter to convince the artist once he has made a decision.

The Landamman, naturally warned immediately, declares that he will not allow the expedition of which the Baron de Vautremesse has just been appointed the leader to leave.

I meet Monsieur Hamard at about midnight at the door of the Hôte Alpenhof. He has been warned about the plot that is being hatched.

"It's absurd!" he exclaims. "We're going to alienate the sympathies of the Swiss. We're going to complicate the conflict with thoughtless actions. I have no means of preventing the Baron de Vautremesse and Monsieur Clépent from trying to take the Fortress, but they'll fail. The only result will be to aggravate the situation of the captives, and to alienate the Swiss government and the Landamman, who are entirely on our side."

In spite of all Monsieur Hamard's objurgations, the Baron de Vautremesse has spent the day organizing a expedition, which will depart tomorrow morning.

It is necessary to expect grave events.

Barbarus

P.S. Madame Peinassols, who is getting better, is also of the opinion that the parents of the victims should not hesitate or delay.

AN INTERVIEW WITH DR. FLAX, BY WILLIAM TRISSON

New York, via P.Q.

The Chicago *Morning Star* has published a sensational interview with Dr. Flax by the famous Trisson, who has become a newspaper correspondent following his resounding judiciary blunders.

The text is undoubtedly the one that the American telegraphed, off the cuff, as soon as he arrived in Melchtahl, whose drafting was observed by an indiscreet colleague.

The ex-detective relates that he has been able to get into the Fortress, converse with the surgeon, the Comtesse and the Hingertil brothers, and that he has seen some of the children.

Dr. Flax has not abandoned himself to excessive confidences with Trisson. He has simply told the American reporter that the motives for which he built the walls of Frutt will soon be revealed. The surgeon has nevertheless let it be understood that all the abductions have been for the objective of vengeance, on the subject of which he is, for the moment, maintaining silence.

The skillful Comtesse, it appears, even in the Alpine heights, wears dresses of the greatest elegance. She has confessed, in that conversation, to having been the doctor's mistress for a long time.

The Hingertil brothers have only played minor roles in the affair. They are merely simple employees paid for specific tasks.

The children are well. They are suitably cared for and nourished. They all sleep in a big dormitory whose windows are decked with nice cretonne curtains. A few of the little ones, having tried to resist their jailers, have been the victims of the worst punishments. The surgeon has thus subdued the rest, of course. Three of the children subjected to these excessive punishments have died.

According to William Trisson, the means of defense at Dr. Flax's disposal are not considerable. The surgeon is only protected by the thickness of the walls. If such an occurrence happened in Chicago, the reporter adds, in conclusion, the children would have been rescued two hours after the discovery of the place where they had been hidden.

We are, of course, only publishing the news sent by William Trisson for informational purposes, without the slightest guarantee, and, so to speak, with smiling skepticism.

The celebrated policeman, who arrested the secretary of the King of the Belgians, has accustomed us too much to those American Gasconades that are known as bluff. We cannot accord him the slightest credence today.

Let us remark that we do not know how he got into the Fortress, by what magic he was able to go up there, stay there and come back down again without having been seen by his colleagues.

We have, for the sake of amusement, telegraphed Bernard to ask him to interview William Trisson about his supposed exploits. The American lent himself to it gravely. He maintained energetically, and in spite of the most blatant implausibility, the veracity of his information. As a scorer of coups William Trisson outdoes his most inimitable compatriots in that genre, and God knows that he exhibits an extraordinary aplomb.

Clovis Binard

AT MELCHTAHL
THE FAILURE OF THE VAUTREMESSE EXPEDITION
WHO WARNED FLAX?
AN UNEXPECTED EVENT

Monsieur de Vautremesse is a marvelous organizer. It only required a few hours for him to assemble a veritable army, with all sorts of siege apparatus that one would have thought it impossible to discover within the bounds of a remote canton.

All kinds of ladders have therefore met up under the walls of Frutt. All kinds of grapnels and hooks have been brought by the local men, with an indescribable good will and enthusiasm.

We left early this morning to conquer the Fortress.

Our troop, composed of fathers gathered at Melchtahl, mountain men recruited by the Baron and a hundred journalists, is numerous. In addition, two or three hundred villagers from the neighborhood have left their houses, with their wives and children, to watch the attack.

The Landamman has not even tried to impede the impulsion of the crowd, as might have been feared.

Nevertheless, at the place where the mountain path leaves the main road, a gendarme is stationed, grave and stiff. Without saying a word, he lets the armed troop pass, but, notebook in hand, he writes down the names of all those who file past him whom he knows.

The ascent commences in an extremely picturesque order.

The Baron de Vautremesse, who everyone salutes as leader, has attached to his arm, as the sole distinctive symbol, the white leather belt normally tightened around the waist of the proprietor of the Hôtel Alpenhof.

Behind him march fifty peasants armed with military rifles. They climb with a fine and determined martial stride. Truly, a land that has such defenders in similar gorges has nothing to fear from external enemies.

This group is followed by the fathers of the young victims and the troop of curiosity-seekers.

Sometimes at the front, sometimes in the middle and sometimes at the back, the journalists, somewhat reminiscent of horseflies, offer lavish advice that no one wants.

The cold, dry weather and the pure air favor the songs with which the Swiss accompany their march. Man and women adjust their pace to the slow measure of the heroic choruses. To low and profound voices high and sometimes strident voices respond. Then the rhythm of sparkling yodels, prodigious Tyrolean roulades, shakes the echoes of the mountains, reverberating in the distance. It is a superb spectacle. It is always quite beautiful to see an enthusiastic and disciplined crowd advancing, whose catchy songs awaken the interior flame.

Half way up, the column is joined by Werner Dürrer.

The guide has hesitated before coming with us. He is too closely linked to Rudolph Hermlein. At first, he wanted to show solidarity with the sulkiness of the painter, who has stayed in Melchtahl to emphasize his opposition. But Dürrer has been unable to resist the thought that the children might be freed without him. After having given us a start, he has hurried to catch us up.

When the troop arrives about half an hour from the Fortress, the Baron de Vautremesse makes a broad signal with the arm to which the singular captain's badge I mentioned is attached. From top to bottom of the column snaking upwards along the narrow path, silence falls.

Then, the order is transmitted from mouth to mouth: "No more noise; no more singing."

It is necessary not to warn the inhabitants of the Fortress of the enemy's approach.

That precaution is, alas, futile. The first people who reach the door stop dead, stupefied. A handwritten notice is stuck there with the aid of four drawing pins. It reads:

Go back to your homes. Your efforts are stupid.

You will not get in. You will not achieve anything.

If you persist in not leaving me tranquil, I will show you that I do not make vain threats.

I will immediately use against you the least of the natural forces obedient to me.

I hope that that correction will suffice, and that, having observed your impotence, you will not oblige me to make use of more murderous engines to rid myself of you definitively.

A brief discussion is held then before that notice, between Clépent, de Vautremesse, Werner Dürrer and Holeman, from Sarnen, whom the Swiss troops have elected as lieutenant and interpreter.

"It's his madness continuing," cried the Baron. "Pay no heed to it, I implore you."

That prayer is heard. Some volunteers, however, are already a trifle discouraged. They were counting on taking the surgeon by surprise. How—by whom—has he been warned of our plans?

The Baron de Vautremesse deploys his men around the door of the Fortress. He enjoins a few mountain men to play a police role and keep the curiosity-seekers away from the danger zone. He makes the reporters promise not to impede the assailants by an excess of curiosity.

The first operation consists of placing a large ladder against the wall of Frutt, in order to try to see inside.

A mountain man, a sergeant of firemen in a small village in a nearby valley, is charge with that prelude to the battle.

Scarcely has he grasped the ladder, however, than a hum is heard: a muted, precipitate vibration; a profound, unexpected roulade.

Everyone looks on, slightly fearful, with the conviction that the Fortress, silent a little while before, no inhabitant of which is perceptible, and which is not pierced by any loophole through which a rifle might be fired, will nevertheless put up a formidable resistance.

The man tries then to stand his ladder up against the wall. Extraordinarily—which strikes us with further amazement—the ladder has scarcely been set against the walls than it is abruptly toppled, as if an invisible spring had hurled it backwards. Immediately afterwards, the mountain men who are furthest forward turn round and flee with loud cries.

I beat the retreat with them, suddenly gripped by a strange sensation: the sensation of blood flowing into the veins, causing them to swell, about to burst out of its envelope—a mysterious, crazy, intolerable sensation.

It is, apparently, as if we have been electrocuted by a fluid that now surrounds the walls of Frutt to an extent of ten meters. It is no longer possible to approach the walls. The boldest, who risk it, are the victims of those muted discharges, which, although they are not mortal, are terribly painful.

So, Flax has not lied. He is the master of some exceptional invention, some new machine, against which all our efforts break like glass.

So, Flax is not mad. He threat was not dictated by a delirious brain, but by a mind conscious of realities, sure of itself.

And it is necessary to go back down to Melchtahl as we came, to go back without having done anything or obtained anything, stopped by a barrier all the more insurmountable because it is mysterious and invisible.

I cannot describe the discouragement of the fathers of the children during the descent. They are convinced, now, that Flax is invincible within his walls, that his rascality is shielded from all punishment.

But what is the strange and powerful fluid that the surgeon has at his disposal?

Barbarus

207

9 August

THE DAY AFTER THE FAILURE
THE OPINION OF THE LANDAMMAN
OF UNTERWALDEN

Melchtahl

The failure of the Vautremesse expedition has left everyone dazed.

Even those who predicted its failure were unable to anticipate the singular means of defense that D. Flax has used. The nature of the fluid surrounding the walls of Frutt with an armor more solid than if it were composed of iron and steel is discussed endlessly.

The local people who have climbed up to those diabolical heights today have told us that the hum has ceased, that it is possible once again to approach the door. However, no one has any doubt that if a new attack took place, the surgeon would be able to make use of his curious machine again.

The mothers have come to Melchtahl today in numbers, and it has been a day of tears and despair.

I have been to wait for the Landamman on the road to Sarnen. He had returned to the town in order to confer with a few members of the government of Unterwalden.

"The French," he told me, "have been punished for their sins. I cannot affirm, however, that we would have succeeded if we had been given the time to prepare an assault at our ease. Who could have imagined the unimaginable resistance that the bizarre refugee of Frutt has mounted?

"The defeat of the Baron de Vautremesse and his troops dictates new duties to us. No one can any longer claim that Dr. Flax's threats are those of a madman. They are the considered threats of an astonishing man, a man of genius who will not be mastered easily. He has written that he has domesticated the forces of nature. He has indeed domesticated them. The proof is there.

"I have just consulted a scientist in Sarnen to try to obtain an explanation of the phenomenon that drove you all away from the walls of the Fortress as if with a hand. He was unable to respond. The hypotheses he put forward have no more value than those the ignorant were formulating yesterday evening. The conclusion remains, nevertheless, that it is more necessary than ever to take precautions and not undertake anything lightly. Your friends' adventure will have had one result, at least. The expedition that we were in the process of organizing rapidly will be postponed once again, until further notice."

Barbarus

WHAT IS FRUTT?
HOW WAS THE FORTRESS BUILT?

While Barbarus was accompanying the Baron de Vautremesse's expedition, I was occupied in a meticulous investigation to determine exactly what the domain of Frutt is, and what kind of construction the doctor has built there.

Frutt is a high valley, extremely uneven, filled with ravines and crevices, at the bottom of which grow thousands upon thousands of the pretty Alpine roses that climbers are so fond of weaving into large bouquets, trophies of their excursions.

The mean altitude is about 1,880 meters.

High mountains surround the valley. At dusk, they design formidable rows of teeth upon the darkening sky, whose aspect is grandiose.

Some of these summits are celebrated among mountaineers: the Boni, the Spicherfluh, the Abgschutz, the Glockhaus, the Wild Geissberg, the Rothsandnollen, and above all the Erzegg, the Balmereghorn and the Hohenstollen. The last-named summit is visited by all true Alpinists who pass through the region. It is famous for the beautiful space it discovers, and for the marvelous view that one enjoys therefrom, but the excursion is not recommended for casual climbers who have faint hearts and fear vertigo.

The mountains in question vary between 2,000 and 2,800 meters. They are thus small fry by comparison with the great colossi nearby, especially the Titlis, whose marvelous hump of snows and glaciers is visible from Frutt.

The valley of Frutt is well known to botanists, who encounter the rarest mountain flowers there. In the summer, in the midst of holes, crevasses and a few snowfields that the sun never succeeds in melting, there is an astonishing flowering of pale yellow or red gentians, blue thistles, saxifrage, Alpine myosotis, veronicas, buttercups, cyclamens, mosses and curiously complicated lichens.

The region, which the friction of ancient glaciers has polished or dislocated, according to the location, sometimes resounds to the piercing whistles of marmots, which wake up in spring from the lethargic sleep that paralyzes them during the winter months. Occasionally, one sees a fickle hare or a snow partridge suddenly making off. From time to time, a vulture in search of prey soars high in the sky, in slow, tranquil and menacing flight.

Not one tree; the last firs stop at the threshold of the valley. A fairly extensive lake is hollowed out at the foot of the mountains that border Frutt. They are mirrored in that water, bluer than the sky. By moving around the marshy banks one can contemplate the neighboring summits, one by one, in its depths.

Before the purchase of Frutt by Dr. Flax, the region was populated by immense herds of the little cows of the high Alps, which, surrounding a bull with a low head, raise their heads as humans pass by, examining them with anxious eyes. A few cheese-makers' cabins, where the harvest of milk was centralized every day for the manufacture of Gruyère cheese were scattered around the lake. Two hotels of a charming simplicity, built of wood, were insufficient during the two months of high summer to lodge the Alpinists faithful to the wild reason.

They flocked there, not only to climb in the neighboring mountains but to visit profound caves whose limits were unknown and to admire the outflow of the Lac de Melch. There, in fact, the water pours into an enormous hole and falls to unknown depths to be lost in the bowels of the earth.

The domain of Frutt and the adjacent region, which is known as the Tannenalp, were communal land. It was, therefore, to the communes that Dr. Flax—or, rather, the Hingertil brothers who represented him—had to address themselves four years ago to obtain the cession.

The sale was completed by a vote of the popular Parliament, the Landesgemeinde, which brings together all the citizens of the canton once a year for the elaboration of the principal laws. One of the conditions stipulated in the contract was that the Hingertil brothers would replace by purchases in the surrounding areas the pasturelands lost by the local livestock-owners. Flax's surrogates did not bargain, and paid without argument a price that silenced all protests. The doctor also bought the houses constructed on the plateau and the two hotels.

I have been to see Monsieur Reinhardt, who ran the more prosperous of the hotels in Frutt.

"The conditions that the Hingertils proposed to me," he said, "were so attractive that I could only accept. But what can he be doing up there, your surgeon?" The hotelier extended his hand, mutilated by a lightning-strike during an expedition to the summit of the Hohenstollen, toward the mountain. "The country is only habitable for three months of the year, and it's not easy to get supplies up there."

Once the Frutt plateau was the property of the Hingertils, foreign workmen were seen arriving in the region, French foremen with Italian crews. They set about working the rocky ground as best they could to establish foundations and construct, to begin with, an encircling wall enclosing a large area all around the lake. After that they erected a large building that had no fewer than forty windows on one side. The two hotels were not destroyed and remained annexed to the complex.

In the center, on the shore of the lake, the workers raised an enormous construction whose purpose no one ever divined. It appears that it has the form of an immense gasholder pierced with tiny windows.

When everything was complete, the inhabitants of the lower valleys observed the transportation of furniture, quantities of beds and all the utensils indispensable to life. In one wing, the Helvetic Society of Zurich installed powerful dynamos, which, I am told, can furnish as much as thirty thousand horsepower. An exceptional large steam-engine was similarly set up by the Escher-Wyss Company of Winterthur.

All these arrangements were, naturally, much discussed in the region. People wondered for a long time what extravagant individual was going to take up residence up there, in that beautiful and picturesque but inhospitable region.

There was talk of an industrialist who had found a means of extracting some rare product, perhaps gold, from the rocky matter—the construction of a factory by an inventor as rich as he was crazy.

The local people interrogated the workers, who did not know anything. Even the overseers were building without knowing the purpose of their endeavor. The French architect who came to supervise the work from time to time was impenetrable.

As for the Hingertils, they contented themselves with smiling vaguely when they spent a few days in the locale and anyone asked them who the eccentric was on whose account futile millions were being lavished on those heights.

In the end, the curiosity abated.

For a long time, the strange establishment at Frutt went unused. Once finished, the buildings were locked up and remained under the guard of a mountain man. The latter lived in the former Hôtel Reinhardt and never went into the other buildings. Recently, a few weeks before the arrival of Flax, one of the Hingertils spent a few hours at Frutt. On the day before the first children were brought to the fortress, he came back and dismissed the former watchman, to whom he gave a handsome gratification.

We know now, and I have already recorded, that Flax and the Comtesse came to Frutt later, via another route, which, departing from Meiningen, continues through Innetkirchen on the other side of the valley.

All these details are of no use in clarifying the mystery.

Why have Dr. Flax, the Comtesse de Houdotte and the Hingertil brothers kidnapped children in order to take refuge with them in this remote elevated region, behind insurmountable walls and an iron door?

Alain Bernard

In the midst of all our excitement an idyll has flourished. Today we are celebrating the engagement of our friend Barbarus and Madame Peinassols.

Paris, 10 August

INTERVIEW WITH M. D'ANGLINEY

I have been to ask Monsieur d'Angliney for his impressions of the extraordinary news that has been sent to us from Frutt. What is the opinion of the celebrated physicist and physiologist regarding the fluid with which the surgeon has armored himself, if it is permissible to say that one can armor oneself with a fluid?

The scientist did not attempt to hide his perplexity.

"The adventure of Dr. Flax," he declared, "seems to me to be increasingly enigmatic. When children's skulls were discovered in the Rue Cassette I thought we were at the end of our confusion and that the truth regarding Dr. Flax's actions was about to be made clear. You can well imagine that his flight, and that of the Comtesse, did not astonish me. It was to be expected, after the charge-sheet that my colleagues and I had drawn up against the child-stealers. But I confess that all the events that have followed it have plunged me into doubts from which I cannot escape. I've turned the problem over in my mind endlessly, but I can't glimpse any key.

"Now that it has been determined that the children's skulls in the Rue Cassette were simple anatomical preparations, such as can be found in many laboratories, and it is gradually being confirmed that all the children are gathered in the Fortress of Frutt, in truth, I no longer know what to think."

"My dear Master, are you not of the opinion that the surgeon and his companions are insane?"

"Insane! That's very premature. If they are insane, theirs is no ordinary inanity. The very originality of all this makes me believe that they're of perfectly sound mind."

"How, then, do you explain the surgeon's emigration to a region that is, in sum, uninhabitable?"

"Oh, I renounce explanation. I merely observe that Dr. Flax has, once again, made a very interesting discovery. I knew, like everyone else, that the man of genius in question had singularly extended the domain of science in physiology. I did not know that he was a physicist."

"Have you given any thought, my dear Master, to the fluid mentioned in the dispatches from Melchtahl?"

"Yes, but the result of my reflections isn't brilliant. I suppose, vaguely, that it's a matter of electricity—without, however, being able to affirm it. Your colleague wrote that he felt as if he were electrocuted. As he has doubtless never been electrocuted before, it's quite possible that he was mistaken about the nature of the sensation that drove him away from the all of Frutt so violently. In any case, if the fluid is electricity, as, strictly speaking, the installation at Frutt of powerful steam engines alongside powerful dynamos could lead one to suspect, then Dr. Flax has invented a previously unknown means of surrounding a large area with a profound and broad electric zone. But don't take that information too literally. It's necessary not to draw overly bold conclusions from the vague indications that it has been possible to telegraph to you from Switzerland."

"Permit me, my dear Master, to ask you whether you still believe, in spite of everything, that Flax is a criminal?"

Dr. d'Angliney remained thoughtful for a few moments. Then he went on: "Would you like to know what I think, deep down? Well, perhaps it's necessary to expect revelations that will make us change our opinion about Dr. Flax's actions, completely."

Monsieur d'Angliney would not consent to explain further. I retained the clear impression that he is no longer as ardent in his opposition to the surgeon of the Rue Cassette.

"You know," he said to me, in concluding the interview, "you ought to pay a visit to Frantz Jourdain. He might be able to give you useful information. I learned yesterday that he's the one who drew up the plans for the Fortress."[34]

AT THE HOME OF THE ARCHITECT OF THE FORTRESS

Naturally, I did not need that invitation to be repeated and I raced to the house of the celebrated architect right away.

Frantz Jourdain, whose distinctive physiognomy and keen eyes are well known in Parisian society, lives amid trinkets and paintings that reveal an artist and a poet. It is very much the home of a man who, against contrary winds and tides, against fossilized palettes and ancient brushes, dared to organize an autumn Salon, to the advantage of young and bold painters.

"I can guess the object of your visit," he said to me, smiling. "I promised Dr. Flax to remain silent. I've kept my word, but everything comes out eventually. Well, yes, I built the Fortress of Frutt."

"Can you show me your plans?"

"No, no. I repeat that I made a promise, on the first day that the professor made me party to his projects, never to reveal anything about my endeavors."

"You were a friend of the doctor?"

"I wasn't, but I am now. Yes, since the opportunity presents itself, I have no hesitation in proclaiming that, in spite of everything, I stand four-square with the doctor, the Comtesse de Houdotte and the Hingertil brothers."

"With the Hingertil brothers too?"

"Yes. What brave men! Not at all the coarse and rustic peasants that some of your colleagues have described. Remarkable and rare minds, in their rude and massive envelope! They too are learned men, scientists, true philosophers—not

---

[34] Frantz Jourdain (1847-1935) was the architect of numerous buildings in Paris from the 1880s onwards. In 1903 he was the founder and first president of the *Salon d'automne*.

professors of philosophy or litterateurs, but great and simple souls who dominate humankind from the height of a considerable and modest science. Oh, an hour's conversation with those fellows consoles you for a year's interaction with our 'very Parisian' minds and our performers."

"And the Comtesse de Houdotte?"

"She's likewise a woman of great worth. There's no one I think, even among the friends who've abandoned her today with a certain excessive ease, who claims otherwise."

"And Dr. Flax?"

"Flax is a man of utter genius, of superhuman genius. I know him well. Every time I've had the opportunity to spend an hour of intimacy with him, I've retained a unique impression: that of finding myself in the presence of a sort of demigod, whose brain gives birth to ideas so elevated that they far surpass the understanding of the most learned and independent men.

"Transport a Chinese peasant from central China suddenly to the Opéra and play him *Tristan und Isolde*, and he would think that he had been brought into a society of monstrous and supernatural people. Dr. Flax has always shown a certain scorn for his contemporaries because, when he talks to one of them, even among the most intelligent, it is as if he were playing *Tristan und Isolde* before the Chinaman from central China.

"So, without knowing anything about Dr. Flax's projects, without even attempting to understand why he has locked himself away at Frutt with the children he abducted, I affirm loudly, with all my conviction and from the utmost depths of my conscience, that the surgeon is pursuing a goal out there for which humankind will have to congratulate him."

Thus Frantz Jourdain expressed himself. Those statements caused me some surprise. Given that Dr. Flax has such men to defend him, and given that a scientist like Monsieur d'Angliney, long considered as the surgeon's adversary but not hesitant, seems, at the very moment when the professor's culpability appears certain, more indulgent toward him, it is not impossible to imagine that this affair might conclude in a manner very different from the one anticipated.

Clovis Binard

OPINION IN MELCHTAHL
THE AUTHORITIES NO LONGER AGREE
THE EFFORTS OF OUR REPORTERS

Melchtahl

Recent events have once again put off the time when an official expedition will take possession of Frutt. The delay is not merely due to the precautions that need to be taken in order to be sure of success, however. There is a conflict between the government of the small canton of Unterwalden and the federal government in Berne.

According to the constitution, the central authority of the Swiss Republic has the sole right to negotiate with foreign states, but the cantons have reserved the prerogative of maintaining particular links with regard to questions of political economy, neighborhood and, above all, policing. These arrangements cannot, of course, contain anything contrary to the general conventions signed by the Confederation.

In the matter of Dr. Flax, the Landamman of Unterwalden and the authorities in Berne are not in agreement of points of detail. The Landamman would like to be able to deal directly with Monsieur Hamard, while the central government prefers to negotiate with our minister in Berne. A Councilor of State had just arrived in Melchtahl to try to put an end to this disagreement.

You have announced that a captain of artillery from Thoune has been appointed to direct the police expedition against the surgeon. That officer has arrived, but he has not yet received orders. He is waiting, spending his days solving chess problems.

The general opinion here is that Flax, from the first day that he proposed becoming the owner of Frutt, had the intention of taking refuge here at a given moment, with stolen children.

The abductions were, therefore, already decided more than four years ago, when the Hingertil brothers were negotiating the initial acquisition of the terrain around the Lac de Melch.

The entire organization of Frutt was planned in order to serve one day, long after, as the refuge of the surgeon and his victims.

I am equally convinced, not only that Flax has not killed any of the children, but that they are all gathered, at this moment, within the walls of the fortress. Not one of them is lacking, in my opinion.

Rudolph Hermlein, Werner Dürrer, Alain Bernard and I are leaving tonight for a slightly hazardous, perhaps even a trifle heroic, expedition, which might perhaps procure us some interesting new information.

Permit me not to say any more today, and to keep a surprise in store for you.

Barbarus

THE DEATH OF ALAIN BERNARD
A VICTIM OF PROFESSIONAL DUTY

It is with sadness mingled with profound amazement that we learn today of the unexpected death of our worthy comrade Alain Bernard.

Just the day before yesterday we published one of his articles.

Our readers will regret as much as we do the disappearance of that serious and reflective intelligence, whose sole ambition was to satisfy them, of that worthy, hard-working man, who was also a courageous man.

Our profession, so difficult and so exhausting, which already grinds temperaments down like a mill, counts its obscure heroes and martyrs in greater numbers than might be thought.

Great reportage has its battles, in which the most noble of us fall, often fatally.

Alain Bernard has perished, a victim of his devotion to our profession.

His memory will remain among us.

Alain Bernard died on the field of honor.

Clovis Binard

Here are the dispatches that informed us of the misfortune. We publish them in the order of their receipt.

Melchtahl, 7 a.m.
To the Editor-in-Chief, Paris

I am hastening to send you the news that your colleague Barbarus transmitted to me earlier this morning, via a mountain man. I am transcribing it as best I can decipher it. It is scribbled on a scrap of paper:

Please telegraph Paris as soon as office opens. Complete failure of expedition announced yesterday. Alain Bernard killed, Rudolph Hermlein wounded.
Barbarus

Permit me to add to this communication, which has put us all in mourning, the condolences of the fathers of the children gathered here. I am serving as their interpreter.

Alain Bernard was such a devoted man! He had devoted himself wholeheartedly to the work of rescuing our children.

Please indicate to me the situation of his wife. Indicate to us the extent of our duty.

Horace Clépent

AN UNFORTUNATE EXPEDITION
ALAIN BERNARD'S FALL
A FORTY METER LEAP
RUDOLPH HERMLEIN'S COURAGE

Melchtahl, 10 a.m.

Such is my emotion and fatigue that I can scarcely succeed in tracing these words on returning from the expedition in the course of which our friend died.

Rudolph Hermlein had indicated a bizarrely formed crag to us from which it was possible to slide down into the Fortress. The enterprise demanded a boldness and self-composure proof against anything.

Behind the Lac de Melch there is a sheer mountain slope that rises up for more than four hundred meters. The wall that encloses the surgeon's property runs along the base of that formidable rock-face. The highest part of the block protrudes into the air, seemingly scornful of the laws of equilibrium. Underneath, the wall slopes inwards in such a fashion that the base is ten meters behind the extremity of the summit. A plumb-line launched into the void would thus fall inside the barrier behind which Flax appears to be invincible.

The disposition of the location permits the plan made by Hermlein and Alain Bernard to be deduced. It was calculated on the plan of the famous eagle-hunt that the Swiss had once organized, with which my unfortunate colleague entertained his readers in his first dispatch from Sarnen. The two friends proposed, as you will already have understood, to follow the course of the plumb-line through the air.

We departed for the fatal operation yesterday evening, at ten o'clock.

There were eight of us: Alain Bernard, Hermlein, the guide Dürrer, four mountain men—robust fellows—and me.

The instruction had been given to meet up in the last house in the village, on the road to Frutt. Hermlein had hidden there, in the course of the afternoon, ropes, pulleys, pitons, axes, hammers, etc.

As soon as we were assembled, he distributed the loads, and we set off, silently, through a damp and heavy night.

I shall not give details of the ascent, which seemed to me interminable and made me suffer cruelly. If the people of the plain knew how lucky they are!

After a hundred turns and detours, ten climbs in which my friends had to hoist me up like a parcel, and during which we were subjected to curious optical illusions, we finally reached the summit of the rock that overhangs the Fortress.

I risked going to the edge.

In the complete, diabolical darkness at my feet, I saw a tiny light scintillating.

With the aid of binoculars, I was able to see that it was the window of a lighted room.

217

The Swiss rapidly set to work.

In anticipation of the operation, two of them had felled a sturdy fir-tree during the day, which they had dragged up to those heights where trees can no longer survive. They stripped the accessory branches, fixed a pulley to one of the extremities and fitted a 420-meter rope to it. The fir was then laid down so as to protrude into the void by a quarter of its length. The other three-quarters were fitted with cables and solidly moored to pitons planted at the rear.

Those preparations sent chills down my spine.

I understood then the folly of letting oneself descend on a rope into such a deep precipice, in pitch darkness. The wind was blowing quite strongly. It was tempting God! A sudden gust might, at any moment, break the bones of the audacious individual suspended in the void—a dangling weight devoid of resistance—against the wall of rock.

I tried to make Bernard listen to reason. He replied, in a cavalier fashion: "You're boring me."

"But don't you fear the surgeon's fluid?"

"The fluid runs around the fortress, not over the top."

He and Hermlein then disputed the honor of departing first. They ended up playing heads or tails. Chance favored—if one can put it that way—Bernard. It was agreed that Hermlein would follow immediately afterwards, and that, once their exploration of Flax's realm was concluded, we would haul them back up by the same route, but that Hermlein would have the disadvantage of only being brought up second.

Bernard put on a sort of leather framework, two straps of which served as a seat. Two others supported the back. The apparatus was attached to the long rope. Our friend put on a pair of gloves, slipped a telephone receiver into his pocket whose wires would unwind during his descent and permit us to remain in communication with him.

Finally, he asked us, tranquilly: "Are you ready?"

"I'll count one, two, three," replied Hermlein, with equal composure. "At three, you let yourself fall into the void. Are you ready, men?"

"We're ready," replied the four Swiss, in chorus, clenching their fingers around the rope and bracing themselves on their legs.

"*Bonsoir!*" cried Bernard.

He lay down prone and crawled along the fir-trunk.

In charge of the telephone, I stuck the second receiver to my ear, and nervously took hold of the rope with the other hand.

"Here goes! One...two...three!"

A little quiver told us that Bernard had let himself fall. I'd expected a big shock. I had not reckoned on the powerful arms of our Swiss.

"Gently," Hermlein commanded. "Release the rope, unhurriedly, ten centimeters at a time. Go! Go! Go!"

Can you imagine the grandeur of that scene, those five men riveted to the ground, with all their energy, brain and muscles taut in the common effort of lowering a man into a gulf?

Can you picture them in the darkness, clinging to the rope, retaining with all their strength the fall of the precious burden, listening anxiously to determine whether the song of the wind is rising or falling, whether their companion's chances of avoiding being dashed on the rocks are increasing or diminishing? And the pulley, ill-greased, grinding atrociously, accompanying each turn of the wheel with its shrill cry?

Bernard telephoned me: "Exquisite!... All's going well!... Not a hint of vertigo... To begin with, I can't see a thing... Gently!... It's swaying a little strongly... The wind's dropping... Like being in an armchair, old chap!"

The rope extended. Bernard got closer to the ground, continuing to joke. Suddenly, I heard: "Stop!... Stop!... Back up!... Quickly!...."

A long sigh terminated the sequence. An "Ah!" of distress caused my heart to leap.

At the same moment, the Swiss collided with one another. The resistance that the counterweight was offering to them had suddenly disappeared. Bernard was no longer on the other end of the rope!

"Forty-five meters from the ground!" howled Hermlein. "What's happened? At least forty-five meters! He's killed himself!"

Feverishly, the rope and the telephone wire were hauled back up.

"Damnation!" said Hermlein, when he had the two extremities in his hand. "The wire's broken, the rope cut, immediately above Bernard's head. The section's clean, as if made by a knife. I want to go down. I want to know."

I tried to stop him.

Why two victims?

The Swiss wouldn't even listen to me. He wrapped himself in the rope and was ready in the blink of an eye. Unfortunately, we no longer had a telephone with which to communicate with him. Bernard, as he fell, had taken his receiver with him.

So Rudolph Hermlein was lowered in his turn. At first, everything went smoothly, but when he was fifty meters from the ground of the Fortress, the four Swiss stopped, astonished.

Increasingly violent shocks were agitating the cable.

Once again, they were nearly dragged away. They didn't hesitate, and tugged the rope toward them once again...

"Is Hermlein still on the end of it?"

"I don't know," Dürrer murmured. Sometimes it feels heavy, sometimes it feels light. It's extraordinary!"

He had scarcely finished speaking when a whistling sound was heard, increasing in strength, and suddenly, Hermlein's body, launched like a cannonball, was hurled toward us, against the fir at the edge of the precipice. Werner Dürrer succeeded in grabbing hold of it and drawing it toward us.

The courageous artist as still wrapped in the rope, as at the beginning, but at least a hundred meters of cable still remained to be brought up.

Rudolph Hermlein was injured, unconscious. We transported him as best we could to the village. As I write this telegraphic dispatch, he has not yet recovered consciousness.

It is beyond doubt, this time, that Flax has a new force at his disposal, unknown and infinitely redoubtable. In my opinion, our two friends have been victims of the fluid that guards the fortress better than an army.

Permit me not to write any more today. I am at the end of my tether, physically and mentally exhausted.

Barbarus

P.S. Rudolph Hermlein has finally recovered consciousness. He has told a fantastic story of his adventure. He has seen Flax.

Barbarus

RUDOLPH HERMLEIN'S STORY

Melchtahl

Still under the impact of yesterday's events, today we have all been further disturbed by Rudolph Hermlein's story.

After a day of prostration, the courageous artist has completely recovered his senses. He is still complaining of internal pains, but the physicians, without yet daring to pronounce anything with certainty, hope that he is out of danger. No fracture has been found.

This afternoon, I was admitted to the injured man's bedside.

He welcomed me with a brave smile in his beard. "I had a lucky escape, eh? But poor Bernard!"

"Alas!"

"I saw him, you know?"

"Oh!"

"Lying on the ground of the Fortress."

"How?"

"Like this... When I was abandoned to the grace of God, on the end of the rope, I only had two overriding ideas. It's necessary not to think about too many things when one is clinging to a thread in a perilous situation. My first thought was to avoid crashing into the rocks. The second was to look down, to try to pierce the opacity of the darkness.

"To begin with, the first idea held sway over the second. From the tenth meter of rope onwards I felt that I was nothing any longer but the wind's plaything. I spun and I swung, without being able to resist. Fortunately, the wind was blowing parallel to the mountain. Depending on its strength, which changed from one second to the next, I went back and forth, an obedient pendulum. I was subjected thus to oscillations of at least fifty meters—an unpleasant sensation, damn it! One could exploit it at fairgrounds. The lovers of roller-coasters, looping the loop and other machines to make you vomit with delight, would flock to it in crowds, I'll wager, and..."

"Don't joke, Hermlein. Tell."

"In brief, I felt the kiss of the rock on my skin three times. Fortunately, to each of those caresses, I presented—by pure hazard—the fleshiest parts of my body. I've never rejoiced so much in being naturally well-upholstered. The upholstery is slightly damaged today!"

"Get to the important part, Hermlein."

"I can assure you, Barbarus," the intolerably obstinate fellow replied, "that the state of that upholstery is a very important matter, for me at least. Ultimately, though, I don't want to bore you with the petty incidents of the first part of my descent...

"So, I had made a short journey of fifty meters like that when I decided to dart a rapid glance downwards. I was convinced of the futility of that glance—you remember how black the night was. Can you imagine my astonishment? Six lights arranged in a semicircle were shining at the exact spot where I was expecting to come down—very bright lights."

"Bah! So our endeavor had been discovered by Flax?"

"You'll see. If, at that moment, I'd be able to signal to you to bring me up. I would have. I'd been gripped by the throat, I confess, by one of those infamous panic attacks that instantaneously turn the marrow of your bones to mush. I was convinced that my last day, if one can say one's last day when it's the middle of the night, had arrived. That's excusable; the mystery of Bernard's accident was clarified for me. He'd been the victim of people on watch below, and who had, by what means I don't know, cut the rope before the end of the descent...

"And still, perpetually, ten centimeters at a time, with frightful slowness, the rope was lowering me toward those implacable enemies. I deduced that I was about to suffer the same fate as Bernard. Oh, Barbarus! It wasn't amusing at all! For half a minute, old man, I shut my eyes, waiting for the fatal blow...

"Then I reproached myself for letting my teeth chatter like a feverish child. I'd never been afraid in my life. Was I about to start just at the moment when it would be truly excellent not to tremble? Oh, Barbarus, what sentiment is more powerful than pride? There was no gallery, no one was observing me. I could have been cowardly, trembling at my ease. No one would ever have known. Well, I was ashamed of myself. I was my own spectator. I blushed at my own weakness...

"Then, old man, a formidable oath rose up from my heart: A thousand million damnations of the shit of Hell! And, grabbing the rope with my right hand, I leaned over to see. I was about half way. The lights had grown. I could clearly see a man and a woman kneeling down beside a sprawling body.

"Bernard's?"

"Obviously! As I got closer, the details became clearer and clearer. The two silhouettes leaning over, almost lying on Bernard, were those of a man and a woman."

"Flax and the Comtesse?"

"Probably...to begin with, the doctor and the woman didn't seem to be paying any heed to me. What were they doing to Bernard's corpse? I don't know. They seemed to be motionless. If they seemed indifferent to my slow approach, however, three children, by contrast..."

"Three children?"

"Yes, three children never took their eyes off me. I could make them out clearly because they were standing close to the lights, while the surgeon and the Comtesse were in a kind of penumbra. One of the children was holding something like an enormous phonograph funnel, larger than him, and connected to a small machine by a short, wide rube. The second was standing on the upper extremity of a large trampoline. The third was armed with a long staff.

"As I got closer to that group, I wondered what attitude to adopt. I was perplexed. Were they enemies? Were they about to oppose my presence? That was possible—probable, even. But Bernard's fall might, after all, have been caused by an unexpected accident…all the same, that machine down below worried me. In brief, I was indecisive. I was in suspense mentally as well as materially.

"In the meantime, the rest of you were lowering me toward my destiny with a marvelous regularity. As a precaution, I took hold of my revolver, determined to fire at Flax at the slightest sign of aggression."

"You were attacked then?"

"Yes and no."

"You fired. We examined your revolver. Three bullets were missing."

"I fired, yes, but into the air, and later. I hoped that you'd hear the shots, that you'd guess that something was wrong, and that you'd have the good idea of bringing me back up."

"We didn't hear the shots."

"I suspected as much. The wind carried the sound away. I fired at hazard."

"Why?"

"Listen…I was about forty meters from the ground, approximately the height at which Bernard must have fallen, when I perceived a slight whistling. Flax and the Comtesse stood up. The child who was on the trampoline got down, ran rapidly backwards, and placed himself as if he were about to make a leap. Then the Comtesse threw herself toward the little chap and took him in her arms. I saw that he was struggling and that the woman was having great difficulty holding him back.

"At that moment, very close to me, ten meters behind me, I heard a child's voice shout: 'To you, Ambroise.'

"I turned my head, sharply surprised. A fourth child, palely dressed, whose form I could vaguely make out, was at my height, clinging to a spur of rock. How had the boy been able to climb up and cling to the rocks? He repeated: 'To you! To you!'

"In response to that call, the child carrying the funnel started turning a little wheel. I couldn't see the wheel, but I deduced it from the movement that was activating it…"

"The fluid machine?"

"Perhaps. Then, Barbarus, a cold sweat chilled me again, abruptly, from top to toe—a sudden blast of frightful panic. The thought that the machine was undoubtedly the one that had provoked the rout at Frutt overwhelmed me. I expected to be struck down.

"So it really was the fluid that cut the rope above Bernard, precipitating our comrade to the ground?"

"It's probable. Again, I shut my eyes, like a coward, and his time, I no longer had the presence of mind to blush at myself. Feverishly, I fired the three revolver shots at the clouds and, while clenching my teeth, I thought, in the midst of a swarm of terrors, of a heap of insignificant things...

"I remembered, for example, a little reseda that I cultivate in a sandstone pot on my window-ledge at Engelberg. I remembered that I owed ten centimes to a newsvendor who would lose them if I were killed. I also remembered the heartbroken gaze of a chamois that I finished off with a knife-thrust after having wounded it during the last hunt. How stupid one becomes at such moments!

"Finally, I was woken up from all those stupidities by a curious sensation. A gust of wind, accompanied by a rapid whistle, lifted me up slightly, and then let me fall. It was followed by a second gust, then a third, a fourth and a fifth, which succeeded one another with increasing rapidity, getting closer together and becoming more violent. The sixth sent me five or six meters up in the air. I no sooner fell back to the point at which the rope was taut than I was projected again, higher still, and so on!

"At each of those leaps, the amplitude of which was increasing incessantly, I felt crumpled, bruised by the force that was hurling my skywards, bringing me plunging back toward the ground, and then launching me higher still. I'm incapable of explaining to you, of course, who was maltreating me like that and the method by which I was the victim of that game of blanket-tossing. It's another of Flax's devices, of course. I don't believe much is supernatural powers, except for God, but that man must know some diabolical tricks.

"Yes, I was the puppet of an invisible force. I spun around, sometimes feet down sometimes feet up..."

"All this is very strange!"

"Oh yes! Oh, I undertook very strange and perilous leaps between the heavens and earth! A winged ant tossed by a storm-wind, would be able to tell you a story similar to mine. Which is to say that, in truth, having arrived at this point in its story, it wouldn't be able to tell you anything else at all. For, worn out, exhausted, out of breath, my mouth full of the blood that was running from my nose, I lost consciousness. The only other thing I can remember vaguely is a sudden light in the darkness, a flash of lightning...

"Then I don't know any more until the moment that I realized that I was in a nice bed, very soft, that every time I moved a finger, my body made me howl in agony, but that, although I couldn't move, I was enjoying a voluptuous sensation of peace and security...

"And now, my dear friend, I'm tired; leave me in peace. Go away. Telegraph. Me, I want to sleep."

Such is the story that Rudolph Hermlein told me, lying peacefully in warm white sheets.

And I haven't told you anything about the mystery of the White Child, who is the object of all conversations here.

The White Child?

In truth, are we mad, or is it reality that is going mad?

Barbarus

13 August

A NEW QUESTION MARK
THE WHITE CHILD?

Melchtahl

The atmosphere of overexcitement in the midst of which we are living in Melchtahl, added to the supernatural nature of the events to which we are the closest witnesses, is giving birth to a new, more or less fabulous legend by the hour.

I avoid being an accomplice to all the fairy tales whose threads are tangled by my press colleagues. It is ridiculous to invent and exaggerate facts when the truth already seems insensate and hard to believe.

That is why I have not yet telegraphed anything on the subject of the White Child—but today, actuality drives me, and compels me to abandon my prudent reserve..

What is the White Child?

Since yesterday, we have given that name to a vague, ungraspable little phantom, an apparition that all the inhabitants of Melchtahl have seen.

On the other hand, an incident that is both shady and disturbing, and sharply so, has affected some of us.

How dare you, people might say, talk about apparitions and phantoms in our epoch of exact sciences?

Let our readers be reassured. I am not inclined to any mental weakness. I do not believe that I am either a child or a simpleton. No one is less inclined than me to bow down before magic. I am only making use today of words borrowed from the vocabulary of sorcery for want of anything better, because I cannot employ more precise terms to characterize phenomena of which I, along with many others, have been a astonished, but not a credulous and superstitious witness.

It was Alain Bernard who, during the expedition of which he was the victim, was the first to see "the White Child."

You will find a mention of that incident in the dispatch that recounts our fatal adventure. I did, in fact, speak, albeit in passing, about "optical illusions" that troubled us along the way.

My poor comrade was marching at the head of our little troop in the dark, when, after going around a mass of rock, he suddenly stopped dead and lifted up his lantern to cast its light further. Then, without saying a word, he continued on his way. A hundred meters further on, he repeated the same abrupt gesture, and asked Rudolph Hermlein, who was behind him: "Can't you see something down there, not far away?"

"Yes!"

"Something white?"

"Yes…which is moving."

"What is it?"

The white thing that was moving in the darkness disappeared, then reappeared, only to disappear and reappear again. Our mountain men made it out several times. As for me, I can affirm that I saw it ten times during the journey. It was a kind of bright moving shadow standing out against the nocturnal background.

We were eight men incapable of being frightened by that specter. We fell into agreement that we were the victims of an optical illusion. I even admitted, later, the hypothesis of a kind of collective hallucination. The fatigue of recent days, the incessantly-renewed emotions, the psychological influence of darkness, the tension of our visual nerves exasperated by the dark, and the expectation of the perils that we were facing, all placed us in ideal conditions to be the victims of a waking dream.

Sometimes preceding us and sometimes following us, the little pale patch accompanied us all the way to the summit of the huge rock that overhangs Frutt. Then it vanished.

It would have remained in our memory solely as a merely curious phenomenon, were it not for the fact that today, the entire village began talking about an analogous vision. Thirty inhabitants have seen the phantom since the evening of our departure. Some of the witnesses are above suspicion.

Monsieur Clépent, the Baron de Vautremesse and Monsieur Flaquette declare categorically that they have contemplated the White Child. The first caught sight of it on the bank of the Melchaa. The second saw it fleeing through the garden of the Hôtel Alpenhof. The third encountered it near a drinking-trough at the sawmill.

All the sightings are concordant, but remains vague. All of them saw something through the darkness, but not can say what it was they saw.

Only one detail seems definite: that the White Child did not appear in Melchtahl again after ten o'clock in the evening, the hour at which Alain Bernard, Rudolph, Hermlein, the mountain men and I left for the heights of Frutt.

However, two old women who live together claim to have distinguished the apparition from their window at about midnight. It was kneeling on the road, in a position of prayer, and bore a sparkling nimbus around its head. I cannot guarantee the assertions of these good women. It is probable that the unusual events of recent days are beginning to turn weak heads.

One more important testimony is worthy of note. Rudolph Hermlein, who is up and about today, never tires of repeating, to the curiosity-seekers who never tire of interrogating him, that, a few seconds before being hurled into the sky, he saw the enigmatic phantom.

"I've already told you," he recounts, "that when I was about forty meters from the ground, a child's voice sprang from the nearby wall and shouted: 'To you, Ambroise!' Well, the child to whom that voice belonged projected a bright patch on the rock resembling the vaporous form that had precedes us or followed us during the ascent. But perhaps it's only a coincidence."

It is in consequence of that story that the apparition, which until then was neither chalk nor cheese, has been baptized "the White Child" by popular parlance.

To that frame of mystery, on which superstitious souls embroider so easily, a new and even more unusual element has been added.

The attempt to descend into the Fortress, which terminated in the death of our colleague, was decided after a long discussion that took place in Alain Bernard's room a few hours before being put into execution. It was attended by the four mountain men who were to join Dürrer, Hermlein, Bernard and me.

The plan was discussed in low voices. We feared being overheard by other hotel guests. Hermlein swore us to silence. Each of us promised to work on the preparations without allowing a single word to escape that might permit anyone to deduce that we had the intention of departing on an expedition that evening. We desired to avoid the unwelcome presence of any of the foreign reporters who were dogging our footsteps—Bernard and me—as soon as we showed any sign of being on the hunt for news. I telegraphed you the news in advance because it could only appear at a time when everything was concluded.

A strange incident marked the end of our conference. We were about to retire when Hermlein said, in astonishment: "Look, Bernard—the door communicating to the next room is slightly ajar."

"Impossible!" exclaimed our comrade, amazed. "I checked the bolt this morning, when I got up. It was locked."

"It is open, though."

"Doubtless the maid, when she made up the room, opened it. But that's bizarre and deplorable. Just as long as my neighbor didn't hear anything—if rumor of our expedition get around, there'll be fifty of us at Frutt tonight, and everything will be spoiled."

"Who is your neighbor?"

"I don't know."

"Did anyone notice that the door was open when we came in?"

"I thought that it was closed," I replied.

"Me too," replied the others, in chorus.

"It must have opened while we were talking, then."

"That's improbable."

"Bah!" said Hermlein. "We need to find out who's staying in the next room and swear him to secrecy."

"Indeed," murmured Bernard, "that would be best."

Rudolph Hermlein pushed the door.

A little boy about six years old, with blond curls, dressed in a bright beige costume, was sitting at a low table and innocently looking at a picture book. He leapt out of his chair in response to that invasion of bearded men.

"Are you alone?" asked Bernard.

"Yes, Monsieur," stammered the child.

"For a long time?"

"Yes, Monsieur."

"What is your father's name?"

"Alexandre Barlatescu."

"Ah!" said Bernard, addressing himself to us. "He's doubtless a second son of the Rumanian chancellor in Paris. He has a brother, little Nicolas, imprisoned in Flax's fortress."

"Yes, Monsieur," the child replied, apparently believing that Bernard was questioning him.

"Is this your father's room?"

"Yes, Monsieur."

"Are you staying with him?"

"No, Monsieur, I'm staying somewhere else, far away, with Mama. We came to see Papa today."

With a lazy and vague gesture the child indicated the direction of Sarnen. We knew that, like the majority of the mothers, Madame Barlatescu had gone to stay at the Hôtel Nunalphorn on the road to the town, while her husband remained at the front line, in Melchtahl.

"How is it," Bernard continued, "that your parents have left you here on your own?"

"They went out to visit a sick lady, Madame Peinassols, but they're coming back."

"Did you hear what we were saying in there, next door?"

"No, Monsieur. I was looking at my pictures."

"Has the door been open for a long time?"

"I don't know."

"Bah!" said Hermlein. "Let him alone. The child's incapable of saying anything about our plans. Even if he heard, he won't have understood."

Bernard closed the door again, remarking: "He doesn't give his children much soup. The child is pale; he looks as if he can hardly stand up."

And we went about our business, each in his own direction, after having saluted one another with a cordial "See you later!"

But imagine my stupefaction this morning! I met Monsieur Barlatescu at the barber's shop in the village. I hadn't seen him for two days. I offered me his condolences.

"Poor Bernard had the room next to mine," he said.

"I know. By the way, did your son tell you that we came into your room?"

Monsieur Barlatescu opened his eyes wide. "My son? What son?"

"Your child, of course."

"I don't understand. I only have the one child that Flax stole from me and..."

"You don't have two?"

"No. I only have one—just one."

I felt weak at the knees.

So, the child who was in Monsieur Barlatescu's room was not his son. It was a stranger who had got in there, who had introduced himself into it, who had put on an act for us, and deceived us.

With the aid of Rudolph Hermlein I have gone from house to house in order to find the little liar. We wanted to elucidate the mater at all costs. No one has seen him.

Combine that surprise with the mystery of the White Child, and you will have some idea of the suppositions in the midst of which, at present, in our valley, the most serious and calm minds are going astray.

Barbarus

14 August

THE WHITE CHILD?

Professor Flax's letter, sent to the Landamman and posted in Lucerne, without anyone being able to figure out how the satanic surgeon got it to that town, the doctor's threats, full of implication, the matter of the notice pinned to the door of the Fortress, the fluid that drove the besiegers away from the walls of Frutt, the death of Alain Bernard, Rudolph Hermlein's story and the matter of the child who passed himself off as Monsieur Barlatescu's son, have ended up completely bewildering all the inhabitants of the region.

The local people only speak in hushed voices now, as if their words might attract the wrath of an omnipotent supernatural being.

A few journalists are sustaining the hypothesis that the child who invented the deception of which we were the victims might be one of those that Flax has gathered in the Fortress. That idea might seem absurd at first glance, but it is nevertheless supported by certain considerations.

The false Barlatescu child has not been recognized, from the description we have given of him, by any of the inhabitants of Melchtahl or the surrounding area. He is certainly not a local child. The proof is not hard to find, for he spoke French with a slight southern accent. Now, the Swiss children by whom we are surrounded, even if they know a few words of our language, deform them in a entirely characteristic fashion. The child is, therefore, a foreigner.

We have investigated as to whether the little trickster might, by chance, have been one of the children that the Parisian mothers resident in the vicinity brought with them. There too the enquiry had no result. None of those boys came to Melchtahl on the day that Hermlein, Bernard and I left on our expedition.

The pallor and unhealthy appearance of the child, which are, in my opinion, typical signs, have not awakened any memory in any mind.

The child was very blond—the blond color that attracted so much comment in the Parisian newspapers at the outset of the affair of the abductions: a very pale blond. His eyes were blue.

That description corresponds well enough to that of little Urbain Godedouins, who was among the first children stolen, or of Pierre Candelaur, who was the fifth child to be kidnapped.

Nevertheless, both of them, according to their parents, were quite well at the time when they were kidnapped, neither pale nor ill.

And then again, how did the child, if he is Urbain Godedouins or Pierre Candelaur, escape from the walls of the Fortress?

How did he come to be in that hotel room, next to the one in which Alain Bernard was lodged?

Why did he invent that story?

How was he able to make it plausible by invoking Monsieur Barlatescu's name?

What has become of the child?

And might that child have been the White Child who preceded us in the darkness on the road to Frutt?

All questions that I will not take responsibility for answering.

Some claim that the boy was a spy whom Flax sent to find out what was happening in Melchtahl.

That supposition is truly too romantic. It is presumed that the children are not having a good time in Flax's home. If one of them had found himself in the village he would surely have stayed there, only too glad to have escaped the surgeon's custody.

MISCELLANEOUS NEWS

Melchtahl, 3 p.m.

Monsieur Hamard left yesterday evening for Paris. The Head of the Sûreté has gone to seek instructions. He left us, it appears, convinced that it is necessary to act on a very large scale if any result is eventually to be obtained. He will submit to his superiors a complete plan of what, in his opinion, is necessary to a definitive action.

The Landamman of the canton of Unterwalden has sent a long report to the federal government, in which, after have related the circumstances in which the Baron de Vautremesse organized his attack on Frutt, he asks for legal action to be taken against the fathers who were accomplices in that expedition and the mountain men who helped them, making use of State weapons. If that infraction of the law goes unpunished, Adalbert Hochberger adds, the will not answer for order in the valley of Melchtahl. According to him, the people of the region are so overexcited by the events of recent days that only a strict obedience to the law will avoid the troubles that the slightest incident might whip up.

I know that the authorities in Berne do not share that opinion. They are closing their eyes precisely because the circumstances are exceptional, because the fathers of the children are truly excusable for not having wanted to wait, and because, finally, the local people who took up arms were acting with the best of intentions.

Barbarus

DR. FLAX AND THE COUNCIL OF MINISTERS

At the Council of Ministers today, there was a long discussion about Flax and his Fortress. Monsieur Hamard, who arrived this morning, had previously met with Monsieur Clemenceau, the Minister of the Interior. It is considered in high places that it is inadmissible that Flax can defy the law of two nations. Important decisions are imminent.

Clovis Binard

SWISS GOVERNMENTAL MEASURES
FLAX HAS FOOD SUPPLIES

Melchtahl, 5 p.m.

Forty gendarmes arrived this morning, coming from all parts of the canton. They have been reinforced by thirty soldiers sent from Lucerne, where they had assembled for exercises. The whole forms a small army that has been lodged as well as can be—not very well—in the school buildings.

The Commissaire of Police from Sarnen, Monsieur Bergenholler, tell me that orders have been transmitted to organize as soon as possible a reconnaissance of Frutt under the orders of the artillery captain from Thoune.

Stung by attacks in the newspapers, which deem that the government in Berne is really not showing due urgency in the affair, the latter has decided to do something in order to appease its critics. No one any longer believes in the success of this petty governmental expedition, however. People are quite convinced that Flax is unassailable. Everyone thinks that he can only be brought down by organizing a veritable blockade, eventually starving him out.

It is known today that the surgeon has food supplies in abundance at his disposal. A grocer in Geneva has furnished him with no less than five thousand livres of chocolate. A wine-merchant in Lausanne has sent him three thousand bottles of champagne. Evidence has also been found of other suppliers who had addressed merchandise to a house in Meirigen where it has been established that the Hingertil brothers organized a large storehouse.

That house, whose doors and shutters were closed, has been opened today by authority of the law. It is empty. All the goods it contained have evidently been taken up to Frutt.

Flax thus has what he needs to nourish his small garrison for some time. It will be necessary to wait patiently for the exhaustion of those provisions to oblige the surgeon to surrender.

It is proposed to organize a cordon of armed troops around the walls of Frutt, at a sufficiently great distance from the region of the fluid. They will be content to watch the eventual effects of the famine. Unfortunately, it is too often overlooked, when reasoning like this, that if Flax is obliged to reduce the rations, it is the children who will suffer the most.

And how long will all that take? It is also necessary to bear in mind that the temperature, at Frutt, is not that of the plain, and that, if a long siege is necessary, considerable precautions will need to be taken to guarantee the men charged with the blockade against the cold and tempests of snow and ice.

233

In that regard, news has come from Frutt, the authenticity of which I cannot guarantee as yet. The legend-mongers are having such a good time at present!

A Spanish journalist, a mountain man, two Englishmen and a postal employee from Kaegiswil went up to Frutt this morning to examine the wall of the Fortress. It is a pilgrimage required of all the inhabitants of the region and all foreigners who obtain permission to pass over the Melchtahl bridge.

They say that that arrived at Dr. Flax's domain in the middle of one of those squalls of snow, of which those who have never attempted to climb high mountains in bad weather can have no idea.

Frozen and numb, their faces battered by a cutting wind blowing like razor blades, they were amazed to suddenly to find themselves, at the end of the road, in a veritable oasis of sunlight and warmth.

The clouds heaving laden with snow were circling around Frutt, covering the surrounding summits with a thick mist, but letting the rays of a benevolent sun pas abundantly over Flax's domain.

There was, according to them, a kind of circular hole in the immense cloud that was covering the region, situated directly over the fortress, through which the azure of a resplendent sky gladdened the heart.

This phenomenon cannot, according to those who observed it with astonished eyes, be due to hazard. The section of the firmament above Frutt was too neatly circular.

Is this information accurate? Is there no exaggeration in it? If it is the truth, might it not be due to hazard? Those are yet more question marks whose curl I cannot yet straighten out.

Barbarus

THE SWISS EXPEDITION
THE INTENSITY OF THE FLUID IS AUGMENTED

Melchtahl, 6 p.m.

We all prophesied it. The Swiss governmental expedition has had no more success than that of the Baron de Vautremesse.

The soldiers and the gendarmes, animated by a fine ardor, climbed up to Frutt in driving rain. Arriving at the famous wall, they witnessed the amazing phenomenon that I described yesterday, and which seems incredible. While it was raining on them, Dr. Flax's domain was spared, not being attained by a single drop of water. The clouds formed an enormous funnel above the Fortress, through which a beautiful clear sky was radiant.

That miracle of sorts, which has lasted with an astonishing persistence since yesterday, astounded the men and depressed their courage. They were immediately convinced that Flax is some kind of sorcerer, one of the powers that secretly rule the world. They only approached from then on with a perfectly understandable timidity.

I wonder, when I reread my telegrams, whether people in Paris might be anxious about the integrity of my mental faculties. More than one of my readers must be saying that I have lost my senses, since I seem to believe all the implausibilities that I am transmitting to you.

Fortunately, I am not alone in sending you these details! Fortunately, all the telegraphic agencies in the world and all the great newspapers have representatives here afflicted with the same madness as me.

The Baron de Vautremesse's adventure was repeated, point for point.

When one of the gendarmes attempted to set a ladder against the wall it was thrown backwards. The sinister hum resounded, the assailants were shaken by formidable discharges, probably electric. But whereas the local people and fathers of the first expedition only retained the memory of disagreeable sensations from those incredible shocks, the soldiers struck this morning by the fluid are presently in a very bad way.

They have been brought back to Melchtahl, and after eight hours, fifteen of the unfortunates are still unconscious, giving only feeble signs of life.

No trace of burns has been observed. The bodies are intact.

The fluid has also extended its range. It now drowns the perimeter of the fortress over a breadth of nearly twenty meters.

It was extremely difficult to withdraw the men thrown to the ground by the current from the dangerous zone. It was almost necessary to give up. Fortunately, the hum stopped for five minutes, leaving the way free for a brief interval. As soon as the wounded soldiers had been brought out during that interval of respite, the fluid recommenced its overwhelming promenade around the walls.

Everything ended as it had the first time.

The artillery captain commanding the little troop dared not persist, and soon gave the order to retreat. He was gravely afflicted by the fluid himself; his right arm and left leg were completely paralyzed.

It is increasingly felt that force is impotent against the surgeon.

Rudolph Hermlein suggests that during Vautremesse's expedition, Flax only wanted to inflict an initial warning on those who were attacking him. He did not give the fluid all the devastating force of which it was capable. He launched it with a certain economy. But this time, to prove that it is possible for him to act far more energetically, he augmented the intensity of the implacable and invisible breath in which he can submerge us.

Barbarus

AT THE COUNCIL OF MINISTERS

The Council of Ministers was occupied again this morning with the affair of Dr. Flax.

A proposal, still kept secret but which, we understand, is of the utmost importance, has been sent to the Swiss government.

Convinced that the children cannot be liberated by the ordinary means at the disposal of the gendarmerie and the police, our ministers are increasingly convinced, if the little neighboring Republic will consent, not to procrastinate any further, and to employ large-scale means.

Clovis Binard

A PROFESSIONAL TRIBUTE TO ALAIN BERNARD

There was a general meeting today of the Syndical Professional Association of Republican Journalists. Monsieur Mario Semet, the secretary general, in an emotional speech, recalled the life and devotion of one of the best-loved members of the association, our unfortunate colleague Alain Bernard. By a unanimous vote, the assembly has, on the proposal of Monsieur Paul Desachy, the managing editor of *Le Siècle*, decided to send our friend's family a letter of condolence in the name of the association.

C.B.

ANOTHER COUP DE THÉÂTRE
ALAIN BALERIN BERNARD NARD

Melchtahl, 9 p.m.
Another surprise

It is such that, even though one is gradually, after having been disinclined to believe anything, coming to believe everything, it surpasses is unexpectedness the most implausible news that has previously astounded us to the marrow of our bones.

I have just received a telegram, which was brought to me at the abode of Madame Peinassols, at whose bedside I happened to be, with Messieurs Clépent, Lévy and de Gobely-Franthéon. I opened it in front of them and my face must have expressed a very violent sentiment, since the same question hastened at the same time from all their lips.

"What is it?"

"I've just received a dispatch from Alain Bernard."

Simultaneous exclamation: "From Alain Bernard!?!?"

"Yes."

And, in the midst of a silence that you can easily imagine; I read:

Frutt (the text will be sent by wire from Lucerne)

My dear Barbarus, reassure our friends, telegraph Paris.

Cannot do it myself.

Not enough money for international toll.

Am relatively well in site of forty meter fall.

Will tell you tomorrow, if possible, how was saved, thanks to almost magical circumstances. You will receive my letter tomorrow, to be transmitted to Paris.

Will contain revelations.

ALL THE CHILDREN ARE AT FRUTT, WITHOUT EXCEPTION!

I don't know whether my telegram will reach you in full. Am like prisoner of Hingertil brothers. Text will be submitted to censorship by Dr. Flax. I don't know whether he will let it pass.

Have not yet seen surgeon or Comtesse.

Have been cared for by Parisian Sister of Charity.

AFFAIR OF CHILD-STEALERS NOT AT ALL WHAT HAS BEEN SUPPOSED.

Alain Balerin Bernard Nard

I transmit this text to you without further commentary. I will only call attention to the stamp that it bears. It has been sent from the office at Lucerne.

Barbarus

The authenticity of the telegram that our colleague Barbarus has sent to us is not in doubt so far as we are concerned.

If it were the work of a trickster, it would be necessary that the latter were familiar with all our journalistic habits.

In fact, to insure ourselves against malicious jokes, always to be anticipated, our colleagues, when they are sent abroad for an important mission, have adopted the habit of complicating their signatures. They add conventional words to their names, varying according to the day on which the dispatch is send. The words Balerin and Nard are those that, by virtue of the key in question, Alain Bernard adds to his telegrams when they are written on a Monday.

It is, therefore, certain that our colleague really is alive, that he has been miraculously saved, and that he is, at his moment, in the hands of Dr. Flax.

INVESTIGATION AT LUCERNE

On receipt of the telegram by Barbarus, we immediately telegraphed our correspondent in Lucerne. On our order, he carried out an investigation to discover how and by whom the telegram sent by Bernard was handed into the office.

This is his response:

Lucerne

The employee of the telegraph office to whom the text of the dispatch was brought was, when he counted the number of words, vividly struck by its contents.

The man who brought the dispatch is a simple commissionaire in the town, whom I was able to find without difficulty.

The porter told me that he was stationed on the dock of the boat arriving from Stanz when he was summoned by a small blond child, very pale and very thin, who handed him the telegram in an envelope, asking him to take it to the post office. He received three francs for his journey in addition to the cost of expedition.

The commissionaire was not astonished to receive that mission from the hands of a young child. It seemed to him that a lady who was on the far side of the causeway was waiting for the child.

The commissionaire has been summoned to the Commissariat of Police, where he has been interrogated. The employee of the telegraph office had, in fact, alerted the authorities. The Commissaire of the Lucerne Police has tried in vain to locate the child.

The letter that Alain Bernard announces to Barbarus, and which we are awaiting with impatience, will, we hope, cast some light on the increasingly troubling problem of Frutt.

ALAIN BERNARD AT FRUTT
FIRST DETAILS

Our colleague Barbarus has transmitted the latter that Alien Bernard told him yesterday to expect.

Frutt

I am writing to you in a pretty little room in which the most cheerful sunshine is playing, while the mountains in the distance are gray and misty. I am writing to you with the joy of a man who has felt death seize him by the throat and was not released by the frightful claw until the very moment that he thought himself definitively doomed.

If my friends could see how I am dressed, they would laugh out loud, after having pitied me. I, who have always had a weakness for well-tailored garments, trousers that hang in an elegant fashion and cravats to make Monsieur Le Bargy[35] pale with envy, am clad from head to toe in bandages and pharmaceutical dressings. My head is surrounded by a kind of white turban fastened at the front by a large safety-pin. My arms and legs are wrapped like sausages in the same way and my torso corseted by a similar procedure.

My poor body has been subjected to all the contusions and abrasions of which the human surface is capable.

But, as this little preamble will indicate to you, my good humor has returned and, although I cannot write with stenographic rapidity, I am writing with pleasure and a mind at ease.

It will be difficult for me to tell you what happened at the moment of my terrible fall. I no longer have any but vague and confused memories of it. It even seems to me, sometimes, that it was not me who was lowered the other night at the end of a cable by our friends from Melchtahl. Had that adventure happened to someone else it would certainly not be any less vividly marked in my memory.

I only recall that when I arrived about forty meters from the ground I saw something moving beneath me. I leaned over to get a better view and perceived scintillating lights.

By their gleam, shadows and a kind of trampoline appeared to me.

Suddenly, one of the shadows was precipitated on to the trampoline.

A kind of bolide brushed me. Then the bolide fell back to the ground.

---

[35] The actor Charles Le Bargy, a stalwart of the Comédie-Française.

Alarmed by the phenomenon, I telephoned Barbarus to tell him to take me back up, but the order had not been executed when the shadow was launched on to the trampoline again…toward me…

I had the sensation that it cut the rope. I screamed into the telephone…and I fell…

That's all I remember.

I cannot send any further information about what happened thereafter, until the moment, yesterday morning, when my consciousness emerged from a long faint, a complete torpor, in the little room where I still am today.

My awakening was a profound astonishment for me.

I did not know where I was or what had happened to me.

It seemed to me to be miraculous to perceive a woman beside my bed, a Sister of Charity, who was knitting without looking up.

I examined her for a long time before speaking to her. It took me more than a quarter of an hour to succeed in reconstituting my own identity, entering into my individuality again and restoring temporal sequence to the recent incidents of my life.

I thought at first that I was in Melchtahl, in the hospice of the sisters from the school. Perhaps my friends had succeeded, after my fall, in pulling me out of the Fortress and transporting me down to the plain in order to care for me.

Finally, I decided to speak. "Sister, would you be kind enough to tell me whether I'm very ill?"

She shuddered slightly at my voice, stood up, moved nearer to the bed and said to me softly, in the purest French: "No, Monsieur. The damage is not enormous. You were more frightened than hurt."

"Sister, I've been neither frightened not hurt, for, in truth, I'm emerging from oblivion. Now that my ideas are reborn and coming together, it would be very kind of you to go and inform my friend Barbarus. I'd like to talk to him."

She smiled, and replied, tranquilly: "I don't know who you're talking about. I don't know your friend Barbarus. He isn't here."

That response struck me with amazement. "Where am I, then? Am I not in Melchtahl?"

"No, Monsieur Bernard. You're at Frutt, in Dr. Flax's fortress."

I jumped—which extracted a cry of pain from me and demonstrated that immobility was still, for the time being, the best policy.

"In the Fortress?" I exclaimed.

"Yes, Monsieur. Dr. Flax had you transported here one night. He cared for you himself. I didn't even think of asking him how you came to find yourself in his domain, for one doesn't ask Dr. Flax questions, and I'm not curious."

"You might not be curious, Sister, but I am. For one thing, it's my profession. Who are you?"

"I'm Soeur Thérèse. I was employed at the children's hospital created by Dr. Flax."

"You're Soeur Thérèse?"

"Yes."

"The one who disappeared from Montretout on the day of the mothers' procession?"

"Yes."

"Dr. Flax asked the police to look for you at that time. Where were you, then?"

"At Frutt, where I took almost all the children, one by one. Dr. Flax only alerted the police to divert suspicion away from me. He knew perfectly well where I was. I've never done anything except follow his orders."

"Aha! Speak, Sister."

"I've said too much already. I anticipated your questions in order not to tire you out. What more can I add? That I have a blind confidence in the doctor. The man is so far above the commonplace! I've always obeyed him, without even trying to understand. When he brought you into the infirmary of which I'm in charge, he simply said: 'I've brought you a Parisian journalist, a worthy fellow who made the mistake of wanting to poke his nose into what doesn't concern him. He hasn't broken anything. He fell forty meters, but we deadened the fall. Look after him well. I'll come to see him tomorrow morning, at seven.' That's it, Monsieur. I won't add another word."

"Would you please call Dr. Flax, Sister?"

"I'll only disturb the doctor if your condition worsens. I leave him to his work. The minutes of such a man are sacred."

"Will you tell me, Sister, everything you've done since your departure from Paris?"

"No. I've told you all that I can tell you. I respect the other secrets, which aren't mine."

"Sister, I'd like to see Dr. Flax."

"I repeat that I won't take it on myself to disturb him. However, I'll tell someone else, to whom I'll repeat your request."

She raised her voice and called: "Wenceslas!"

The door opened immediately, very softly. I didn't even hear the sound of the catch.

A child, whose beautiful chestnut colored hair fell in curls over his shoulders, came—or, rather, glided—into the room.

"Wenceslas," she said, "go tell one of the Hingertils that Monsieur Bernard is asking for him."

The child went out, after having darted a glance at me all the more radiant with fever and intelligence because his eyes seemed larger by virtue of the pallor of his skin.

"Who is that child, Soeur Thérèse?"

"It's Wenceslas Lévy. He helps me to look after the infirmary."

The boy came back after a few minutes with the youngest of the Hingertil brothers—the one who answers to the name of Numérien."

"Ah! You're awake at last!" the latter cried.

"Yes—as you see."

"And how do you feel?"

"Quite well. Well enough to be primarily preoccupied with knowing how I come to be here and what will happen next."

"My God, Monsieur, Dr. Flax hasn't yet given any orders in your regard. Our Master hopes that tomorrow morning you'll be back on your feet and able to walk. He foresaw that you would recover consciousness this morning, and asked me to come and tell him as soon as you woke up."

"Well, run along. I won't be sorry to greet him."

Numérien Hingertil left the room for a few minutes.

As soon as he had gone, young Wenceslas Lévy approached me and set about opening the safety-pin that secured the bandages surrounding my head.

I thought it was childish mischief. I protested. But the sister, come back toward me, smiled and said: "Let him do it, Monsieur. It's time to change the dressings. Wenceslas is very adroit. There's isn't a nurse in Paris who can apply a compress or tighten surgical bandages like him."

And, indeed, climbing on to a chair, the child unwound the bandages, washed my wounds, and then refastened over the hydrophilic padding the gauzes, lead-plasters and my medical turban with a marvelous skill, rapidity and dexterity.

I noticed, during the operation, that the child had a bloody scar under his right ear, in the process of healing.

Numérien Hingertil soon brought back Dr. Flax's response.

The doctor refused to see me, but he authorized me to send a dispatch to reassure my friends.

He gave me permission, in addition, to write a more complete letter to Barbarus, while warning me that he would not allow any information that did not suit him to pass.

I am concluding in haste. Numérien Hingertil is pressing me to hand him the letter, or else it will not go out today.

Just as I am about to sign, an enormous hum suddenly makes the walls of my room tremble.

Soeur Thérèse says, softly: "Don't worry. It's nothing."

But the enormous Chrysostome comes through the door like a whirlwind and cries: "Come on Numérien; they're attacking. We need you."

"What's happening?"

"A new assault..."

"The Baron de Vautremesse and his men again? Is he mad?"

"No—the Swiss this time, gendarmes and soldiers."

"The machine's working?"

"Yes."

"We'll have to increase the dose a little. Then they'll leave us in peace, the imbeciles."

These words lead me to think that the Swiss governmental expedition has set out, and is attacking Frutt as I write. You must know about that. Shall I be rescued by my friends from Melchtahl? I doubt it. Numérien Hingertil looks so calm!

I will do everything possible to send you more news.

Alain Bernard

Monsieur Hamard's trip to Paris did not last long. Indefatigable, the Head of the Sûreté returned to Melchtahl this evening. What are his new instructions? What have the government resolved?

"I can't answer you," he told me. "Diplomatic negotiations, very complicated and very delicate, are under way. Following an exchange of notes, the French government has made the Swiss Republic a proposition, slightly strange at first glance, but which, when one thinks about it, is the only one that might have useful effects. Be patient for a few more days. Events will certainly take a new direction."

While waiting for that prophecy to be realized, existence at Melchtahl is becoming tedious. Inaction is weighing heavily upon everyone. The interminable card games organized here are insufficient to kill the time.

Since yesterday, however, Bernard's correspondence has reanimated the conversations vividly.

A few of the fathers have left for Paris, being unable to neglect their business affairs any longer. Curiosity-seekers are flooding in again, because surveillance on the Pont de Melchtahl has been relaxed somewhat.

The tourists do not fail, as soon as they can, to go up to Frutt to see the wall behind which something is going on. The boldest go up to the summits from which the gaze can look down into the Fortress. One cannot lend any credence to all the stories that are brought to us. Many of the visitors, however, claim to have seen, with the aid of binoculars, small groups of children walking with mechanical and jerky steps.

No further letter from Bernard.

Barbarus

FLAX AND BERNARD'S TELEGRAMS

The telegraph operator at Lucerne received a letter this morning slipped into the special box where his correspondence his placed. It contained a telegram addressed by Bernard to us, plus a thousand-franc bill. That money was intended to pay the expenses of transmission and to make provision for future transmissions.

It is evident that Dr. Flax is taking all his precautions. It will therefore suffice for him to put the texts of telegrams in the post. Flax's messenger will no longer risk being denounced by an excessively talkative commissionaire.

Clovis Binard

BERNARD HAS SEEN THE CHILDREN
THE SCAR UNDER THE LEFT EAR
FLAX WILL SPEAK

Frutt (by wire)

Dr. Flax has just authorized me to enter into telegraphic communication with you. he is advancing me the necessary sums of money. In fact, I only had a few francs on me when I was lowered down on the end of the cable.

I was obliged to terminate my last letter when crepitations were shaking the infirmary.

The strange noise did not last long.

Soon afterwards, Numérien Hingertil came back. He had a painful burn on his arm. Wenceslas Lévy coated it with a nauseating yellow substance.

Dr. Flax, as you must know, has once again repelled an attack directed against Frutt. The fluid must have done its work.

In the evening I too was massaged by young Lévy, who is decidedly a first-rate nurse, active and silent. In the wake of that operation I slept like a log. Today, I couldn't be better. I've been able to get up, walk and dress myself, making use of clothes belonging to Numérien Hingertil. Soeur Thérèse has shown me the jacket and trousers I was wearing when I fell; they're riddled with holes. If I dressed in them my appearance would hardly be decent.

At eleven o'clock this morning Chrysostome Hingertil came into my room. I was chatting to Soeur Thérèse, who is a woman of great devotion.

"Dr. Flax wants to see you," the giant told me.

At those words my heart beats faster. Perhaps I am finally going to have the key the great enigma.

The enormous Chrysostome takes me downstairs and across a vast courtyard in the middle of the barracks-like building of which there has already been mention.

There I encounter three of the children kidnapped by the surgeon.

They go past me, absolutely indifferent, as if my presence is of no interest to them. They walk like certain ataxics, in long jerky strides, their hands behind their backs, heads bowed, absorbed in profound meditation. All three have scars under their left ears, still bloody, of the same design as the one I noticed on little Wenceslas Lévy's head.

After traversing a long corridor, Chrysostome Hingertil, in order to open a door, operates a heavy lock that seems to me to be an extraordinary complication, and we find ourselves in the open air, on a path bordered by walls. By that route we reach the bank of Frutt's lake.

"We need to go across," says my guide. "We'll take the boat." In a Stentorian voice that makes the echoes of the mountain tremble, the giant shouts: "Frantz!"

In response, a child, whose extraordinarily blond hair immediately reminds me of the initial abductions, emerged from a little cabin constructed on the shore.

"What do you want?" he asks Chrysostome nonchalantly, without sparing me a glance.

"I want to cross over with Monsieur."

At a weary pace, the child heads toward the cabin and brings back a large packet of gray cloth, bending under its weight. He unfolds it.

The fabric is fitted with a copper framework, which suddenly stiffens under the pressure of a trigger, and the whole takes the form of a small dinghy.

The blond child goes back to the cabin and this time, comes back dragging a minuscule motor fitted to a light tiller. He fits that apparatus to the back of the canvas boat. Chrysostome and I get in, followed by the child, who sits at the back, still maintaining his impassive attitude.

"Where do you want to go?" he asks Chrysostome.

"The doctor's residence."

The boat moves off abruptly under the action of the motor, which seems rather paltry but must furnish a considerable force to the propeller.

The boat moves almost soundlessly, with the rapidity of an arrow. Scarcely have we departed than we arrive. After disembarking, I ask to examine the jewel of navigation that has transported us, but Chrysostome prevents me from doing so.

"No, no," he says. "If Dr. Flax wants to show you all these inventions, he will. Personally, I have orders to take you to him, and I shall merely obey that order." And he takes me by the arm, a trifle rudely.

I am conducted thus to another building smaller than the large barracks but equally severe in its aspect.

"You have only to go to the end of the corridor," Chrysostome tells me, "and you'll find a door. Knock, and enter when you're invited."

He leaves me alone in a long corridor, whose walls are varnished fir-wood.

I hastened to the door in question. When I reach it I stop, my heart pounding. Yes, I'd be lying if I didn't admit that a sudden feverish warmth burned by temples then.

A simple panel of wood now separates me from the strange beings whose extraordinary actions have attracted the attention of the world. I have only to push that panel and the mystery might perhaps be unveiled.

Into what world of terrors and follies will I be entering? All that I have already see and all that I have deduced multiplies my curiosity, which is mingled with dread, a hundredfold. A kind of hesitation retains me; fear prevents me from turning the door handle immediately.

But the door opens abruptly, snatched by a violent movement. A small boy appears on the threshold. He fixes me with a furious stare, the gaze of a dog that is about to pounce and bite.

"I told you he was there! He was listening at the door, this Monsieur!" cries the child, who seems to want to prevent me from coming in.

246

From inside the room, a woman's voice calls: "No, Ange, no. Let him be. Come here, Ange—come on!"

And I go in.

In a large room, whose bare walls and whitewashed, Dr. Flax and the Comtesse de Houdotte are sitting.

The surgeon is half-sprawled in one of those large and comfortable but heavily-built armchairs that the English have made fashionable. His steely gaze fixes upon me.

The Comtesse gets up. With a welcoming gesture she extends her hand to me, while the child places himself behind Flax's armchair and continues to examine me with a hostile gaze. Without greeting me, Dr. Flax cuts off the polite formula that I begin to express.

"Monsieur," he says, "I don't have time today to talk to you. I'm very busy. Know this: your foolish enterprise in penetrating into my domain without my permission will be compensated. I've decided not to remain silent any longer. Since you're the correspondent of one of the largest newspapers in the world, I shall make you responsible for destroying the absurd legends that are running around in my regard. I will, therefore, see that your telegrams reach their destination. You will only have to write, and you may write what you will. I am counting on your honesty. For the moment, content yourself with sending a few preliminary items of information. At present I have an operation to conclude. I cannot put it off. Come tomorrow morning, then, at ten o'clock. You can go back now. Chrysostome Hingertil is waiting for you at the entrance door."

The doctor dismisses me. The Comtesse, who has not said a word, salutes me with a nod of the head and a smile. The child follows me, suspiciously, all the way to the exit. Outside, I find Chrysostome.

We go back by the same route, with the aid of the vessel steered by the child who responds to the name of Frantz. He is Frantz Vetyolle, the son of the harp-teacher at the Conservatoire. I had already recognized his blond, almost white hair.

Alain Bernard

I have just telegraphed Barbarus to ask him for certain clarifications. It seems to me that the information that Bernard has sent us today, combined with recent correspondence from Melchtahl, permits the resolution of the enigma of the White Child.

Clovis Binard

FIRST REVELATIONS FROM FRUTT
CURIOUS INVENTIONS
THE COMTESSE DE HOUDOTTE
THE GENIUS OF ESPIONAGE?
THE WHITE CHILD AND THE GENIUS OF PNEUMATISM?

Yesterday evening I moved out of the infirmary.

Soeur Thérèse has installed me in an absolutely delightful little room in the left wing of the large barracks that is visible from the neighboring summits.

My descriptive talent is insufficient to depict for you the artistry, the tastefulness and the comfort with which the room is decorated. The walls are covered with exquisite frescoes with charming subjects. They represent, in idyllic mountain landscapes, on the edges of lively spring, lovers' kisses and amorous excursions. One cannot imagine more cheerful designs or prettier colors. Whoever painted these walls is a master.

The furniture is similarly expert in its design, pleasant to behold and yet perfectly comfortable.

My bed, which is very low, requires no gymnastics in order to climb into it. The part on which the head rests can be raised or lowered gently by means of a small electric button placed to the right on the bed-head. It is sufficient to reach out a hand and exert an insignificant pressure to be lying higher or lower.

The wardrobe door, fitted with a mirror, opens and closes by means of an analogous mechanism. It disappears upwards into the body of the cupboard, as if the mirror were a blind capable of being rolled up.

The sash windows of the room are similarly controlled by electric buttons, one of which is set in the little desk on which I am writing to you. I can open them, narrowly or widely, or close them without getting up.

Everything is attractive. A thousand minor marvels of mechanics and construction, a thousand of those inventions that certain novelists have predicted for future times, have been realized here.

At the time fixed by Dr. Flax, Chrysostome Hingertil comes to fetch me. I repeat yesterday's journey and soon find myself in the whitewashed room where Dr. Flax received me. I only find the Comtesse de Houdotte. The surgeon is not there.

"Monsieur Bernard," says the Comtesse, "please excuse the doctor. He thought he would be free this morning, but one of our little gentlemen has had an accident. The doctor can't leave the child, who needs urgent care. He is therefore postponing your great conversation until later. Nevertheless, if you can content yourself with the information I can give you, I'm ready to answer your questions."

All these words are pronounced in the most amiable tone, with a smile.

The Comtesse de Houdotte is wearing a long dress, the corsage of which is extended into a fitted waistcoat. The bust is superb. When a strong woman is also slender and arched in the back, she realizes one of the most perfect types of feminine beauty.

Is it possible that this admirable and seductive woman, whose forehead, beneath lush dark hair, seems to contain a world of thought, is the accomplice of the abduction of children? That it is her who has caused so many maternal tears to flow, who has participated in so many acts of cruelty?

The Comtesse reads in my eyes that I am trying to read hers. Before making me pronounce the first of the hundred questions that are pressing upon my lips, she says: "Have sufficient insanities been related on our account? Enough follies and implausibilities? We have been treated as vulgar criminals!" She opens a cupboard fitted into the wall, and continues: "Look, Monsieur; I have arranged here the articles from the principal newspapers that have followed the so-called affair of the child-stealers. I amuse myself from time to time by reading them. I have begun to believe that human beings are made in the fashion that makes it absolutely impossible for them to reason sanely. Certainly, the world is unaware of the underlying reasons for our actions, but the visible, known and verified facts ought nevertheless to prove to the most imbecilic individual that neither Dr. Flax, not the Hingertil brothers, nor Soeur Thérèse, not I can possibly be the lunatics, the odious criminals that so many people consider us to be."

"Oh, Madame, don't accuse my unfortunate colleagues of ignorance and injustice. You have caused us to pass through so many extraordinary twists and turns, and have led us from one astonishment to another, that it is perfectly excusable for us not to have discovered the truth..."

"I can assure you," the Comtesse replies, "that it is all perfectly simple. The doctor will give you the clearest explanations. For myself, I shall be content to satisfy your curiosity regarding the accessory details. But first, sit down at this table. Read the papers. Since the day of your fall, many events have occurred of which you're unaware. It will be as well, I think, for the clarity of your correspondence, to reconnect the threads of your thought."

The Comtesse hands me the latest issues of *Le Matin*, where I read the telegrams from Melchtahl.

"You receive these newspapers at Frutt, then?"

"Yes indeed. We are not as isolated from the world as people think."

"How do you receive them? Who brings them to you?"

"If I answer those questions, my answers will immediately lead to others. It's better to take up the thread of story from the beginning, in order not to have to go back over the same explanations twice."

Assuming that the latest problems that have excited public curiosity ought to be elucidated first, and having read the correspondence from Melchtahl, I ask the Comtesse: "What is the White Child?"

"The White Child's name is Paolo Palavacoccini. And in fact, he's the very person who keeps us supplied with newspapers. By what means, I don't know. The son of a spy, he is our little spy, and I can assure you that history has never known one more cunning or more artful. The doctor has trained him, in a matter of days, to keep us informed of everything happening around us. The slightest of your actions is reported back to us by him. He slips in everywhere, he hears everything, he understands everything. And he's indefatigable in his mission, although he seems weary.

"He slipped into the Hôtel Alpenhof when you were discussing, with your friend Barbarus, Hermlein and the others, your plan to descend into the Fortress. You caught him in the next room, but he got himself out of it by passing himself off as young Barlatescu. He followed or preceded your expedition. It was him that you saw in the darkness, all along your route, like a pale phantasmal apparition. In fact, he wears pale clothes that the doctor has rendered faintly phosphorescent. In the darkness, that phosphorescent makes a deep impression on the local people. It's not inconvenient to our projects that the people of the region regard our presence with a certain superstitious dread.

"It's the same Paolo Palavacoccini that your friend Rudolph Hermlein saw perched on the spur of rock at the moment when the painter felt the first effects of the apparatus that threw him back toward his comrades, over the mountain. Paolo Palavacoccini, Monsieur, has a genius for espionage. It's impossible to be any cleverer."

"What, Madame, is the force capable of throwing into the air a man as heavy as Rudolph Hermlein, with such energetic power?"

"Compressed air, the release of which is triggered by a little machine—the one that your friend made out from the height of his rope, and which he compared to a phonograph. The apparatus was invented by one of the children here, Ambroise Riffelart, who has a genius for pneumatism..."

I am about to demand the hundred explanations that those words seem to me to necessitate, when Soeur Thérèse arrives in haste to summon the Comtesse. Dr. Flax was asking for his companion.

I wait for three hours without seeing anyone return.

At the end of that time, Chrysostome Hingertil comes to tell me that my audience is concluded for today, that the Comtesse de Houdotte has been obliged to assist Flax in a delicate operation, and, finally, that the surgeon has promised—formally, this time—to grant me an hour of conversation tomorrow and to reveal to me the secret of what the giant calls "the doctor's Work."

Alain Bernard

FLAX SPEAKS
A GREAT HUMANITARIAN PROJECT
THE SCIENTIFIC PRODUCTION OF MEN OF GENIUS

Frutt

I have been able to converse at length with Dr. Flax.

I finally know the motive that has led the extraordinary surgeon, and the people that I no longer dare to call his accomplices, to act as they have.

How far above all the accusations of which they have been the object their project is!

In truth, I remain astounded in thinking about the immensity of their goal, and the prodigious science of the man who dared to conceive it.

How far we have come today from the various events that marked the origin of this affair and impassioned the world!

The work of Dr. Flax is worthy of attracting universal attention, no longer as a sequence of inexplicable crimes, but by the grandeur, the extent and the novelty of his conception.

Dr. Flax and the Comtesse de Houdotte received me this morning in the large whitewashed room that I have described.

"Monsieur," said the doctor, "I am going to reveal to you the key to our story. Let me speak, without interruption."

And, walking back and forth, with his hands behind his back, in his long gray dressing-gown, his forehead bowed toward the ground as if searching it for his thoughts, he said—or, rather, dictated—the following:

"Some time ago, *Le Matin* published an article by your friend Binard about the Comtesse de Houdotte's salon. He related how the Comtesse chose her guests. On Mondays she received anyone at all, and then, from Tuesday to Friday, filtered the people according to their intelligence, in such a fashion as to gather in her drawing room on Saturdays only 'the profound,' an exceptionally select society that consisted entirely of men of very rare intelligence, men of genius. The Comtesse obtained a particular pleasure in the midst of those high minds.

"That was what gave me the idea of realizing the work that I am carrying out today, and which I meditated for long years. But I would certainly not have launched myself into the enterprise had I not been supported by this female hand."

Passing behind the Comtesse, Dr. Flax, illustrating his words with a gesture, grasped his friend's wrist and lifted up a long white hand with an aristocratic wrist. Slightly surprised at first, Madame de Houdotte withdrew her hand gently, smiling.

"Because," he continued, "I love the Comtesse de Houdotte; I love her with all my heart, every fiber of my being. That love has given me the energy necessary to dare to attempt a vast, unique and superhuman enterprise..."

"There is," the Comtesse put in, "an agreement between the doctor and me. I do not respond to his amour, but we will marry when he has finally realized completely the Work that we have conceived together, when he has rendered himself worthy of being loved by realizing our great common dream."

While he affirmed his passion, in a curt and clipped voice, the surgeon's eyes were fixed on those of the Comtesse, in which they seemed to want to embed their steely gaze.

"One day, therefore, Monsieur," he continued, "I understood that the fashion in which the Comtesse selected her guests could be singularly ameliorated by the scientific method. The Comtesse liked to surround herself with men of genius, but men of genius, as you know, are not very numerous. Humanity is infinitely more miserly in that regard than the earth with diamonds. Could not a means be discovered of creating them artificially, in the same way the agriculture and animal husbandry have been ameliorated? Might it not be possible to improve the human brain scientifically?

"That idea, which had haunted me for a long time, I expressed one day to the Comtesse. She replied to me in a few sentences that have remained engraved in my mind. Permit me to recall them in her presence.

"'The entire modern civilized world,' she replied, 'is preoccupied today with social improvement. Human progress, solely due to the action of a few men of genius, has been such that we are impatient for further progress that will permit us all to live better, and to enjoy the pleasure of life more. The expectation of that progress, the impatience of waiting for it, has been translated into violent social upheavals, by revolutions, by political struggles that are akin to the reflex gestures of the sick.

"'People want something, want it ardently and violently, but do not know exactly what it is that they want, and do not know, above all, the veritable means to bring about the realization of their confused desires. Now, it lies uniquely in the augmentation of the number of men of genius. Unfortunately, the leaders of popular movement who express the impulsive discontentment of those whom the men of genius have not yet been able to deliver from poverty, employ methods diametrically opposed to the end to be attained. Every popular revolt, like every battle, is injurious to the production of men of genius. They can only develop in a calm environment that leaves the field entirely free for the flight of their thought.'"

"Yes, Monsieur," put in the Comtesse, who had been listening, impatient to speak, "the solution of the social problems that oppress all of humankind today, does not lie in vain agitation, in theories contrary to the law of nature, in the unconscious anger of peoples. It lies in the production of a greater number of men of genius, who will invent machines progressively reducing human labor, remedies against diseases, new objects of utility for the needs of existence, and new works of art for the needs of intelligence."

"Primitive humans," Flax went on, "were obliged to live in caves. Every living moment was used up by the almost unique preoccupation of not dying of starvation. Gradually, they constructed shelters, initially refuges made of wood and foliage; gradually, they transformed them into houses. That progress was never the work of a collectivity; it was the work of a few individuals of genius. It was to them alone that came, in the long run, the idea of successive ameliorations, which they imposed on the routine and the stupidity of the crowd."

Having made that profession of faith, the doctor and the Comtesse, exciting themselves with the sound of their own words, continued their demonstrations, enthusiastic phrases overlapping and colliding.

"When the houses were constructed," the Comtesse continued, "the men of genius found the means to contend with the night, to illuminate the hours when the sun withdraws its light from us. They discovered means of warming themselves without being inconvenienced by smoke and vapors."

"Then, the doctor resumed, "one by one, the items of progress piled up as the men of genius accumulated them..."

"Look around. The men of genius have improved on nature prodigiously..."

"Thanks to them, the poorest individuals today live better than the richest ten thousand years ago. As for our fellow citizens who have some wealth at their disposal, they can boast of being scarcely preoccupied with the struggle for existence..."

"People, principally in the working classes, would like to have everything immediately, and they imagine that it is sufficient for that to take it from those who possess it..."

"That means is contrary to the very end envisaged. The problem does not consist of impoverishing the rich. For all those who study the progress of society scientifically, it appears evident that the sole result that can emerge from that procedure will be, by virtue of a rebound, an even greater impoverishment of the poor..."

"It is indispensable, in order for humankind to advance, that the capital so dearly coveted, the capital that can be defined as an accumulator of force, can be, at a certain moment, in the hands of the few who will put it, when they find it advantageous, at the disposal of the men of genius. In the hands of the men of genius, capital will increase, the natural forces that have been tamed will be increased tenfold. Finally, everyone will have profited..."

"Let us take an example. One of the most obvious human needs is that of being able to move around more rapidly than natural means permit. That gave rise to the invention of the locomotive, but the need is less for the poor than the rich..."

"If capital had been equally divided between humans, in mediocre measure, at the moment when Stephenson invented the first locomotive, the inventor would not have found a sou with which to exploit his idea. But, the need to travel more rapidly being a need of wealthy people, born of that same wealth, Stephenson's invention was welcomed and sustained until our own day by the most formidable capital..."

"Now, in our epoch, the need to travel more and more rapidly had gradually extended to the popular classes, by contagion, and we have succeeded in satisfying that need at progressively lower cost. Today, the poorest people enjoy that advantage, which was once reserved for the most fortunate, and they enjoy it a hundred times more. The proof is thus provided, and provided a thousand times over, that humankind is good as it is, and that the only means of making it better is not to exhaust itself in social evolutions but, on the contrary, increasingly to aristocratize the world by the production of men of genius, who are the leaven of universal happiness."

There was a long silence.

My pen was running rapidly over the pages of my notebook.

The doctor gave me time to write it all down, and then he went on.

"Monsieur, the great principles that the Comtesse de Houdotte summarized for me in one day, which I shall remember all my life, responded to my most secret meditations. The question of human genius had always preoccupied me. I had thought for a long time that genius might be stimulated by scientific methods. Our entire adventure is contained in those meditations. Since then, I have carried out long and patient research on the human brain.

"I can now declare to you, today, that it is possible for me to produce human genius surgically. All the children I have abducted have been submitted to my treatment. Today, they are children of genius. They will become, as they grow older, adults whose genius will advance the progress of society by five or six thousand years. My surgical operations have given me extraordinary results. In a matter of days, I can fashion new and marvelous intelligences.

"I shall show you a few astonishing, unexpected inventions already due to the children of Frutt. Thus, I shall soon have realized the conception of the Comtesse de Houdotte, of resolving the social problem by the creation of individuals of genius."

Fatigued by this discourse, the doctor paused, and then went on: "Tomorrow, I shall furnish you with the proof of what I am saying, and you shall see our troop of young geniuses. Confess, Monsieur, that child-stealers such as us are not the Bohemians who steal children in order to teach them to perform tricks in public squares."

I cannot describe the striking impression that Dr. Flax's grave words made on me. While I was writing my notes I felt myself penetrated, through all the fibers of my being, by one of those superb respects, one of those poignant religious aspirations that seize you in the presence of a grandiose natural spectacle, an immense storm over an unchained ocean.

Alain Bernard

FRANCO-SWISS NEGOTIATIONS FOR THE ATTACK
ON FRUTT CONTINUE

Melchtahl

Monsieur Hamard has returned from Berne.

The Head of the Sûreté has had lengthy conversations with our minister. The negotiations have not been slowed down by Bernard's revelations. The French and Swiss governments are still determined to make the utmost efforts to put an end to the story of the Fortress. In the best-informed circles it is being said that the delay in mounting energetic and efficacious action is due to the protests of a neighboring great power, which does not look kindly on the project under discussion.

Barbarus

REVIEWING THE CHILDREN

I have spent today with Dr. Flax and the Comtesse de Houdotte, reviewing the children resident in the Fortress. Almost all of them were gathered together in the large courtyard of the barracks that serves for their accommodation.

It was a far-from-banal spectacle, but which, in spite of all the admiration I now have for Dr. Flax, tugged at my heartstrings.

All the children have that bloodless appearance of which the White Child furnished us with the first specimen.

They march like little old men, as if they were artificial, as if their joints lacked flexibility.

Some have precocious wrinkles on their foreheads.

All of them are marked below the left ear with a bloody gash that denounces the surgeon's implements.

All of them also remain indifferent to what is happening around them. I walked between their ranks without attracting a single curious glance, and without obtaining any answers to my questions.

Only Dr. Flax, the Comtesse de Houdotte, Soeur Thérèse and the Hingertil brothers seem to have the ability to animate them. The surgeon, in particular, has a considerable influence over them. When he speaks to them they tilt their heads back, their eyes shine, their cheeks color and they reply with an extraordinary volubility.

"This is my Work," the surgeon tells me, extending his hand with pride over the troop of pale children. "These are the geniuses that I have created beneath the conquering blade of my scalpel. Each one has a specialty. In fact, universal genius does not exist. No complete brain exists. The man who unites all perfections within himself is a myth. We can scarcely imagine an individual who could simultaneously be the best physician, the best surgeon, the best mason, the best writer, the best mathematician, the best acrobat, the best soldier, the best architect, the best painter, the best sculptor, the best engineer, the best technologist, the best dancer, the best navigator, the best financier, the best statesman, the best orator, the best actor, the best philologist, the best psychologist, the best bureaucrat, the best explorer, etc., etc. Human genius can only be applied to specialties, and I have, in consequence, only succeeded in creating specialists of genius. Each of these children is today endowed with a unique gift in one of the branches of mental activity."

With a dry voice, the surgeon called: "Ambroise!"

At that name, one of the children, who was sitting sadly in a corner, as if absorbed by his meditations, stood up and ran toward us.

"Ambroise," the doctor said to me, affectionately caressing the back of the little boy's neck, "is the genius of pneumatism. He's young Ambroise Riffelard, the son of one of my colleagues, Dr. Riffelard, a hospital physician. A curious detail: I was summoned to a consultation with his father on the day before the boy's abduction.

"Ambroise is one of those who have given me the greatest satisfaction. A mere four days after his operation his genius for pneumatism had developed marvelously. A week later, he constructed a pneumatic machine of extraordinary ingenuity. He's endowed with a unique facility for all problems concerning the compression of gases. I'll show you the machine that served to blow your friend Hermlein back to his friends. You'll be amazed.

"Thanks to him, we can launch tempestuous jets of wind with hurricane force, directing the violent pressure of a column of air as one regulated a jet of water. The fashion in which Hermlein was lifted by that column of air is comparable to the manner in which, in the firing ranges at fairgrounds, an empty eggshell is made to dance on a jet of water.

"We intended to send you back in the same manner when you tried to descend to Frutt along the rock-face. Unfortunately—or fortunately—Ambroise's machine malfunctioned initially. It was necessary to do something else, so we sent young Philippe Soleillaut, who has a genius for leaping."

The Comtesse de Houdotte raised her hand and called: "Philippe!"

One of the children, who was a long way away from us and walked at the same weary pace as the others, then made a prodigious bound in our direction. It was like a feline pounce. The jump measured approximately twenty-five meters.

I looked at the doctor with a dazed expression

"Oh, yes," said the doctor. "Philippe Soleillaut can, when it suits him, cross considerable distances, in length and in height, in a single bound."

"The doctor," the Comtesse explained, "wanted to prove, by according him that special genius, that many physical aptitudes that are only exercised today either by material means, or by virtue of training from which all intelligence is banished, are also brain-functions..."

"I didn't expect to succeed so completely," the doctor continued. "No jumper as powerful as Philippe Soleillaut has yet been seen on earth. It's necessary to multiply by a hundred the most astonishing prowess to form an idea of what he can do. With a trampoline he can attain such heights that he disappears from view, and his skill in coming down is equal to his skill in launching himself. Unfortunately, I wasn't able to endow that skill in so perfect a fashion. He can only jump about seventy meters vertically..."

"Seventy meters! That's quite a lot!"

"If he tried to do better, he'd risk breaking his bones on the fall back. He's the one who, jumping up to meet you, managed to cut the rope during your attempt to descend into the Fortress. You recounted in your paper that it seemed to you, during your expedition, that a bolide had cut the rope. That bolide was none other than young Soleillaut. He had to go back a second time, having missed his stroke on the first attempt. Then your fall was deadened by a blast of air that emerged from Ambroise Riffelard's pneumatic machine while he was repairing one of its components. It's thanks to that fortuitous circumstance that you're among us, safe and sound..."

"Oh certainly! The doctor wouldn't have done anything to prevent you from killing yourself. He considers that his Work is great enough to dispense with having to worry about a few victims..."

"Indeed! All important adventures have cost human lives. So much the worse for those who are the ransom of general progress. But once I saw you on the ground, grazed, bruised, wounded, the old instinct of the physician that was lying dormant within me woke up. I cared for you."

"Add too," the Comtesse de Houdotte interjected, "that I interceded in Monsieur Bernard's favor. Indeed, I wasn't of the same opinion as the doctor, who wanted to pursue his Work in shadow and silence, without deigning to inform anyone at all until his success was complete. For a long time, I've been convinced that, once the people who have been attacking and pursuing us since the beginning of the affair of the child-stealers knew the objective at which we are aiming, they would let us finish our good work in peace."

"You might be mistaken, my friend," the doctor objected.

"Perhaps, but I think it's necessary for us to emerge from our ivory tower. That's why I urged the doctor to allow you to communicate with your paper."

"But if you want to send another telegram today," said Flax, looking at his watch, "you only just have time to draft it. Paolo Palavacoccicni, the genius of espionage, has to leave soon. They're plotting a new attack against us. I need to know what they're planning."

I would have liked to write at greater length today, but Wolfgang Hingertil is standing beside my table. He declares to me in his thunderous voice that if I don't hand over my copy right away, Paolo, who has to take it away, will leave, sent on an urgent mission, and you won't receive my telegram today, so I can't delay any longer, although I would have liked to tell you about the genius of Charles Clépent, Dr. Flax's masterpiece.

Alain Bernard

21 August

FRANCO-SWISS AGREEMENT
GERMANY PROTESTS
A COMPROMISE
THE GENIUS OF CONDENSATION

Frutt

Dr. Flax summoned me early this morning. He has received news that, although not inspiring the least dread in him, saddens him to the utmost depths of his soul.

Little Paolo has come back from a long voyage of espionage, in which he has distinguished himself once again by phenomenal prudence and sagacity.

He has, therefore, been able to report to the surgeon that the interminable negotiations between the French and Swiss governments have concluded with a bizarre result.

The general conviction that Dr. Flax and his Fortress cannot be mastered without employing considerable means has determined a veritable expedition of war against him, an international expedition.

France will put at the disposal of the Swiss government a line regiment, two battalions of light infantrymen, a battalion of engineers and mountain artillery. That force will come to join Swiss troops, the principal nucleus of which will be furnished by the Frontier Guards garrisoned at Andermatt.

We have also learned, through the intermediary of Paolo Palavacoccini, that the German government, when it learned of these facts, protested energetically, demanding lengthy explanations. It would not have taken much, thanks to the politics of the Wilhelmstrasse, for the expedition to be abandoned. Germany would not tolerate French regiments being able to operate in a neutral country, even for a simple police operation.

Innumerable telegrams have been exchanged between Paris, Berlin and Berne in the attempt to calm the political sensitivity of Germany—which, as we know from the Morocco affair, bristles unhealthily.[36]

In response to the representations of the Swiss government, declaring that if the deliverance of the young geniuses is postponed because of pressure from Berlin, the effect on world opinion would be disastrous, Berlin has proposed a compromise.

---

[36] During the "Moroccan Crisis" of 1905-06 German diplomats attempted to use the issue of Morocco's independence to generate friction between France and England and further their own compatriots' commercial interests in north Africa. The plan backfired, strengthening the Entente Cordiale and enhancing general mistrust of German imperial ambitions—a significant incident in the long lead-up to the Great War.

Germany will send a company of Bavarian infantrymen, and all the united international troops, Swiss, French and German, will be under the general command of the aged and celebrated German Generalfeldmarschall von Haeseler, presently retired.[37]

It is thought that, in the presence of these agreements, the Italian government will doubtless claim the honor of sending a company of *bersaglieri* to join the combined expedition.

According to Paolo Palavacoccini, our Council of Ministers has appointed Général Lacroux as commander of the French troops. The rank of the German officer requires obliges us similarly to choose a leader of the highest status.

"Why this great movement of forces?" Dr. Flax asks me. "Your correspondence has made it perfectly evident that we are not malefactors. Now that, thanks to you, no one is any longer unaware of the splendor of our projects, ought they not to leave me in peace in the solitude I have chosen?"

"Undoubtedly, Doctor. Absorbed by your Work, however, you can't see that, for the French and Swiss police, the problem remains the same. Whatever the result obtained, you're still the child-stealer, the man who has snatched children away from the tenderness of their mothers.

"Place yourself for a moment in the situation of the families that are gathered there is Melchtahl, waiting anxiously. In spite of all my revelations, their sentiments certainly haven't changed. They're still the same way inclined. They want their children back. They're demanding it with all the more desperate insistence because they now know that you've subjected their children to difficult surgical operations. Their hearts are stirred even ore by the idea of the suffering their sons have been obliged to endure. The pressure they're exerting on the authorities is increasing day by day, and public opinion is still with them."

"The families have their reasons," the doctor replies, "but public opinion is, as always, baneful and stupid. What does the unhappiness of a few families matter, compared with the true and rapid solution of the social problem by the production of human beings of genius? Ought not the governments to grant me their aid instead of fighting me stupidly at the behest of a few mothers—justly afflicted, I agree, but unimportant by virtue of their small number—and the appeal of a public opinion dominated by bad reasons of sentiment?"

---

[37] The Prussian military leader Gottlieb Graf von Haeseler (1836-1919) had fought in all the major conflicts in which his homeland was involved from 1853 to 1903, when he was elevated to the upper house of the Prussian parliament. Although it is plausible that Forest was personally acquainted with all the other real individuals who play significant roles in his novel, and might even have obtained their approval for the words he put into their mouth, it is difficult to believe that he obtained licence from von Haeseler—although the general would surely not have found anything to annoy him in the treatment he receives, which is unusually generous for a French writer of the period.

"In a case of conscience of this sort, Doctor, governments always submit to the sentiments of the majority. That's why these military expeditions have ended up..."

"Ended up what?" the doctor interjects, swiftly. "Being organized? Yes— but that's all. In defeating me? No, not yet. I offered peace, but they want to fight, so I'll fight. You know better than anyone, now, that I don't bluff, and that with my young geniuses, I'm capable of resisting all attacks, even by a man of genius and all his soldiers, soldiers of genius."

"Yes, you have machines..."

"Oh, you haven't seen anything yet. I dispose of apparatus against which no modern engine can do anything. I have no fear of the largest cannon. Their shells will crumple here, if I wish, like an old lead cannonball against steel armor-plate."

"It's certain that the electric machine that repelled two expeditions from the walls of Frutt ought to make the governments reflect, and..."

"That machine was invented by Fernand Pig. It conducts high tension jets of electricity at will, through the atmosphere, as Ambroise Riffelard's pneumatic machine permits the direction of blasts of gas."

"With those two weapons alone, you could..."

"I have others still, constructed in a matter of days. Would you care to come with me? I'll show you a new apparatus that will change the face of the world by changing the conditions of agriculture, an apparatus of peace that I can also use, if need be, as an apparatus of war."

I follow Dr. Flax, who leads me into a vast hall equipped with all possible and imaginable machine-tools. That detail escaped the first reporters. No one was aware that Frutt had installed a complete factory at Frutt.

Four or five of the surgeon's little boarders were working there when the doctor introduced me to the workshops. As usual, they paid no heed to my entrance and continued their work without raising their eyes.

The doctor went over to one of them and asked: "Have you completed the trials, Charles?"

"No, Doctor, but I'm well on the way."

"He's a very good boy," Dr. Flax said, turning toward me, while the child's eyes shone with pleasure. "He's my masterpiece—the one who, in his specialty, is the most perfect of my geniuses."

"What is his name?"

"Charles Clépent, the son of the lady who, when the child was abducted, made the confession of adultery that your colleague Barbarus reported."[38]

"And what is his genius?"

"The genius of condensation. He has already improved significantly the condensers of the steam engine that we use here, but that's only a secondary

---

[38] Dropped from the Tallandier edition.

262

invention. At this moment he's studying a problem that has already been addressed, to which a poor solution has been found. I mean the large-scale condensation of atmospheric vapors. If the first experiments succeed, as I have the firm hope that they will, Charles Clépent will soon be able, either to dissolve the clouds overhead, to attract clouds from a distance, or drive clouds a thousand leagues away.

"You can imagine, Monsieur, the immense advantage that we might be able to obtain from that unimaginable apparatus. It means rain at the hour one wishes, wherever one wishes, and for as long as one wishes. It means agriculture freed of all its anxieties. There will never again be too much rain or not enough rain; there will never again be too much sunlight or not enough sunlight. The earth will be watered scientifically; the heat of the sun will be filtered by clouds that will burst or not, according to our desire. It means that immense areas of the earth, arid desert today, will become fertile and luxuriant, again or for the first time. It represents the Sahara transformed into a vast oasis, which will be the most beautiful garden ever dreamed by poets. It represents the great deserts of Asia changed into paradises, along with the interminable Australian solitudes. It represents hurricanes scorned, tempests mollified. It's the safety of maritime voyages over an obedient sea. It represents a general regime of changed winds. It represents fresh breezes in summer, warm breezes in winter.

"When his invention is perfected, Charles Clépent will have realized, for the pleasure of human beings, a progress greater than any other accomplished on Earth since the existence of the globe. We've already experimented on a small scale with the principle dictated to him by his genius of condensation. The other day, while it was raining torrentially on the mountains, Charles deflected the mass of clouds that accumulated above Frutt away from us, and while the downpour inundated the country all around us, the Fortress remained dry beneath a joyful blue sky."

"Ah! That's the curious phenomenon that, according to the newspapers, has struck the tourists and local people who have come to Frutt in recent days with amazement?"

"Yes. Know that during of my first reflections on the possibility of producing genius by means of surgery, I calculated that it would be easy for me to create a genius of condensation. That's even why I installed myself so boldly in this region of Frutt, which the snow and he cold so often renders impracticable…impracticable for others, certainly, but always charming and delightful, if the genius of condensation furnishes us, according to need, with benevolent warmth and melts the snow and ice."

"How can Charles Clépent's condensation apparatus serve you as a defensive weapon?"

"Think about it. What will become of the international troops when the final apparatus is functioning? We'll be able to afflict them with the worst weather. We'll be able to exterminate them with cold and tempests."

Today, I have the absolute certainty that the Fortress of Frutt is impregnable, the Dr. Flax is in the process of bringing about the most formidable revolution of all the centuries here. The governments that have agreed to mount the international expedition would do well to renounce their plans.

In truth, the thefts of children, the despair of families, all become insignificant by comparison with the prodigious work that is being elaborated within the walls of Frutt.

And if anyone insists on sending soldiers against us, there will be a frightful catastrophe, not long delayed.

Alain Bernard

22 August

A STRANGE SOCIETY
GREEN FUCHSIAS AND GIANT GENTIANS

Frutt

I have spent the entire night meditating about the marvelous work of Dr. Flax.

Am I dreaming?

Am I living in an ideal society?

All the new and inconceivable things I have learned have been seething in my imagination all night, and my brain is suffering from an indigestion of excessively new ideas.

This morning, as if to affirm the reality that I doubt at every awakening, I was able to take account of a further prodigy accomplished by one of Dr. Flax's young geniuses.

It is seven o'clock in the morning when someone knocks gently on my door. I assume that it is Wenceslas Lévy, who comes from time to time to change the blessings on my remaining wounds.

I have already explained that my room is a model of comfortable devices. Human effort has been reduced to the minimum here. I have no need to emerge from my silk sheets to go to open the door. It is sufficient to push one of the buttons fitted to the wooden bed-head. It activates a little nickel lock, a veritable gem of solidity and complication. So I extend my arm and the door sides softly into the wall.

Two of the little geniuses come in; Wenceslas Lévy approaches me, and says, in his uninflected voice: "The doctor has instructed Léon Aproli to bring you some flowers. They're here."

"Where?"

"In the corridor. If you wish, we'll place them next to your bed."

"That's fine."

The two children go out, marching with the strange automatic gait that they all have.

They reappear a few seconds later, dragging a little cart of incredible lightness. It is built of steel mesh so fine that, even with a slight push, one can no longer make out the spokes of the wheels. They are surely no thicker than the threads of spider-silk that float over the roads. The armature supporting that invisible mesh is slightly thicker; it is, however, not as strong as the whalebone ribs of an umbrella.

That fairy-tale cart is carrying a relatively considerable weight of superb flowers: Maréchal Niel roses of a unique brightness and an exquisite grace, cuckoo flowers as big as peonies, gray-green fuchsias and giant gentians.

265

The whole is arranged with a delightful artistry. Our most artistic Parisian florists could not have invented designs of surer taste.

I beckon young Aproli to come closer. "Beautiful flowers," I say. "Are they yours?"

I learned yesterday afternoon that Flax has given the geniuses orders to reply to me, otherwise I would not have got the slightest word out of him, but he replies, without a muscle of his face quivering:

"Yes. I have the genius of culture and gardening. They're unique flowers, Monsieur. I had a great deal of difficulty growing them, especially so quickly. Fortunately, Clépent helped me. He made me an apparatus that furnishes plants with the exact atmosphere that suits them. One thus obtains the maximum intensity of life. Oh, if Clépent wanted to continue helping me…we could fabricate, the two of us, flowers such as the world has never known. Alas, Clépent no longer wants to know. I have to ask Dr. Flax for everything, who has to ask Clépent for it, who almost always refuses.

"These gentians are ordinary mountain gentians. I forced them in my own fashion. Now they're enormous. But I don't believe that the goal of scientific gardening is that which is generally proposed—which is to say, to produce giant flowers. It's necessary, above all, to have graceful and useful flowers. Now, you'll notice that my gentians, although large, are very pretty. Their tall stature works to their advantage. Otherwise, I wouldn't have permitted myself to augment their form. Admire, too, how superb that yellow is, how the blue gentians have a bright and dazzling blue. Their massive branched roots are much more efficacious against fevers than the roots of the ordinary gentian."

"Yes," adds Wenceslas Lévy. "We had you take some, Monsieur Bernard, after your fall, to bring your fever down. The results were good."

I thank little Léon Aproli for his attention. He speaks earnestly, with the gestures of a disillusioned old man, and I try to question him. Would the children reveal to me the method by which Dr. Flax had abducted them, how they had arrived at Frutt, and what their impressions had been? Neither the doctor, nor the Comtesse, nor the Hingertils, nor Soeur Thérèse had yet wanted to inform me on that subject.

A curious observation: when it is a matter of talking about their specialty, the two little prodigies do not have to be begged; they even develop with a certain abundance the findings of their inventive minds. That abundance is not animated, though. The eyes remain dull, as if the words were of no interest, not expressing any mental state. However, when one tries to extract a few words from the children outside of the special domain of their intelligence, they reply poorly or falsely, or not at all. It seems that everything not connected with their genius, closely or distantly, does not interest the at all, that they cannot link foreign ideas to their principal preoccupations.

"You must remember," I say to Léon Aproli, "that Dr. Flax abducted you in the Bois de Boulogne?"

"The Bois de Boulogne?" murmurs the child. "Oh, yes, I see…the little pine-wood through which the cyclists are passing! They're beautiful trees, Monsieur."

"Come on, my boy—don't you remember that you were kidnapped?"

Léon Aproli looks at me without replying.

"And you," I say to Wenceslas Lévy, "it was also in the Bois de Boulogne that you were abducted, wasn't it? On the Route de Madrid?"

"Ah!" said Wenceslas. "The air is fresher in the Bois de Boulogne than in the city. The transition is quite rapid. So the people arriving in automobiles risk caching cold, as a result of the abrupt change in temperature. It's prudent, when one comes from the Avenue de la Grande-Armée, to slow down slightly, in order to avoid the lungs experiencing too swift a change."

That is all that can be extracted from Dr. Flax's little geniuses.

It seems to me, all the same, that the surgeon's operations have certain grave inconveniences. They have surely affected the mental integrity of the children. The genius has been bought at the expense of the general equilibrium of the brain.

I have tried to see Dr. Flax or the Comtesse de Houdotte today, in order to continue my revelations, but I have not been received. The surgeon's work is demanding; he does not want to be disturbed.

Fortunately, the Hingertil brothers have become much more obliging. They have gradually decided to talk. I went to visit them today at the former Hôtel Reinhardt, where they live, near the entrance door, and drank beer with the two giants and their brother. We have become friends.

I am glad to observe that they have a fine and delicate intelligence, when they take the trouble to show it, in spite of their rough and heavy frame. Numérien, especially, has a glib, reasonable and charming wit.

Our conversation was principally concerned with the manner in which the doctor organized is abductions.

As the Parisian police deduced long ago, all the abductions were premeditated and patiently organized. Dr. Flax only kidnapped children he had selected in advance, and whom he had studied.

"The children," Wolfgang told me, "were not taken at hazard. The doctor can only induce genius in certain predisposed brains. Not everyone is capable of such rapid and considerable development. We had, therefore, complete information about the children, which permitted us to believe that they would be able to blossom into geniuses under the Master's scalpel. For example, Dr. Flax knew the two sons of the Baron de Vautremesse well, since he had cared for them. Similarly, we had precise indications regarding Bernard Flaquette and Émile Loubé. The former stayed for three days at the hospital at Montretout, where he was cured of an attack of the croup. As for the latter, we had treated one of his relatives, a cousin whose mother, in chatting to Soeur Thérèse, recounted that she had a little nephew, Émile Loubé, who was at school in the Rue

267

Portalis and was of exceptional intelligence. Furthermore, the doctor has invented a curious apparatus that permits him to recognize the quality of a child's brain rapidly, as they pass by in the street. Perhaps he'll tell you about it."

"It's true, then, that you only abducted highly intelligent children."

"Naturally. Just as lush vegetation doesn't grow in arid and stony ground, so genius doesn't germinate in unrefined brains. It was necessary to choose our subjects carefully."

"It would be better if you got Dr. Flax to tell you all that," Numérien put in. "We're always afraid of divulging secrets that he wants to keep. He alone knows what it's permissible to say."

Dr. Flax has let me know that he will be at my disposal tomorrow morning. I intend to interrogate him about the means he employed to abduct the children with so much skill, without ever leaving a trace sufficient to guide the police, however, skillful and vigilant they were.

Alain Bernard

THE CONQUEST OF FRUTT

Melchtahl

The news sent from Frutt had not reduced the zeal of the government. Whatever the goal might be that Dr. Flax is pursuing, it is necessary to return the children to their mothers as soon as possible and put a stop, by force is necessary, to the surgeon's pitiless experiments.

As it is believed that the Fortress will not surrender unless a major military effort is mounted against it, it has been decided to organize a powerful expedition.

It is strange that Alain Bernard has been able to send us the information, discovered by unknown means by the young spy Paolo, before anything was released in Paris regarding either the resolutions of the French and Swiss governments or the obstacles raised by Germany.

All the difficulties have now been smoothed over.

Tomorrow, we shall enter into the period of execution, and our soldiers will depart for the conquest of Frutt.

Clovis Binard

23 August

GERMAINE PLAIZANCE'S SCREAMS
WHY THE DOCTOR ABDUCTED THE CHILDREN
THE QUESTION OF BLOND HAIR
NOT ALL CHILDREN CAN HAVE GENIUS
NECESSARY CONDITIONS

Frutt

This morning, the astonishing phenomenon that has amazed all visitors to Frutt, which is due to the genius of condensation, was repeated majestically.

While the surrounding mountains disappeared in the dull opacity of fog, fine sunlight cheered up the Frutt plateau.

I went for a walk with the doctor in that marvelous atmosphere, filling my lungs with the light air and enjoying the mildness of the heavens. For half an hour we strolled around the large cylindrical building that, when seen from the mountain, resembles a gasholder.

"That's my laboratory," the doctor told me. "I'll show it to you. It's not banal. That's where I work, and conclude the creation of geniuses."

As we passed a little opening, a kind of little window reminiscent of a porthole, I heard heart-rending screams—the screams of a child.

"It's nothing," said the surgeon, coldly. "I operated on little Germain Plaizance yesterday morning. She's screaming because she's in pain. In endowed her with the genius of maternity..."

He continued, with a vague smile: "For one thing, that's really all that women are good for. All the girls I abducted will have that genius. There's really no point in trying to germinate another in their imperfect brains."

Every time that our stroll brought us back to the opening of the laboratory, the incessant, exasperated plaints of Germaine Plaizance upset me, making me feel ill, but the doctor did not seem to hear them. He seemed indifferent.

Once, however, he perceived my pallor. He understood, and exclaimed, with a kind of brutal impatience: "Don't get emotional, Monsieur. It's a law of nature. Human progress is only bought by suffering..."

And, as if to make me forget the child's pain, Dr. Flax continued to tell me the story of the abductions, which had been interrupted the other day.

"I told you, Monsieur, that when I took account of the possibility of creating men of genius by means of a surgical operation, I made the Comtesse de Houdotte, who was pursuing a dream akin to mine, party to the discovery. We immediately decided to put my work into execution. But how? Could I carry out my great Work in the open, in the glare of publicity?

"Oh, Monsieur! All the poor minds, all the petty, unintelligent but squeamish souls, all the whiners in the world would have been revolted, if I had said to them: 'I need young children. I shall open their skulls. I shall insufflate them with genius. And the world will be better!' The antivivisectionists already howl when one sacrifices a rabbit to the advancement of humankind, and, as a side-effect, the advancement of the world of rabbits too. What cries would they not have uttered if I had publicly claimed the right to carry out experiments on children? My discovery would have been lost forever."

"Indeed, Doctor—but does not morality forbid it?"

"Morality, Monsieur, is a necessary law, but it only obliges mediocre and average souls. Great minds can and must create a morality of their own, appropriate to the needs of their intelligence. They therefore have the right to permit themselves what is forbidden to others. Without the slightest modesty, with the consciousness of what I am and what I can do, I consider myself, Monsieur, as one of those great minds, above the laws that regulate the near-totality of humankind. That is why I have dared actions that, inscribed in the account-books of another man, would be to his debit, while they are to my own credit."

"How did you organize the abductions?"

"First, I recruited the Hingertil brothers, who understand me and would give their lives for my work. They were the ones who had the idea of organizing the Fortress of Frutt. It's an exceptional situation for me. It's isolated. I can work here is calm and peace. The atmosphere here is one of the purest. My little geniuses recover rapidly here from the shock of the operation. Finally, it's very defendable. I can resist all attacks here, if the governments disposed to public force do not end up yielding to the beauty and grandeur of my hopes...

"So, the Hingertils bought and organized this territory, without attracting too much attention. The construction was carried out in accordance with the plans of a Parisian architect, Frantz Jourdain. When it was finished, the difficult problem began."

"Procuring the children?"

"Yes. I didn't want to waste my time trying my method on imperfect brains. We therefore gathered information about the children meticulously. It was only after having determined that they possessed special aptitudes, brains of the first order, that we kidnapped them. We had, at the same time, taken note of the habits of the parents, in order not to neglect any precaution in executing the necessary abductions."

"Doctor, the kidnapped children are all highly intelligent, all city-dwellers, all between six and seven years old, and almost all from rich families. Why?"

"They're the indispensable conditions for making the seed of genius germinate in the nascent brains. It's necessary..."

"Pardon me, Doctor, would you care to give me a preliminary explanation. Why, at the outset, did you set out only to abduct very blond children?"

"Ah!" Dr. Flax replied. "That was an error—the only one I made. I believed, for a few days, that exceptionally intelligent children who were exceptionally blond were more intelligent than if they had had brown hair."

"For what reason?"

"Because there is a correlation between the brain and the quality of the hair. Coarse people have coarse hair. Refined people have refined hair. It would require a volume to explain how I was induced to adopt the erroneous belief that very blond children were more likely than others to have genius. The error did not last long; I soon abandoned that false trail, and we then chose children with hair of all colors. As we abducted them in the order in which we had studied them, the result was that the blond children were kidnapped first."

"Public opinion was keenly excited by those repetitions."

"Fortunately, brown- and chestnut-haired children can also be endowed with genius. We would have had a great deal of difficulty procuring thirty subjects if we had had to limit our efforts to those with pale blond hair."

"So, Doctor, if I've understood correctly, the children of rich families and city-dwellers are more apt to develop into individuals of genius than those of poor families and country-dwellers?"

"Exactly. Genius only grows in well-cared-for and refined ground. The father and mother of a man of genius do not need to be individuals of genius themselves, but it is necessary that they have the leisure that permits them to develop the child's intelligence. They also need a long atavism of culture, without which it is futile for their son to have the flame of genius. It would be extinguished by the first breath...

"In the same way, genius is the child of cities. It is only born in environments where there is a brisk exchange of ideas, among fevers and passion. There is no rural genius. The air of the fields is harmful to great brains, with need and atmosphere of conflict and overexcitement. That, Monsieur, will explain the petty mysteries that stimulated Parisian curiosity. You know now why certain children were kidnapped rather than others."

At that moment, Numérien Hingertil interrupted our conversation.

"Doctor," he said, urgently. "Germaine Plaizance is poorly. Her fever is rising."

"Excuse me," said the doctor, and went away at a run, followed by Numérien.

As I passed the porthole of the laboratory, I heard the little girl's screams of pain again, and went back to my room trembling and distressed.

Alain Bernard

THE MILITARY EXPEDITION AGAINST FRUTT

As we were led to understand yesterday, the diplomatic skies are clear and bright again. Germany is satisfied. She had, it appears, demanded the holding of an international conference at Bayreuth to regular the Frutt affair. Thanks to the intervention of England, a repetition of the Algeciras coup was avoided.[39]

The complete expedition will therefore depart.

The third battalion of the 51st line regiment, garrisoned at Beauvais, has been selected to go to Melchtahl. It will be accompanied by its commander, Colonel Cordelong. A special train has been organized. It will depart tomorrow or the day after; the exact time has not yet been fixed.

The soldiers of the 51st will meet up in Melchtahl with the 13th battalion of the Alpine light infantry, garrisoned at Chambéry. We also know that military engineers are being sent from Versailles; the appointments are not yet official.

For their part, the Swiss are concentrating three companies in the location, under arms at this moment and commanded by Colonel Loender. They are German-speaking troops from the canton of Berne and Soleure. The men in question will be based at Meiringen.

A number of these soldiers, who are known in Switzerland as Gardes de Sûreté, and form a little known but veritable permanent army, will leave Andermatt with cannons and machine-guns. They will travel via the Furka and Grimsel passes to Meiringen, and will set up camp at the foot of the Titlis, near Engstlen.

These are veritable strategic dispositions.

One can observe on the map that the Fortress of Frutt will be invaded from three directions at the same time, the only ones from which it is accessible. Starting off at great distances from one another, the troops will converge on that point.

The Italians have decided to abstain. They will only be represented by one officer.

The German feldmarschall, von Haeseler, who will take general command of the troops, with meet Général Lacroux in Lucerne.

I am leaving for Munich, from which the German troops will depart, in order to interview the Prussian generalissimo regarding his project against the Fortress of Frutt.

Clovis Binard

---

[39] The Algeciras Conference, called to settle the Moroccan Crisis, was held between January and April 1906. The intended "coup" backfired as al the nations represented except Austro-Hungary ganged up against Germany.

THE ART OF CHILD ABDUCTION
THE POINT OF FASCINATION
THE GENIUSES ARE IMPERFECT
THE FLAW OF SPECIALIZATION

Frutt

Dr. Flax does not seem troubled by the news that is reaching us from Melchtahl and Paris.

"Bah!" he says. "I've said that I'll resist, that I have the wherewithal to resist. I'm not in the habit of pronouncing vain words. So much the worse for the deaf who don't want to hear. No one in the world will prevent me from continuing my cultivation of children of genius."

And without further comment on the expedition being prepared against us, he continues to dictate further details of his Work.

"I explained to you yesterday," he said, "the reasons for which I only abducted the children of city-dwellers and rich families."

"Pardon me, but little Émile Loubé and Bernard Flaquette, alias Bobichon, were exceptions."

"Yes, to confirm the rule. The principle tolerates a certain flexibility. I'll now explain why I only attacked children between six and seven years of age."

"Will you permit me one question?"

"Go on."

"How did you abduct thirty-one children, mostly in broad daylight, without being caught in the act?"

The doctor smiles and replies: "Because we took the most studied and careful precautions. There's nothing easier that committing the most blatant crimes in Paris, in the middle of the day, in the midst of the crowd, if one has a great deal of presence of mind and a good deal of psychological science and intelligence.

"The five of us—the Hingertil brothers the Comtesse and I—prepared the abductions so well that we hardly ever suffered any hitches. It's no more difficult, when one knows what one is doing, to make a child disappear from a street, than it is for a conjurer to make a card disappear before the eyes of a numerous audience. I never had any anxiety. My only worry was the great height of the two Hingertils. I always feared that the presence of the giants in the vicinity of the abductions would eventually attract attention. That's what happened, but too late to prevent the abductions I had planned.

"How is it that the children went with you so easily, without protesting or crying out?"

"In the course of my research, I had discovered in young children, slightly below the elbow, a location that I call the point of fascination. When the child is gripped there, in a certain fashion, and one applied the index finger to it very precisely and violently, the child is not only incapable of resistance but will follow you meekly, as if he were acting entirely of his own accord. It was by that means that I drew the children either to my coupé or one of the automobiles."

"Why did you undress your victims?"

"In order not to leave the slightest trace of their identity. Once in the vehicle, I lowered the blinds and undressed the children, and one of the Hingertil brothers of the Comtesse parceled up the clothes. As soon as that part of our work was done, my traveling companion generally got out of the vehicle and disposed of the clothes. The coachman or the chauffeur was always one of the Hingertils. Once the child was undressed we went home as quickly as possible, sometimes making a slight detour. The children were then locked in one of the rooms in the house, and I operated on them as soon as possible."

"Locks of hair were found in the abandoned parcels. What sentiment led you to leave those precious souvenirs for the mothers?"

"My God, Monsieur, if the examining magistrate and the police had followed through with their deductions—some of which, it's necessary to admit, came close to the truth—they would have suspected, from the detail of the locks of hair alone, that there was a woman in the affair.

"It certainly wasn't me, Monsieur, who had the idea of cutting those locks. It was the Comtesse de Houdotte's inspiration. She wanted to attenuate the grief of the parents slightly…personally, I scarcely gave a thought to the pain I was causing them. What does it matter, I repeat, in comparison with the extraordinary benefit that will result for everyone when the world s regenerated by my men of genius? A few tears scarcely count in the face of that immense blossoming of the happiness of the many. They will dry up very rapidly in the sunlight and the radiant heat that, thanks to me, will one day warm all humanity, from the top of the social scale to the bottom.

"But the Comtesse de Houdotte, being a woman, cannot, like me, abstract herself from the present by means of a vision of the future. She's still troubled by the sufferings of which we're the origin. It was, therefore, out of sentimentalism that she begged me leave the mothers a lock of hair. I didn't refuse her that small favor. It was, you'll understand, indifferent to me…"

"You mentioned just now, Doctor, the point of fascination that permitted you to take possession without difficulty of the children selected for abduction. Not all the children allowed themselves to be taken so easily, however. Some of them struggled. When Barbarus found Charles Clépent's clothes, it was observed that the buttons were ripped off, that the child had defended himself…"

"Indeed," the doctor replies. "The fascination doesn't last. In some subjects it disappears within a minute. Little Charles Clépent did, in fact, struggle fearfully. To prevent him from crying out in the carriage I was obliged to force him to breathe chloroform."

Dr. Flax recounts his acts of violence with an imperturbable calm. His eyes fixed on his goal, he remains cold before the means. He takes no account of the fact that his auditor is distressed, troubled by the cruelty of his words.

"I interrupted you, Doctor, when you were about to explain why you only abducted children between six and seven years of age."

"It's impossible for me to carry out the operation of 'genification,' of which I'm the inventor, on brains that are already formed or too young. The age of six to seven is the most favorable. It's at that moment that the skull, which previously consisted of scantly resistant matter, begins to take on its definitive form. It's then that the medio-frontal suture takes on consistency and the large vertebra that expands into a capsule at the top of the head to round out the skull finally possesses a more solid frame. Nevertheless, that resistance of the bones of the heads is not yet considerable enough to prevent the veritable work of sculpture that I'm obliged to accomplish with my scalpel.

"At that age, too, the neural cells of the brain have not yet been affected by overly vivid impressions. They are still all new. One can, if I might put it like that, direct their energy in the direction one desires without them being tugged this way and that by memories that inhibit their action and flight."

"Are your discoveries completely original, or did you have a master?"

"I had a master—a great master, unjustly forgotten today. I'll tell you about him tomorrow, and unveil many of the curious particularities of the human brain, which is the least known machine in the world. I'll also show you what my method consists of. You'll know the whole of my secret. I don't want to hide my work. I retreated here in order to complete it, not to hide it. You will deliver it to the discussion of scientists. I don't fear the light, and I'll even allow you to watch the final operation, when I open the skull of Louise Accesson to sow the genius of maternity therein."

"Permit me, Doctor, to interrupt our conversation once again to ask you a new question that intrigues me greatly. All your little geniuses look unhealthy—pale, anemic and weary. They all have a scar under the left ear, and..."

"The scar is easily explicable; it's the trace left by my instruments. It will disappear. After an interval of time, nothing will remain of it. On the other hand, the children lose a good deal of blood while I'm working on their genius. Hence that pallor. It will take them some time to recover the vigor of full health.

"As for the indifferent and weary expression, of, Monsieur, that is the weak point of the work; it's in that respect that it's still imperfect, that it requires further study, investigation, long reflection. I have given them genius but, unfortunately, at the expense of other mental faculties.

"I have made all the vital force of their neural cells converge on a single focal point, to the detriment of other regions of the brain. An image might help you grasp my meaning better. On a table in the middle of a room, arrange a dozen candles in a circle. If the flames are of equal strength, they will light the whole room equally. The walls at the back and the front, the right and the left, will be illuminated in the same fashion. Now take a reflector and place it behind the candles. Immediately, one part of the room is illuminated more intensely than it was before, and, by contrast, all the other parts will fade into shadow.

"A similar phenomenon occurs with my little subjects. I've concentrated on their genius all the little light-sources in their brain that previously illuminated it entirely, back and front, right and left. Now, certain aspects of their intelligence remain in darkness and don't develop in proportion to their sovereign faculty, which soaks up all the light.

"That's why they have the apathetic appearance that you've noticed. That's why they walk with a stiff and mechanical gait—for genius is also acquired at the expense of the motor functions. They walk poorly because they think too much...

"Come to my study tomorrow, and I'll explain the sequence of studies I went through before arriving at an endeavor that, in spite of its imperfections, will be the salvation of the world."

Alain Bernard

THE ART OF REVEALING THE FUTURE OF NEW-BORN CHILDREN
BLANCHET'S SYSTEM

Frutt

Obedient to the doctor's invitation, I went to his study today.

There, the surgeon of Frutt revealed to me, for the benefit of our readers, many curious details regarding the function of the mysterious laboratory that is the human brain.

"Sit down at this desk," he says. "And now, listen to the origin of my research. I'll dictate it to you. It is, Monsieur in this little book."

From a small rotating bookcase, the surgeon takes a pamphlet carefully bound in red morocco.

"This book," he continues, "appeared in 1841 in Cherbourg, published by Beaufore and Locauf, lithographic printers. It is entitled: *The Physical, Intellectual and Moral Future of the Child, Discovered at Birth by a Very Simple Method*. The author's name is Blanchet.[40] He was the chief surgeon at the civic hospital in Cherbourg.

"The work was very remarkable in its era. When the newspapers announced that Monsieur Place, the secretary general of the Société Phrénologique de Paris would read the Cherbourgian surgeon's observations during the presentation of his annual report, it caused a considerable stir in the intellectual world. The seats were grabbed. The great hall of the Athénée Royal was too small. A number of the members of the Institut and the Académie Royale de Médecine honored the Société Phrénologique with their presence that day, and well-dressed ladies affirmed by their attention that certain aspects of science do not deter elegance. The name of the surgeon Blanchet was much acclaimed.

"The scientific interest of his studies, Monsieur, was perhaps less attractive to general curiosity than the promise it contained of being able to reveal the future of new-born children. Tearing away the veil of future time has always been a human obsession. It has made the fortune of all the tricksters who have allowed it to be believed that they enjoyed special insights on that subject—all the sorcerers and sorceresses, all the fortune-tellers...

---

[40] The pamphlet in question, *L'Avenir physique, intellectuel et moral de l'infant: découvert à son arrivée au monde, au moyen d'un procédé très simple* by-lined "M. Blanchet, chirugien en chef de l'hospice civil de Cherbourg" was, indeed published by Beaufore et Locauf, 1841; the Bibliothèque Nationale catalogue records it as having been published by Feuardent in 1842, but that is simply a rebound version—available on *gallica*—which adds the report of the phrenological society to which Flax refers. It was obviously the rebound version that Forest saw. Dr. Blachet had previously attracted considerable attention by virtue of his pioneering work on mending bone fractures.

"Now, Blanchet was a scientist, a true scientist, a serious and well-informed researcher. It was the first time that science had announced a concurrence with readers of the Tarot and tea-leaves. It was worth the trouble of investigation. It's necessary to add that snobbery also contributed to Blanchet's success. The discoveries of Gall, he inventor of phrenology, were still recent. The disquieting problems of the human brain were impassioning the scientists and the ignorant alike."

The surgeon pauses momentarily, draws breath, and then concludes: "It is, therefore, my dear Monsieur, to Blanchet that I owe the commencement of my reflections on the possibility of endowing men with genius surgically."

Professor Flax, who is striding back and forth, stops again, and collects himself while applying his hands to his temples; then, resuming the movement of a wild beast in a cage, the continues the speech he is addressing to me.

"Doctor Blanchet," he says, "began his original work by examining the skulls of a hundred infants at the age of nine months. After which, with the inalterable patience that is half of the scientific spirit, he waited for conclusions. He waited for between twenty and twenty-five years, during which time he never completely lost sight of his subjects as they grew up. When they reached adulthood, he drew up a table of their various mentalities, their various destinies.

"If, he thought, all these infants who presented the same phrenological phenomena when they were nine months old, offer clear similarities of character and talent, intelligence or the lack of it, when they reach adulthood, there are good grounds for claiming that one can foresee the future of infants at the breast.

"And, indeed, the result of his study was that children of the male sex—Blanchet had only observed males—bear, as soon as they are born, indications of the height, the penchant, the character and the degree of intelligence that they will have as adults.

"Then, in more detail, Blanchet affirmed that: one, by the length of the child's skull at birth, one can predict his adult height; two that an infant's head bears indications of the penchant, character and intelligence that he will have at twenty five, and that it sufficient, to ascertain those things, to study his skull in a certain fashion; and thirdly, that the quantity and quality of intelligence depend on both the form of the skull and the extent of its development at the front and the rear."

Dr. Flax interrupts himself at this point to remark that this conclusion of Blanchet's was partly inexact.

"That semi-error," he says, "does not harm the basis of Blanchet's system. The Cherbourgian surgeon, in his fine study, committed more than one error of reasoning, and even of science—but Monsieur, one does not judge a theory by its errors. Only the verities are important.

"The other laws discovered by Blanchet are: fourthly, that education masks natural defects, but does not obliterate them; and fifthly, that out of 75 individuals—Blanchet had observed a hundred infants, but twenty-five did not survive to adulthood—nature produced seven men deprived of common sense, one idiot, five endowed with considerable wit, two endowed with superior genius, one with blatant and cruel arrogance, fifteen of above average intelligence, two of very great intelligence, thirty-three of good common sense, two with rounded heads, who were eccentric and exceedingly vicious, and seven with heads disproportionate to their bodies, who were stupid.

"Such were, Monsieur, the observations that Blanchet made in Cherbourg. They were the result of various very delicate measurements of the skull carried out by the scientist on the same skulls, at twenty-year intervals. The surgeon was thus able to establish a very reliable rule, unjustly forgotten today, which permits an adroit phrenologist to foresee, from birth, the character, and hence the future, of the children whose skulls he measures.

"It was Blanchet's theories that were my point of departure. It only remains for me now, Monsieur Bernard, to indicate the journey traveled and the point of arrival."

THE WHITE CHILD BRINGS NEWS

At this moment, we are interrupted by the arrival of Paolo Palavacoccini. The little spy is bringing very important news.

He has been to Lucerne.

It appears that the international troops will arrive much more rapidly than we thought.

The various governments involved seem to be in a hurry to take action.

"Since they're in haste, Monsieur," Dr. Flax says to me, "I must make haste too. I can only be sure of defending myself to the last when Charles Clépent has successfully completed his final experiments in condensation. It's that little genius who will save us.

"In addition, Isidore Bimorel is putting the final touches to a little apparatus that will be very useful to us in the defense of the fortress. Isidore Bimorel has the genius of ballistics…excuse me; I must go check on their endeavors. It's urgent. I'll take up the thread of my demonstration tomorrow."

Alain Bernard

OUR TROOPS IN SWITZERLAND

The French battalion will leave Beauvais this morning, at two minutes past eight. It will go directly to Bâle and Lucerne.

The municipality of Bâle has requested that our soldiers make a halt in the town in order to be fêted there.

It must not be forgotten that in a square in the large Swiss town, in front of the railway station, there is a beautiful monument, erected in memory of the hospitality that the Swiss gave the Alsatians in the war of 1870. It is a work by the sculptor Bartholdi, which was offered to the town of Bâle as a tribute by the Alsatian Baron Hervé de Gruyer.

A ceremony of our troops marching past that beautiful statue would certainly have been a fine and moving sight. Nevertheless, it has been decided not to delay, even by an hour, the campaign that our young soldiers are to undertake against the Fortress of Frutt.

Our infantrymen will therefore go on to Lucerne without stopping, where they will spend the night. The Alpine infantry from Chambéry will not leave until tomorrow, traveling via Geneva, Interlaken and Brunig.

A few Swiss newspapers are mounting a campaign against their government, which has permitted the entry of foreign soldiers to its territory. They claim that their republic is big enough to police itself.

We deem this criticism to be unjust, and that Swiss self-esteem is wrong to take offense.

It is, in truth, a highly exceptional police operation. It is necessitated by the insensate actions of a Frenchman. It is entirely natural that we should participate in the difficulties of an affair of that sort, and that we take responsibility for inflicting on the surgeon of Frutt the exemplary punishment merited by his insane enterprise.

Clovis Binard

FLAX'S LABORATORY
THE OPTICAL INTRUMENT FIR MEASURING SKULLS
THE DESICCATION OF BRAINS
THE NATURAL INFERIORITY OF FEMININE INTELLIGENCE
RADIUM-FLAXIUM

Frutt

I have finally penetrated the singular laboratory that the doctor has constructed at Frutt.

Imprisoned for several days in the Fortress, I have gradually become acquainted with the surgeon's discoveries.

The strange scientist seems to be taking a malign pleasure in only initiating me gradually.

To my request to circulate freely in his domain, to visit as I please the barracks, the laboratory and the workshops of the little geniuses, he has opposed a curt refusal, I am obliged to obey. It is, therefore, only today that I have been able to enter the enormous cylinder, the "gasholder," the giant paunch where the surgeon elaborates his unprecedented discoveries.

That laboratory does not resemble any other. It is a vast room that takes up the whole of the cylindrical space within the building. The iron walls, painted bright blue, circle around a concrete floor. They are only pierced by sparse round openings. All the daylight comes from high above. Imagine an immense drum whose upper skin has been replaced by a glass roof.

That glass is not blank. It is tinted slightly blue, so that all objects seem blue, except for yellow ones, which look green. As Dr. Flax has yellow-brown skin, he is pale green in that light.

Today, the surgeon is wearing a large Spanish cloak and a broad-brimmed hat, He this appears to be completely transformed. I no longer have the celebrated Parisian physician before me, but a Chilean bandit.

The laboratory is divided into small compartments by sheets of white cloth, extended to slightly more than a man's height. One marches in the midst of a labyrinth with textile walls.

Dr. Flax invites me to sit down in one of the boxes formed by these broad ribbons. Its only furniture consists of two chairs and a large desk.

On panel resting softly on a bed of immaculate padding I perceive a small piece of an unknown substance that shines with a fulgurant gleam—an unsteady glow that comes and goes, dancing. It is sufficiently dazzling that, in order to follow the doctor's words, I am obliged to turn my back on the flamboyant object.

Dr. Flax resumes the conversation at the point where he left it yesterday.

"You know now, that it was reading Blanchet that opened the first horizons to me. To be sure, the Cherbourgian scientist made many errors, but he unrolled the conductive thread that guided me through the darkness. It is thanks to his method that I was able to detect, at such an early age, children susceptible of one day becoming men of genius—but I ameliorated that method and only employed it myself to children between six and seven years old. Thanks to procedure of my own invention, a kind of tiny telescope, the relatively complex measurements of Blanchet's system were replaced by simple ocular examination. If one examines the head of a child from a distance with the aid of that instrument, one can immediately well whether it is or is not capable of receiving genius.

"Now, listen carefully. I'll give you my great secret. Thanks to the vast print-run of your newspaper, you'll be able to submit it to discussion by scientists the world over.

"Know, therefore, Monsieur, that the human brain contains a considerable quantity of water. Now, that quantity is in inverse proportion to intelligence. The more water, the less intelligent you are. The more intelligent you are, the less liquid it contains.

"The brain of an adult in full possession of his means always contains less water than the brain of that same man had when he was a child, or will have when he is old. that is why the female sex in endowed by nature with an inferiority, by comparison with the male sex. All feminist theories break like glass against that observation. Women are, necessarily, more stupid, less rational, less capable of logic and intellectual development then men, because their brains are cooking-pots that contain too much water. It is also the reason why the only genius that can be evoked in the little girls I abducted is that of maternity—which is not, as I've already told you, genius, strictly speaking, but an instinct."

"Oh, Doctor—you'll have all women against you."

"What does it matter, if the truth is with me? So, intelligence and, with greater reason, genius—which is the perfection of intelligence—is a kind of flame, which too much water puts out. It can only flare up easily if the brain is relatively dry, and will burn more brightly as that dryness becomes greater. Men of genius, naturally, have naturally dry brains; my children of genius have brains desiccated artificially by surgical procedures.

"What is the schoolmaster who develops the intelligence of a child doing? He is simply drying his meninges. By his example, simulation, competition and punishment, the professor overexcites the neural molecules of his pupil. He thus produces a mild fever, a slight augmentation of the temperature of the brain. That warmth causes a certain amount of water to evaporate, and the child thus becomes more intelligent, more capable of acquiring and retaining new notions that would otherwise have been inundated and drowned, as it were, by an excess of liquid.

"My method of the genification of children derives from the same principle. I begun by choosing, thanks to the Blanchet system improved by my optical instrument, children susceptible of becoming more intelligent. After which, I dry out a certain part of their brain."

"By what means, Master?"

"Ah! That's the nub! I make use of a marvelous kind of matter—the one that is shining so brightly before your eyes."

"What is that dazzling object?"

"It's the mysterious product, simultaneously inert and alive, that has already created a good deal of noise in the world. It's…?"

"Radium?"

"You've guessed it—but a radium that I have strangely improved. To be fair, I ought to confess that the improvement in question was largely the work of Chrysostome Hingertil, a physicist of great learning. He has not only succeeded in producing the radium that was prepared and described by Pierre and Marie Curie, but also of alloying it with another new substance, which has been named flaxium in my honor. From that combination, a kind of brilliant stone emerges, which crumbles easily. A grain of the powder thus obtained develops a prodigious intensity of heat and light.

"To produce genius in the brain of one of my boys, I introduce a particle, a grain, of radium-flaxium into the exact place where that faculty is located, the intellectual function of which I want to increase a hundredfold."

"One might say, therefore, quite literally, that each of the little geniuses 'has a grain'?"[41]

Dr. Flax does not seem to get the joke—which is, I must confess, not very funny.

After a brief silence, which is exceedingly embarrassing for me, he continues: "In brief, therefore, Monsieur, my operations consist of drying out, with the aid of radium-flaxium, the cervical matter of children, in order to obtain the maximum desiccation at the particular location in their meninges where I am trying to produce genius.

"So, under the influence of the marvelous substance, the neural force of my little subjects is multiplied tenfold. Then their intellectual forces are all attracted to the light that I gave slipped artificially into the brain. In the same way that fever, by increasing the temperature of the brain, provokes in everyone an abnormal abundance of new ideas, the local fever created by the radium-flaxium in a chosen corner of the gray matter determines the magnificent flight of the great specialized thoughts to which we give the name 'genius.'

"Now you know my theory, Monsieur. I shall soon give you the opportunity to contemplate the practical application of my method on flesh and blood. Louise Accesson, whose operation I was forced to put off because she had a cold, will be genified tomorrow. I'll show you how I introduce the radium-

---

[41] This pun does not translate; "avoir un grain" [to have a grain] is used in much the same sense as the English phrase "to have a screw loose."

flaxium into the encephalum with the aid of special needles, in order to develop the genius of maternity in little girls."

Such were Flax's words, as I noted them down today.

I confess that the prospect of watching Louise Accesson's operation tomorrow scarcely delights me. I can still hear the screams of little Germaine Plaizance, howling in pain, and I have the misfortune to have a sensitive heart.

Alain Bernard

OUR TROOPS AT MELCHTAHL

After spending the night in Lucerne, The French troops have gathered at Sarnen. He infantry from Beauvais and the Alpine infantry arrived in the town two hours apart. They were followed by fifty Engineers from Versailles.

Our soldiers are in a very good mood. They consider this expedition against Dr. Flax as a pleasure trip. They have no suspicion of the difficulties that await them.

The population of Sarnen welcomed them with the warmest demonstrations of amity. Refreshments were provided at municipal expense, and cigars distributed liberally.

Our troops have gone on to Melchtahl on foot; there they have been lodged in hastily-erected barracks. They are awaiting the order to go up to Frutt.

The timing of the attack depends on the arrival of the Bavarians sent by Germany, who have gone to Andermatt, from which they will cross the Furka pass with the Gardes de Sûreté from Saint-Gothard.

Thus, our troops, armed to the teeth, are a few hours' march from the fantastic Fortress. We are on the eve of great events.

Barbarus

LOUISE ACCESSON'S OPERATION
THE LITTLE GIRL'S TERROR
THE MOBILE SKULL'

Frutt

What a frightful spectacle a surgical operation is! And how much more terrible it is when it is not necessitated by an affliction to be cured, suffering to be calmed or a mortal threat to drive away.

At the appointed time this morning, Wolfgang Hingertil took me to one of the fabric rooms into which Flax's laboratory is divided.

There I find the surgeon, the Comtesse de Houdotte and Soeur Thérèse, all clad in long white smocks. The Comtesse de Houdotte is cleaning the surgical instruments; Soeur Thérèse is preparing pads and bandages. Dr. Flax, his eyes equipped with dark spectacles, seems to be sorting out flamboyant gains of radium-flaxium with some sort of awl.

When Wolfgang brings me in, the doctor gives him an order: "Go fetch the child."

The giant goes out, and comes back a few minutes later carrying Louise Accesson, the last little girl abducted in Paris and the only one not yet subjected to the gash of genius, in his arms.

Terrified by that formidable grip, and horrified by everything she has seen since arriving at Frutt, the child remains silent at first when she finds herself in our presence, looking at us one after another, her eyes wide with fear.

The giant deposits his living burden in an armchair, and, in a voice that he tries in vain to soften, in order to reassure the child, says: "She's very good, Doctor, very reasonable. She understands that everything that's going to be done to her is for her own good."

But Louise Accesson does not seem to be touched by the words that, in Wolgang's view, ought to comfort her. She stands up abruptly, jumps down from the chair and tries of run away.

In four strides the giant overtakes her and, having grabbed her round the waist, drags her toward the doctor.

"Don't hurt her," says Soeur Thérèse, reproachfully.

"I'm not," the giant replies, completely convinced of the gentleness of his actions.

"Come on, come on," says the doctor. "Let's not waste time." And, without paying any attention to the girl's howls, pleas and tears, with the calmness of a man working on inanimate matter, sculpting wood or modeling clay, he draws the child's head toward his breast and plunges her nose into a handkerchief soaked with chloroform.

The effect does not take long to makes itself felt.

Louise Accesson struggles, then rapidly calms down. When she is asleep, the doctor entrusts her to Soeur Thérèse, who lays her down on a camp bed and undresses her in haste.

In the meantime, Wolfgang prepares a kind of operating-table in the form of a long box supported by a large foot of robust appearance. At one end of the box, underneath, a hole large enough to admit a hand has been bored.

When Soeur Thérèse has finished, Wolfgang Hingertil picks up the child and sets her down in the box as if in a coffin. He places her in such a fashion that the child presents her left ear to the opening. Then he hoists the box up, the foot elongating like a folding telescope.

It is thus no longer possible for me, not being very tall, to see the body of the victim. All that I can still perceive, as I look up, is her poor little ear, her temple and a fragment of forehead near the left ear.

"Here's the chloroform," says Flax, passing the rag steeped in the soporific liquid to his aide.

Wolfgang sits down at the extremity of the box and watches the girl's slumber from the height of his giant stature.

In the meantime, the Comtesse de Houdotte explains to me that it is necessary to create, by means of Dr. Flax's methods, future mothers who will, in addition to the love of abundant families, the genius to raise them well.

"They'll be wives for our little geniuses," she tells me. "He hope to obtain thus, by crossing men of exceptional intelligence with women to have the cares and virtues of their role to a rare degree, a marvelous race that might perhaps be able to dispense in the future with the operations that are indispensable today."

Dr. Flax then takes a pair of scissors from a long sheath and slowly cuts Louise Accesson's hair all around the ear. After that, Soeur Thérèse hands him a soap-dish with a brush and a razor. He moistens the place deprived of hair with a little soap and sets about giving it a close shave, like an expert barber.

When the skin is perfectly clear, he takes possession of an instrument, turns toward me and says: "This is a trepan of my own invention. With the aid of this tool I can perforate the skull without leaving a trace. I'm going to make a fairly large opening in the skull. I shall remove the bone, and, when I've introduced a fragment of radium-flaxium into the location I've selected, I'll reclose and reseal the hole by replacing the piece of bone, like a cork."

I feel my legs becoming weak, my temples bathed with a mist of sweat.

Perhaps I am less troubled by the sight of that section of head that appears through the plank, than by all that surgical apparatus, and the horror of the blood and vital material that will suddenly escape a little human body by virtue of the striking calm of the two men and the two women.

They work without the slightest appeal of conscience. The peace of their souls is that of people who have faith.

Does a person have the right to damage and deteriorate a vigorous and sound human organism, which only wants to live according to natural laws? That is a question to which they give scarcely any thought.

Nothing in their gestures or their words betrays any doubt, hesitation or remorse.

Furthermore, their confidence and precision indicate that a kind of phlegmatic ardor—if those two words do not protest at being linked—is animating and guiding them.

With a pencil, Dr. Flax draws a small circle around Louise Accesson's ear. Then, with curt and rapid movement, he cuts.

And the flesh is lifted up, the bone laid bare.

Then the surgeon brings the trepan into play, and the frightful drill penetrates the skull, allowing a kind of sawdust to fall, white at first and then red.

"Look," Dr. Flax instructs me. "I'm uncovering the *dura mater*. That membrane, with which the brain and spinal column are wrapped, as if in a parcel, is agitated by a pulse. Oh, Monsieur, the first time I pushed my awl through that membrane, in order to slide a parcel of genius into one of my subjects, I was gripped by a great emotion. Although sure of myself, I wondered whether I might not be overstepping my rights as a surgeon and a scientist. I soon reassured myself. I was too certain of the result. There are moments in life when it is necessary to take risks."

Four times Dr. Flax sinks his trepan into Louise Accesson's cranial bones. When four holes have been bored, he removes the intermediary wall with the aid of a saw, the teeth of which, as it cuts through the skull, hurt my heart.

Then, defeated, I close my eyes.

I know little more about the operation that followed than what the doctor said to me. I therefore know that he pierced the three membranes of the encephalum, that he inserted a long thermometer into the soft matter in which the mysterious force of our intelligence shelters.

"Come closer," the operator commanded, not perceiving my cowardice at first. "You can read on the instrument the temperature of Louise Accesson's brain. I'm using a special thermometer manufactured in Paris according to the instructions of Angelo Mosso, professor of physiology at the University of Turin, to whom we owe very interesting studies of the different temperatures of the brain.[42]

"In order for me to succeed in my work of genification, it's necessary that the temperature remains at 38.30 degrees. If I don't obtain that favorable level, the Comtesse de Houdotte will pinch the child violently in her belly. That stimu-

---

[42] Angelo Mosso (1846-1910) was one of the leading neurophysiologists of his day, who devised numerous new measuring devices for monitoring physiological and neural activity. The instrument employed here was presumably one described in *La Temperatura de cervello* (1894)

lation will suffice to raise the temperature at the place I've just perforated. But that isn't necessary yet, for my thermometer is marking exactly 38.30 degrees."

Saint Augustine recounts that when he watched a gladiatorial combat he began to being sickened, that all his flesh quivered, and that he closed his eyes in order to longer to see the disgusting spectacle—but he had the misfortune to reopen his eyes; he could not close them again, fascinated in spite of himself by the spectacle of the blood and the palpitating flesh.

That memory crosses my mind, and I risk opening an eye, telling myself that I might perhaps get used to contemplating the surgeon's abominable work. Unlike Saint Augustine, I cannot bear that sight. In that second, however, I have time to make one observation.

"For what reason?" I ask Dr. Flax, "do you hold your little patient in that strange position?" The box in which the girl is lying is tilted, the head much lower than the feet.

"The reason is purely scientific. The brain is not immobile within the skull. On the contrary; it's a mobile mass. It moved back and forth at the whim of our movements. When we do to sleep on our back, it slides back and forth, filling a space that it finds free between itself and the frontal bone. When we're standing up, it heaps up. When I place my subjects like this, it's simply to bring the thinking matter closer to my instruments, by virtue of its weight."

Dr. Flax continues his operation slowly while talking to me. My eyes still closed, I follow his explanations as if in a nightmare.

Finally, he introduces the radium-flaxium into the encephalum…and henceforth little Louise Accesson has the genius of maternity.

When it is all over, Wolfgang Hingertil takes hold of the box in which the girl is lying, and the little patient is taken to the infirmary, where she will remain in the care of Soeur Thérèse and the little nurse of genius, Wenceslas Lévy.

As we leave the laboratory, the smiling Comtesse de Houdotte says to me: You shut your eyes!"

"Yes, yes," exclaims the doctor. "You haven't yet been able to rid yourself of the vain scruples and prejudices that are pursuing you. You wouldn't have protested if I'd extracted a rotten tooth from the child. There is, however, no comparison between the good that would result from the extirpation of a damaged molar and the result that I'm obtaining today for that child…

"Can you imagine the world in twenty or thirty years, when, thanks to the children of genius, there will finally be perfect happiness, when there will be no more poor people or sick people, no more suffering, madness or degradation? Will it not be a marvel well worth the price of drilling holes in the skulls of a few children with my trepan?"

I made no reply to Dr. Flax.

Alain Bernard

28 August

Melchtahl

The Bavarian troops leave Munich tomorrow. While awaiting their arrival, our men are training for mountain marches. Two captains have gone up to Frutt to reconnoiter the area. No one any longer wants to leave anything to chance.

Barbarus

THE ANTIVIVISECTIONIST LEAGUE PROTEST

Taking advantage of the general indignation against Dr. Flax's crimes, the Antivivisectionist League has had the following text displayed on posters throughout France.

Manifesto of the Antivisectionist League of France

It had to happen!

The scientific madness that immolates in vain experiments millions upon millions of rabbits, guinea-pigs, white mice and poor dogs has followed a fatal slope. It has ended today in carrying out on children the infamous methods of scientific research that are fashionable in all the physiology laboratories in the world.

Are not the indifferent, finally enlightened as to the cruelties of Dr. Flax, going to open their eyes?

Are they not finally going to realize that we are right when we protest against the barbarity of physicians who attempt to solve the problems dictated to them by a scientific imagination in delirium, by means of experiments on poor inoffensive creatures?

The madness of Dr. Flax is the final phase of the aberration that we pursue with so much ardor.

It was foreseeable that one day, one of these insensate scientists would continue on living, healthy human beings, the experiments commenced on animals taken from the pound.

We hope that the government will not allow itself to be stopped by any influence, that it will punish Dr. Flax in a suitable manner.

The Antivivisectionist League of France

THE WOMEN'S PROTEST

The theories of Dr. Flax, affirming that the female brain is physiologically inferior to the male brain, and that it can only aspire to the genius of maternity, has excited protests from a large number of women and all their feminist friends.

289

Among others, we have received a long letter signed: "A group of indignant women." We read therein:

"By his beautiful generous theories, and his marvelous visions of a sublime humanity, Dr. Flax has gradually lulled to sleep the anger aroused against the child-stealer. Yes, people forgot, or wanted to forget all that…

"And now the great mind allows himself to descend to ideas that all highly cultured individuals abandoned a long time ago. What a pity! Let him look around himself, then. He will see the Comtesse de Houdotte, who is certainly not a banal intelligence, nor a petty character..."

WITH THOSE AT ANDERMATT!

The company of Bavarian infantry, which the German government demanded to send, in order that no one else on earth could breathe without being monitored from Berlin, left Munich yesterday evening.

We have sent Clovis Binard to the capital of southern Germany to accompany the journey of the troops. He will then rejoin the Swiss soldiers at Andermatt who are also heading toward the Fortress via the Furka, the Grimsel and Meiringen.

Thus, all three of the reporters whom we launched to assault the affair of the child-stealers at the very start are now in the Swiss republic.

Barbarus will remain in Melchtahl in the midst of the French troops. Alain Bernard will continue to supply information from inside the Fortress itself. Clovis Binard will accompany the German and Swiss troops.

It will be granted that our reportage service is well-organized, and that in the adventure of Dr. Flax we have, as always, in the novelty and precision of our information, beaten the best-equipped of our sister papers hands down.

TO MUNICH!
FELDMARSCHALL VON HAESELER
AN ADMIRER OF FLAX
TOWARD FRUTT

I should have been in Munich days ago. I had even announced my journey to my readers. I was obliged to put it off at the last moment, having been advised that Marschall von Haeseler, whom I had been commissioned to interview, had been summoned to Berlin by a telegram from the emperor. It was said, in fact, the Wilhelm II is particularly interested in the scientific ventures of Dr. Flax, and that, after having received a long report from the German Ambassador in Paris, he wanted to give instructions personally to the old soldier charged with representing him.

It was, therefore, not until today that I disembarked in this fine and fortunate city.

Munich!

O old city of beer, fatherland of fuming sausages, land of tranquil and heavy men, fat men with fluid bellies, it is with pleasure that I see you again after many long years, between your walls, behind which, blond, brunette or black, the divine beer tickles the taste-buds and puts the mind to sleep!

Unfortunately, I have not had time to revisit all the old taverns that are the soul of this great city, where I spent entire months when I was a student, training my ardor as a neophyte drinker.

I scarcely had time to go shake hands with my friends, the artists of that extraordinary periodical of political caricatures, *Simplicissimus*: Resczinec, a sketcher of supple elegance, of silhouettes seen by an eye accustomed to the broadly-corseted figures of German beauty; Thoeny, the ferocious satirist of the incredible middle-aged officers under whose spur obedient Germany still tolerates life; Bruno Paul and Heine, artists of the pencil who do not scourge mores while laughing, but with tooth and claw, tearing away the flesh.[43]

As the train that was due to transport the Bavarian troops left an hour after the arrival of the express that brought me to Munich, I had to reduce to a minimum the pleasure of reawakening old memories in a city where I once lived, carefree and happy. I therefore set out, in haste, to track down Marschall von Haeseler.

Feldmarschall von Haeseler, overall commandant of the international troops directed against the Fortress of Frutt, is an old warrior, considered in Germany as the last representative of the great generation of generals in the mold of Moltke.

I was able to exchange a few words in a corner of the station with that stiff and angular old man, who gives the impression of being sculpted in some knotty tree-trunk.

The former governor of Metz and head of the troops that Germany piles up in Lorraine is emerging from retirement today in order to command the international troops. Guided by the kind of symbolic intelligence that is his alone, Wilhelm II has chosen this debris, venerated on the far side of the Rhine. He wanted to show, by designating the most glorious warrior of contemporary Germany for the expedition, that he is claiming for his nation a kind of right of military policing throughout Europe. He has only sent one company of Bavarian soldiers, but he is imposing on the common effort of the three nations an aged leader whose presence is as significant as a flag.

Marschall von Haeseler speaks French fluently, with a kind of arrogant grace. "What do you want, Monsieur?" he asks me.

"To ask you what strategy you intend to employ against D. Flax."

---

[43] The satirical magazine *Simplicissimus* was under attack in 1906—not for the first time—because of its relentless lampooning of Prussian army officers and Wilhelm II. The editor, Ludwig Thomas, was jailed for six months in that year, ostensibly for blasphemous offenses against the clergy.

"Oho!" he replies, smiling. "You think you're a war correspondent, do you? Do you think that a general would reveal his secrets to a reporter?"

"Marschall, your smile proves to me that you're not taking your objection very seriously. It's not a matter of an expedition of war."

"Indeed. And that's why I'm not formulating any kind of strategy. I shall respond to events—and, while having command of a few international troops, I shall do nothing without perfect agreement with Général Lacroux and Colonel Fahrlander."

"Have you read the correspondence of my colleague Alain Bernard, Marshal?"

"Certainly. I must confess that, at the moment when His Majesty's favor brought me out of retirement, I was beginning, thanks to Alain Bernard, to acquire a considerable sympathy for Dr. Flax. Oh, Monsieur, what a man! A superman! One of those individuals who surpass our banal humanity! We're going to disrupt that scientist's fabulous dream. Perhaps we're wrong! Perhaps it would be good to let him continue his work on the summits of Frutt. I've arrived at an age when the best one can do is to pass one's time in reflection. One has accumulated so many experiences! One ruminates them; one ends up extracting the principle, the essence and the sap therefrom. Well, it's from the heights of those meditations that I express my admiration for the boldness of the surgeon's conceptions."

"Your intention, then, is to treat him with respect?"

"What do you mean by respect? I shall fulfill my duty. I shall obey my orders. I shall make every effort to deliver the surgeon into the hands of the Swiss authorities—but that won't prevent me from treating him with the utmost consideration while he's in my power."

"Do you think that he'll put up lengthy resistance? Do you have means to counter the famous fluid and the condensation machine with which you're threatened?"

"No. Perhaps we'll fail. Perhaps we'll run into insurmountable difficulties. But if we fail in our objective, our very defeat will prove that I'm right, and that it's necessary to let minds of that caliber work in peace."

At that moment, one of those wooden staff officers who are a German specialty comes in. After a stiff salute, he informs the Marschall that the military train is ready to depart. The Marschall extends his hand to me and draws away, adding: "Until next time, Monsieur."

Ten minutes later, I take the same route as the troops, by the following train.

Marschall von Haeseler and Général Lacroux will meet tomorrow in Lucerne.

Clovis Binard

DR. FLAX'S MANIFESTO

Frutt

Dr. Flax has asked me to transmit the following manifesto, which he drafted this morning:

To the Civilized World,
To all men of intelligence and reason,
To all those whose minds, soaring above the preoccupations of everyday life, hope for a better humankind,
I write this:

I have disdained thus far to respond to the attacks of which I am the object in the world's press.

I grew accustomed a long time ago to considering the immense majority of humans as inept, incapable of free thinking, stupid and brutal to the point of being not much better than beasts.

I am profoundly scornful of what is mistakenly called public opinion, for public opinion is never an opinion. It is always an impulsive, irreflective pressure, which imposes itself on peoples like cold and warmth, by virtue of laws on which logic and reason have no purchase.

I have, in consequence, never taken account in my determinations of the judgments of the crowd.

Unfortunately, that public opinion, intellectually negligible as it is, might hamper the momentum of my discovery. I disdain the criticism of the masses, but I cannot disdain its effects, since they are now drawing three governments to form a coalition against me, in order to shackle my endeavor.

So, although I am powerful enough to immure myself in arrogant silence, and to fight, in order to be certain of being able to shelter my studies and my science from barbarians, it seems to me to be useful to appeal to a few veritable scientists. I simply want to put an end to the futile debates that currently divide, in my regard, the few rare individuals whose admiration I value.

This is where I am coming from and where I am going:

I have sounded the utmost abysses of the radical impotence of ameliorating humankind by the ordinarily advocated means. All the governmental formulae of happiness are either chimeras, optical illusions devoid of value, or the charlatanesque speculations of unfortunates who, in order to help people live, do not hesitate to bring about their death.

No economic doctrine being capable of ensuring the destiny of humankind, I have been led to think that general amelioration can only be obtained by surgical methods.

But what is the goal to be attained?

This:

The fortunate humankind will be that in which humans, thanks to perfected technology, will only have a minimum of actions to carry out in order to satisfy the essential necessities of life.

The human being for whom one minute of labor per day would be sufficient to ensure quotidian wellbeing will have all the rest of his time to cultivate his body, pleasurable sensations, fine sentiments and great ideas.

The fortunate humankind will be, in sum, that in which leisure will have been created.

That is already the way it is.

The man who has a servant is more fortunate than the man who has not, because, if he is not a fool, an idler, an alcoholic or an invalid, he has valuable leisure at his disposal, which he would not have if he were obliged to do his own cooking and make his own bed.

By the same token, France is a more fortunate nation than the majority of other nations, because the French citizen has, without being deprived of anything, more leisure than elsewhere, because many French investors possess property abroad—which comes down to the same thing as saying that the French collectivity has, in a number of less civilized lands, a large number of servants obliged to work for it, in order that it can live better than if each of its investors were obliged to bake his own bread and manufacture his own garments.

Social happiness can therefore be defined as the state in which one conquers, with the minimum of effort, a maximum of comfort and leisure destined for the perfection of human nature.

That happiness will be the work of a succession of men of genius, or it will not be.

Only geniuses are capable of developing technology to such a point that all the labor imposed on human beings will consist solely of operating a few switches, of effortlessly directing the great forces of nature.

Only thus will we arrive at the blessed state in which it will no longer be true, as Biblical language puts it, that a man is obliged to earn his living by the sweat of his brow. He will earn it while enjoying himself—and there will be paradise on earth.

That is what I have dreamed.

That is the goal that I finally have within arm's reach.

Can the imbeciles not comprehend that the prestigious success of my science ought to make everyone—even souls crippled by sensitivity—forget the few holes that I have been obliged to drill in a few skulls with the aid of my trepan and my saw?

Flax

FELDMARSCHALL VON HAESELER AND GÉNÉRAL LACROUX
FROM LUCERNE TO GOESCHENEN AND ANDERMATT
THE INSOUCIANCE OF THE TROOPS

Andermatt

The German soldiers, after a two-hour halt in Lucerne, have left again on the line to Saint-Gothard.

The anticipated meeting between Feldmarschall von Haeseler and Général Lacroux has taken place at the Hôtel National. Nothing was released after that conversation.

From Lucerne onwards I traveled in the same train as the German troops and disembarked with them at Goeschenen, at the entrance to the Saint-Gothard tunnel.

Throughout that beautiful journey, first along the shore of the lake and then through the audacious corkscrew tunnels that lead to Fluelen and the entrance to the Saint-Gothard massif, the German soldiers never stopped singing slow, sad songs.

At Goeschenen, the little troop quit the railway line to go on foot to Andermatt, a large village situated above the famous tunnel at an altitude of 1,444 meters. The march was very picturesque, along the sinuous road and through the gorges of Schoellenen, where the powerful torrent of the Ruess cascades, seething tempestuously.

Having arrived at the famous Pont du Diable, Commandant Kahlenbeck, who was at the head of the Bavarian troop and gives the impression of being a devilish fellow himself, bought each of his men a picture postcard of that tumultuous region. Many blonde Gretchens will receive that souvenir bathed with tears and the dirty water that the torrent projects over the road at that point.

Having given the order to depart again, the commandant directs his men to file in ceremonial fashion past the monument to Souvaroff, the great Russian cross erected near the bridge in memory of the famous general who, returned in 1799 from beating the French in Italy, lost thousands of Cossacks in that terrible gorge, ill-designed for the convenience of armies.

We then pass before an entire series of fortifications. At frequent intervals mountain is pierced by iron doors. One assumes that behind those openings all kinds of engines are is readiness that would prevent the ascent of any army bold enough to threaten Swiss neutrality.

Passing over the debris of a recent avalanche, we gradually approach, via the Uri pass, the great fortresses of Andermatt. As soon as we emerge into the high valley that overlooks the village we perceive that we are in the location where Swiss military engineers have elected to concentrate all the artillery that command the road to the Lac des Quatre-Cantons, the road to the Rhine, the Saint-Gothard pass and, further away, the valet of the Rhône, in the direction of France.

Before the distribution of their billets, the Bavarian soldiers are assembled by their officers in the middle of the great firing range at the entrance to the town. After a heartfelt speech from Commandant Kahlenbeck, who asks them to be polite to the inhabitants, they disperse in groups.

In the evening, the village offers a curious spectacle.

Andermatt is animated all year round by its garrison of Gardes de Sûreté, permanent troops that the complication of modern fortresses and big guns have imposed on the Swiss whether they like it or not, their democratic spirit preferring the militia system.

Those soldiers are paid four francs a day. The engineers can earn up to 3,200 francs a year. That is a tidy sum when one lives in a remote region at an altitude of 1,400 meters, where living is not expensive and mores are patriarchal. So the village of Andermatt is sometimes singularly lively, and, in the evening, all the little taverns fill up with clients who have money in their pocket.

Then, one sees balls of a Biblical simplicity organized in those establishments. Soldiers who possess harmonicas play them with an indefatigable ardor, while other soldiers dance with one another. From time to time the serving girls put down their trays and waltz until the call for service causes them to abandon their partner, to whom they return as soon as the requested tankard has been served.

These are innocent distractions. The Bavarians whom Commandant Kahlenbeck has just brought from Munich do not feel out of place among these pleasures of people devoid of nerves. Although wearied by a long journey, they dance until eleven o'clock, taking the Gardes de Sûreté as obliging partners for waltzes.

Needless to say, these are not the dances of sylphides. You can imagine the heaviness of the steps that hammer the ground beneath boots fitted with mountaineering crampons. Nevertheless, the spectacle has its charm and its poetry, all the more so by virtue of the tranquil joy of heart's content in the insouciance they reveal.

Almost all these men will be exposed, doubtless as early as tomorrow, to the infernal inventions of the genius of Dr. Flax. How many of them will remain forever on the steep slopes of Frutt? And yet, not one of them is thinking about the imminent battle, and perhaps-imminent death.

And they are dancing!

Clovis Binard

GÉNÉRAL LACROUX AT MELCHTAHL

Melchtahl, noon

Général Lacroux arrived in Melchtahl yesterday evening.

He immediately went to the Hôtel Alpenhof, where the Landamman welcomed him on behalf of the canton of Unterwalden.

After that polite exchange, a great conference was held in which the French officers took part, along with Monsieur Hamard, the Commissaire of the Sarnen Police, the Master of Melchtahl and the Swiss Captain Herner, the staff officer attached to Général Lacroux by the Swiss government.

As soon as the debate opened, Général Lacroux sent for Rudolph Hermlein and the guide Werner Dürrer. The painter and the mountaineer responded immediately to that invitation. They played a leading role in the discussion.

Rudolph Hermlein's opinion is categorical. He thinks that the conquest of the fortress is almost impossible.

"The general confidence of your officers and soldiers is truly astonishing," he repeats to me. "It can only come from a kind of skepticism. They don't believe in Dr. Flax's machines. It's necessary to have felt their power in the flesh, as I have, to be convinced. I dread bloody disillusionments."

An overhead telegraphic wire has been established between Melchtahl and Frutt, some two hundred meters from the Fortress. As soon as the troops have reached the plateau, a wireless telegraphy mast will be erected. Another mast will be planted at Engstlensee for the Swiss soldiers and Marschall von Haeseler's Bavarians.

Barbarus

A great dinner will take place this evening at the Hôtel Alpenhof, hosted by Général Lacroux, for the fathers and mothers who are still in the village.

A SUPERB MEAL
THE GENIUS OF CUISINE
THE IDEAL CUTLET
ATAVISM

Frutt

Dr. Flax and the Comtesse de Houdotte have invited me to lunch. It's the first time that they have done me that honor. It was an exquisite lunch, ultimately refined in its quality and the delicacy of its dishes.

I have never eaten anything so supremely good, so ideally perfumed, so perfectly perfect.

What sauces! Aromatized with what science, with what artistry, worthy of the gods!

Nothing is more ordinary than mutton stew, but there is mutton stew and mutton stew. The one that I tasted at the doctor's table was a marvel, a masterpiece, a miracle, and Lucullus dining *chez* Lucullus could not have offered himself a more extraordinary gourmet experience.

Naturally, I offer my compliments to the mistress of the house. My enthusiasm overflows all the more because, until then, the cuisine at Frutt had left much to be desired. The menu, prepared by the Hingertils, had never been very delicate: eggs, meat cooked to varying degrees, ham and vegetables, generally hard. So the change was most agreeable. Damn it! I am positively carried away by the g…oulache,[44] as a distinguished Hungarian once said to me

I therefore perform as a good trencherman should. The doctor smiles on seeing me eat with such a hearty appetite. "Good, isn't it?" he says, his eyes radiant.

"Oh yes!"

"This cutlet," the Comtesse de Houdotte observes, while sucking a bone, "is truly the ideal of cooking, a veritably sensuous experience."

"Yes," the doctor says, "It's scientifically perfect. One cannot imagine a better one, as much in terms of its seasoning as the quality of the cooking."

And it is the same throughout the meal.

The Comtesse marvels, the doctor is ecstatic, at every course.

While judging that enthusiasm just and well-merited, I cannot help thinking that one might nevertheless change the topic of conversation at least once. I try several times to introduce a different subject, but without success.

The Comtesse de Houdotte notices my stratagems and says: "We're so happy, Monsieur! Finally, two days ago, our cook began to manifest signs of the genius that the doctor has sown in him. He's given us a great deal of anxiety, that child. We thought, for some time, that the operation had failed. The blossoming has been belated, but the result is now evident. That's why you see us so delighted with regard to these beans and potatoes."

"What is the name of the child to who you have attributed the genius of cuisine?"

"André de Vautremesse."

"What! The Baron's son?"

"Yes, Monsieur."

"That's not a very aristocratic genius."

"In the world of which I dream, there will be no aristocracy except that of genius. The cook of genius is equal there to the engineer and the physician of genius."

---

[44] This pun does not translate, being based on the meanings of the French *gout* [taste] and *lache* [loose].

"Why did you choose that child rather than another for the specialty in question?"

"I acted in full knowledge of the case. André de Vautremesse had an innate talent for that métier. He obtained it—the Vautremesse family is doubtless unaware of it—by virtue of atavism. A Vautremesse once married the daughter of Vatel, the celebrated maître d'hôtel of the great Condé, who committed suicide for fear of not having sufficiently salted the supper that his master was offering to the king at Chantilly."

"So it's not at hazard that you distribute genius?"

"No, Monsieur. I only ever develop my subjects' essential aptitudes. That's why the son of Pietro Palavacoccini, the remarkable spy, has become a spy. Frantz Vetyolle has the genius of navigation..."

"But his father is a harpist! It's not by scraping sonorous strings that one invents boats."

"Certainly—but Frantz Vetyolle counts among his ancestors the grandfather of the great Nelson. I quickly realized that, among all the qualities with which that child is endowed, those of the famous seaman are reproduced most strongly. Atavistic particularities often make great leaps. They are lacking for four, five or ten generations, and then reappear all of a sudden, at the moment when one least expects them. Little Clépent has an aptitude for studying the phenomena of condensation. His father doesn't have it; he's a good stockbroker and nothing more. But Général Clépent, who went with Napoléon to Egypt, left marvelous studies on the formation of clouds."

Such is the conversation that I had with Dr. Flax and the Comtesse de Houdotte while guzzling the products of the genius of André de Vautremesse. Although well aware of everything that is being planned against us, the doctor continues to be confident. In spite of the imminence of the attack, he scarcely touched on that subject during lunch.

Numérien Hingertil has told me that young Isidore Bimorel, the genius of ballistics, has invented a new rifle, compared with which the weapons of our troops are children's toys.

I have asked the doctor to give me a list of the different geniuses he has created. I will send it to you as soon as I have it. It will interest the families of the children stolen by the doctor.

Alain Bernard

A NEW EXPLOIT OF THE WHITE CHILD

Melchtahl, 9 p.m.

During the dinner that Général Lacroux offered to the fathers and mothers still at Melchtahl, Dr. Flax's spy, the famous White Child, Paolo Palavacoccini, was found hiding in a cupboard in the dining room that is almost never opened.

No one had seen him enter.

That child's cleverness surpasses all imagination.

He refused to tell us how he got into the dining room and into the cupboard.

The scamp does not give the impression of being a prisoner. He replies to all questions frankly, but in an extinct voice, as if worn out be fatigue.

We examined him very attentively. Dr. Riffelard, the father of the young Riffelard who, according to Alain Bernard, possesses the genius of pneumatism, examined the scar the Paolo Palavacoccini has beneath his left ear. The observation did not, however, lead to any interesting observation. Dr. Riffelard proposes to continue the examination of little Paolo attentively, in order to be able to make a report to the Académie de Médecine as soon as possible.

Paolo Palavacoccini has been locked in a hotel room under the guard of two Alpine infantrymen. We shall still have gained, by virtue of his capture, the advantage of leaving Dr. Flax in ignorance of our plans.

Barbarus

Melchtahl, 10 p.m.

The White Child has just escaped.

Barbarus

Frutt

As he promised me yesterday, Dr. Flax has given me a list of the young geniuses, with a few notes added for my usage by the Comtesse de Houdotte. Here is the curious enumeration, as I received it this morning:

THE LIST OF GENIUSES, WITH OBSERVATIONS
FOR THE BENEFIT OF ALAIN BERNARD

Bernard Flaquette, known as Bobichon, has the genius of engraving.

Paolo Palavacoccini has the genius of espionage.

Urbain Godedouins has the genius of jewelry

Ange Pompaigne has the genius of amity. This was the child who welcomed you so poorly, Monsieur Bernard, on the first day that the doctor summoned you—the child who divined your presence behind the door and warned us, like a guard dog. Ange Pompaigne is the son of parents who cherished him beyond measure. It is because he has retained something of that immoderate love that the genius of amity has devolved to him. He is our friend—the doctor, the Hingertil brothers and me. He watches over us, and strives to give is pleasure. He only lives for us. He is also our joy. All the other geniuses have hard hearts; there is no point in expecting the slightest mark of affection from them. They are only capable of pride and stimulation. They do not act for the pleasure of others; they are pure egotists. That is why the doctor has created a genius of amity, who introduces a hint of softness into all that hardness, and who will give the world, in the midst of the fecund egotism of other geniuses, the good example of tenderness and generosity.

Pierre Candelaur has the genius of poetry. He has recently written a hymn to glory, which is one of the most admirable songs ever sung in human language. That hymn to glory has been set to music by...

Nicolas Barlatescu, who has the genius of music, and whose brain composes the most beautiful sonorous harmonies.

Frantz Vetyolle has the genius of navigation.

Jules Bimbaleau has the genius of painting. He is the one who painted the adorable subjects ornamenting your bedroom.

Fernand Pig has the genius of electricity.

André de Vautremesse has the genius of cuisine.

Charles Clépent has the genius of condensation.

Godefroy Pomme has the genius of aerostatics; he has invented a kite that he has succeeded in launching outside the terrestrial atmosphere. He has thus been able to capture a certain quantity of the interplanetary ether, which

Vincent Montier, who has the genius of chemistry, is in the process of analyzing.

Léon Aproli has the genius of gardening and agriculture.

Bouquet de Gobely-Franthéon has the genius of lockmaking.

Philippe Soleillaut has the genius of leaping.

Isidore Bimorel has the genius of ballistics.

Wenceslas Lévy has the genius of nursing. He too is a good example of long-range atavism. In him an aptitude was revealed that had been dormant in his family since the death on a pyre in the era of the Inquisition of his ancestor, the Spanish Jewish physician Rabbi Mardocke Lévy.

Justin Chipé has the genius of animal husbandry. Before the operation, he was already greatly interested in the rearing and training of animals; remember the letter to his grandmother found in a pocket of his garments, in which he was talking about giraffes and elephants with a kind of affection.

Ambroise Riffelard has the genius of pneumatism.

Émile Loubé had the genius of sculpture.

Gontran de Vautremesse has the genius of fashion design. I deem that the art in question, taken to the extent that this young genius will soon develop it, will be considered as the most perfect of that time, above that of painting and sculpture.

Louis Maneuil has the genius of fermentation and distillation.

Philippe Ordin-Rosier has the genius of architecture.

Aristide Peinassols has the genius of furniture. He was the one who furnished your room.

Finally, the six girls:

Germaine Plaizance, Victorine Artésy, Alice Poliarre, Alice Change, Fernande Bonnéglise and Louise Accesson have the genius of maternity. Their genius is, naturally, still useless, since they are only six years old. It will develop gradually and will only appear in its plenitude when they are sixteen or seventeen years of age.

Such are the geniuses that the doctor has created for his initial trials. An entire series is missing therefrom, which he will fashion as soon as his success is imposed on the world, the peoples of which, with a unanimous voice, will demand that he continue his Work and will generously provide him with subjects on whom to operate, to genify.

THE CONFIDENCE OF THE BESIEGED

Add to that list the names of Dr. Flax, the three Hingertil brothers, Soeur Thérèse and the Comtesse, and you will have calculated all of the small garrison that Dr. Flax intends to oppose to the assault of the international troops.

I do not count myself among the combatants. I shall retain until the end an impartial historiographer, nothing more.

302

Our garrison, you might think, is scarcely considerable: four men, two women and thirty-one children, six of whom are girls, against battalions of infantry and mountain troops.

"Bah!" Wolfgang Hingertil replied to me, to whom I pointed out the small number of Frutt's inhabitants. "One of our little geniuses is worth a hundred thousand men. If Charles Clépent finishes his machine in time, we'll take on the entire world and emerge victorious."

Alain Bernard

FLIGHT OF THE GENIUS OF ESPIONAGE

Frutt

Paolo Palavacoccini has just returned. He has told us that he was captured voluntarily yesterday evening at the Hôtel Alpenhof, but escaped later having succeeded in introducing a narcotic into his guards' beverage.

Alain Bernard

Melchtahl

Paolo Palavacoccini put the two soldiers charged with guarding him to sleep. Cleverly, he poured a substance whose nature has not yet been verified into their cups. He escaped then through the window, letting himself slide down into the street along two bed-sheets tied together.

The alarm was raised a quarter of an hour later. The "White Child" has not been recaptured.

The Swiss and Bavarian troops will arrive at Engstlensee tomorrow. As soon as they are gathered in that locale, on the far side of Frutt, we shall go up to the Fortress, in numbers this time.

Barbarus

THE GERMANS AND SWISS ON THE FURKA ROAD
FINAL DISPOSITIONS

Meiringen

I have accompanied the Swiss Gardes de Sûreté and machine-gunners who, preceding the Bavarian column, are showing it the way from Andermatt to the Furka and Grimsel passes.

The signal for departure was given at three-thirty a.m., in icy darkness. Fortunately, the colonel in command at the square of Andermatt lent me a horse. I don't know how I would have been able to follow otherwise, for the route seems interminable. It is, however, so grandiose, the air there so rich, that one can tolerate fatigue there that would seem unbearable elsewhere.

Eyes filled by the marvelous spectacle of glaciers that a chilly sun was painting with pale gold, we climbed solely toward peaks eternally covered with vast snow-fields.

Unused to such landscapes, the Bavarians often pause. Their trumpets sound then, to warn the Swiss, who are marching ahead, to slow down.

At the Furka pass, black coffee was served to the troops. It was not a luxury, for we arrived there in the middle of a snowy squall that suddenly descended upon us without warning, chilling us to the bone—after which the sun reappeared, and it was in a dazzling atmosphere that we descended as far as the Rhône glaciers.

A large meal was served outside the tavern in Gletsch, in the open air, facing an enormous stairway of blue and white ice, which gradually melts and becomes animated, to form the thin trickle of water that is the nascent Rhône.

After a halt of two hours, it was necessary to go up the linked slopes all the way to the Lac des Morts, to descend again between rugged crags to the hospice at Grimsel.

From there the troops went to Handegg. We made a long halt alongside the sixty-five meter waterfall, a frightful bound that the river Aar makes at that spot.

Four hours later, we finally reached Meiringen, where, exhausted by fatigue, the Bavarians did not have to be begged to go to bed. A very excusable urgency! A brisk walk of 71 kilometers accomplished in seventeen hours, in ups and downs, was weighing on their legs.

The Swiss soldiers, used to marching in the mountains, arrived as fresh as on departure. They are hearty fellows who don't look very pretty but are as solid as their rocks. One can demand the greatest efforts from them.

People here are asking which the Bavarian troops were obliged to take a long detour. It would have been simpler to transport the Germans by rail from Lucerne to Meirginen instead of obliging them to make that forced march. It appears that it was at the express request of the Emperor of Germany that the men were subjected to that fatigue. Wilhelm II wanted, by means of a difficult military march, to accustom the Bavaria soldiers to the atmosphere of the high mountains and familiarize them with landscapes of ice and snow before they established a base at Engstlensee, at the foot of the formidable massif of the Titlis.

We leave tomorrow for Engstlensee, and operations will immediately commence against Dr. Flax. It will take us five or six hours to climb from Meiringen to Engstlensee.

As soon as the Germans have left Meiringen, they will be replaced by the three Swiss companies charged with investing the Fortress directly from that direction.

Marschall von Haeseler is already at Engstlensee. He has made the entire journey from Andermattt to Meiringen by landau, and from there, the indefatigable old man has continued on horseback.

It can be assumed that, tomorrow afternoon, operations will be definitively commenced against Dr, Flax. Events are about to accelerate.

Clovis Binard

One of our most celebrated professors of medicine has sent us the following article. We are publishing it, although it is anonymous, for reasons that everyone will understand. It expresses frankly the secret opinion of many scientists,

BOLD OPINION OF AN ANONYMOUS MEMBER OF THE INSTITUT
IN FAVOR OF VIVISECTION
SURGICAL EXPERIMENTS ON HUMANS ARE A NECESSITY OF SCIENCE

The dispatches of reporters confirm one another. Mobilization is today general around the Fortress of Frutt, and the doctor is making his final preparations to withstand a siege.

Can the outcome of the struggle be foreseen? It is certain that, thanks to the inventions of the child geniuses, the doctor possesses reliable and very powerful weapons. All the apparatus and strategy of modern military art are worthless in confrontation with the inventions of Frutt.

Dr. Flax is several centuries ahead of us in terms of equipment for war. Our troops in Switzerland today are what Caesar's would have been had they, on invading Gaul, run into modern France with her long-range rifles and improved artillery. What, in spite of all their bravery, all their discipline and all the genius of their leader, could the Roman legions, armed with swords and lance, possibly have done? Exterminated beneath a rain of shrapnel and machine-gun bullets, a hundred thousand men would have been easily defeated by a hundred of our infantrymen and a single artillery battery.

It is the same for the international troops at Frutt. It is not without a constriction of the heart that one thinks that those brave men are going to sacrifice their lives for an impossible task.

In these conditions, opinion is beginning to realize that it might perhaps be better, instead of exposing those human lives to the reprisals of Flax's geniuses, to leave the surgeon to his work, to wait, to temporize.

There will surely come a time when the man that the voice of the people calls "Dr. Hell" today will emerge from that strange Fortress. Then, one of two things will be the case: either he will have succeeded completely, and humankind will have the profit of his endeavor; or he will have failed, and there will still be time to capture and punish him.

"What!" people will cry. "You're proposing to sacrifice thirty-one children, consenting to their imprisonment? You're renouncing any attempt to rescue them? But that's abominable!"

Is it not more abominable still to expose a thousand men to certain destruction? Between two evils, we should choose the lesser.

It is worth noting that some of the surgeon's most determined enemies have completely changed their attitude since they learned the reason for which the surgeon carried out his numerous abductions.

All of them were energetically opposed to the doctor while they were ignorant of the motive for his crimes. Outraged by his dissimulation, outraged by having been duped by him when he dared to set himself at the head of those who were investigating the child-stealers, and outraged against his accomplice, audacious enough to have made a resounding speech at the Trocadéro, to have organized the mothers' procession, and to have spoken on behalf the victims even in the reception rooms of the Élysée, they launched themselves flat out against those odious liars.

But now, everything has changed, everything is explicable. Everything is almost excused.

Certainly, I would never permit myself to attempt a project analogous to Flax's—but his great success is a redemption such that no one in the scientific world can any longer cast a stone at him.

Yes, he had reason to dissimulate, to lie; he had reason to surround himself with every precaution, without which he would not have been able to create his geniuses, for his discoveries will mark an important revolution in the world, will overturn humanity from top to bottom.

In those conditions, our change of mind is explicable. It is entirely due to a saner appreciation of the situation.

Of course, the anti-vivisectionists are having their say. They have found a marvelous opportunity to exploit the stupidity of the human heart. They go everywhere, repeating the same old refrain that no progress in medical science has been achieved by experiments on animals.

Now, the opposite is the case.

None of the great achievements of modern therapeutics has been obtained without the sacrifice of millions of animals.

And then again, let's be frank. For a long time, already, physicians have been trying out their remedies and their instruments on human beings. In 1835 William Wallace injected subjects with venereal disease in order to prove contagion.[45] Recently, the scientists Klingmuller and Bachmann injected humans with microbial products. The American commission studying yellow fever in Havana worked on living subjects who were paid to undergo practical experiments. That is how Cuba was rid of the fever that was terrifying its population.

One might object that the victims of the American commission consented to the sacrifice of their health, which Flax's children are victims of force. I would not give two sous for consent obtained from someone dying of hunger

---

[45] The reference is to William Wallace of Dublin (1791-1837), a surgeon at the Jervis Street Infirmary, still celebrated for the illustrations of skin diseases composing "the Wallace Collection." The subsequent reference is more obscure, although "Klingmuller" is presumably the German medical researcher Victor Klingmuller.

when one offers him bread and a scalpel on the same plate. Flax has simply extended somewhat the methods of scientific context that have become a contemporary necessity.

I will add that there has not yet been a complete sacrifice, that the children are alive. I will say more. The parents have only to congratulate themselves on the fortunate transformation of their children.

That slightly bold opinion will probably not be to the taste of all my readers, but it is nevertheless, however unpleasant and inhuman it might be, a perfectly defensible philosophy.

Doctor X
Member of the Institut

THE TROOPS AROUND FRUTT

Melchtahl, 11 a.m.

The French colonel and the Swiss colonel have led their infantrymen to Frutt. The troops have been disseminated up there in a long cordon of surveillance arranged around the domain of Frutt, about two hundred meters from the wall.

On arriving at our destination, we saw above Frutt, on the promontory of sorts from which Rudolph Hermlein and Alain Bernard let themselves down into the Fortress, Swiss soldiers who had come from Meiringen and were already mounting guard overhead.

With the aid of my binoculars, I was able to observe all the movements of the men, clad in dark blue trousers, blue trousers and shakoes with peaks and neck-covers. They have hoisted a cannon up there. What is good for? Nothing, since any bombardment is out of the question.

The wireless telegraph had sent us orders from Engstlensee to camp around the Fortress for the night. Tents and blankets have been sent up.

The cold is intense in the hours when the sun is not shining. The men will doubtless suffer considerably.

Engstlensee, 2 p.m.

Marschall von Haeseler has made his first dispositions for battle.

The path between Engstlensee and Frutt is very good. It slopes up gently, except for one place, where it suddenly rises, among the pasturelands and chalets of cheese-makers, in a steep and stiff slope, over a kind of enormous step in the mountain.

The Bavarian troops and the Swiss Gardes de Sûreté advanced as far as that step. Then, after an hour's rest, they reached the environs of the Fortress.

As I am sending this by telegraph, we can distinguish, a short distance away, on the other side, the French putting up their tents. Further away, we can see the three companies of Swiss infantry that have come from Meiringen under the command of Colonel Fahrlender.

The Gardes de Sûreté have established an entire line of machine-gunners, behind which we are camping.

It is assumed here that Marschall von Haeseler's objective is to overwhelm the Fortress beneath a general assault, acting by surprise.

The doctor is giving no sign of life. The Fortress looks dead. The fluid machine is not humming.

Perhaps the attack might even be mounted tonight.

Clovis Binard

FLAX'S SPEECH TO THE GENIUSES
A BLACK SPOT

Frutt, 5 p.m.

Dr. Flax has just gathered all the little geniuses in his laboratory. He seems to be extremely worried. A visible disquiet is furrowing his brow.

"My children," he said to them, "stupid men are trying to prevent you from developing your precious genius. Men, jealous on seeing children surpass them in intelligence, have seen an army against us. It is a matter of defending ourselves. To be sure, we have nothing to fear. Charles Clépent, the genius of condensation, and Ambroise Riffelard, the genius of pneumatism, can ensure our safety. Add to our weapons the precious information brought to us by Paolo Palavacoccini. The peril is therefore slender. But it is indispensable that you help one another, instead of seeking, as you do, to harm one another and prevent one another from working. All our results might be compromised by the stupid jealousies that are increasingly dividing you. I will be obliged to take punitive measures if I perceive, one more time, the ill will that is making you implacable enemies. Go."

The children listened to the admonition tranquilly. They went their separate ways without any evidence of either approval or protest—but it is certain that they are not united. Perhaps that is the reason why Dr. Flax seems preoccupied.

I have the impression that something serious is happening here, and that, in consequence of some fact of which I am unaware, the surgeon's defensive situation is not as solid as I thought.

309

THE BLACK SPOT?
ISIDORE BIMOREL'S NEEDLES

Frutt

An order has been relayed to me by Chrysostome Hingertil not to put my nose outside today.

The doctor fears that the Swiss installed on a rock overlooking us might have orders to fire on anyone appearing inside the Fortress.

A conversation with the Comtesse de Houdotte has confirmed the suspicions that I telegraphed to you yesterday. I encountered Dr. Flax's friend in one of the subterranean tunnels that have been revealed to me this morning, which link together all the buildings in the Fortress.

While she was speaking to me, the Comtesse's face was sad and distraught. Combine that with the visible discouragement of the preoccupation that I read in Dr. Flax's eyes yesterday, and you will reach the same conclusion that I did.

I tried to seek information for the reasons for this melancholy from the Hingeril brothers, the only people who know everything that is going on, but the big men don't say anything that they don't want to say.

Dr. Flax's position remains very strong, however, to all appearances.

A little while ago, Wolfgang Hingertil showed me a little instrument invented by Isidore Bimorel, the genius of ballistics, in collaboration with Ambroise Riffelard, the genius of pneumatism.

"A difficult collaboration," Hingertil tells me. "Those diabolical kids don't want to help one another. The doctor and I have to force them, and that's not an easy task. In then end though, they've succeeded, all the same, in making us a little device that will cool the zeal of our enemies in a singular fashion."

I examine the little tube, twice the length of a finger, that he giant holds out. It's a ling of hollow wand made of hard wood, fitted with nickel rings. Inside it, one can distinguish a complicated mechanism through a tiny glass window. A kind of mobile viewfinder, like the ones in certain kinds of photographic apparatus, is screwed on top, approximately equidistant from the two ends.

"What does the rod do?"

"It's a rifle. Does that surprise you?"

"A little."

"You're not unaware that in modern weapons, the makers of rifles have a tendency to reduce the caliber of the bullets. Isidore Bimorel has taken that process of improvement to its conclusion. The projectiles launched by this weapon, which is pneumatic, are needles. Look, here's one of them."

Hingertil hands me an extremely slender but not very flexible blue steel needle.

"With that little rifle we can launch these new projectiles to a distance of 4,200 meters. They always fly point forward, in such a way as to penetrate directly into the flesh. Furthermore, the special viewfinder permits an almost mechanical precision. Once can strike wherever one wishes—in the eye, the throat, the legs; one has the choice."

"Are the wounds mortal?"

"Less so than the bullets used by armies. One of these needles can go straight through a man, in and out, without occasioning fatal tears. But the points are dipped in a liquid concocted for us by Vincent Montier, the genius of chemistry. One molecule of that liquid, brought into contact with blood, provokes an intolerable burning sensation throughout the body, a pain so intense that the most heroic soldiers quit the battle and refuse flatly to expose themselves again to such sensations. In sum, this marvelous weapon of war is one of the most humanitarian. It is content to put combatants out of action, to inspire such terror in them that they're no longer willing to return to the ranks. It doesn't kill; it just creates a distaste for battle. The defensive result is the same."

This description of Isidore Bimorel's rifle proves once again that Dr. Flax will not have any difficulty resisting. The international army have to contend with an enemy who will almost certainly defeat them with the novelty of his machines and methods, unless...

Unless a little wisp of straw whose existence I suspect without being able to see it intrudes into the doctor's work, to corrupt it and render it fragile.

Alain Bernard

AN INTERVIEW WITH EDISON

New York, via P.Q.

Our American sister paper, the New York *Sun*, has interviewed Edison, the most famous contemporary inventor, about the case of Professor Flax. This is how the conversation went:

"What do you think of the affair of the child-stealers?"

"An embarrassing question, even for a mind prompt in decision. I won't compromise myself, however, by telling you that it's not a criminal affair like any other."

"I thought that for you, contrary to the opinion of some scientists, that it *is* a criminal affair?"

"I say 'criminal' because if the doctor is caught, he'll be tried and condemned as a criminal, but I don't say that he *is* a criminal."

"So, if you were a judge, you'd acquit him?"

"It's necessary never to condemn or to acquit people when one is not their legally-appointed judge, when one does not have all the documents in the case in hand, and the means of clarifying doubts. Otherwise, one risks being mistaken or indulging in journalism. I can't tell you what I would say to you if I were a judge, because I'm not."

"If you had been in Flax's situation—if you had invented what he has invented, discovered what he has discovered, would you, in order to make sure of your experiments, have done what he has done?"

"No."

"So you would have preferred to lose the fruit of your labors rather than try them out on young children?"

"Yes."

"However, it's been argued that the general benefit that might emerge from the discoveries of the French professor is greater than the particular evil inflicted on a few children."

"Indeed. There's no comparison."

"Your conclusion, therefore, is that a scientist has no right to carry out experiments on humans, even if the result of his studies would be a considerable improvement of the conditions of life for the generality of human beings?

"Yes."

"So, Flax didn't have the right to act as he has done?"

"He didn't have the right."

"So, if he didn't have the right, he's culpable?"

"Yes."

"Well, my dear master, if he's culpable, it's necessary to condemn him. You've answered the question that you refused to answer just now."

"Wrong! Professor Flax is culpable, but his culpability is of an entirely exceptional nature. I admit not only the possibility of an acquittal, but even of an acquittal with acclamation. Or the judges might condemn him, and at the same time congratulate him, in order to offer him a statue in the principal public square of Paris—a decision that wouldn't seem absurd to me. Flax has made himself illustrious with the most important discovery of the centuries."

"Those are somewhat contradictory sentiments, my dear Master, and subtle."

"Humans are obliged to live in the midst of contradictions, to accommodate illogicalities. If one wanted to reason scientifically in the Flax affair, one would reason differently than in reasoning practically. One would say: the goal of science being to ensure the wealth and progress of the greatest number, any particular evil from which that wealth and progress germinates does not count, is non-existent for the scientist. Thus, Flax was right. And yet, he was wrong. He was wrong because humankind cannot establish that verity as a moral law, because that verity is too dangerous, because all the imbeciles, all the semi-savants and all the social climbers that encumber the academies would make use of it for futile, shameful or stupid projects."

After this interview with Edison, our readers may be sure that Flax is increasingly finding loud voices to defend or absolve him. The opinion of the celebrated American will certainly win the favor of thousands of scientists.

Frutt, the Swiss Camp

I have visited the Swiss camp to our right and contemplated for some time the famous place from which Alain Bernard allowed himself to be lowered into the Fortress.

From that position one can look down on the entire scene, and all the preparations for the attack.

One can see the Bavarian troops on the far side, whose tents are aligned around one of those little mountain chapels, the cottages of the good Lord, that one encounters everywhere in Switzerland, in the remotest locations.

To their right are massed the Gardes de Sûreté from Saint-Gothard.

A great activity reigns in that camp. The soldiers are exercising actively with wooden ladders and ropes.

To the left, the French flag flutters above a large octagonal tent, which is used by Général Lacroux.

In the general opinion, Marschall von Haeseler has been too adventurous with the international troops. They are too close to the Fortress.

It is feared that Dr. Flax is only tolerating that immediate neighborhood in order to be better able to get rid of his enemies at a single stroke.

A sentinel has fired at the White Child, but without hitting him.

Barbarus

IMMINENCE OF THE ATTACK

Engstlensee

It is not true, as rumor has it, that Marschall von Haeseler wants to temporize. He has, on the contrary, decided to strike a heavy blow, to risk everything, no matter what the cost. I am in a position to affirm that a general attack will take place tomorrow morning, irrevocably.

Clovis Binard

313

3 September

A CATASTROPHE
INTERNATIONAL TROOPS ROUTED
SERIOUS REVERSES

Melchtahl. 10 a.m.

We were going to attack the Fortress this morning! We have been put to flight, and how!

What a frightful tempest! All the calamities that intemperate weather can accumulate over the heads of men, by means of rain, cold, snow, ice and wind, fell upon us this morning at six o'clock.

It was already an hour since the trumpets and bugles of the international troops had sounded for the various awakening services and had had their response, awakening he echoes of the mountains. Beautiful sunlight illuminated the neighboring snow-fields. The day promised to be clear, beautiful and joyous.

Suddenly, white clouds appear on the surrounding crests, like the vapors of volcanoes. They thicken rapidly, join together, melting into one another, while circling the Fortress completely, as if to spare it. Then, abruptly, the immense cloud sinks downwards, and drowns us in a fog that could be cut with a knife.

The inhabitants of London have never sought to find their way in an atmosphere more opaque or drearier. It is impossible to distinguish anything clearly more than half a meter ahead of one. At sixty-five centimeters one can scarcely make out the indecisive and blurred silhouette of a man. It's worse than night.

We remain thus for more than an hour, immobilized in that semi-obscurity, which no artificial light can pierce. It appears that large electric searchlights have been illuminated twenty meters away from the place where I am groping my way through that vaporous cotton wool, but I can't even see them.

Gradually, that icy vapor penetrates us to the marrow of our bones.

We shiver, and our teeth chatter.

I yearn for my cloak, in vain. I can't find my tent, set up at the entrance to the road to Frutt, behind the troops. Where the devil is it, in this atmospheric smoke?

I wander like a soul in torment, in the midst of other souls in torment, who are stumbling, bumping into one another, looking under their noses without being able to see what they're looking for, in the midst of an inexpressible confusion. Numerous are those who fall into the thousand holes garnished with Alpine roses, the thousand excavations with which the ancient glaciers have riddled the locale.

But that pitiless fog is only the anodyne commencement of a frightful finale.

While our teeth rattle with cold, a great wind rises.

Far from chasing away the mist, it seems to be concentrating it, heaping it up upon us.

That wind is turbulent, glacial, cutting. It stings us with razor-like thrusts. Lips are instantaneously chapped. Breath solidifies in moustaches. It is something atrocious, to make one scream.

I encounter three men I don't know. Instinctively, with similar movements of self-preservation, we huddle together. And clutching one another, hugging one another, we turn our backs, if I might express myself thus, to that new and sudden tempest.

That wind lasts for ten minutes or so. It is followed by an inundation such as the records maintained by pluviometers have never registered. The heavens have never opened their floodgates so wide.

Is it rain? It's a torrent that is collapsing. It is the Deluge of ancient times renewed, an ocean that has broken its dykes.

After the rain comes the snow, thick and heavy, with large flakes that look like cow-pats. It is, in spite of everything, a relief. One can finally breathe in the white whirlwind, whereas the flood of water almost choked us.

But what now?

Are we going to be buried by the accumulating snow? It is soon up to our knees. Where can we run? How? The fog, in the midst of precipices, retains us better than if we were wearing iron shackles.

Finally, the snow stops.

But then, a new joy, a hailstorm breaks over our heads. The hailstones fall so violently, so harshly, than at nearby tent whose fabric I feel is riddled with holes.

My right ear is torn away.

It is as if Rudolph Hermlein's jacket has been ripped apart with a knife. Werner Dürrer has been undressed. There is not one among us who is not carrying wounds inflicted by the pebbles of ice with which we have been bombarded.

At the height of the tempest and the hailstorm, we hear the bugle, vaguely, sounding the retreat. The commander gives the order to get away, as quickly as possible, from that inhospitable region—but how? It's impossible to walk in the wind...

I end up protecting myself, gradually, by lying face down on the ground, and covering my head with four large stones pulled over my hair.

Oh, the bugle can sound. I don't obey. And then, what a croak the bugle is making!

Fortunately, the tempest suddenly stops.

I'm out of breath.

One last assault of more violent wind concludes the atmospheric tragedy. As if a magic wand has been waved, everything calms down. The storm of water, ice and fog vanishes, and a resplendent sun illuminates the scene.

What a disaster!

All the tents are flattened, shredded and soiled.

Not a single pole has remained upright

Not a single rope has held firm.

A spectacle of desolation.

Soaked to the bones, hair stuck to our heads, sick, feverish, brutalized, bleeding from wounds inflicted by hailstones, the men try to find their officers, to regroup.

No one has obeyed the signal to retreat.

As best they can, the officers assemble around their general. The decision is made to retreat to Melchtahl as soon as possible. Medical attention will be given there to the most seriously injured.

As we are about to depart, a messenger appears, covered with filth from head to toe, a living mud. It is one of the frontier guards under the orders of Marschall von Haeseler. He has come to announce that the Bavarian and Swiss troops are in a lamentable state, and that they are retreating to Engstlensee.

With my binoculars, which have miraculously escaped disaster, I can see that the Swiss from Meiringen have also abandoned their positions.

We descend, at the double, toward Melchtahl, leaving the Fortress of Frutt in the beautiful warmth that is now falling from the skies, and seems to be mocking us, radiant and gently.

At Melchtahl, by order of the medical officer, all the men massage one another furiously. It is hoped by that means to avoid the serious chills that the inundation to which we have been subjected gives reason to fear. Fortunately, there are no serious injuries to deplore, but all the baggage is ruined. All the equipment that was to serve in the assault is ruined, all the rifles rusted. That will not hasten the taking of the Fortress.

Barbarus

The following dispatch from Alain Bernard explains the catastrophe described by Barbarus:

A FEAT OF THE GENIUS OF CONDENSATION

Frutt

Chrysostome woke me up very early.

"Quickly, quickly, Monsieur Bernard. You're going to witness a fabulous spectacle.

I get dressed in a hurry. The giant takes me to the laboratory, where I find the Comtesse de Houdotte, Dr. Flax and the other two Hingertils.

Little Charles Clépent is with them.

"Go, now," Flax orders him, as soon as I arrive. "Give us a sample of what you can do."

The young genius of condensation presses a button. The wind rises.

In the space to ten minutes, the mountains are covered with cloud, sealing the Fortress in a great circle of mist, and the phenomenon that has caused so much comment is reproduced.

While the vast clouds swell up around us, the sun continues tranquilly to illuminate our little domain. Then the wind increases, surrounding us with frightful rumbles, gusts, roars and whirlwinds—but not a single breath raises a ripple on our placid lake, whose water reflects before our eyes a large patch of blue sky framed with gray.

"It's the work of Charles Clépent's condensing machine," the doctor declares, triumphantly. "It isn't yet functioning perfectly, but nevertheless, it already has an unimaginable power."

"Ah!" the Comtesse remarks, sadly. "If only our little geniuses didn't hate one another. Dr' Flax's Work would appear, from now on, with all the characteristics of perfection. Unfortunately, in spite of all our efforts, they're jealous of one another, and as they grow in ability, they're less and less inclined to help and support one another."

"Can you imagine," added the doctor, "that Isidore Bimorel and Ambroise Riffelard have refused to participate in our defense because Charles Clépent has been charged with it alongside them. Bimorel has declared that he won't make use of his little needle-firing rifle. Riffelard has affirmed, no less energetically, that he won't furnish the compressed gas necessary to activate that extraordinary instrument if I accept the aid of Charles Clépent. At present, they're sulking in corners, and I can't get anything out of them."

For more than an hour, the tempest that spared us ravages the surrounding area. When it dies down rapidly, as if exhausted, and the mist surrounding us vanishes, Dr. Flax invites me to go up to the top of his laboratory.

One can, in fact, walk on the roof, which one reached by means of a small spiral staircase.

From there, one can see a long way.

The hurricane has completely devastated the surroundings of Frutt.

"What has become of the international troops?" I ask, quite astonished.

"They've fled, vanquished by Charles Clépent's condensing machine. As I foresaw, the genius of condensation has saved us. Look at what remains of the French and Bavarian camps. And doubtless nothing remains of the Swiss camp set up over our heads to the right, of which we don't have a complete view. The tempest has swept them all away more effectively than a hundred machine-gunners. Will that shower calm our adversaries down, or will it be necessary for the genius of condensation to prepare another artificial Berezina for them? I'm waiting for Paolo Palavacoccini, who's in Melchtahl. He'll inform me of the moral effects of our victory.

Alain Bernard

For his part, our colleague Clovis Binard writes:

Engstlensee

Marschall von Haeseler's troops have suffered, without combat, the same checks as the other French and Swiss columns. The Marschall has retreated to the Hôtel d'Engstlensee, from which he has telegraphed the Swiss camp at Thoune for them to send him, as soon as possible, new equipment the shelter his men.

C.B.

A GREAT TURNABOUT
THE DISSIDENT SCIENTISTS RETURN TO THE STAGE

It is an infatuation, almost an enthusiasm.

From all directions, protests are rising against the three governments making war against Dr. Flax.

To tell the truth, some Flaxists are exaggerating slightly. To hear them, the surgeon is the only victim.

It proves yet again that might is always right. Defeated, Flax would probably not have found so many defenders. Triumphant, he is drawing noisy friends in his wake.

These morose reflections are only aimed at the opportunists and self-advertisers who are trying to obtain a little publicity by acclaiming the name, branded with disgrace by the crowd, of Dr. Flax. They do not apply to the great scientists, the great artists and the noble individuals who are taking the surgeon's side purely as a matter of conscience and as a duty of supreme humanity.

The anonymous article by one of the dissident scientists published here the other day has revealed an interesting reversal of opinion of Dr. Flax's former enemies.

Now his friends are applauding!

THE PROTEST OF LETTERS AND ARTS

This is the text of another protest, which is followed by the most important signatures in the world of letters and arts:

The undersigned contend, in accordance with Edison's opinion, that the case of Dr. Flax is an entirely unique case, which cannot be judged by reference to ordinary law or morality.

They contend that the sending of international troops has been a double and serious fault, firstly because it was futile to expose the lives of brave men to the effects of invincible machines, and secondly because the superhuman science of Dr. Flax merits other consideration than the organization of an international police expedition.

They contend that, the solution of great social problems being, in our era, the permanent anguish of all men of feeling and intelligence, the work of Dr. Flax and the Comtesse de Houdotte cannot be judged in the same way as a case of burglary and a case of drunkenness.

They contend that, in spite of the cruelty of the means, that work is fine and praiseworthy. They contend that, even if the surgeon of Frutt has partially failed, it is one of the most noble ever conceived by a human brain.

The contend, like him, that the tears of parents are a small matter by comparison with social happiness, even merely glimpsed; that the suffering of a few is the necessary ransom of the joy of all; that the dolor of a few individuals is the necessary fertilizer of a universal flourishing, in the same way that a single rotting carcass at the foot of a rose-bush will soon blossom in a thousand healthy and perfumed roses.

Among the signatures that follow the text, we find those of Anatole France; Victor Margueritte; Théodore Cahu; Camille Flammarion; Séverine; Jean Ajalbert; the painter Besnard; André Honnorat, the former deputy of Monsieur Dubief at the Interior; the celebrated composer of music Mroczkowski; Marcel Prévost; Millerand; Coquelin the elder; Gabriel Trarieux; J.-H. Rosny; Abel Deval; Jules Bois, etc.

THE FLAW IN THE WORK
JEALOUSY AND GENIUS

Frutt

I have made you party, in my recent correspondence, to the anxiety and worries that have been furrowing Dr. Flax's brow for several days.

The Comtesse de Houdotte and the Hingertil brothers have, as you know, explained the reasons for this preoccupation to me.

Now, the situation is aggravating with disconcerting rapidity.

The victory of the genius of condensation has put the other little geniuses in a rage, overexciting their jealousy.

They are ferociously scornful of one another today; they hate one another mortally.

The doctor is direly fearful of the excess of these hostilities, which he despairs of curing, or even attenuating.

A compliment that the Comtesse de Houdotte gave Charles Clépent yesterday, to thank him for having put the troops to flight by means of his machine, almost provoked a revolution. Each of the geniuses demands exclusive praise; praise addressed to another is considered as an insult.

There have been acts of vengeance.

The superb flower-beds that Léon Aproli has carefully designed have been entirely vandalized during the night. Nothing any longer remains of the new flowers that the young genius of gardening had succeeded in growing in a matter of days. It is suspected that Ambroise Riffelard, with a jet of his pneumatic machine, has scythed down all those plants.

I have already recorded the fact that the genius of ballistics, Isidore Bimorel, has refused to collaborate in the defense of the Fortress. It is to that manifestation of vanity that our soldiers owe their escape from the needles of the little rifle.

Soeur Thérèse is desolate.

"It's been ten days now," she mourns, "since the character of our little geniuses has been modified and embittered. They demand, imperiously, that one expresses profound admiration for them. It's necessary to heap them with hyperbolic eulogies and enormous flatteries—and still on condition that one does not do likewise for the others. We've been obliged to separate the most intractable of them from their comrades.

"Can you imagine that little Chipé has allowed a herd of goats on which he had begun a fascinating work of selection, to die of hunger? Why? Solely because I had the audacity to claim, in his presence, that Godefroy Pomme, who has succeeded in launching a kite beyond the atmosphere, and succeeded in a very interesting experiment. Their jealousy is becoming unhealthy, acquiring an irritability that you can't imagine. I'm heartbroken."

"Bah! These are minor inconveniences. I don't understand why Dr. Flax is allowing himself to become so obviously depressed by this minor flaw of character in his geniuses."

"Minor flaw! Say immense vice, which might compromise the entire work. Even assuming that they don't exterminate one another one day, you must understand that their intimate collaboration is the key to the vault of miraculous progress that we're counting on for humankind. If Godefroy Pomme refuses to furnish Vincent Montier with the transatmospheric ether captured by this kite, it will be a vain conquest, a useless acquisition. That ether is only interesting if a specialist chemist can analyze it, study it and extract al the consequences from the acquisition. Without that, the discovery remains vain and sterile.

"Can't Dr. Flax correct the character of his geniuses?"

"Yes, but that would require a further operation. Dr. Flax would undertake it without hesitation if he had not, in spite of everything, been badly affected by all the anger that he has aroused in the world. The Master believed that as soon as he had proved the reality and the solidity of his discovery, he would no longer have to do anything but throw open the doors of the Fortress—that not only would the governments not form a coalition against him, but that they would come together to assist him, in order to permit him to continue his studies in the best conditions possible.

"He's been deeply disappointed. Will not the partial failure, which is preventing the geniuses developing normally because of the unexpected action of the microbe of jealousy, give new strength to his countless adversaries? Are they not going to criticize him even more bitterly than before? Well, he's hurt by it—and he's hesitating."

I am reporting this conversation with Soeur Thérèse to you; it seems to me, in the present circumstances, to be of the greatest importance.

Remember that, since my arrival in the Fortress, I have scarcely been able to get the inhabitants to talk. As soon as I attempted to ask questions, I ran into evasive responses. I was referred to Dr. Flax.

Today, tongues are loosening of their own accord; the situation must be serious, and difficult.

I shall try to see Dr. Flax.

If I can draft a telegram in time, you will receive explanations on the subject of the curious incidents that are preoccupying the inhabitants of Frutt so gravely.

Alain Bernard

Melchtahl

In sum, Flax has inflicted a veritable rout upon us, and a ridiculous rout.

People are mocking us.

The international troops have fled, but the number of dead and wounded—I mean seriously wounded—is zero. We are scarred by the scratches of the hail, but we are quite well. The sunlight that accompanied us from Frutt to Melchtahl dried us out so conveniently that, with the aid of massages, chest infections have been avoided.

We cannot look at one another without laughing. If the discouragement of the fathers and mothers of the little geniuses were not so profound, our disaster would be positively cheerful.

The most extraordinary aspect of the affair is that, even here, Dr. Flax is gathering more sympathy. Our soldiers have a boundless admiration for him. The cold shower has made them grateful. It is a very curious result. The officers are loudly professing the same opinion. As before, they will be obey orders, but if they are sent to renew the assault of Frutt, they will say to themselves quietly that the order is absurd and stupid.

It is rumored that the three governments are even more determined to take extreme measures.

Will they mobilize an army? But what can an army do against "atmospheric warfare"?

Barbarus

UNEXPECTED NEWS
IS FLAX SURRENDING?

Melchtahl, stop press

Rudolph Hermlein and Werner Dürrer, who went back up to Frutt this afternoon, one of them to try to find his binoculars and the other a pair of boots lost during the storm, have just returned to Melchtahl.

They have brought extraordinary, incredible news.
A white flag has been hoisted over the Fortress.
Does Flax, although victorious, intend to surrender?

FLAX CAPITULATES
THE REASONS

Frutt

A *coup de théâtre* that will strike the world with amazement: yesterday evening, Dr. Flax hoisted the white flag over his laboratory, thus announcing his decision to surrender to the troops sent against him.

That decision is uniquely motivated by the increasing discord between the children.

Dr. Flax is not discouraged, but the hatreds that have increasingly paralyzed the impetus of the geniuses have obliged him to change his plans.

It appears that even the genius of amity has led Ange Pompaigne, out of amity, to all sorts of acts of violence. His amity for the Comtesse de Houdotte and Dr. Flax has become frightfully egotistical. He cannot bear others to have amicable relations with those he loves. He bit Numérien Hungertil's finger because the doctor thanked his three bodyguards for their absolute devotion and ardent and disinterested collaboration, in emotional terms.

In operating on the children, Dr. Flax thought of everything, except for the essential law of human nature that all geniuses are jealous of one another, and detest one another more, the more genius they have.

It therefore seems proven today that a society entirely composed of men of genius could not survive, that it is condemned to a thousand intestinal disputes that would radically compromise its existence, and that, in the final analysis, all things considered, it would not be superior to a society of worthy individuals of mediocre or average intelligence.

What good are extraordinary discoveries if they only serve to annihilate one another, in permitting the geniuses to harm one another?

That is one of the true reasons for Dr. Flax's capitulation.

Wolfgang Hinteril is becoming loquacious in misfortune. He has revealed to me another flaw in the surgeon's work. The doctor had already touched upon it, but I had not realized that the vice was so disastrous.

All the geniuses of Frutt are narrowly specialized. Each mind, exclusively drawn toward a single magnetic pole, cannot attach itself to anything other than a single obsession, which directs it. The specialist of genius—musician, aeronaut, cook, chemist, etc.—is so impassioned for his specialty that it is all that interests him. Everything else seems futile, inconvenient, and harmful.

Charles Clépent judges it extravagant and insane that anyone can enjoy the verses of Pierre Candelaur or the music of Nicolas Barlatescu. That is one of the reasons why he is so exasperated when he learns that Dr. Flax and the Comtesse de Houdotte have sent for those two little geniuses to distract them in the evening. Poetry and music are, for him, arts that are not merely inferior but non-existent. He cannot conceive that anyone might find pleasure and stimulation in anything but the problems of condensation.

That detail explains in another fashion the indifference and apathy marked on the faces of all the little geniuses. Nothing awakens their attention outside of their essential preoccupations. They are only susceptible to two sentiments: that of pride when their own genius is admired, and that of envy, or insane rage, when the genius of another is admired.

In a society exclusively composed of geniuses, therefore, social relationships would become impossible. For lack of a few common ideas and admirations, the geniuses would die of starvation alongside one another, without understanding why.

That prospect has changed the surgeon's plans without destroying his hopes. He expects to continue his work.

"Why am I surrendering at the moment when I'm victorious?" he says to me. "I'm surrendering because I've made a grave error of calculation, in not taking into account the destructive jealousy of the geniuses. That error, I can redeem in my subjects within six months—for I have reason to believe now, in spite of everything, that I will be allowed to correct my work in Paris, in better conditions than those at Frutt. The scientific world is rising up universally in my favor. Tomorrow, the French government will beg me to continue my experiments. So, what am I risking? I've fought without displeasure, at Frutt, against the international troops, but it would be difficult for me to sustain a perpetual battle here against me little geniuses. I prefer to recommence my endeavor in Paris and perfect them in peace at my hospital in Montretout."

"But what if you're mistaken? What if the courts, obedient to the crowds that detest you, and to the law, condemn you?"

"Don't worry. They won't condemn me. Think that men like Edison have come to my defense. Edison is worth as much as a crowd. I consider that, at this moment, there's no longer any danger for the Comtesse, the Hingertils, or Soeur Thérèse, or me, in coming back down from these mountains to the civilized world. And if there is a danger, well..."

"Well what?"

"Say that I'm not afraid and that I have more than one means today of emerging victorious. I hope that I shall be spared the necessity of having to astonish the world once more..."

At ten o'clock, trumpets sound on three sides at once, informing us that the detachments of international troops are within sight of the Fortress.

I run in haste outside the walls.

A few moments later, my worthy friends Barbarus and Binard run to meet me.

We shake hands with an inexpressible emotion. We embrace one another.

Oh, how good it is to find one's friends again, after so many adventures!

Barbarus and Binard precede Général Lacroux and Marschall von Haeseler, who arrive together.

The two senior officers, who are joined by Colonel Fahrlender, hold a brief conference outside the gate.

The following protocol is adopted: Marschall von Haeseler will enter the Fortress first to receive the surgeon's surrender officially; from that moment on, it will be the French general who is deemed to be in command of the international troops. That mode of action has been anticipated by the diplomats, in order to establish an equal balance between France and Germany, and not to offend any patriotic susceptibility.

But now the three Hingertil brothers appear, dressed in their Sunday best. It is necessary to have seen Chrysostome Hingertil in a frock coat to understand the effect of our fashions on an elephant,

"Marschall," says Numérien Hingertil, emotionally, "Dr. Flax is waiting for you. I have orders to take you to him, with your officers."

There are twenty seconds of hesitation. Might it be a trap set by Dr. Flax? Without my presence, they would have taken great precautions before penetrating into the Fortress, but in a few words, I explain the reason why the surgeon does not want to take resistance any further, and we go in.

In agreement with Barbarus, I am now passing the pen to Clovis Binard.

Barbarus and I are exhausted by this rude campaign. By virtue of the agreement, today—the day of the arrest of the child-stealer—marks the end of the competition of reportage and cannot change the result.

It is up to our readers to designate the winner.

Alain Bernard

FIRST MEETING OF MARSCHALL VON HAESELER AND DR. FLAX
THE CHILDREN WILL NOT BE RETURNED TO THEIR PARENTS
UNTIL TOMORROW MORNING

Marschall von Haeseler chose a dozen officers to accompany him to meet Dr. Flax.

After a rather complicated march through a labyrinth of walls, our company arrives at the Lac de Frutt.

There, the first incident occurs. Frantz Vetyolle, the young genius of navigation, suddenly flying into an inexplicable rage, sets fire to the extraordinary boat he has constructed, which Alain Bernard has described. In the blink of an eye, the launch is reduced to ashes.

Preceded by the Hingertil brothers, who are marching heavily with sad expressions, we finally reach Dr. Flax's laboratory. They introduce us, and, in the first fabric chamber, we perceive Dr. Flax, the Comtesse de Houdotte and Soeur Thérèse standing in a group.

Dr. Flax salutes us with a broad gesture, and a vague smile in his hollow eyes. The Comtesse de Houdotte bows. I glimpse a tear in the corner of her eye. Soeur Thérèse is weeping copiously.

Marschall von Haeseler advances toward the surgeon and holds out his hand affectionately.

Is that an enemy accepting the surrender of a defeated adversary? No. The old officer ostentatiously translates, in his grip, all of his high esteem for the miraculous scientist.

"Doctor," he says, "my emperor's orders oblige me to consider you as my prisoner. Naturally, I obey those orders. But I can ennoble my mission with the respect that is due to you. How do you wish to be treated?"

"Marschall," the doctor replies, "I'm touched by your words. I thank you, both on my own behalf and that of my friends, now your prisoners, as I am. This is the program of capitulation that I propose. Leave me in the Fortress for one more night. I need a few hours to put my papers in order, and to record a few more scientific observations to which I attach a very high value. Whatever the future has in reserve for us, it is not detrimental to the good of science to let me record my experiments, my results and my theories. Also, since you want to be agreeable to me, don't take delivery of the children until tomorrow. I want to examine them individually, one more time. Will you please, n consequence, forbid the parents entry into the Fortress until the morning. I will then place myself, as well as my friends, at the disposal of the French general who, from that moment on, will do with us as his orders and his conscience dictate."

These proposals made by Dr. Flax are accepted by Marschall von Haeseler, and we immediately leave the Fortress.

When the fathers and mothers gathered behind the troops guarding the gate of the Fortress learned that they must wait until tomorrow to have the right to embrace their children, we witnessed a furious revolt.

In a fit of anger, the Baron de Vautremesse even struck a junior officer who, faithful to his orders, refused to let him pass.

That incident will have no consequences. The officer refused to make a complaint, excusing an almost unhealthy nervousness, exasperated by days of anguish and continually disappointed hopes.

The return of the children to their parents thus promises a moving spectacle.

Clovis Binard

THE GENIUSES AND THEIR PARENTS
A TERRIBLE DISILLUSIONMENT

Frutt

This morning, at nine o'clock, the return of the children to the parents took place, in the presence of Général Lacroux, today the commander-in-chief, and Marschall von Haeseler.

A grave and poignant scene!

The mothers and fathers are lined up in front of the large door of the barracks where the little geniuses reside.

They are waiting feverishly, their faces contracted with impatient anxiety.

Monsieur de Vautremesse, his fingers clenched, is twisting and tearing his moustache. Madame Peinassols, Barbarus' fiancée, who cannot walk yet, has been carried up to Frutt on a stretcher; she has the wooden shafts of her litter nervously, and is digging her fingernails into them, quivering because she cannot stand, cannot run to her child when he comes out.

At the appointed time, Chrysostome Hingertil opens the door and appears on the steps. The giant is greeted by a long, hostile murmur. Cries of rage burst forth. Fists are waved at him.

"Scoundrel!"

Monsieur de Vautremesse, who has already resorted to acts of violence yesterday, is prey to an extreme agitation. The French general moves closer to him and admonishes him gently.

"You need to calm down, Monsieur, or I shall be obliged to have you removed. What good is this excitement? It's utterly futile, and can only cause trouble. Master it. Set an example. What will the women do, if the men can't control themselves?

Chrysostome Hingertil seems quite nonplussed by this hostile welcome. Like Flax, his accomplices cannot comprehend the execration of which they are the object. They cannot even imagine the implacable hatred of the parents. Why this relentless hostility? Has the surgeon not rendered the children a service by increasing their intelligence?

Timidly, with awkward gestures, the giant speaks: Dr. Flax," he says, in a voice that is loud but tremulous with emotion, has ordered me only to release the children to you one by one. It is necessary, to avoid the incidents of jealousy that would surely arise if I were to release all the geniuses together, at the same time."

The parents shout, whistle and protest. "We've waited long enough! Immediately!"

The general is obliged to intervene again. "It will be done," he orders, curtly, "in accordance with Dr. Flax's wishes."

Then, at a sign from Chrysostome Hingertil, Soeur Thérèse opens the door and comes forward, holding a pale and listless child by the hand: Louise Accesson.

A great groan goes up from the audience.

"My daughter! My daughter!"

And a woman runs forward, her features convulsed, almost fearful with overexcited maternal love. She holds out her arms to the child and pounces.

"Madame," observes Soeur Thérèse, "don't shake her, I beg you. The operation is recent. The child is still very weak. It will take a full month for her to recover completely and..."

Without replying, the mother carries the little girl away in her arms. Like a dog that has stolen a bone and takes it away in order to gnaw, she retreats behind the group of fathers and mothers in order to get a better look at the child, to embrace her more conveniently, to savor her happiness egotistically, out of sight of the others.

The other five girls then emerge from the barracks.

As each one appears, the same crisis follows. Loud cries, tears, and the mother's flight, as if she feared at that the child-stealer might change his mind, and take back the possession that she had finally recovered.

At each appearance, too, the anger seething in the hearts of the others, those who are still waiting, increases and swells. The paltry appearance, the unhealthily diaphanous complexion of Dr. Flax's victims, torment all the unfortunates with a pity sharpened by the aguish of anticipating the imminent sight of their own child, equally faded, lacking in strength and blood.

The girls having been returned to their parents, the boys are brought out one by one in the same fashion by the second giant, Wolfgang Hingertil. He begins with Aristide Peinassol, the genius of comfortable furniture. Barbarus takes the child by the hand and takes him to the stretcher on which his mother is waiting attentively, rendered desperate by her forced immobility.

Then come Philippe Ordin-Rosier, Louis Maneuil, Vincent Montier, Émile Loubé, Ambroise Riffelard and the others, almost in the inverse order of that in which they were abducted and operated on.

While the first one before whom the door to liberty opened seem delicate and unsteady on their feet, the later ones, who went under the scalpel a long time ago, are visibly more robust and solid—but they all walk with that extraordinarily jerky gait, like puppets moved by springs.

Gradually, as the number of returned children increases, a veritable concert of noisy tears and sobs rises and propagates among the fathers and mothers. All of them are astonished and distressed by a frightful observation.

In the first moment of expansive tenderness, the first passionate enlacement of arms, they have not perceived that their children hardly recognize them. They are soon obliged to yield to the evidence. The geniuses remain cold to the most persuasive appeals. It is not that they do not remember the familiar faces and smiles, but that they have, in gaining intelligence, completely lost the memory of the heart.

"Do you recognize me?" Monsieur Clépent asks his son, in front of me.

"Yes. You're my papa, and this is my mama."

"And you're not kissing her, your mama?"

"What's the point? Would that help the progress of the machine for condensing clouds?"

"We're going back to Paris. You'll find all your toys, and Maria, the maid who spoils you so much."

"I'd rather stay here where I have my tools. If you want to take someone back to Paris, take Ambroise Riffelard, who annoys me and has a grudge against me."

This conversation with the young genius of condensation, who maintains a serious impression, and the attitude of a disillusioned old man, gives some idea of the mortal remarks to which the dolorously surprised parents are obliged to listen.

Their disillusionment is bitter and heart-rending. They expected great demonstrations of love, cries of joy, a babble of foolish tenderness; they find icy, wicked little creatures, egotistical brains inaccessible to emotion: strangers.

The pupil of Dr. Flax who offers the most disconcerting spectacle is Ange Pompaigne. The genius of amity struggles furiously in the embrace of his mother and his father. The poor people who attempted to commit suicide a few weeks ago, in the despair of losing their son, are in the presence of an unchained demon.

Not only does the child not respond to any caress, but he protests desperately against the idea of accompanying his parents to Paris. Howling with rage, he demands Dr. Flax and the Comtesse de Houdotte. He does not want to leave them. It is to them that he remains attached by heart and mind. In the attempt to get rid of his father and mother he ends up punching and kicking them.

Soeur Thérèse runs up and intervenes to put an end to that tragic scene.

"Dr. Flax foresaw this," she tells the tearful parents. "Ange won't allow you to take him away. If you insist, if you hurry the child along, he's capable of throwing himself out of the window of a carriage, at the risk of killing himself, in order to get back to his friends. It's necessary for you once again, and gradually, to win the amity of your son. To facilitate that process, Dr. Flax requests that you entrust the boy to him. Ange will accompany the doctor and The Comtesse de Houdotte to Paris. They'll work on his during the journey, and get him used to the idea of living with you. If you prefer, you can travel with them. You can thus, with the benevolent mediation of Dr. Flax, pay court to your child and gradually reconquer his affection.

Monsieur and Madame Pompaigne immediately accept this bizarre plan. Preceded by little Ange, who departs like an arrow to find his great friend the doctor, and by Chrysostome Hingertil, they quickly disappear behind the massive door of the barracks.

In spite of the almost general resistance, a few of the geniuses are taken away without delay by their families. A little caravan is thus organized for the descent to Melchtahl. Fifteen children depart in that fashion.

The others want to spend the night at Frutt. It is on Dr. Flax's advice that that decision is made by the parents. According to the surgeon, it is necessary to treat some of the little geniuses with great care. Too abrupt a change of habits might be disastrous, and might drive them to frantic revolt. The parents ought first to walk with their children for an entire day in the environment to which the little ones are now accustomed to living.

So beds are set up in various rooms, where the mothers and fathers will spend the night.

DOCTOR FLAX AND THE PRESS

It is not until tomorrow, at a time that is not yet fixed, that Dr. Flax, the Comtesse de Houdotte, the Hingertil brothers and Soeur Thérèse will be taken away by Marschall von Haeseler and Général Lacroux, who, as soon as the prisoners reach Melchtahl, will hand them over to Monsieur Hamard and the policemen charged with returning them to Paris.

The Swiss newspapers, which, so long as Flax was only reproached for the abduction of children, had agreed that the surgeon and his accomplices should be tried in Paris, have changed their opinion.

In fact, they say, by virtue of his resistance to the Swiss authorities, the surgeon has rendered himself guilty of a crime that concerns the local judges. Most of the injuries and incapacities that he has caused, including the contusions and sufferings of Alain Bernard and Rudolph Hernmlein, and all the effects of the fluid, have been inflicted on Swiss subjects. Flax ought, therefore, to be tried in the Swiss courts, in the opinion to the newspapers.

But would there not be a veritable disappointment in society if the individuals formerly besieged in Frutt were stolen from French justice?

That is also the opinion of the Swiss government. It has decided to derogate the customary rights. It has been announced today that a general assembly composed of the national council and the state councils will authorize the federal council to allow Flax to be tried in a French court.

Frutt
Marschall von Haeseler has hosted a big dinner this evening at Frutt. Numérien informs me that Flax has a surprise in store for the German officer's guests.

C.B.

THE MARSHAL'S BANQUET
BOUCHÉES FLAX
ORGAN MUSIC
THE NOBLE APEARANCE OF THE PROFESSOR
HIS PERSUASIVE ELOQUENCE
ENCHANTMENT

Yesterday evening, as we announced yesterday, Feldmarschall von Haeseler hosted a large farewell banquet in Dr. Flax's laboratory for the officers on the international troops who took part in the astonishing Frutt campaign. He had also invited the fathers and mother who were still in the Fortress and a few reporters.

It was thus that I had the great joy of rediscovering our friend William Trisson, still a drunkard and still triumphant. The American policeman-turned-journalist formally affirmed to me that he holds the record for sensational news since the flight of Professor Flax. I don't doubt it. The question remains as to whether the sensational news in question contained a single accurate fact.

The Marschall's banquet was very animated. The word "banquet" is really a trifle ambitious; the menu included in fact, neither ortolans nor rare vintages. Marschall von Haeseler, refusing to touch Dr. Flax's provisions had charged Bruster, the hotelier in Sarten, to send up the elements of the dinner in haste. The menu was, therefore, Spartan in its simplicity: ham and eggs, breaded veal cutlets, *bouchées Flax*, "floating islands," beer and coffee. Even then, there were not enough veal cutlets for everyone; the guests who missed out were compensated with a double ration of ham.

Official feasts are rarely as meager, but war is war! That frugality allowed us the advantage of avoiding the odious "federal sauce" in which three hundred thousand morsels of meat float, untenderized by the bath in question, at ten thousand Swiss *tables d'hôtes*.

That stoical repast was, however, redeemed by one dish of divine softness, whose savor tickles my palate even in memory. I recommend *bouchées Flax* to all our gourmets. Brillat-Savarin would have wept with love. They had been prepared by young André de Vautremesse, the fist child stolen, in whom, by courtesy of the doctor's scalpel, the savory genius of cuisine had been incarnated.

The Baron de Vautremesse had attempted to prevent his son from preparing the dish, but the father had been obliged to give in, the child having been shaken, as a result of that prohibition by a serious fit of convulsions.

Never have I tasted anything finer, more supremely exquisite, than those mouthfuls, prepared, it appears, with calves' liver fried in little pieces in an oil perfumed with certain mountain herbs.

At the end of the meal, while the palate was still enchanted by that delicacy, when we were in the process of nibbling a few excessively dry raisins and even drier hazelnuts, Marschall von Haeseler got to his feet and made a short speech in French.

"Messieurs," he said, "Our task is complete. It has concluded, I confess, much better than I ever dared to hope. If the doctor had wanted to continue his resistance, our efforts would undoubtedly not have succeeded in defeating him, so true is it that in our modern times, science is the universal mistress, the universal dominatrix. In our day, the weak man is the man who knows nothing. The word 'weak' will soon disappear from the language, or simply become a synonym of the word 'ignorant,' and the man who is stronger than another will be the man who knows more.

"In the course of this brief campaign, Dr. Flax has, so to speak, illustrated those truths, which will be the great guiding principles of life in times to come. And now"—the Marschall turned to the fathers and mothers—"I shall ask Professor Flax's victims to make a great effort. However much they hate him, let them not crush the great French surgeon! Be indulgent! He deserves it. Take it upon yourselves to calm, with wise words, the excitement that has been translated with so much violence in the majority of your newspapers.

"Now it only remains for me, *Messieurs les officiers*, to thank you for your good will, and your fraternal aid. I shall always retain the memory of our excellent relations."

In a few brief words, the French general and Colonel Fahrlander thanked Marschall von Haeseler for his words.

I owe it to the truth to record that the exhortations to indulgence had no success among the fathers and mothers, increasingly outraged as they took account of the changes that Dr. Flax's operation had wrought in the mental equilibrium of their children.

When the speeches were over, we were about to get up from the table when all of a sudden, from behind one of the sheets of fabric that divided the laboratory into smaller sections, extremely beautiful and moving organ music rose up—music of genius.

Then, all conversations die down, and all hearts unite in a fervent silence. It is Nicolas Barlatescu who is playing the organ—an organ whose sound is poignant. It appears that the instrument has been improved by Ambroise Riffelard, the genius of preumatism, who has discovered a new means of blowing air into the roaring tubes.

The harmonious vibrations envelop us in a mystery as beautiful as a summer night. They seem to propagate in our souls, in intimate intellectual shudders. We are all gripped by those rhythms, which are murmuring and speaking to our entire sentimental being, when a woman's voice—a marvelous voice—suddenly accompanies the grave sounds of the organ.

It is the Comtesse de Houdotte who is singing, accompanied by Nicolas Barlatescu , the *Hymn to Glory* composed by Pierre Candelaur.

The heroic music adapts so well to the words, and the words are a breath so superhuman, and the voice that is singing is singing with so much lyricism, that soon, moved to tears, Marschall von Haeseler's guests remain as if intoxicated by a strange, new and sweet intoxication. Even the faces of the fathers and mothers, incessantly wrinkled by anxieties, mark the forgetfulness of sufferings passed, vanished in the inspiration of the miraculous music.

And then, when, as the *Hymn to Glory* is concluded, Dr. Flax appears, surrounded by the three Hingertil brothers, Soeur Thérèse and the Comtesse de Houdotte, we all rise to our feet in a single movement, and we bow respectfully to our proud prisoners. Even the Baron de Vautremesse, whose excessive nervousness is always to be feared, who has sworn to kill Dr. Flax with his bare hands, finds himself mute, gripped, immobilized, mastered by the aureole of superiority in the midst of which the doctor walks—an aureole that no one can see, but which everyone divines around the professor's head; a powerful and invisible light that illuminates us in the utmost depths of our souls.

Dr. Flax stops in front of Marschall von Haeseler. A soon as the organ ceases to move the air with its sonorous waves, he speaks, in a vibrant voice that continues the harmony if the metal quivering under the pressure of air.

"Behold!" he says, as the final organ note slowly dies away. "Behold our Work! Behold the results that we have obtained in a few days. I address myself to the fathers who want me dead; I address myself to the mothers I have tortured—and I ask them whether they too have not felt, in the most unyielding fibers of their soul, that there is something grandiose and superb in that—so grandiose and so superb that there has never been anything in the world so grandiose and so superb?

"And I present myself before you to say to you: I have consented to surrender, when my work was not finished, when it still requires numerous perfections, when all the ideas that I have here"—he slaps his vast brown forehead—"have not yet been realized. Will you leave those ideas sterile? Will you not permit me to continue at leisure, wherever I would like, under the surveillance of the scientific world, in broad daylight, the experiments so triumphantly commenced?

"Be judges now. I am so convinced of the grandeur of our Work that you, who have suffered, will, I feel sure, he my aides and supporters henceforth. It is you that I request to be the advocates of my cause—yes, you. Forget the petty maneuvers of which I have been obliged to render myself guilty in order to abduct the children, to work in secret. Do not look backwards any longer; more than that, close your eyes to the as-yet-imperfect present. March on, your gaze fixed only on the future.

"If you want to follow me, that future will soon by more beautiful than the most extravagant utopians have ever imagined. I leave to your consciences the care of judging us. In order that each of you should have before your eyes the evident proof that we are not impostors, that our Work is a reality, Soeur Thérèse will distribute rings to you all that you may keep in memory of me. They are reproductions of a ring that Bernard Flaquette sculpted recently. We have given the ring, in order to distinguish it from others, the name of Love-Ring. It is a perfect masterpiece, worthy of the best museums. So, when you contemplate on your fingers that little pieces of silver on which the genius of engraving has traced a few rare lines, you will think of Dr. Flax, and you will find a new courage to defend his discoveries before those exasperated by a vain sentimentalism, a sentimentalism that it is necessary to qualify, when one thinks about it deeply, as an inimical, inhuman sentiment."

Having spoken thus, Dr. Flax salutes us again, and slowly retires, followed by the Comtesse de Houdotte and the Hingertil brothers, leaving us under the impression of his warm and persuasive eloquence.

Soeur Thérèse distributes the Love-Rings to us.

They are, indeed, pure masterpieces. One does not know which to admire more, the modeling of all the tiny figures, their finesse and delicacy, or the artistry with which they are grouped. They represent humanity made happy by human genius, by the influence of geniuses.

Alain Bernard, my neighbor at table, whispers in my ear: "Isn't it marvelous? Aren't you now under the charm? Personally, though, I can still hear the sinister screams of little Germain Plaizance lying on her lamentable framework. And I ask myself why, in truth, all these beautiful things can only be obtained by suffering. I ask myself whether the doctor's opinion is true—essentially and naturally true—that all human progress is acquired in sobbing and in dolor; whether one cannot hope that there will be smiles unless there are tears today."

All meditating on similar grave thoughts, we leave the laboratory and spend the night outside.

The moonlight is bright.

The white light descending from the heavens extends over all the surrounding white summits. All those gleams, which deepen around us the nocturnal shadows of the fortress, plunge us into living dreams in which we follow the genius of Dr. Flax, as our gazes follow over the distant hump of the Titlis, over the snowfields of the colossal mountain, the slow and changing march of the moonlight.

Clovis Binard

THE GENIUSES AT MELCHTAHL

Rudolph Hermlein had just come up from Melchtahl. He tells us that the geniuses who arrived in the village with their parts are veritable little furies, and that they have turned the population upside down. Trouble is feared.

C.B.

THE CONCLUSION OF THE REPORTAGE CONTEST
THE VICTOR
WHO LOSES WINS

Our reportage competition is concluded. The result was not in doubt. Alain Bernard has been chosen by our readers as the victor in the tournament. He has emerged, celebrated and popular, from a struggle in which he nearly lost his life. He is the one who will receive the prize of 25,000 francs. Everyone applauds his success.

Clovis Binard has been awarded second place. He will have lost nothing, either, by his reportage. He has, in fact, just been informed that the 15,000 francs promised by the police, as in the Humbert affair, to the person who denounced the guilty party, have been sent to the committee of dissident scientists that designated Dr. Flax in their memorable accusations. The committee met one last time and, having recognized that the first capital proof was furnished to them by Clovis Binard's work on the map of Paris, has decided that the sum of fifteen thousand francs should be passed on to our colleague.

As for Barbarus, who appears to have won nothing, the is perhaps the most fortunate of all, having conquered in the course of the affair, the heart of the widowed Madame Peinassols, a charming woman who owns a dozen houses in Paris. The marriage will be celebrated on the eighth of next month.

FLAX LEAVES THE FORTRESS
TO MELCHTAHL...
THE DOCTOR'S ENIGMATIC THREAT

This morning, an hour before the time fixed for the departure, all the discoveries of the little geniuses were destroyed.

That was ordered by Dr. Flax.

Godefroy Pomme's transatmospheric kite has been burned; Ambrose Riffelard's pneumatic machine has been smashed; Charles Clépent's great condensing apparatus, Fernand Pig's electrical fluid projector, Isidore Bimorel's rifle, etc. etc., no longer exist.

What motive was the doctor obeying in this work of extermination? He refused to reply when I interrogated him.

At ten o'clock Général Lacroux came to fetch his prisoners in order to take them to Melchtahl. Marschall von Haeseler has taken his leave of them and returned to Engstlensee to meet up with is Bavarians. The Germans will go back down to Meiringen, from which, this time, they will be repatriated directly by railway.

The Swiss Gardes de Sûreté will take the road to the Grimsel and the Furka in order to rejoin the forts at Andermatt. The troops of the Aufzug, the Swiss elite that formed our right wing, will be distributed again to their various garrisons by Colonel Fahrlander. The latter accompanied us as far as Melchtahl.

The descent was very picturesque, a rare and original cortege.

At the head, marched Soeur Thérèse and Chrysostome Hingertil, then Numérien and Wolfgang Hingertil, then the Comtesse de Houdotte. alongside Général Lecroux, then Flax, on his own, and then the father and mothers, leading their recovered children by the hand.

Behind followed the crowd of spectators, the journalists, a contingent of Alpine infantrymen who had come up to Frutt with the French general, and finally the stretcher of the widowed Madame Peinassols, carried by two sturdy mountain men.

I made the journey with Alain Bernard and Barbarus, in front of Werner Dürrer and Rudolph Hermlein. One of the Alpine officers told me that Général Lacroux has asked for the cross of the Légion d'honneur to reward the two Swiss who have aided the parents with so much abnegation and courage.

Dr. Flax came out of the Fortress without, at first, darting a backward glance. One wondered whether he was going to go down without bidding farewell, with his eyes, to the world that he had created. When he arrived at the last bend in the path from which one can still embrace he landscape, however, he stopped abruptly, as if reluctantly, and slowly turned toward the place that he had once chosen in order to carry out his work.

From there, the gaze can contemplate the entire circle of the mountains, the little lake, the little chapel next to which the frontier guards had camped, and the whole of the Fortress.

The sun, already high over the horizon, is splashing one entire half of the horizon, while the other remains dark, veiled by a large could. The snow of the high speaks, the Wendenstokes, the Titlis, the Graustock and the Boni, seem to be redoubling the bright light in order to salute the surgeon's departure. In the midst of those summits, on the great cutting of the Joch pass, the chain of mountains sinks down, a symbol of faded hope, in the midst of hopes that are still superb.

Suddenly, the surgeon closes his eyes, in order no longer to see, and then he leans toward the Comtesse de Houdotte and murmurs to her: "Perhaps, my dear friend, we have left all of our existence there! Perhaps we are cradled by illusions, and are now going down into the tomb."

The caravan resumes its march then, gliding slowly over the stony slopes of the path to Melchtahl. As we get closer to the village, the road fills up with curiosity-seekers. Général Lacroux has to make the troops intervene to clear us a narrow passage between the rock and the precipices.

In the plain, on the cart-track, a line of local people dressed in their Sunday best has been waiting for hours. The inhabitants of the canton bear the doctor no resentment. On the contrary, they seem proud of the fact that their region has been chosen for these resounding experiments, for they are aware that the name of Unterwalden is now known to everyone on earth who reads a newspaper.

All the peasants and mountain men take their hats off as we pass by. In that salute there is a hint of religious dread, a little of the fervent terror that takes possession of all simple souls before mystery.

The little geniuses have been well-behaved during this descent. Even the weakest have stood up well to the fatigue of the journey.

On our arrival in Melchtahl, we are told that the children who spent the night in the village have, by contrast, all become intolerable.

Léon Aproli has vandalized the curé's flower-beds, under the pretext that the flowers there are pitiful. Isidore Bimorel, the genius of ballistics, has amused himself breaking all the windows in the Hôtel Alpenhof with the aid of small pebbles launched from a considerable distance with a mechanical contraption of his own invention. At table, the chemist Vincent Montier has mixed a little powder of his confection with the mustard, which has violently purged all the guests, etc. etc. There is not one of the little geniuses who has not indulged in these acts of eccentricity, to the great displeasure of the neighbors.

Thus, the arrival of Dr. Flax in the midst of the parents who have just supported all these practical jokes due to their children's genius is very poorly welcomed. The doctor and his friends are once again the butt of threats and insults, which contrast with the warm welcome of the local population during the descent from Frutt.

Dr. Flax and the Comtesse de Houdotte are lodged under a strong guard in the school. Alain Bernard has visited them there. He has asked the surgeon what his future plans are.

"My plans?" the doctor replied. "That depends on the fashion in which I'm received in Paris. If I'm left at liberty, authorized to continue my work, well then I shall resume my existence where I left off, and I shall work at my hospital in Montretout instead of working at Frutt. But if, contrary to my expectation, as almost all the French newspapers are imperiously demanding, they want to put me on trial and treat me as a criminal…oh, then…I'll think again.

"You can write that I have no fear, no anxiety. If the government is cowardly enough to obey the frantic injunctions of the fools who are demanding my head, I have a means to get us out of trouble—my friends and me: a radical and reliable means."

Alain Bernard has tried to find out what that means is, but the doctor closed his mouth with a peremptory and categorical: "It's pointless to persist."

A special train designated for the fathers, the mothers and their children will depart and seven p.m. from Sarten. It will be immediately followed by another train, in which the French general, Monsieur Hamard and his men will travel with the surgeon, the Hingertil brothers, the Comtesse de Houdotte and Soeur Thérèse.

I have obtained authorization to accompany the latter train. Alain Bernard and Barbarus will travel in the train with the mothers and fathers.

Clovis Binard

THE DEPARTURE FOR PARIS
OVEREXCITEMENT OF THE CROWD
WHAT WILL HAPPEN IN PARIS?

All Switzerland has come together to witness our departure. The approaches to Sarnen are black with crowds. The inns are overflowing. All the slopes from which the road on which our carriages are traveling can be seen are swarming with curiosity-seekers.

As we get further away from Melchtahl, sympathy for Dr. Flax is visibly decreasing. The professor has become a prophet in the narrow valley; he remains a monster for more distant populations.

Here and there, hostile cries greet the passage of the landau in which the surgeon is sitting, in the company of Soeur Thérèse and the Comtesse de Houdotte. Those insults find facile echoes. The natural calm of the majority of peasants prevent their manifestation, but it is evident that they are with those who are shouting and protesting.

Having booked my seat in the train of the father and mothers, which is due to depart with the doctor's, I wanted, before leaving the man who appears to me today, in spite of all his hopes, as a kind of fallen god, to shake his hand and bid him *au revoir*.

"Thank you," said the doctor, squeezing my palms. "I shall never forget that you have written nothing contrary to the truth, or calculated to harm me. If, as I am beginning to dread, the hostility that I observe around me increases between Sarnen and Paris, well, Monsieur Bernard, I shall soon have some fine reportage in store for you. Have no fear; I shall give you a sign when the time comes."

I could not obtain any information about the significance of that enigmatic statement, the second of the same kind that I have obtained from the doctor's lips.

Before quitting her, I permit myself to address an indiscreet question to the Comtesse de Houdotte: "It's rumored, Madame, that whatever events might follow henceforth, you intend to marry Dr. Flax. Is that true?"

"Perhaps," replies the woman who has been the surgeon's guide and mainstay.

Alain Bernard

Sarnen

Dr. Flax's train is on the point of leaving the town.

It is just in time.

The French troops who have been keeping order, before being taken to the frontier by the following trains, have nearly been overwhelmed by the spectators, who are beginning o be intoxicated by the destructive vertigo of crowds.

The train whistles in the midst of cries of "Death to Flax!"

That presages a fine arrival in Paris, where the overexcitement is even greater than it is here.

Barbarus

Paris, 9 September

FLAX ARRIVES IN PARIS
THE MULTITUDE
THE NEWSVENDDORS
A COMPLAINTE

An enormous crowd, the crowd of great events, has headed this morning toward the Gare de l'Est to await the arrival of the little geniuses and their parents, preceding that of Flax and his accomplices.

It is the movement, the excitement and agitation of great days. The population of Paris has been overexcited by the newspapers, the great majority of which are inveighing against the man that is still being called a torturer of children, Dr. Hell, and so on—a campaign that had not been attenuated either by the manifestations of the dissident scientists, today the most moderate, not the opinion of considerable individuals such as Edison, Marschall von Haeseler, Anatole France, etc.

Since yesterday, all Paris has been getting ready to receive the surgeon of Frutt with one of those jeers that raise up all hearts unanimously with the same lever.

So, from all directions and very early, newsvendors, the benevolent heralds with which civilization clutters our sidewalks, are howling the names of papers and the headlines.

Certain gazettes, which only appear when great events torment opinion, to disappear as soon as the agitation eases, are indulging in the luxury of enormous headlines: *NEW REVELATIONS!! INTERVIEW WITH THE COMTESSE DE HOUDOTTE!! UNPUBLISHED DETAILS,* etc., etc.

And, as happens every time an individual attracts public anger, a black-bordered bereavement notice surmounted by a cross is being sold in the streets, which reads:

You are invited to participate in the funeral procession and burial of
DR. PROFESSOR FLAX (GEOLET)
Chevalier d'industrie, grande croix (palm) de la Légion d'honneur
AND THE NOBLE LADY COMTESSE DE HOUDOTTE
Née de Barbote, de Crachote, de Tripote, de Complote, de Banknote.
Both deceased on their return from a voyage to Switzerland...
Which will be held one day soon, at the Palais de Justice,
to the applause of the entire world
On behalf of the parents Flax-Alif, Flax-Ifilé, Flax-Gorneur, Flax-Grandélit,
Flax-Tuosité and Houdotte-Eronome, Houdotte-Riche

and Houdotte-Quejycours.
Do not pray for them.

The authors of these kinds of production, which are born who knows where on the Parisian sidewalks could, I think, be accused without injustice of lacking wit and rather poor imagination were it not demonstrated that their pieces of paper sell like hot cakes and that large numbers of worthy people take delight in this very special literature, which occasionally makes the fortune of certain editors.

And naturally—another phenomenon that always follows great crimes—the hawkers are singing a new *complainte* in the streets. It relates, from end to end, the story of Dr. Flax, the Comtesse de Houdotte, Soeur Thérèse and the Hingertil brothers.

Like the author of the bereavement notice, the author of the *Complainte du docteur Flax* has not overtaxed his brain. He has chosen the tune that was once borrowed for a song about the king of Saxe by a witty dentist, Catelan, when he wrote the famous, unforgettable and unforgotten *Complainte de Fualdès.*[46]

The verses that recount the adventures of the surgeon of Frutt are, in addition, directly inspired by those that entire generations have learned by heart. There are, is as conventional, seventy-eight couplets, from the beginning to...the guillotine. Popular wrath is pitiless!

THE COMPLAINTE OF DOCTOR FLAX

Listen, people de France.
Or the kingdom of Peru,
The people of Russia too,
And other provenance.
To the crime of a professor
And his three accessors

That savant hatched a plot
A crime without precedent
And encountered at that moment
The Comtesse de Houdotte
Not before the Pantheon
But near a wall at Charenton

"O Flax," that woman said,

---

[46] The Fualdès Affair, occasioned by the murder of a former imperial prosecutor in 1817 was a landmark in the history of such scandals, *La Complainte de Fualdès* was adapted to the tune of a popular song, the *Air du Maréchal de Saxe*, by the dentist in question, who has no other claim to fame.

342

"You're a genius unspied."
"Yes, that's true," he replied.
"Then it's daft, 'pon my head,
"Amazing Doctor Flax
"To treat asthma and anthrax.

"There's better things to do.
"You could enhance intell
"-gence with your scalpel
"For all, no matter who.
"Everyone will be your debtor
"If you make the world better."

Such literature gives an idea of the sentiments that are agitating the crowd. Not the slightest comprehension of Dr. Flax's projects, of the humanitarian goal that he was pursuing, and claims that he might yet attain.

In the face of this upsurge of blind rage, the Prefect of Police has been obliged to take extraordinary measures. Since this morning, Monsieur Lépine has personally distributed long cordons of agents in the streets neighboring the Gare de l'Est. The force responsible for keeping order is under the direction of Monsieur Norioy, the divisional commander, and Monsieur Lebon, a peace officer of the reserve brigade.

At the station, the gates to the main concourse have been closed. Parisian horseguards are circulating, clearing the roadway. In the concourse, a hundred guards are waiting with their horses, with the bridles under their arms.

Monsieur Touny, the director of the municipal police, has been charged with maintaining order in the Boulevard de Strasbourg and the Boulevard de Sebastopol. That is the route that Dr. Flax will follow. Support is provided by Messieurs Murat and Descaves, peace officers, whose task is very difficult.

A compact crowd is blocking the sidewalks. Men, women and children are packing the windows.

Finally, the train carrying the fathers and mothers enters the station.

Monsieur Lépine greets the passengers. He makes all kinds of recommendations before allowing them out into the street. Closed landaus are at the disposal of the surgeon's victims.

The emergence of the carriages provokes thousands of cries in the crowd. Those of "Death to Flax!" are the most frequent. They are soon replaced by those of "Die, Flax!"—which seems more euphonious to the popular ear.

The little geniuses pass through the midst of that racket, that noisy curiosity, still cold, still indifferent. They are not interested by the crowd massed on the sidewalks, whose members, craning their necks to catch a fleeting glimpse of something behind the windows of the landaus, stare at them passionately. They are scornful. The children are not even moved by the sinister howls addressed to

Dr. Flax. It is certain that although these geniuses are obedient to the surgeon, attentive to his instructions, it is only because they realize that he alone appreciates their genius at its true value. They have no sincere amity, nor even sympathy, for the Master.

Given the increasing excitement of the spectators, Monsieur Lépine soon decides that, in spite of all the precautions that have been taken, the transport of the child-stealers to their prison by the planned route would be perilous. And suddenly, at the moment when everyone expects that Flax is about to disembark in his turn, at the moment when attention is multiplied a hundredfold, at an order from the peace officers, the barrages of agents are seen to disperse. The Parisian guards mount their horses again and calmly ride away, as if their task were concluded.

Disappointed and tumultuous, the crowd then spreads into the streets.

Numerous spectators affirm, which a persuasive certainty, that Dr. Flax has passed through in one of the parents' landaus. Some claim to have seen him, others maintain that they have recognized the Comtesse de Houdotte.

The truth is that, as it passed through the eastern fortifications, the driver of the train transporting Flax received orders to retrace his route as far as Pantin. There, the carriage containing the surgeon, his friends, Ange Pompaigne—who still does not want to leave the doctor's side—and the father and mother of the genius of amity is shunted into a siding. Half an hour later, automobiles sent from Paris finally take the prisoners away to the police cells.

Numerous important people in the scientific and artistic worlds have already put in requests to visit Dr. Flax as soon as he arrives. Will their requests be granted? The anti-Flaxists, a noisy majority, think that the surgeon is being treated too gently, and that he does not merit any exceptional consideration.

The examining magistrate who has followed the affair of the child-stealers from the outset has already interrogated Dr. Flax. All the accomplices to the abductions of children have also passed through the anthropometric service.

While Monsieur Bertillon was doing his job it was necessary to restrain Ange Pompaigne by force, who wanted to hurl himself upon the chief of the anthropometric service and the examining magistrate to score them with his fingernails.

The Comtesse de Houdotte, Soeur Thérèse and the Hingertil brothers lent themselves to the procedure with very good grace, and even with a certain curiosity. It was not the same with the doctor, who only submitted to the formality after a brief but energetic protest.

"I have not committed any crime," he said to the chief of the service. "There is no point in measuring me. I am not a murderer or a thief. I am a benefactor of humanity. But, even though I might be considered by idiots as a murderer or a thief, I warn you that your operation is futile and vain. One way or another, my friends and I will be out of your cells within three days. Take my word for it. If I am not set free tomorrow, and if I observe that the continuation of my work has become impossible, warn the government that I will act as I see fit."

After having repeated the mysterious threats made in Melchtahl, the doctor went to take his place before the photographic apparatus of the anthropometric service, which has reproduced the images of all the great villains of the century.

Clovis Binard

10 September

Numerous groups have been stationed outside the police station all night. From his cell, Dr. Flax has been able to hear the cries demanding his death, the croaking of the poor anonymous crows who do not understand the first thing about the professor's great attempt of human deliverance.

The surgeon of Frutt occupies a large, brightly lit, relatively comfortable room. In spite of the demanding cruelty of the anti-Flaxists, the prison regime has been attenuated as much as possible for these remarkable prisoners.

Dr. Flax and the Comtesse de Houdotte have been authorized to receive a few visitors early this morning, and the quality of the courtiers if misfortune is by no means mediocre.

They are either former guests of the Comtesse de Houdotte's Saturdays— the "profounds"—signatories to the manifesto by which famous contemporaries asked for indulgence for an exceptional genius, or imply friends: Camille Flamarion, Bréal, Tristan Bernard, Anatole France, Briand, Antoine, Séverine, Moczkowski, Besnard, André Honorat, Pierre Veber, Henry de Gorsse, Milleraud, Pozzi, and even d'Angliney and Henri de Vorigno.

"Yes," Henri de Vorigno said to me, when he emerged from the police station after visiting his former enemy, "I went to ask Flax to forgive me. He did so wholeheartedly, without the slightest embarrassment for him or for me. That intelligence, of such vast scope, understood the motives that guided me. In the same circumstances, perhaps he would have adopted the same attitude. Could I have guessed, when I accused him, that he was in the process of accelerating several thousand years of evolution necessary to global society? We embraced one another. I will not hide from you that tears rose to my eyes during that embrace."

In spite of the most powerful interventions, the government cannot remove Dr. Flax from the severity of justice. No democratic government could resist such formidable pressure.

Monsieur Laudet has proceeded once again with the interrogation of the guilty parties. The magistrate has never had such obliging perpetrators. They reply with the best will in the world, and do their best to facilitate his task.

Beginning at the beginning, the magistrate attempts to confirm the history of the child thefts. Several as-yet-obscure questions have been elucidated.

It was the Comtesse who, gripped by compassion on reading the stories in the newspapers, sent money to the parents of little Émile Loubé.

It was Flax who carried out, with his own hands, the abduction of Gontran de Vautremesse at the Nouveau-Cirque. The Comtesse de Houdotte only intervened to distract the attention of the Baron momentarily as he left the performance.

It was Flax who sent me, a few minutes before that abduction, the letter in characters cut out of a newspaper article. The surgeon wanted, in order to deflect suspicion, to distract public opinion with exotic procedures. Was it not improbable in the extreme that a man like the surgeon would devote himself to that kind of correspondence?

It was Numérien Hingertil who bought the glue and paper for that note at the Librairie Veneziani.

It was Dr. Flax's carriage that Madame Clépent saw fleeing along the Rue de Thann. The deductions that Barbarus recorded then have been partly confirmed.

It has also been revealed today that the Hingertils disguised themselves on several occasions, which explains the variety of the descriptions that confused the police.

The reasoning of Monsieur Laudet, following Gilbert Bartoulou's deposition, regarding the itinerary followed by the doctor's coupé as it returned from the abduction of Gontran de Vautremesse was, as has also been demonstrated today, largely correct. It only contained one minor error, for which the magistrate cannot be blamed. That night, Numérien Hingertil, who was guiding the horse, made a detour because his master wanted, before returning to the Rue Cassette, to put a letter in the post-box in the Rue des Saint-Pères.

Thus, today, all the petty mysteries that created so much fuss have been clarified and explained.

Clovis Binard

THE EXRAVAGANCES OF THE GENIUSES
AN INTOLERABLE SITUATION

The father and mothers, finally in possession of their children, are going completely crazy. Life in the presence of the little geniuses is intolerable. The demands of Flax's pupils are becoming intolerable, their eccentricities infernal.

Desperate protests are rising up from all sides.

To make himself a small experimental pond, in order to try out at home the various machines he devises, Frantz Vetyolle has opened the kitchen tap fully and flooded the landing. The entire house has been inundated. The tenants are demanding collective compensation.

Nicolas Barlatescu claims that darkness inspires him, and only plays music at night. Attempts have been made to take away his piano, precipitating frightful temper tantrums. The parents have been obliged to give in. Nicolas has thus given them a marvelous serenade, but which prevents them from sleeping, along with their neighbors above and below.

Bouquet de Gobely-Franthéon has demolished all the locks in the paternal home. They are, according to him, stupidly crude and do not respond to necessity. In order to oblige his father to provide him with a locksmith's workshop, he has blown up all the mechanisms and the door handles.

Wenceslas Lévy has run away from home. He ran to the Hôtel-Dieu, and slipped in to the first ward behind someone who was going in. There, without having received orders from anyone, he completely revised—in a much improved fashion—the dressings of an apache who had just been brought in, whose jaw had been fractured by a bullet during a brawl.

The genius of leaping, Philippe Soleillat, is devoting himself to his favorite sport in the streets. He leaps into the upper decks of omnibuses with a single bound, jumps down again, then up again, into the crowns of trees on the boulevard, on to the roofs of houses, and back down again in the same fashion, sowing alarm everywhere he goes.

"What are we going to do?" laments Madame Chipé, whom I have questioned. "I no longer recognize my little Justin. That infamous doctor has transformed him completely. The child is insupportable. Not only has he worn us out with his demands, but he treats us as if we were strangers. He talks to us like an old man who is taking out on those around him the bitterness of a character that age has rendered profoundly egotistical. What's more, alas, he exerts I don't know what attraction on all the animals in the neighborhood. Yes, thanks to his genius of animal husbandry and acclimation, he has an extraordinary authority over all the dogs and cats he encounters. As soon as he opens the window, all the sparrows, pigeons and rooks in the vicinity come running to his call. In twenty-four hours, Monsieur, my drawing room has become a menagerie. It can't go on—it can't go on!"

The unfortunate mothers no longer know which saint to pray to.

Alain Bernard

THE AUTHORITIES PERPLEXED
WILL FLAX OBTAIN HIS LIBERTY BY FORCE?

A meeting has taken place, rather late in the evening, between Monsieur Laudet, the public prosecutor, Monsieur Hamard and Dr. Flax.

The gentlemen requested the surgeon to use his influence to put a stop to the various extravagances of the little geniuses who have been returned to their parents. The unusual actions of the children are causing chaos in the areas where they live. Putting an end to their follies is a matter of urgency.

The surgeon replied with a proposition that seemed unacceptable at first glance, but to which it will be necessary to submit if we want to put an end to the bizarre excesses of the little geniuses.

"I'm not surprised," the doctor said, "by the children's immoderate actions. The intemperance of their genius is explicable not only by the error I made, but also by the lack of education. I am no longer there to restrain their immeasurable and overweening passion. They would all have benefited from a few more months of schooling in the solitude of Frutt. Abruptly thrust into contemporary life, without transition, their genius is crossing at a stroke the narrow boundary separating it from madness, and turning to fury.

"There's no remedy, then?" asked Monsieur Laudet.

"Yes, but I am the only one who can apply that remedy. I shall only apply it if the law renounces our pursuit and we are set free, unconditionally."

"What is the remedy?"

"A further operation. In the same way that I could perfect the genius of the children with a further application of my scalpel, I can remove from their brains the particles of flaxium-radium that are directing their will. I can guarantee, with complete scientific certainty, that I can return complete mental integrity to the children. By the time the scar that I shall be forced to reopen will have healed, there will no longer be the slightest remaining trace of my experiments. The children will then revert to the character, ideas and intelligence they had before, without the slightest lacuna. The parents will not be able to perceive any evidence of the fact that the little ones have, for a few weeks, been unique and amazing geniuses."

Such is Dr. Flax's proposition.

It became known rather late in the evening.

Dr. Flax has given the authorities twenty-four hours to reply. That delay passed, he will refuse to intervene again, and the little geniuses and their families will be abandoned to their baroque and heart-rending fate.

The government thus finds itself in a very difficult dilemma.

If it accepts Dr. Flax's proposition, and sets the child-stealers free, it will run into the most violent attacks by the anti-Flaxists. If it does not accept, it will be oblige the parents, inhumanely, to maintain custody of the thirty-one little lunatics that the surgeon has created, and whom he could, in fact, return to reason.

What decision will be made? Opinions are sharply divided.

The Minister of the Interior has urgently summoned three professors of medicine. He will ask them whether the operation proposed by Dr. Flax is possible, and whether the surgeon is not abusing his ability and his science.

It is evident today that the surgeon of Frutt was not bluffing when he repeated, several times, that he hoped to be released from prison on his return to Paris. Perhaps he will be able to oblige the authorities to realize his hopes.

Barbarus

GRAVE DIVERGENCE OF OPINIONS

Dr. Flax's proposition fills the front page of all the newspapers. It is being discussed, attacked and defended with equal energy.

Some contend that Dr. Flax cannot succeed in the new operation that he is offering to attempt, others that one can expect anything from the skill of such a hand. Some consider that even if it possible for the surgeon to undo what he has done, it would be better to leave the little geniuses as they are. In general, the bargain that the surgeon wants to make is considered inadmissible.

"What!" says the *Lanterne*. "Is the scoundrel to be set free? That would be a total negation of justice. This is a guilty man, guilty of one of the worst crimes imaginable, but who would be strolling tranquilly along the boulevards tomorrow, rubbing shoulders with you, while unfortunate wretches who have stolen a pair of shoes will be going to prison!

"Let the little maniacs remain mad, so long as justice follows its course, equal for all!"

The majority of the parents of the geniuses, however, are in favor of the doctor's proposition.

I have been to ask the Baron and Baronne de Vautremesse what they think of Flax's new plan. They approve of it, energetically and passionately.

"Let's not lose a minute. Let the government make an immediate affirmative response to the doctor. Let him be set free and let him restore the former intelligence of our children. People will object that the doctor might not succeed in the operation. He will succeed. We hate him with all our might, but we can't deny that he's a miraculous surgeon. And even if he doesn't succeed, he can't return our children to us any less transformed or more impossible than they are. Whatever he does, the result probably won't be worse than the present situation. I hope that our supplications—those of the victims, who will surrender our children to the doctor's scalpel hopefully—will be heeded."

Similar opinions have been expressed in the Clépent family, the Franthéon family, the Plaizance family, the Bonnéglise family, etc., etc., where I was also received. I heard a contrary opinion, however, in the home of Monsieur Flaquette.

"Certainly," the mother said to me, "our little one is no longer the same, but his genius is inoffensive. Provides that one gives him plates of gold and silver, and his tools, he's satisfied. He's very good, never moving, creating admirable engravings. A rich dealer in New York has reserved all of Bernard's products for six months. He offered us 400,000 francs. Let the child stay as he is. We don't want to subject him to the surgeon's instruments."

The mother of Urbain Godedouins, the genius of jewelry, is of the same opinion.

"Of course, she exclaimed, "my little one has changed completely. On the other hand, he designed marvelous jewelry, which he didn't do before. One can't imagine anything more artistic, more beautiful. The jewelers in the Rue de la Paix are sending him gemstones. The rings, ear-rings, brooches and pendant he makes are selling at a premium on the market. What's more, as I adore jewelry and admire the items he contrives so much, we've gradually become the best of friends. I'll never surrender my child to the surgeon."

Barbarus

DR. FLAX PROTESTS
THE SURGEON WANTS TO REOPERATE ON ALL
THE CHILDREN WITHOUT EXCEPTION
A CRUEL DILEMMA

Dr. Flax sent the Minister of the Interior the following letter today.

Monsieur le Ministre,

For what reasons have you consulted surgeons before replying to me? To discover whether it is possible to reformulate the intelligence of the children such as it was before? What can my colleagues, even the most eminent, tell you? They don't know anything.

Confident of what I know, I reiterate, Monsieur le Ministre, the proposition that the public prosecutor has transmitted to you.

I will operate again on all the children—all of them, without exception—on condition that you set me and my friends at liberty.

No trace of my instruments will remain except for a slight scar near the hairline. As it grows back, the hair will rapidly cover it. I cannot even be reproached for harming the beauty of my so-called victims.

And since my previous achievements are insufficiently convincing, I declare now that if the children cellulo-radiotomated by me and returned to their previous condition do not become exactly what they were before, entirely and completely, without restrictions, I shall tear up the bargain that I am imposing on you.

If the slightest accident occurs, if the result announced is not obtained, even for a single one of the children subjected to the operation, I renounce, for my five co-accused and myself, the liberty I am demanding today. We will then consent to appear in court and allow ourselves to be convicted.

I draw your attention, Monsieur le Ministre, to one passage in this letter. I have written to you that if I operate again on the children, I must operate on all of them, without exception.

In fact, I have realized that, given the state of public opinion, it will not be possible for me to complete the endeavor that I have undertaken.

Certainly, the sympathy of a few great minds consoles me for the almost general antipathy, but my work requires calm and silence, and I can no longer continue them today without governmental consent and aid.

That peace and that support are both lacking.

I therefore renounce my work—but I want to renounce it completely, and do not want to leave imperfect traces of it. That is why I am adding a further condition to the one I have already set before you. I will not operate on the children unless I am allowed to operate on all of them.

Please accept, Monsieur le Ministre, etc.

Flax

That letter has unleashed thousands of disputes.

With the exception of rabid anti-Flaxists, it is admitted in many circles that Dr. Flax's proposition, as it was known yesterday, was acceptable. However strong the desire for vengeance against the surgeon might be, it was, after all, necessary to think about the misfortune of the parents. Since they welcomed joyfully the risk of a further operation, it would have been cruel to be obstinate in a solution that would further augment the already-lengthy list of their sufferings.

But not all of those who thought the bargain offered by the surgeon acceptable are still in accord now that he has added a new and grave condition. They accept that the doctor should operate again on those children whose parents consent to that sacrifice, but they refuse to oblige to that cruelty the parents who will not consent to it.

Since some mothers and fathers are satisfied with the genius of their children, and are accommodating themselves to their eccentricities, why force them to deliver their sons and daughters to the surgeon's knife again?

It is therefore necessary, in the negotiations with Professor Flax, that the government obtain the agreement of the surgeon only to reoperate on the children whose parents consent. The other geniuses will remain as they are.

If the doctor submits to this condition, he might, we believe, be set at liberty, along with his friends. Gradually, public opinion will settle down, understanding that it was necessary to bend to the demands of the master of Frutt out of charity for the victims.

Unfortunately, it is to be feared that the doctor, an energetic and determined intelligence, will refuse all discussion and remain obstinate in his demand: all or nothing!

Clovis Binard

We have learned that the government has just accepted Dr. Flax's proposal, without any restriction. All the children, therefore, will pass once again over the surgeon's operating table—even those whose parents resist.

This news will provoke the most vigorous effervescence among the anti-Flaxists. They are numerous.

The affair of Dr. Flax might yet have unexpected events in store.

GREAT SESSION IN THE CHAMBRE

The divergence of opinions excited throughout the land by the affair of Dr. Flax could only be definitively settled by a vote in the Chambre.

The representatives of the nation had to determine the new judgment of Solomon, the enigma of justice and equity in the midst of which the public were struggling.

So, after having decided yesterday to meet the conditions of the surgeon of Frutt in their entirety, the government took a step backwards, having received an interpellation from Monsieur Georges Larry, the député for Paris.

Going back on its resolution of the previous day, the Council of Ministers unanimously rallied in support of the sage advice expressed by Monsieur Leygues. The former minister declared that, in his opinion, the Executive ought not to take the responsibility of removing the guilty parties from the jurisdiction of the courts, from the laws that regulate the entire nation. Parliament alone has the right, in the interests of public peace, to vote on such an exceptional measure.

The anti-Flaxists were demanding imperiously the rejection of the surgeon's proposition, his trial and his condemnation—and, as a side-effect, the condemnation of the thirty-one little victims to lifelong madness.

The Flaxists, for their part, were demanding no less fervently to see the transactional project of the creator of geniuses accepted, and to see the prison gates opened to their hero, in exchange for operations on all the children of Frutt, without exception.

Finally, a third party, born yesterday, admitted the liberation of the doctor and his accomplices, admitted the operation on all the children whose parents will consent to it, but protested energetically against the doctor's demand to reintroduce his scalpel even into the skulls of the children whose parents refuse that second surgical intervention.

The Chambre had to settle that extraordinary conflict, that confusion of conscience, which was being discussed from one pole to the other, in the smallest villages in Japan and in the farms of the pampas.

The Palais-Bourbon thus offered today an enormous treat to the lovers of great parliamentary sessions. The immense hall was full to bursting. The tickets had been snapped up. The spectacle announced outside was maximal in its effect.

Pretty dresses, socialites.

Numerous administrative, political and literary personalities witnessed the debates. A few names, jotted down at hazard:

Jules Clarétie;

Nansen, the Norwegian explorer, passing through Paris;

Fauré, the director of the Conservatoire, alongside Brunau;

Chenu, president of the bar;

Finot, editor of the *Revue des Revues*, between Maurice Donnay and Feydeau;

M. de Selves, the Prefect of the Seine, with the new Prefect of Seine-et-Oise, M. Autrand;

Abel Hermant;

Santos-Dumont;

the two Coquelins, the elder and the younger;

Mademoiselle Lavallière of the Théâtre des Variétés;

Mademoiselle Dieterle, currently at the Théâtre de l'Athénée, alongside Yvette Guilbert and Mademoiselle Dorgére, prettier than ever;

etc., etc.

The diplomatic bench is full, as if the question were important to world equilibrium. One notices, in particular:

Comte Van den Playgs;

the Italian ambassador, whose sympathy for Dr. Flax and the Comtesse de Houdotte is no secret for anyone;

his first secretary, Comte Léonardo de Valmali, an Italian more Parisian than many Parisians;

Comte Monoto, the former Japanese ambassador in Paris, presently ambassador in St. Petersburg;

Munir-Bey, the minister of the Sublime Gate;

etc.

Seated on the ministers' bench are Messieurs Clemenceau, Briand, Leygues, Cruppi, Étienne, Thomson and Dujardin-Beaumetz.

The session is opened at two-forty under the presidency of Monsieur Brisson.

After a few preliminaries, Georges Larry comes to the podium. The député for Paris drinks a mouthful of water. All gazes are upon him. A great silence descends. The drama begins.

Georges Larry declares that, in his opinion, the government has always acted with the utmost incompetence in "the affair of the charlatan who has not created the genius of charlatanism in his collection because he has kept it for himself." After having terrified the population of Paris during his thefts of children, the minister has permitted the country, momentarily appeased, to catch fire once again without any necessity.

M. Clemenceau, *Minister of the Interior*: "What would you have done?"

M. Larry: "I don't know. I would have done something. I'm not the government."

M. Rabier protests.

George Larry concludes by declaring that one cannot have any confidence in a government that allows a simple matter concerning the police and the law to degenerate into a public quarrel.

Monsieur Aynard, taking the podium: "Dr. Flax is one of the most prodigious intelligences of all time." (*Energetic protests. Applause. "It's True!" Tumult. Cries of "Enough!" Censure!*) The services that a man of that stripe and that intellectual caliber might render a nation are such that not only must he be set at liberty..." (*Cry to the right: "In Berlin!"*) "...but that it is also necessary to offer him, in profusion, all the means to perfect his work in total security, without allowing him to be stopped by any vague sentimentality."

M. Ribot applauds M. Aynard.

A rare event! Voices from the extreme left support the moderate député. One might almost believe, momentarily, that the Chambre is about to vote felicitations to Dr. Flax, that it is even about to authorize him to continue his gigantic Work of the perfection of the human race by the artificial creation of men of genius.

M. Dudry Bisson: "I request the floor."

The floor is given to M. Dudry Bisson, the aged *enfant terrible* of the Parliament.

M. Dudry Bisson: "The debate that has opened in the Chambre is strange. As the song says, my honorable colleagues have spoken very well." (*Laughter.*) "It would only remain for us to drink to their health..." (*Laughter.*) "...if some of us, of whom I am one, did not think that the final word of the subject has not been said. The orators who, from the height of this podium, have poured the waves of their eloquence over us... (*Ironic exclamations: "Oh! Oh!"*) "...are accustomed to ask their listeners to raise the level of the debate. I should like, for once, permission to lower it. We have been discussing the subject of Dr. Flax, thus far, with the arguments of passion, sentiment and philosophy. I shall address myself, Messieurs, firstly to your common sense and secondly to your egotism. I hope to be understood in the former instance; I'm sure of being understood in the latter." (*Laughter.*)

"It is necessary, Messieurs, in my opinion to prevent Professor Flax from ever having the possibility of continuing his experiments, interesting as they are. It is necessary, however, since he offers us the alternative, that he emerges from prison, and retransforms the children of genius he has created into ordinary children, in order that the little ones in question can become ordinary adults, adults without genius, like you...and me..." (*Amused protests.*) "I pray those of my colleagues who are protesting that they are men of genius to make themselves known." (*Laughter.*) No one names himself. I am therefore correct in claiming that there are no men of genius in the Chambre. I think that conclusion is near to the truth." (*Laughter.*)

"Furthermore, given our political system, which expels all superiorities, I am not far from believing that we form the prettiest collection of mediocrities that one could bring together in our beautiful France."

A voice: "You're going a bit far."

M. Dudry Bisson: "Perhaps I am going a bit far, but I'm not far off the truth."

M. Sembat: "Be careful you don't shave it." (*Laughter.*)

The president rings his bell.

M. Dudry Bisson: "Now, Messieurs, composed principally—let's be polite—of average brains, and careful of its rights and prerogatives, the Chambre cannot authorize a man to manufacture, by the gross, electors of exceptional intelligence. What would become of us, Messieurs, and our children who have not been subjected to the surgeon's regenerative scalpel, in the midst of so many children and so many adults of genius? They would soon end up considering us as negligible quantities, of rapidly throwing us out of our electoral fiefs and privileges.

"Yes, Messieurs, we and our children would soon disappear from the stage where we have been very content to play the leading roles, if we had to contend with too great a number of high intelligences. That is why, Messieurs, it is necessary that Dr. Flax operates again on the little geniuses, why it is necessary that not the slightest trace remains of an invention that, by creating too many superiorities, would rapidly bring down the gravest prejudices upon the mediocrities who are, incontestably, the majority in the country."

The Chambre listens to Monsieur Dudry Bisson's speech with joyful amusement, but the députés who are laughing allow themselves to be quietly convinced, without allowing the conviction to show. There is some truth in the orator's irony.

M. Jaurès goes up to the podium, after M. Dudry Bisson. He makes a very fine, very violent speech. He opposes the scientists who want to go too far in the matter of experiments on living flesh. He nevertheless renders homage to the "sovereign humanity" that has guided Dr. Flax.

The Minister of the Interior replies. In his opinion, the Chambre must dictate to the government the course of action to take. It is a case of conscience that Parliament must decide.

A voice from the right: "The fear of responsibility."

The Minister of the Interior: "No—but the conviction that the legislative power ought, in a case of this sort, direct the government. No political principle is at stake. It is a matter of taking census of minds divided by a unique and novel moral problem. The government does, however, have an opinion, and has stated it: that Dr. Flax's proposal should be immediately accepted. The parents who have requested that the surgeon operate again on their children are, in fact, in the great majority.

"On the other hand, the parents who are refusing are guided purely by self-interest. Thus, Émile Loubé, the genius of sculpture, has just received a commission from the American billionaire Mr. Vanderbilt, for a bust for which he will be paid 600,000 francs. The Chambre will doubtless not allow itself to be stopped by considerations of that sort. It will consider that it is necessary to sacrifice certain individual interests to public tranquility.

"The solution indicated by the government will restore calm, but it is not the only one that will attain that result; thus, the Ministry, while indicating its preference to the Chambre, is ready to accept any motion not containing an expression of a lack of confidence."

M. George Larrry demands priority for a motion of that kind: "The Chambre, regretting that the Ministry has not yet found a reasonable solution to the affair of Dr. Flax, disapproves of the actions of the government."

It is rejected by 280 votes to 203.

A motion proposed by MM. Couyba and Steeg is then passed by 294 votes to 180, with 30 abstentions: "The Chambre, confident in the government, authorizes it to accept Dr. Flax's propositions, in their entirety."

Animated conversations follow this vote. The benches are agitated. The anti-Flaxes are furious.

The parents of Émile Loubé, Urbain Godedouins, Bernard Flaquette and Philippe Ordin-Rosier, who are present at the session, are determined to resist by all possible means, including violence.

"There is no law in the world," Monsieur Flaquette declares to me, that can oblige a father and mother to let their child be cut up by a surgeon's knife. We shall defend ourselves."

RELEASE FROM PRISON
THE FURTHER OPERATIONS

Dr. Flax had not deceived us.

That fabulous man is always sure of himself.

When he told us that if he were not allowed to pursue his studies in transcendent surgery, he would oblige the government to set him, and his friends, at liberty with the briefest possible delay, he was not boasting. He was merely expressing an intimate conviction, conscious of his strength.

The vote of the Chambre des Députés had not been acquired for an hour when Dr. Flax, the Comtesse de Houdotte, the three Hingertil brothers and Soeur Thérèse emerged from prison, embraced and congratulated by their friends, who were weeping with joy.

Soeur Thérèse immediately went to the Gare Saint-Lazare, where she took the first train to Saint-Cloud.

The children are to undergo their further operations at the hospital at Montretout, and her intention was, as soon as she arrived there, to put the doctor's laboratory in order and prepare the operating theater.

The Comtesse de Houdotte will take up residence in a new abode with the doctor, for the adventure of he celebrated child-stealers will terminate in a marriage. The banns will be published immediately. The union of Professor Flax and his collaborator is imminent. It will be celebrated as soon as the legal formalities are completed.

At six o'clock this morning Dr. Flax, accompanied by Numérien Hingertil, climbed into an automobile and had himself taken to the hospital at Montretout.

The little geniuses were all there, with the exception of Émile Loubé, Bernard Flaquette, Urbain Godedouins and Philippe Ordin-Rosier, whose parents had been obstinate in their refusal.

When the surgeon enters the large hall where the parents and children are waiting, a great silence falls: a silence of emotion and fearful hatred.

The surgeon crosses the room with an uncontrived attitude of fine nobility, exempt from any affectation. It is a Master who is passing by, a Master who dictates his will, who is obeyed by virtue of the strongest laws of all, profoundly mysterious. Having reached the second door the surgeon pauses momentarily to count the little geniuses present.

"They're not all here!" he cries. "Thus, as I have sworn, I shall not begin until all thirty-one children are gathered in this room."

Accompanying his words with a peremptory gesture, the surgeon disappears behind a glazed door into the corridor that leads to his laboratory.

Cries and protests are heard. Messieurs Clépent and Gobely-Franthéon telephone the Minister of the Interior in Paris. They are told that the police are in the process of bringing to Montretout the four little geniuses whose parents have tried to escape the necessity imposed by the doctor and, in consequence, by the Chambre des Députés.

Little Émile Loubé had been hidden the day before with friends of his father's, but Monsieur Hamard, anticipating that trickery, had established surveillance, and the child's whereabouts were, therefore, known. In the homes of Messieurs Flaquette and Odin-Rosier, the authorities were similarly obliged to use force.

At eleven o'clock in the morning, the four little geniuses thus abducted from their parents for a second time arrive at Montretout under a strong escort.

Professor Flax immediately sets to work.

Numerous physicians have come to watch him at work, but he refuses to operate in front of spectators. Only Soeur Thérèse and Numérien Hingertil assist the surgeon.

At four o'clock in the afternoon, Soeur Thérèse comes to announce to the parents that the thirty-one children have once against been subjected to the surgeon's scalpel, and that everything has gone as well as could be desired.

The children will be cared for at the Hospital in Montremont until they are healed, which will not take long.

THE ENGAGEMENT CELEBRATION
THE HINGERTILS' DISCONTENTMENT
A PESSIMISTIC PREDICTION

After completing that task, Dr. Flax returned to Paris. The automobile took him to his house in the Rue Cassette, where he spent more than an hour, with Numérien Hingertil, sorting out the papers that the examining magistrate had returned to him.

For her part, the Comtesse de Houdotte, after a long visit to her former domicile, transported various objects to her new dwelling.

At seven o'clock, Dr. Flax and the Comtesse received friends invited to dinner informally, to celebrate their engagement.

I have been invited to this meal by a very amiable note reminding me of my adventures in Frutt and the days spent in Dr. Flax's domain at the foot of the snow-capped mountains.

The guests are all those devotees whose rare amity resisted the misfortune or, indeed, germinated within the misfortune. I note, in addition to names previously cited, Amiral Fournier, Octave Mirbeau, Georges Lecomte, Dr. Maurice de Fleury and Comte Noailles-Amboise, Madame de Houdotte's uncle. The two last-named are to serve as witnesses for Dr. Flax's fiancée at her imminent marriage.

The Comtesse is wearing, as usual, a long dress of regal design, fabricated from a single piece of rich maroon fabric, fastened at the side by a row of large tortoiseshell buttons. On the front she is wearing a little brooch engraved by young Flaquette, into which Urbain Godedouins has inserted gems. The little brooch is a masterpiece. On her finger shines the celebrated Love-Ring engraved by Bobichon, replicas of which were distributed during the dinner at Frutt.

The doctor astonishes us slightly.

He has trimmed his beard to a point and shaved off his moustache. His modified visage would now gives him the banal appearance of an actor or a clergyman, were it not for his imperious jaw, every muscle of which furrows the skin with knotty grooves, marking the mask with a relief like that of a medallion.

Thus transformed, Professor Flax, who has never had any pretention to resemble Chérubin,[47] is frightfully ugly, but with an ugliness akin to pure beauty. He seems thinner thus, more emaciated than he did at Frutt, and his tall frame is stooped. The eyes are less brilliant, as if veiled with mist. I wonder whether the master of Frutt has not been touched more deeply than he will admit by the disillusionment that has smashed his enormous dreams.

During dinner, I chat with the Hingertil brothers. A curious conversation! They are very discontented regarding the projected marriage between Dr. Flax and the Comtesse de Houdotte. They do not hide the fact, and speak overtly, unconcerned that they might be overheard by their masters.

Their devoted intransigence will not admit what Chrysostome frankly calls the violation of an oath.

"They had promised not to marry," he says to me, "until the day when their work had taken flight throughout the world. The work has failed. Therefore, they should not marry. It's bad."

"For one thing, it will bring them misfortune," Wolfgang grumbles. "I didn't want to refuse to be the doctor's witness, but I'll be putting my signature at the bottom of a baneful document. Wait and see, Monsieur, wait and see. The future will prove me right."

At table, the talk is dull and heavy, in spite of the men of great intellect gathered around the doctor and the Comtesse.

A storm is weighing over Paris, oppressing breasts, slowing the pace of life.

But above all, it appears to all the guests that this joyless meal, which concludes the hour when two destinies almost surpassed humanity, has something cramped and paltry about it: it is a pitiful ending, and we are witnessing an unmerited, unjust decline, a small death.

The soul of desolation presides over that agape.

---

[47] A character in Beaumarchais *The Marriage of Figaro*, who became a type-specimen of a handsome adolescent.

The vast low black clouds that are slowly creeping over the city impregnate us with effluvia of discouragement. No one dares react against that dire sentiment of apprehension and vague anguish, the professor and is fiancée even less than anyone else. They have the air of exiles.

After the dessert, at coffee, as we pass into a little drawing room, Dr. Flax takes me by the arm and does not seek to conceal his state of mind.

"Life for us, henceforth, will be frightfully empty," he tells me. "After frantic agitation, and incessant fever and a thousand hopes swelling our sails, we are now sent into retirement before our time. How can we adapt our brains to that polar calm?"

"We shall try, my friend," says the Comtesse, who has overheard, "to overcome out thoughts and our disillusionments. We shall try to forget our marvelous dreams." Looking at me, she added: "Oh, Monsieur, don't laugh; I've bought a game of bezique, which will replace the evening conversations of old, when we brought impassioned inspirations into collision."

"We have fallen from a height," Flax continues. "Perhaps it will be difficult for me to forget, when I still have within me, here, in my head, beneath this cap of flesh and bone, the certainty of being able to succeed whenever I wish, whenever I am allowed to do so."

I examine "Dr. Hell" attentively while he pronounces that statement. He has a sardonic smile. His temples are furrowed. A bitter wrinkle squeezes the corners of his mouth.

Will he be able to reconcile himself to the idea of allowing the fecund power that is seething within him to fade away, uselessly, without any profit for anyone?

Naturally, I attempt to offer a few words of consolation.

"Certainly, Doctor, the transition from a life of superhuman dreams to the peace that is imposed on you, is bound to be difficult and painful. There's something unusual and heart-rending in the silence that will surround you. Permit me, however, to congratulate you on the calm that you will finally savor in the joy of your marriage, the union of two beings who have understood one another completely."

"Bah! Don't congratulate yourself too soon. Wait a little—doubtless not long...tomorrow."

I also note a response made by the doctor to Marcel Prévost.

"Bah!" the great novelist says to them. "All great ideas find an hour when the crowd does them justice. The condemnation of Galileo did not prevent his triumph, because it could not stop the movement of the Earth. Your time will also come. Then you will resume your experiments, and...."

"No," the doctor interjects. "It's impossible. We are excessively distant precursors, and precursors are accursed, by virtue of the laws of human nature."

"Well, then, let the irreflective anger fade away slowly and abandon problems that are too vast. Apply your minds to more down-to-earth problems, simpler for the crowd. You'll be better understood. The people who abuse you to-day and consign your names to the flames of Hell will then applaud the unique and unprecedented gifts of your intelligence."

"No, my dear friend. When one has, like us, almost attained the summits; when one has, like us, looked down at the world from such a high vantage, one can no longer consent to a mediocrity of thought. No, we shall remain idle. We shall disappear, we shall bury ourselves in indolence, which will be a kind of antechamber to our tombs."

It is midnight. We take our leave of the Comtesse de Houdotte, Dr. Flax and the Hingertils. We leave them all depressed by a heavy sadness, as ponder-ous as the atmosphere.

"How discouraged they are, those individuals that we believed to be com-pounded out of rock and bronze!" remarks Dr. Maurice de Fleury.

"Alas, I glimpsed the knell of infinite despair in their voices," adds Anatole France.

Wolfgang Hingertil accompanies us to the street.

As he crushes my hand in a final *bonsoir*, the giant murmurs to me: "A funny engagement, eh? You'll see, you'll see. It will bring them bad luck. They shouldn't marry. They're breaking their oath. It will bring them bad luck...before long..."

Alain Bernard

14 September

SUICIDE OF THE HEROES OF FRUTT
AN UNUSUAL TESTAMENT
THE ROSE-BUSHES OF SARNEN

Is it written somewhere, in the Book of Destiny, that the adventure of Professor Flax and the Comtesse de Houdotte would be a tissue of violent and dolorous events until the very end?

It was assumed that the noisy affair would fade away slowly and gradually into the peace of history. It will not.

By contrast with people of the theater, who do not know when the time has come to quite the stage, clinging on to the public to offer them the spectacle of their decrepitude, the strange actors of the drama of Frutt wanted to depart in full glory, if one can call their fantastic notoriety glory.

Who would have thought that, the day after I announced the marriage of the scientist and his friend, I would have to record their end, that the engagement of yesterday was merely a funeral vigil and an alliance for death.

Not long before noon, this morning, I received the following telegram:

My dear friend.

You have been the almost faithful and always sincere historiographer of our lamentable adventure. Come quickly. We shall furnish you with a supreme epilogue, the ultimate full stop of your narrative.

Sigismond Flax

The letter is urgent; the mystery that it allows to be read between its lines anguishing.

I remember Flax's enigmatic voice when he said to me, twice, the previous evening: "Wait a little—doubtless not long…tomorrow."

I run to the Rue de Valois, for it is there, in an apartment overlooking the Palais-Royal, that the doctor and the Comtesse have retreated, on emerging from prison.

The street is packed with people.

I catch stray words: suicide, poison, Flax.

They respond clearly to my silent questions.

After negotiating with the agents clearing the vicinity of Flax's house, I climb the stairway in haste.

Leaning his full height against the frame of the entrance door, Chrysostome Hingertil is mounting guard.

The enormous Swiss crushes my phalanges in a grip into which he puts all his soul.

The mountain man conducts me into a bedroom, whose drawn curtains and closed shutters veil it with an oppressive penumbra.

My eyes, too full as yet of the bright sunlight that is inundating Paris with its joy outside, have difficulty adapting to the gloom.

Vaguely, I distinguish silhouettes bending over in the darkness, where everything is spangled.

The giant Hingertil takes me by the arm and leads me to the foot of the bed.

"Look," he murmurs, in a hoarse voice.

Then, slowly, as my eyes adjust to the vague ambient light, two pale patches appear, against an exceedingly dark background. Gradually, they become more precise, taking shape, becoming three-dimensional, and I recognize, still elongated by death, the faces of the incredible heroes reposing on garnet velvet cushions.

I stand for a moment, trembling, contemplating that extinct flesh, those skulls, illuminated yesterday by two exceptional flames, abolished forever today.

On turning round, I finally recognize the spectators of that inertia, which speaks so forcefully to our imagination.

They are almost all there, the people who witnessed the engagement yesterday, the combatants of an unusual cause, in which justice soared to such heights that rare were the elect who were able to perceive it.

In one corner, Camille Flammarion, Anatole France, Millerand and Georges Lecomte are conversing in low voices; d'Angliney and Pierre Veber are murmuring words of consolation to Numérien and Wolfgang Hingertil.

Wolfgang is curled up in an armchair. He gives the impression of an immense, mortally wounded beast, gathering himself for one last bound, formidable and devastating.

Octave Mirbeau, Besnard, Mroczkowski, André Honorat, Marcel Prévost, Antoine and Franz Jourdain are standing, lost in reflections, and one senses passing through those skeptics a hint of the invisible and powerful breath that, in naïve souls, sows faith, superstitions and legends.

I ask Théodore Cahu: "You're their neighbor—how did it happen?"

Numérien has overheard the question. "At eleven o'clock the doctor called us. His fiancée was beside him, smoking a cigarette. Without any preamble, he read his testament to us. After which, he added, calmly:

"'My friends, at quarter past eleven I shall open the window of the drawing room that overlooks the garden of the Palais-Royal. I shall play the organ, and the Comtesse will sing. We should like the passers-by to say to one another that such harmonies and such a pure voice could not be born of the fingers and the throat of evil and wicked individuals.

"At eleven-thirty, my fiancée and I will commit suicide. I possess a new, rapid poison that does not destroy the features

"At eleven thirty-five, you will come into our room. It will be finished. Don't touch us. You will leave us in our beds, as we are lying. On the mantelpiece, you will find telegrams prepared for our friends. You will take them immediately to the box, and you will make as many copies of our testament with the typewriter as the number of people we have invited for a final visit. They will be a copy for each of them..."

"Then," says Wolfgang, with a sob that shakes him like a coughing-fit, "the Comtesse got up from her chair, held out her hand to us and said: 'Adieu, my friends,' and the professor repeated: 'Adieu, my friends.'"

"And we," Chrysostome adds, "replied: 'Adieu, friends,' and we left."

"What!" cries Georges Lecomte. "You didn't oppose it?"

"We've always obeyed them," Wolfgang interjects.

"At the appointed time," Numérien goes on, "we heard the organ playing and the voice of the Comtesse. The professor was accompanying the *Hymn to Glory* composed at Frutt by little Pierre Candelaur and Nicolas Barlatescu. It was magnificent. The organ made the house tremble. All three of us listened, pressed against the door. The song grips you by the throat, it's so poignant, celestial, powerful...in the garden, a crowd gathered. They listened silently, until the end...

"For the rest, we did as the professor had asked of us. We have no more to do than give you the copies of the testament."

Wolfgang passes them to us. He takes the original and reads it aloud:

"This is our last will, with the reasons that dictate it to us:

"We have tried, engaging ourselves in order soon to marry, to realize the recompense that we had fixed for our work, giving us a poetic illusion. But we have observed that our union, so long dreamed, will not bring us any interesting satisfaction.

"One day was sufficient for us to understand that our marriage was a function of our Work, and that, our Work having been annihilated, it was no more than a vain formality devoid of heartfelt joy and of hope.

"Better, then, to die.

"We shall not even attempt to distract ourselves from our dream by mingling ourselves with contemporary life. We feel indifferent to it, as a repeated experiment. This morning's newspapers talk about horse races at Vichy, a mysterious scandal in the Rue de Temple, the German emperor's new uniform, Monsieur Le Bargy's next production and a complementary election of a député. What would we do in that world? We would be like aged scientists obliged to live in a circus.

"Better, then, to die.

"We both recognize also, honestly, that perhaps we never loved one another, veritably and truly. We were not infatuated with one another; we were only infatuated with the same ideal. That ideal having disappeared, finished, we now remain mere neighbors, disenchanted and disoriented. Tomorrow, we would be at odds.

"Better, then, to die.

"We are dying without dread, and we are dying without hatred.

"We have suffered the fate of all those who have sincerely sought the good of humankind, all those who, to hasten the advent of a better world, have run into the irreducible barrier of stupidity, the paltry passions of a majority impoverished in ideas, composed of simple torch-bearers lost in the frightful night of human ignorance.

"We have been able to wrench an immense secret from rebellious nature. We have been able to communicate that secret to the deaf who did not want to hear...

"The Hingertil brothers will be alone is accompanying us to the cemetery. They will transport us in a simple hearse and arrange things in such a fashion that our burial passes unperceived.

"The metal of the precious objects that we possess will be melted down into ingots.

"Our precious stones will be removed from their settings and delivered to the lapidary.

The product of these alienations and the rest of our fortune in bonds and immovable property will revert to the Hingertil brothers, charged with the execution of the present testament.

"All our papers all our books, all our clothes, all our furniture and everything else that belongs to us will be burned, in order that no trace of us will remain.

"Since we have not been permitted to bequeath to civilization our completed, perfected Work, we wish to disappear totally.

"We ask that our bodies also be burned, but that our remains should not be kept in the vicinity of the crematorium oven, uselessly contained in a funerary urn. Let the Hingertil brothers buy a garden somewhere. Let them plant beautiful roses there, and strew our ashes around those rose-bushes, to fertilize the soil.

"We shall thus live again next spring, in the sap of flowers; we shall blossom in healthy verdure, in petals, in embalmed flower-beds.

"We have vanquished nature; she will thus take her revenge, by bending us in our turn to her chemical and organic laws, and we, who wanted to go too quickly, shall collaborate, without haste, in the slow progress of the world.

"Let the brothers Hingertil, every year, pick those roses and sent bouquets of them to our friends, in order that the latter might thus breathe in a little of our spirit.

"That is all that we desire, before disappearing."

The letter concluded, Numérien adds: "The document that has just been read to you was written by the doctor, as far as the passage concerning ashes, the garden and the roses. The rest is in the Comtesse's handwriting."

Marcel Prévost smiles, sadly. "Women," he says, "cannot dispense with poetry, even before dying."

"They have both signed with a firm pen," remarks Antoine. "They did not tremble. It's honest, frank. They weren't actors, those two."

Séverine raises her voice, and says, dully: "Messieurs, let us bid the eternal adieu to those mysterious and noble intelligences."

Then each of us, in turn, advances, leans over the dormant cadavers and deposits a kiss on their rigid foreheads.

"And what will become of you?" Camille Flammarion, who is twisting his beard, profoundly troubled, asks the Hingertil brothers.

"We'll return to Switzerland," Wolfgang replies. "We'll buy the garden to plant the roses and sow the ashes. We'll built a house near the lake at Frutt. We'll live there in summer. In winter, we'll come down to Sarnen. And we'll wait for death, while remembering them."

Alain Bernard

Afterword
Transcendental Surgery and Human Progress

"*Le Voleur d'enfants*" is a work that could not have been published, in the first instance, in any other format than that of a daily newspaper serial, to which it as specifically adapted. Its adaptation as a book requires that the reader be aware of that initial format and sensitive to its implications. On the other hand, seen in retrospect, it is obvious that the serial in question would have appeared to any editor of a daily newspaper to have been effectively unpublishable, because it was simply too provocative in the development of its concluding section, in which Dr. Flax is not presented as the kind of stock villain standardized by popular *feuilleton* fiction, but as a problematic item in a sharp *conte philosophique* posing a conundrum in what American pragmatist philosophers of the era called "situational ethics."

The fact is, of course, that the serial *was* published—but one suspects that it was only published because it was *not* seen in retrospect, and seemed very different in vague anticipation. In effect, it was published by stealth, masquerading in its early section as a melodramatic mystery story with a cheerful edge of satirical comedy. Although the element of satirical comedy is never entirely lost in the course of the story, it changes its tone considerably; the humor becomes black and subtle, and the eventual "solution" to the initial mystery is devoid of any hint of the surge of moral satisfaction that is conventionally supposed to attach in popular fiction to the revelation, arrest and punishment of criminals.

The logic of that "solution" leaves a good deal to be desired, in that the loose ends that the author condescends to tie up are disposed of in a manner that is as cursory as it is unconvincing, while some awkward enigmas still remain conspicuously unanswered (How did Paolo Palavacoccini get Alain Bernard's telegrams from Frutt to Lucerne? How did Soeur Thérèse manage to transport the children from Paris to Frutt—allegedly one at a time—when the timetable of abductions seems to have left no time at all for the necessary journeys?) In fairness, however, it ought to be noted that many of the great exponents of make-it-up-as-you go feuilletons, most conspicuously Paul Féval and Ponson du Terrail, were far more cavalier in leaving loose ends awkwardly strewn around, and that Louis Forest at least had the excuse of having transformed his narrative into a kind of story that reduced the intricacies of its supposed mystery to mere trivia.

The conclusion of the story, in addressing the question of the possibilities of human progress, the potential contribution to be made to that progress by technological invention, and the best way to foster technical invention, was not breaking entirely new ground for *feuilleton* fiction, but it was certainly breaking that ground far more brutally than any implement that had been applied to it in the medium before.

Le Matin had published fiction with elements of *roman scientifique* before; indeed, one of its most prolific *feuilletonists*, Paul d'Ivoi, routinely introduced technological innovations into his Vernian adventure stories—but he did so with even greater delicacy that the publisher Pierre-Jules Hetzel had forced upon Verne himself, rigorously condemning such motifs to the margins of adventure stories that that steered well clear of moral and philosophical questions likely to offend the sensitivity, or startle the complacency, of the average reader. However, the newspaper had never published anything that thrust future technological possibilities into the foreground, not as mere playthings, but as goods with a heavy price-tag attached, in order to ask and leave deliberately unanswered the question: "If this were the price of authentic social progress, would it be worth paying?" Editors do not like authors to do that sort of thing—even though authors often yearn to do it—because editors are eternally convinced that there is nothing the majority of readers hates more than being asked, even politely, to think.

In taking on motifs of *roman scientifique*, the final section of "*Le Voleur d'enfants*" only bears a distant relationship to Vernian adventure fiction, but it bears a much closer relationship to a kind of deliberately combative *roman scientifique* rarely found in *feuilleton* form, which was consciously carrying forward the Voltairean tradition of ideative challenge. Indeed, it belongs to an interesting series of speculative narratives dealing specifically with what is described in the text, in relation to Dr. Flax, as "transcendental surgery"—the use of hypothetical biotechnological methods to transform human beings in the interests of progress.

A search for the earliest significant works of that kind could go back as far as Louis Ulbach's "Le Prince Bonifacio" (1860)[48] and the brain-manipulating surgeries of Dr. Marforio, but that *conte philosophique* is a straightforward political satire whose speculative content is primarily an ironic narrative device. A far more important forefather of Dr. Flax is Dr. Gael, the ambitious human vivisector featured in Louise Michel's *Les Microbes humains* (1886)[49], who figures in that novel as a kind of ultimate Gothic villain with only slight redeeming features, but is transformed in the sequel, *Le Nouveau monde* (1888)[50]—planned as the second item in a six-volume series, although no others were written—into a kind of demigod potentially capable of steering the pure in heart through an impending world catastrophe to an interplanetary utopia, by means of ingenious transformations of the flesh.

A far more sophisticated work, in both literary and philosophical terms, is André Couvreur's *Le Mal necessaire* (1899)[51], which features the human vivi-

---

[48] Available in a Black Coat Press edition as *Prince Bonifacio*, ISBN 9781612272283.
[49] Available in a Black Coat Press edition as *The Human Microbes*, ISBN 9781612271163.
[50] Available in a Black Coat Press edition as *The New World*, ISBN 9781612271170.
[51] Available in a Black Coat Press edition as *The Necessary Evil*, ISBN 9781612272535.

sector Dr. Caresco, a less ambiguous villain than Dr. Flax, although his very villainy might have played some part in prompting Louis Forest to take up the themes it develops, and give them a different slant. The extrapolation of Dr. Caresco's career in the sequel, *Caresco surhomme, ou Le Voyage en Eucrasie* (1904)[52], in which his ambitions become even more ambition in shaping the society of a remote Pacific island, represented a process of narrative development and transformation not unlike the one employed by Forest in changing the genre of his evolving serial. Couvreur was to go on to chronicle the exploits of another transcendental biotechnologist, Professor Tornada, in a series of six stories published between 1909 and 1939, which might have browed some inspiration from Dr. Flax by way of recompense.[53]

There was, of course, no reason why ambitious surgeons could not feature as standardized feuilleton villains, and some or all of these literary predecessors might have helped to provide inspiration for Gustave's Le Rouge's long weekly part-work *Le Mysterieux Docteur Cornelius* (1912-13)[54], whose villain, nicknamed "the sculptor of human flesh" mostly helps to further nasty criminal schemes intended to make money. Even Cornelius seems to have another and stranger agenda, however, and readers inclined to look beyond the surface of his adventures—who were probably few in number, but no less precious for that—not only caught glimpses of much more adventurous technical possibilities, but also much more intriguing potential social transformations.

It is difficult now to judge how *Le Matin*'s readers reacted to "Le Voleur d'enfants," because no sign of the feedback the editor received was manifest in the paper's pages. It is, however, noticeable that although speculative fiction had played a very minor role in *Le Matin*'s feuilleton slots prior to 1906, it played a significantly larger role thereafter, albeit in forms far more comfortably adapted to the standard conventions of feuilleton narrative. One writer who joined the newspaper's stable of regular writers not long thereafter was Jean de La Hire, who made his debut there in 1908 with *La Roue fulgurante* [55], a fast-paced and riotous interplanetary adventure of a kind that was to become one of the staples of American science fiction, and *L'Homme qui peut vivre dans l'eau* [The Man Who Could Live Under Water] (1908), a thriller featuring a transcendental biotechnologist named Oxus, who might also have provided some inspiration for Le

---

[52] Available in a Black Coat Press edition as *Caresco, Superman*, ISBN 9781612272542.

[53] *An Invasion of Macrobes, The Androgyne, The Phosphorescent Waltzer, Memoirs of an Immortal, The Biocole, The Case of Baroness Sasoitsu*, soon to be available in a three-volume Black Coat Press edition.

[54] Available in a three-volume Black Coat Press edition, 1. *The Sculptor of Human Flesh* ISBN 9781612272436, 2. *The Island of Hanged Men* ISBN 9781612272443 and 3. *The Rochester Bridge Catastrophe* ISBN 9781612272450,

[55] Available in a Black Coat Press edition as *The Fiery Wheel*, ISBN 9781612272177.

Rouge's Dr. Cornelius. Oxus returned in a sequel, *La Mystère des XV* (1911)[56], which begins—perhaps not entirely coincidentally—with a series of kidnappings in Paris intended to supply breeding-stock for a utopian community of supermen. The popularizer of science and occasional dabbler in *roman scientifique* Camille Flammarion, who makes a cameo appearance in "Le Voleur d'enfants," also makes cameo appearances in both "La Roue fulgurante" and "La Mystère des XV."

Another reporter on the staff of *Le Matin* in 1906, who became a far more prolific *feuilletonist* than Louis Forest, was Gaston Leroux, who had made his debut in that form with *Le Chercheur de trésors* (1903; reprinted as *La Double vie de Théophraste Longuet*; tr. as *The Man with the Black Feather*), a thriller with a fantastic element involving a curious form of atavism akin to reincarnation or quasi-demonic possession. Most of Leroux's subsequent serials, in *Le Matin* and elsewhere, were more modest in their inventions, even when he worked in a Vernian vein, as he occasionally did, but more striking speculative elements cropped up in such *Matin* serials as *Balaoo* (1911; tr. as *Balaoo*), *Rouletabille chez Krupp* (1917)[57] and *La Poupée sanglante* [The Bloody Doll] (1923; reprinted in two volumes, the second of which was translated as *The Machine to Kill*). Although slicker in his plotting than Forest, and a much tighter tier-up of loose ends, Leroux never came remotely close to matching the rhetoric sophistication of "*Le Voleur d'enfants*," but that only helped to ensure his success as a *feuilletonist*, while Forest was never permitted to dabble in the medium again.

Whether or not the example "*Le Voleur d'enfants*" did have some influence on future editorial policy at *Le Matin*—whose editor might, of course, have recruited La Hire and encouraged Leroux to greater imaginative range regardless—its anomalousness presumably came to the attention of the staff of *Le Matin*'s chief daily rival in the early years of the twentieth century, *Le Journal*. *Le Journal* was far more sparing in its use of *feuilleton* serials than *Le Matin*, and certainly did not run them three at a time, but it had been rather more adventurous in the past in its use of *roman scientifique* motifs, notably in *Fleur de bagne* (1901)[58], written in collaboration by the ex-head of the Sûreté who liked to sign himself simply "Goron"—whose memoirs had been a big hit in the same serial slot—and Émile Gautier, the former editor of the popular science magazine *La Science Française*. Although basically a straightforward tale of the glittering career and eventual downfall a criminal mastermind, the story also fea-

---

[56] Available in a Black Coat Press edition as *The Nyctalope on Mars*, ISBN 9781934543467.
[57] Available in a Black Coat Press edition as *Rouletabille at Krupp's*, ISBN 9781612271446.
[58] Available in a Black Coat Press edition as *Spawn of the Pentitentiary*, ISBN 9781612271378.

tures an innovative scientist in his thrall and numerous technological innovations deployed by an against him.

Le Journal made much more use of short stories than *Le Matin*—although *Le Matin* retaliated by introducing a short story feature, under the rubric *Les Mille-et-un Matins*—and a few of the *contes cruels* it routinely features employed speculative motifs, even though the format did not lend itself to their development.

A compromise of sorts was found by one of *Le Journal*'s stable of fiction writers, Edmond Haraucourt, in a series of short serials, which allowed more scope for ideative development than stories contained in a single slot, without requiring the kind of formulaic narrative extrapolation typically associated with feuilletons. In 1906 *Le Journal* published two short series of that type by Haraucourt, which were far more daring in their futuristic speculations than anything seen in Parisian newspapers for half a century, "Le Gorilloide" (January 1906) and "Cinq mille ans, ou La Traversée de Paris" (September-October 1906)[59].

Neither of those stories could have taken any inspiration from Forest's serial, although Forest might well have been interested to note the vaulting ambition and innovative format of the former before shaping his own endeavor, but the next novelette in the loose sequence, "La Découverte du docteur Anguérand" (1910)[60] might well have done, in that it deals with the reaction of public opinion to a biologist's discovery of a technology of longevity, in an ironic and rhetorically sophisticated fashion that has conspicuous similarities to the later chapters of "*Le Voleur d'enfants*." Even if no direct influence was involved, "La Découverte du docteur Anguérand" nevertheless slots quite neatly into the sequence of *romans scientifiques* dealing with the social implications of human corporeal modification.

"*Le Voleur d'enfants*" is, therefore, a significant work in the development of *roman scientifique*, not only because of its theme and the pugnacious fashion in which it displays the supposed implications of that theme, but because of its medium, and the role it played—or attempted to play—in the adaptation of *roman scientifique* to the near-mass market of the popular press. Its achievements in both senses were limited and short-lived; the entire genre of *roman scientifique* faded away into esotericism as editorial experience confirmed what editors surely already felt as a gut reaction—that it did not have sufficient reader appeal to make it worthy of consistent attention, let alone intelligent effort—except in the most carefully anodyne of narrative, but the brief effort was nevertheless interesting, at least in historical retrospect.

---

[59] Translated as "The Gorilloid" and "A Trip to Paris"; both are included in the Black Coat Press edition of *Illusions of Immortality*, ISBN 9781612270753.
[60] Translated as "Doctor Anguérand's Discovery" and included in *Illusions of Immortality*, q.v.

The question raised by the novel, in order to exhibit its awkwardness, still remains unanswered, of course, and for the most part, deliberately unasked.

Brian Stableford

SF & FANTASY

Adolphe Alhaiza. *Cybele*
Alphonse Allais. *The Adventures of Captain Cap*
Henri Allorge. *The Great Cataclysm*
Guy d'Armen. *Doc Ardan: The City of Gold and Lepers*
G.-J. Arnaud. *The Ice Company*
Charles Asselineau. *The Double Life*
Cyprien Bérard. *The Vampire Lord Ruthwen*
S. Henry Berthoud. *Martyrs of Science*
Aloysius Bertrand. *Gaspard de la Nuit*
Richard Bessière. *The Gardens of the Apocalypse*
Albert Bleunard. *Ever Smaller*
Félix Bodin. *The Novel of the Future*
Louis Boussenard. *Monsieur Synthesis*
Alphonse Brown. *City of Glass; The Conquest of the Air*
Emile Calvet. *In a Thousand Years*
André Caroff. *The Terror of Madame Atomos; Miss Atomos; The Return of Madame Atomos; The Mistake of Madame Atomos; The Monsters of Madame Atomos; The Revenge of Madame Atomos; The Resurrection of Madame Atomos; The Mark of Madame Atomos*
Félicien Champsaur. *The Human Arrow; Ouha, King of the Apes; Pharaoh's Wife*
Didier de Chousy. *Ignis*
Jules Clarétie. *Obsession*
Michel Corday. *The Eternal Flame*
Captain Danrit. *Undersea Odyssey*
C. I. Defontenay. *Star (Psi Cassiopeia)*
Charles Derennes. *The People of the Pole*
Georges Dodds (anthologist). *The Missing Link*
Harry Dickson. *The Heir of Dracula*
Jules Dornay. *Lord Ruthven Begins*
Alfred Driou. *The Adventures of a Parisian Aeronaut*
Sâr Dubnotal *vs. Jack the Ripper*
Alexandre Dumas. *The Return of Lord Ruthven*
Renée Dunan. *Baal*
J.-C. Dunyach. *The Night Orchid; The Thieves of Silence*
Henri Duvernois. *The Man Who Found Himself*
Achille Eyraud. *Voyage to Venus*
Henri Falk. *The Age of Lead*
Paul Féval. *Anne of the Isles; Knightshade; Revenants; Vampire City; The Vampire Countess; The Wandering Jew's Daughter*
Paul Féval, *fils. Felifax, the Tiger-Man*
Charles de Fieux. *Lamékis*
Louis Forest. *Someone is Stealing Children in Paris*
Arnould Galopin. *Doctor Omega; Doctor Omega and the Shadowmen* (anthology)
Judith Gautier. *Isoline and the Serpent-Flower*
Léon Gozlan. *The Vampire of the Val-de-Grâce*

G.L. Gick. *Harry Dickson and the Werewolf of Rutherford Grange*
Edmond Haraucourt. *Illusions of Immortality*
Nathalie Henneberg. *The Green Gods*
V. Hugo, P. Foucher & P. Meurice. *The Hunchback of Notre-Dame*
Romain d'Huissier. *Hexagon: Dark Matter*
Jules Janin. *The Magnetized Corpse*
Michel Jeury. *Chronolysis*
Gustave Kahn. *The Tale of Gold and Silence*
Gérard Klein. *The Mote in Time's Eye*
Fernand Kolney. *Love in 5000 Years*
Paul Lacroix. *Danse Macabre*
Louis-Guillaume de La Follie. *The Unpretentious Philosopher*
Jean de La Hire. *Enter the Nyctalope; The Nyctalope on Mars; The Nyctalope vs. Lucifer; The Nyctalope Steps In; Night of the Nyctalope; Return of the Nyctalope; The Fiery Wheel*
Etienne-Léon de Lamothe-Langon. *The Virgin Vampire*
André Laurie. *Spiridon*
Gabriel de Lautrec. *The Vengeance of the Oval Portrait*
Alain le Drimeur. *The Future City*
Georges Le Faure & Henri de Graffigny. *The Extraordinary Adventures of a Russian Scientist Across the Solar System* (2 vols.)
Gustave Le Rouge. *The Vampires of Mars; The Dominion of the World* (w/Gustave Guitton) (4 vols.)
Jules Lermina. *Mysteryville; Panic in Paris; To-Ho and the Gold Destroyers; The Secret of Zippelius*
André Lichtenberger. *The Centaurs; The Children of the Crab*
Jean-Marc & Randy Lofficier. *Edgar Allan Poe on Mars; The Katrina Protocol; Pacifica; Robonocchio; Return of the Nyctalope;* (anthologists) *Tales of the Shadowmen 1-10*
Xavier Mauméjean. *The League of Heroes*
Joseph Méry. *The Tower of Destiny*
Hippolyte Mettais. *The Year 5865*
Louise Michel. *The Human Microbes; The New World*
Tony Moilin. *Paris in the Year 2000*
José Moselli. *Illa's End*
John-Antoine Nau. *Enemy Force*
Marie Nizet. *Captain Vampire*
C. Nodier, A. Beraud & Toussaint-Merle. *Frankenstein*
Henri de Parville. *An Inhabitant of the Planet Mars*
Gaston de Pawlowski. *Journey to the Land of the 4th Dimension*
Georges Pellerin. *The World in 2000 Years*
Ernest Pérochon. *The Frenetic People*
Pierre Pelot. *The Child Who Walked on the Sky*
J. Polidori, C. Nodier, E. Scribe. *Lord Ruthven the Vampire*
P.-A. Ponson du Terrail. *The Vampire and the Devil's Son; The Immortal Woman*
Edgar Quinet. *Ahasuerus*
Henri de Régnier. *A Surfeit of Mirrors*
Maurice Renard. *The Blue Peril; Doctor Lerne; The Doctored Man; A Man Among the Microbes; The Master of Light*

Jean Richepin. *The Wing; The Crazy Corner*

Albert Robida. *The Adventures of Saturnin Farandoul; The Clock of the Centuries; Chalet in the Sky; The Electric Life*

J.-H. Rosny Aîné. *Helgvor of the Blue River; The Givreuse Enigma; The Mysterious Force; The Navigators of Space; Vamireh; The World of the Variants; The Young Vampire*

Marcel Rouff. *Journey to the Inverted World*

Han Ryner. *The Superhumans*

Brian Stableford. *The New Faust at the Tragicomique;The Empire of the Necromancers (The Shadow of Frankenstein; Frankenstein and the Vampire Countess; Frankenstein in London); Sherlock Holmes & The Vampires of Eternity; The Stones of Camelot; The Wayward Muse.* (anthologist) *News from the Moon; The Germans on Venus; The Supreme Progress; The World Above the World; Nemoville; Investigations of the Future; The Conqueror of Death*

Jacques Spitz. *The Eye of Purgatory*

Kurt Steiner. *Ortog*

Eugène Thébault. *Radio-Terror*

C.-F. Tiphaigne de La Roche. *Amilec*

Louis Ulbach. *Prince Bonifacio*

Théo Varlet. *The Golden Rock. The Xenobiotic Invasion; The Castaways of Eros; Timeslip Troopers* (w/André Blandin); *The Martian Epic* (w/Octave Joncquel)

Paul Vibert. *The Mysterious Fluid*

Villiers de l'Isle-Adam. *The Scaffold; The Vampire Soul*

Philippe Ward. *Artahe*

Philippe Ward & Sylvie Miller. *The Song of Montségur*

MYSTERIES & THRILLERS

M. Allain & P. Souvestre. *The Daughter of Fantômas*

A. Anicet-Bourgeois, Lucien Dabril. *Rocambole*

A. Bernède. *Belphegor; Judex* (w/Louis Feuillade); *The Return of Judex* (w/Louis Feuillade); *The Shadow of Judex*

A. Bisson & G. Livet. *Nick Carter vs. Fantômas*

V. Darlay & H. de Gorsse. *Arsène Lupin vs. Sherlock Holmes: The Stage Play*

Séamas Duffy. *Sherlock Holmes in Paris*

Paul Féval. *Gentlemen of the Night; John Devil; The Black Coats ('Salem Street; The Invisible Weapon; The Parisian Jungle; The Companions of the Treasure; Heart of Steel; The Cadet Gang; The Sword-Swallower)*

Emile Gaboriau. *Monsieur Lecoq*

Goron & Emile Gautier. *Spawn of the Penitentiary*

Rick Lai. *Shadows of the Opera: Retribution in Blood; Sisters of the Shadows: The Curse of Cagliostro*

Steve Leadley. *Sherlock Holmes: The Circle of Blood*

Maurice Leblanc. *Arsène Lupin vs. Countess Cagliostro; Arsène Lupin vs. Sherlock Holmes (The Blonde Phantom; The Hollow Needle); The Many Faces of Arsène Lupin*

Gaston Leroux. *Chéri-Bibi; The Phantom of the Opera; Rouletabille & the Mystery of the Yellow Room; Rouletabille at Krupp's*

Richard Marsh. *The Complete Adventures of Judith Lee*

William Patrick Maynard. *The Terror of Fu Manchu; The Destiny of Fu Manchu*
Frank J. Morlock. *Sherlock Holmes: The Grand Horizontals; Sherlock Holmes vs Jack the Ripper*
Jean Petithuguenin. *The Adventures of Ethel King*
Antonin Reschal. *The Adventures of Miss Boston*
P. de Wattyne & Y. Walter. *Sherlock Holmes vs. Fantômas*
David White. *Fantômas in America*
Pierre Yrondy. *The Adventures of Thérèse Arnaud*

SCREENPLAYS

Mike Baron. *The Iron Triangle*
Emma Bull & Will Shetterly. *Nightspeeder; War for the Oaks*
Gerry Conway & Roy Thomas. *Doc Dynamo*
Steve Englehart. *Majorca*
James Hudnall. *The Devastator*
Jean-Marc & Randy Lofficier. *Royal Flush*
J.-M. & R. Lofficier & Marc Agapit. *Despair*
J.-M. & R. Lofficier & Joël Houssin. *City*
Andrew Paquette. *Peripheral Vision*
Robert L. Robinson, Jr. *Judex*
R. Thomas, J. Hendler & L. Sprague de Camp. *Rivers of Time*

NON-FICTION

Stephen R. Bissette. *Blur 1-5. Green Mountain Cinema 1; Teen Angels*
Win Scott Eckert. *Crossovers* (2 vols.)
Jean-Marc & Randy Lofficier. *Shadowmen* (2 vols.)
Randy Lofficier. *Over Here*

ART BOOKS

Jean-Pierre Normand. *Science Fiction Illustrations*
Raven Okeefe. *Raven's L'il Critters; Rave's Faves*
Randy Lofficier & Raven Okeefe. *If Your Possum Go Daylight...*
Daniele Serra. *Illusions*

HEXAGON COMICS

Franco Frescura & Luciano Bernasconi. *Wampus*
Franco Frescura & Giorgio Trevisan. *CLASH*
L. Bernasconi, J.-M. Lofficier & Juan Roncagliolo Berger. *Phenix*
Claude Legrand, J.-M. Lofficier & L. Bernasconi. *Kabur*
Franco Oneta. *Zembla*
L. Buffolente, Lofficier & J.-J. Dzialowski. *Strangers: Homicron*

Danilo Grossi. *Strangers: Jaydee*
Claude Legrand & Luciano Bernasconi. *Strangers: Starlock*